The
Invisible
World

The Invisible World

a novel

John Smolens

SHAYE AREHEART BOOKS
NEW YORK

Published by Shaye Areheart Books, New York, New York.
Member of the Crown Publishing Group, a division of Random House, Inc.
www.randomhouse.com

Shaye Areheart Books and colophon are trademarks of Random House, Inc.

Printed in the United States of America

Design by Lynne Amft

Library of Congress Cataloging-in-Publication Data
Smolens, John.
The invisible world: a novel / by John Smolens.—1st ed.
1. Official secrets—Fiction. 2. Mothers—Death—Fiction. 3. Fathers and sons—Fiction.
4. Massachusetts—Fiction. I. Title.

PS3569.M646 I58 2002
813'.54—dc21   2002018492

ISBN 0-609-60996-3

10 9 8 7 6 5 4 3 2 1

First Edition

For my mother,
Mary Burke Smolens

Acknowledgments

I am truly grateful to my friends and colleagues at Northern Michigan University; to the university for a grant that enabled me to travel to Boston and Salem; to my remarkable editor, Shaye Areheart, and her wonderful staff; to my agent, Noah Lukeman, who looked north; and to my brothers, Peter and Michael; my sister, Elizabeth; and their loved ones. . . .

And always, always, to my wife, Reesha.

'Tis possible, that the Experience, *or, if I may call it so, the* Education *of all Devils is not alike, and that there may be some difference in their* Abilities. *If one might make an Inference from what the Devils* do, *to what they* are, *One cannot forbear dreaming, that there are* degrees *of Devils. . . . Yea, 'tis certain, that all Devils do not make a like Figure in the* Invisible World.

COTTON MATHER, *A Discourse on the Wonders of the Invisible World,* Uttered (in Part) on August 4, 1692

Part I

The Diabolical Familiar

1

My mother died on the second Tuesday of October, at 3:14 P.M., to be exact. For the previous ten days she'd lain abed in the Dana Farber Cancer Institute in Boston. From her sixth-floor window I could look down Brookline Avenue toward Kenmore Square and the lights above Fenway Park. I took some solace in the fact that she died with such a view of the city, but the truth is the last day she was so out of it, she didn't know where she was—the nurse called it last-stage dementia, as though it were some saving grace.

But I had my doubts. Can a seventy-five-year-old woman go from perfectly lucid to drooling stupefaction in less than twenty minutes? I asked the nurse what they had given my mother while I was down in the cafeteria. She said nothing. No painkillers? Nothing—nothing that would bring this on so quickly, so completely. The nurse, a beefy woman with a pink Irish face that almost undermined the steel of her blue eyes, fingered the cross around her neck and suggested that perhaps it was the hand of providence. We were standing out in the fluorescent white corridor, and I stared back at her until she left for her nurses' station.

Petra Mouzakis was sitting on the long bench wedged between two laundry bins, listening to our conversation. She'd been there on the sixth floor all morning. I want to say lurking, but that would suggest that the woman tried to blend in, to conceal herself. That simply wasn't the case. Petra was, like myself, a journalist, and she was the kind that rarely hides. To be fair, she was a working journalist; I was not—had hardly written a word in over a year.

Petra got up from the bench, swinging her sleek dark hair over one shoulder, and walked toward me. She wore black leggings beneath a loose white blouse that hung down over her hips. "Your mother had a visitor."

"When?"

"While you were down in the cafeteria."

"Who?"

"A man." Her large eyes were so dark they seemed incapable of admitting light, even the fluorescent kind. Something admirable in that. "I only caught a glimpse of him as I came out of the women's room down the hall. I think it was your father."

"My father? We haven't seen him in—in years. Are you sure?"

She touched the side of her head with a long hand and nodded. Her nails were green.

"You know what my father looks like?"

"That's why I've been here," she said. "To ask your mother about him. She wanted to tell me things about him, but it was a slow process. She kept going back, skipping around in time. The sequence of events was jumbled."

"In my family they usually are."

"But she wanted to tell me. She wanted to get it out—at last, I think."

"Deathbed confession."

Petra glanced away, embarrassed, as she fingered the thin silver chain that hung about her graceful neck.

"That your brand of journalism?" I asked.

"You used to write for the *Beacon*. You know what it takes to get a story."

"The *Boston Beacon* I wrote for was a very different thing—it was a different time."

Something in her jaw shifted, firmed up. "I know, you wrote for the first *Beacon*—when it was this renegade alternative paper." Petra was in her late thirties, about ten years younger than I was—and this was starting to feel pointless.

"The paper should have stayed folded," I said. "Somebody bought the name and now it's just a lightweight designer rag meant to give boomers flashbacks. Anybody who could really write went to the *Globe*. Or New York. Or Washington."

"Except you," she said.

"Maybe that's because I can't write."

"Maybe," she said, and now she looked me right in the eye. "Though I thought some of your stuff in the *Beacon* was better than that book of yours."

"You a writer or an editor?"

"It was a struggle to finish the book."

"Or maybe a critic?"

She folded her arms and said, "*All right*. I've been looking for your father for years—on and off."

"Have you? And why would you do that?"

"Probably for the same reasons you have," she said. I didn't answer. I started to turn to go back into my mother's room. "That's what she told me," Petra said. "You've been looking for him for years—even when you didn't know it, that's what you've been doing. I think it hurt her that she couldn't help you more. I think she was trying to protect you."

I didn't turn around but said, "You've gotten *all* you're going to get out of her." I entered the room and closed the door. Beyond my mother's bed, the window framed a view of the Citgo sign above Kenmore Square and the lights of Fenway Park on a gray fall day.

MY NAME IS Samuel Xavier Adams. I think. For some time, most of my adult life, I've suspected that little about my family could be stated with certainty. I believe I was born in New York City, and something about my mother's eyes tells me that that fact at least is solid. My father, John Samuel Adams, has been an employee of the United States government since he enlisted in the navy at the beginning of World War II. Exactly what he has done for the government since the end of the war I'm not certain. In fact, he has never actually admitted being a government employee, not directly—it's always been one of the many tacit understandings we supposedly shared. There have been times when my best hunch was that he worked for the FBI, the CIA (and its predecessor, OSS), various branches of military intelligence, and, at one point, a little-publicized federal agency known as SOS, Secret Operations Section. The branch names may change and shift, but I know that since the end of the war he has worked in government (as opposed to *for* the government), though at times I suspect he worked freelance *for* the Mafia (as opposed to *in* the Mafia).

There have been times when I doubted that the man I thought was my father was really my father. Some of the evidence that I've gathered over the years suggests that the real John Samuel Adams died a long time ago—perhaps in combat, though even that is not certain—and that the man I've considered my father from childhood was really some kind of substitute. But despite the weight of that evidence, I've always resisted such a wild possibility. Why? Because of my mother's eyes, my mother's voice—ever since I was young there was something in them when she spoke of my father that suggested that the man she called Jack was indeed my father.

As she lay on her hospital bed, I could clearly see her scalp through her thin white hair. Her face, usually flushed—an Irish flush much like that of the nurse who attended her—was slack and pale. Her eyes were opened, staring at the ceiling, but they didn't appear to comprehend anything.

"Mom?" I waited and there was no movement, no response. *"Ma."*

Nothing.

I sat down by the window. And looked out at Boston.

WHEN I THINK of my mother, I often see her as she was in a photograph that was taken shortly after she was married and, I assume, about a year before I was born. It's a black-and-white photo taken sometime in 1948. Fall or perhaps winter. She's sitting on a couch wearing a finely cut suit with padded shoulders. The wide-brimmed hat shades one eye and around her neck hangs her mother's mink, its little dark eyes seeming to stare out at the camera. Her lipstick is dark, a deep red, no doubt, and she's holding a cigarette in her right hand. Her smile is wide, her eyes are bright, her figure is stunning. She's twenty-six years old. None of the lines of worry have yet etched their way into that face. She's a South Boston girl who's moved to New York City with her new husband, an ex–navy officer with a job in the government. Has there been a more optimistic time in America's history? I once asked her who took the photograph and she said, "Oh, your father took that, in our apartment, the one in the city before we moved out to Lake Success." Since I first saw that photo, I've wanted to be able to somehow beam back to that moment when the camera flashed. Wanted to look around the living room, to smell her perfume, to listen to the rustle of such clothes (she wore not only stockings but gloves), to hear the ice in their Scotches, to smell the smoke of their filterless Chesterfields, lit by a Zippo that had a distinct ring and click every time my father flipped the top open (a sound I have associated with him since early childhood).

There's another photograph taken, I think, about the same time, before either of their children was born. My mother and father are both sitting in a semicircular booth in an Italian restaurant. The tablecloth is white, their hands are poised over ashtrays, their drinks are full, and she leans against his chest. She's wearing a different outfit, this time a print dress, and without her hat her long hair is draped over her right shoulder. She had what used to be called a plait. It's dark in the black-and-white photo, but I know that then her hair was a deep red. My father is wearing a double-breasted suit with a silk tie and a matching handkerchief. It's one of the few photos I've seen of him—all or most were taken during that brief optimistic time, after the war and before they started a family. Apparently taken by the restaurant's photographer (because the photo came in a cardboard frame that said *Giovanni's Grotto* in the corner), this portrait is unique for two reasons: It's one of only a few photographs I've ever seen where my father, who was then about to turn thirty, wasn't in military uniform, and he's grinning. Not smiling. Grinning. Both of them, grinning for the photographer in Giovanni's, somewhere in New York City.

STARING OUT at that fine Boston drizzle, I wondered if it was possible, if my father had really slipped into my mother's hospital room a few hours before she died. I had gone down to the cafeteria for coffee—at her insistence, as usual. Since she'd been admitted to Dana Farber ten days earlier, I'd spent most of every day in her room; but she would insist that I go out and eat, take a break from my vigil. Always she was worried that I was hungry, and she'd tell me to go to a restaurant and get a decent meal. I found the food in the cafeteria quite good and reasonably priced, though a few times when I returned to her room, I made up elaborate descriptions of the clam chowder that preceded the baked haddock. If nothing else, my mother was always content to talk about food.

My guess is that my father had been somewhere on the sixth floor of Dana Farber for some time. He would have been there long enough to determine our routine—how long I stayed in her room, how long I was gone when I took the elevator down to the first floor. He was not a man to leave much to chance, and a chance encounter with his son, his only surviving child, after eluding me for years, was not something that he would allow. Not if it would interfere with his intentions. Or his work, which was what my mother always called it: *work*. When he went away, it was always to work. No wonder I developed such an aversion to the concept.

When he saw me take the elevator, he probably waited a minute to determine the movement of the nurses and floor staff; then, walking slowly but without hesitation, he went down the fluorescent white corridor, stepped into my mother's room, and closed the door behind him. He would not be dressed in a double-breasted suit cut in the forties fashion. His short white hair would ring his scalp, the dome on top shining as though polished, and his clothes would be intentionally inconspicuous: dark slacks, a solid shirt or sweater, and a fall jacket, gray or perhaps forest green. The one thing that would not be different would be his wire-frame glasses, which had varied little ever since that photograph, taken nearly fifty years ago in Giovanni's Grotto. The glasses, the delicacy and frailty of them, were almost a trademark. When they weren't on his face, they were in his shirt pocket. He cleaned them often, carefully, always with a special cloth designed not to scratch the lenses.

I wondered if the sight of my father would have frightened my mother. I think not. In fact, I wouldn't be surprised if she expected to see him. Perhaps it was part of her insistence that I leave the room periodically, knowing that only then would my father take the opportunity to enter her room and stand next to the bed, cleaning his glasses. I was having trouble imagining what they would say to each other, two people who had spent so much of their married life apart, now, half a century after the shrimp scampi at Giovanni's Grotto. With my mother so near death, was it possible in one conversation to clear everything up, to make amends, to express fears and doubts and, certainly, regrets?

I don't know.

Maybe Petra was right. My father wasn't there to talk at all, but to make sure that my mother would talk no more. About him. About his work. Maybe my father was responsible for the fact that when I returned to my mother's room twenty minutes later she was gone—still alive but oblivious. Uncomprehending. Brain dead.

"Mom," I said, leaning down over her. Her eyes were different and her mouth was slack. "Mom? You all right?" She seemed to be trying to look through my forehead at the ceiling above me. *"Mom."* But there was nothing there, no response.

I wondered what he would have done—a pill, or maybe some injection. Something that would quickly drain all awareness, all memory from her mind. And I wondered if he could actually do it, pull the plug, so to speak. To his wife, the mother of his children.

If it was necessary, if it was essential to protect what we always referred to as his *work,* then, yes, I knew that my father could have done it.

2

I had been to the crematorium in Jamaica Plain once before, to pick up my sister's ashes. So when I walked into the stone building adjacent to the cemetery, I felt like I was returning to a familiar venue. When I was young we moved frequently: New York, New Orleans, Houston, San Diego, places where my mother tried to set up a sense of "home" that would sustain us until we packed up again. The purpose, it seemed, was not to be with my father so much as within close proximity to him. My mother referred to it as "within striking distance." We'd position ourselves near him and he'd make brief, often unannounced visits, then vacate the premises with a sense of urgency that, when I was small, I found exciting. When I was about six I went through a spell where I suspected that he might be Clark Kent, always ready to rush off and save imperiled souls.

The crematorium had granite stone walls and a slate roof, and it resembled a fortress: wrought-iron bars on the narrow windows, with whorls and imperfections in the glass that distorted the view of the grounds. My footsteps echoed off the polished floorboards as I walked toward the oak desk at the end of the corridor. The man sitting behind it never glanced up as I approached. He was not the same man who had been at the desk when I came for my sister's ashes, but the black suit was familiar. When I stopped in front of the desk, I saw that he was reading the *Boston Herald*. Back page, sports section.

"B's in Montreal tonight," I said. In Boston it's an icebreaker.

"Did you ever think that both the Bruins and the Canadiens would be so bad?"

"The Habs, no."

He looked up for the first time. Cataracts and a slack mouth. A man in his early sixties. Probably took early retirement and supplemented his pension by putting in a few afternoons here. The kind of man whose jobs required clothes that approached a uniform, a blazer, slacks, a solid tie, much like the security at the Boston Museum of Fine Arts. "How can I help you?"

"Agnes Margaret Byrne Adams." Stating my mother's whole name seemed dutiful. And for a moment it sank through me again, this sensation that had sporadically hit me over the past twenty-four hours, since she died six floors above Brookline Avenue. Perhaps it was grief. Perhaps it was part of the mourning "process." All I know is that it had been fucking up my shit something terrible.

"Adams?" he said.

I knew it right away—there was a problem. With my sister it had been so quick, so efficient and mildly formal. I gave her name and the man in the black suit left this same desk, went through the heavy oak door, and returned with a white box about six inches square. I left feeling as though I had just picked up the cake for a birthday party. Of course, that was a decade ago and I had been drunk through the whole ordeal. Driving away from the crematorium, I got my kazoo out of the glove compartment of my VW bug and played some of our favorite songs by The Band, "Across the Great Divide," "Rag Moma Rag," "Jemima Surrender," "The Weight."

"Adams," I said.

He took a leather-bound register from the corner of the desk and opened it on top of his newspaper. "Agnes Margaret Byrne Adams," he read. "She was picked up at one o'clock." He turned the register around and fingered the entry. "Samuel Adams, her husband, picked her up."

"Shit," I whispered.

"What?"

"Could I use your bathroom?"

You're supposed to want to kill your father. By senior year in high school you know about Oedipus and you know that much of world literature portrays a son driven by the desire to defeat his father. In my generation it was more a figurative killing, accomplished by self-destruction. Guys grew their hair long, drank themselves silly, blew their minds on drugs, burned their draft cards. They refused to become what their fathers expected of them, with the expectation that it would ultimately slay the old man.

I never knew what my father expected—never had such guidance—so even my rebellion was vague and ill conceived. I got fucked up because it felt good. It wasn't a question of not going into business with my father, or joining the club. There were times when I really wanted to kill the bastard. Because he was always leaving me. *Us.* Since I was a boy, it was always my mother, my sister, and I left behind, awaiting his return. His presence was his absence. Days, weeks, months the three of us lived with this sense of anticipation, feeling that something about every meal, every bedtime was incomplete.

Now he'd left again. But rather than leaving me with my mother, he'd taken her with him. What's left of her, the white box of ashes.

It was a good bathroom to dwell in; had the small hexagonal-shaped white tiles, and marble stalls, which gave the chamber a dignified echo. The man in the black suit waited at the front door for me. I suspect that this was the first time he'd had someone leave the crematorium empty-handed. He appeared curious; I had won his sympathy. This happens easily between lifelong Bruins fans.

"I hear they're bringing this kid up from Providence for a tryout." He nearly smiled. There was always hope of finding another Bobby Orr. It was like believing in the Second Coming. You either had faith or you didn't.

"Paper says he can shoot and likes to hit," I said.

"That's what the old Bruins had, the guys who liked to go in the corners and hit."

I was tempted to ask him if he wanted to skip work, go get primed for the opening face-off. Instead, I did an odd thing. I reached out and shook his hand. An impulse he seemed to appreciate and understand.

His hand was firm and warm. "Your father—you share a resemblance, you know—he didn't appear well."

"Really? Did he say anything?"

He let go of my hand, reluctantly I thought. "Something about taking his wife home."

"Home?"

"Perhaps you can find him there?"

I said nothing and he watched me long enough to realize that home, the concept of home, was not easy to define. He opened the door and I stepped out into chilly October air.

THAT NIGHT I broke a vow. I started in a place called Margaret's Shamrock in Dorchester, and when the third period of the Bruins-Canadiens game ended in a 2–2 tie, I was at Sully's in Charlestown, a few blocks from my apartment. Sully's is difficult to find unless you know it's there. It has no sign outside—not since the hurricane of '38 blew it off the front of the establishment. Through the three picture windows you can look across a kind of wasteland—an incredible tangle of elevated highways and a sand and gravel pit belonging to a concern called Boston Sand and Gravel— toward the lights of downtown. Charlestown is where we engaged the British at Breed's Hill, better known as Bunker Hill. It's become a neighborhood famous for its car thieves and bank robbers. The Irish kids of Charlestown still do battle with the Italian kids across the river in the North End. When I walked uphill to my apartment, the Bunker Hill Monument, a tall, granite obelisk, illuminated above me, I didn't regret breaking my vow.

Because I had replaced it with another. In my second-floor apartment of Mrs. Hennesey's house, I went straight to the closet in the bedroom. Up on the shelf, in a shoe box, I found the .38 Smith & Wesson, just as I had left it several years ago, tucked in an old white athletic sock. There was also a small package of cleaning utensils and oils, and a box of hollow points.

In the living room I pushed the plates, the books, the cans of Canada Dry ginger ale to one side of the coffee table, spread out the classified section of last Sunday's *Globe,* and began to clean the gun. Rain tapped on the glass in the bay window behind me; downstairs I could hear Mrs. Hennesey cough as she often did in her sleep. The bristle brush fit snugly in each bullet chamber, creating a fine scratching sound, the sound of a precisely crafted weapon.

When I had cleaned all five chambers, the phone rang. It was a little after eleven. I went into the kitchen and picked up the phone.

"Hello."

There was a pause, long enough that I expected the caller to hang up. "Sam?"

"Petra."

"You're drunk."

"How perceptive of you."

"Thanks."

"So," I said. "So I broke a vow. I've made another."

"You have?"

"I have. And you called to tell me something about my father, didn't you?"

She didn't answer right away. Finally, "Yes."

"Good. Tell me what you know."

Again she hesitated. "I'm not sure now is the right—"

"Don't fuck with me," I said. "I need to find him. He took her with him."

"Took who?"

"My mother. He has her ashes. You know where he is?"

"No, I don't think so, Sam."

"You know *anything?*"

"I'm sorry but not now, not while you're—"

"Listen—" I shouted into the phone.

"No, *you* call me when you're through with this and *then* we'll talk." She hung up.

I went back into the living room, turned out the reading lamp, and lay down on the couch, with my head on the stack of old newspapers at one end. It was raining hard now, the east wind coming in off Boston Harbor. There was a draft from the bay windows and I realized one was opened slightly, water patting on the sill. The air was moist, sweetened by ocean salt.

3

In the morning I took the last three aspirin I had in the medicine cabinet and spent the better part of an hour on the growler reading the *Globe*. The Bruins' new kid, J. P. Proulx, was from St. Foy, Quebec, and had been a standout in junior hockey playing for the Sault Ste. Marie Greyhounds; he played left wing, where the B's needed help. He'd done all right in his first game: skated a regular shift, got an assist on the first Bruins goal, and received an elbowing penalty in the second period (in hockey parlance an infraction is often "received," as though it were a gift, as though the player has no culpability for his actions). Also took a gash in the chin from a high stick, requiring twelve stitches. Welcome to the NHL, Jean Pierre.

When I went into the kitchen for my fourth or fifth glass of orange juice, I noticed the digital light blinking *3* on the message machine, and I hit the button. The first message was dead air for about ten seconds before the caller hung up. The second began with a man clearing his throat.

My father.

"Samuel." There was something strained about his voice, and I couldn't tell if it was emotional or physical. He cleared his throat again. "I'm sorry about your mother, Sam. This isn't an easy time for you, I know, and I suspect you're quite upset with me. There are no excuses and I'm not going to give you any, son. You were always good to your mother"—he paused a moment—"and to your sister as well. Know that I've always operated according to a clear sense of duty. And this is true now." A longer pause, and then a slow inhale: "In a sense I'm fulfilling a promise made a long time ago. I don't expect you to believe that, but it's the truth. Samuel, try to—" The machine shut off.

I sat on the stool at the kitchen counter. There were plates and glasses left from the last time I ate in the apartment, which I realized was at least three days earlier, before my mother had died. A turkey sandwich on pumpernickel bread, lots of Plochman's mustard. I watched a large black ant walk across the plate, carrying a crumb. I took the glass, which had held Canada Dry ginger ale, and placed it upside down on the plate, incarcerating the ant. It walked up to the rim of the glass, touched it with its feelers, and moved to its right, looking for an opening. The ant worked its way around the entire circumference of the glass; then it stopped and began eating the crumb. I removed the glass.

The message machine light was still blinking and I pressed the button to listen to the third call.

"Mr. Adams," a woman with tight nasal passages said. "This is Dr. Ault at Dana Farber. We have the results of your mother's autopsy and I'd like to discuss them with you." There was a faint accent—British, I thought, but perhaps West Indian. "We'd appreciate it if you'd come in to Pathology as soon as possible."

I felt light-headed. The old solution would be to go down to the corner store and pick up a new bottle of aspirin and a six-pack. Instead I went into the living room and stretched out on the couch. The .38 still lay on the coffee table. I turned over and fell asleep.

A SENSE OF DUTY. This was what it had come down to so often with my father. This sense of duty that justified his every move. When I was very young I thought it was heroic; I liked his navy uniforms, the medals, the bars, the gold pins, the patches. But of course that all gave way when Vietnam came along and turned everything inside out. My father had a sense of duty and his worthless son did not. We seldom discussed the war directly— for one thing, he was rarely home, except for a brief period in the late sixties, and I don't think I saw him more than three times during the four years I was a journalism major at Boston University.

His sense of duty was tied to the notion that he was expected to protect and serve. On the phone he said he was fulfilling a promise to my mother.

How do you fulfill a promise to someone who's dead? You take her ashes. You take her ashes and you deny your son, the only other remaining member of your family, the opportunity to have some sense of closure. I hate the notion of closure. There's no such thing. You don't forget as long as you live. So my mother's ashes don't really mean that much to me. In fact, I had no idea what I was going to do with them. Uncle James and the rest of my mother's relatives would insist on a memorial Mass, but her ashes would not be required (nor expected). I had no plans on finding some hilltop at sunset. If I had been able to collect that white box from the crematorium, chances are it would have ended up on the shelf in the bedroom closet next to the shoe box containing my trusty .38, which I hadn't fired in years. But the *fact* that my father had the white box of ashes changed everything; it gave the contents inestimable value. It was a simple matter of possession, as in the law, as in hockey. My mother's ashes were in my father's possession and I wanted them.

Of course, it wasn't the ashes my father was protecting, though they clearly meant something to him. He had some design; otherwise he wouldn't have gone to the trouble of getting that box at all. It was a part of his military demeanor: Rituals were necessary. He told the man at the crematorium that he was taking her home. I didn't know where that was, and that was the worst of it: I had never really known where *home* was, and now, suddenly, my father, who was seldom home all those years, did.

Along with duty, my father had a deep belief in reputation, for that was one thing that outlived us. He wanted to protect not my mother's ashes but her reputation. It was not something she had done, but a matter of association. With him. With what he might have done. With what I had come to believe he had done. With what he would be remembered for after he was dead. If it ever came to light. Which was what my sister and I had sought for years. The bringing to light. The evidence. Clear evidence of what he had done.

My sister, Abigail, was two years younger than I, but she was a senior in high school with me in 1968. The "party line," as we called it, meaning Mom's explanation, was that in eighth grade (we were then living in San Diego) I had had all my childhood illnesses in one year—measles, mumps, and tonsillitis. Thus, I missed so much school that I repeated a year. The fact was I couldn't pay attention in class and deserved to be kept back. My sister, on the other hand, was so bright, so attentive, yet so bored, that she skipped a grade; so when we moved to Salem, Massachusetts, in the fall of 1963, we were both enrolled in the eighth grade. I was fourteen and she was eleven. My mother expressed concern about what effect this would have on me. True, at first it was awkward, but I soon discovered that being older and bigger than most of the other boys was an advantage that outweighed whatever psychic bruise I might have received. But it was Abby who obtained bruises in every way possible—intellectually, physically, sexually. It seemed that through most of her childhood my sister was younger and smarter than everyone else. A terrible combination.

That first fall in Salem I was plagued by pimples and rampant erections, while she began to bleed. Our father was nowhere to be found. Our mother was overwhelmed with the newness of everything: the house, the unpacking, the furniture. She never ignored us, but it seemed that we were suddenly allowed more freedom and I, being the oldest, was responsible for Abby. She was so frail then. We'd walk to school fall mornings, passing the looming, ancient houses of Salem, and she'd determine which of them was haunted. She'd already read *The Scarlet Letter* and *The House of the Seven Gables,* and she already knew much of the long history of the town, the generations of inhabitants in these dwellings. Her large, dark eyes were full of both fear and glee as she talked about the Salem Village witch trials of 1692. She was keenly aware of what the first Puritan settlers in Massachusetts Bay Colony referred to as the Invisible World, which, despite paved roads lined with Fords and Chevrolets, still seemed to be in evidence in the crisp fall air of Salem in the early sixties. After California, with its bland and predictable string of sunny days, chilly New England was, for Abby, invigorating, mysterious, deliciously dangerous. Needless to say, that first Halloween she went trick-or-treating as a witch. And a witch she did remain.

Giles Corey was my favorite citizen of old Salem, the contentious farmer who refused to defend himself in court and who was given the sentence of *peine forte et dure*—to be pressed to death. I remember nights lying in my bed imagining that they were placing the first stone on my chest; and then the second, and the third. Being crushed to death, slowly, stone by stone, was better than being eaten alive by a dinosaur, blown to bits in battle, hanged, beheaded, boiled, or drawn and quartered (though that, too, had its appeal). Pressed to death as punishment suggested a community that possessed fierce rectitude, uncompromising morals, an appreciation for the prescriptive value of pain. A place where the diabolical and the God-fearing were distinct, where the sinners and the saintly shall never inhabit the same pew. And Giles Corey's last words were a taunt to authority: "More weight." What balls.

Meanwhile, lying in the next room, Abby was reading about demons. How male demons—incubi—would come to a woman's bed and have sexual intercourse with her while she slept. How female demons—succubi—would entice sleeping men into unholy congress. As our years in Salem passed, as Abby was transformed from that frail, wide-eyed girl to a delicate, beautiful young woman, she was constantly in search of a glimpse into the Puritans' Invisible World.

For our mother Massachusetts was a return home. We found ourselves surrounded by family, an aunt and uncle in Malden, two uncles in Newburyport, and a spate of cousins from Winthrop to Kennebunk, Maine. At the center of this universe sat our grandmother, who still lived in Dorchester. Extended family was no replacement for a father and husband who came and went, but it made the holidays busy, noisy, tolerable. A good, old-fashioned New England word that: *tolerable.*

DR. MIRIAM AULT's dark face shone as she walked down the corridor of the Pathology Department at Dana Farber Cancer Institute. Her white smock seemed to float on her broad hips, her enormous breasts. She was about thirty years old and she didn't seem too pleased to see me.

"In here, Mr. Adams," she said, opening her office door.

It was a small room with a window next to her cluttered desk; she sat down and nodded that I should sit in the chair by the bookcase. She opened the file folder on her blotter and studied the pages within for a moment. Next to her right elbow was a crumpled brown paper grocery bag; my name was written on it in black Marks-a-Lot.

"We got the report back from the lab," she said without looking up. "Traces of RSP were found in your mother's blood."

"RSP?"

"It's a chemical and we don't know how it got there." She looked at me for the first time since we'd been in the room. "Do you?"

I shook my head. "What's it do?"

Her brown eyes were clear and skeptical. She had full lips and there was a delicacy to her features that undermined her apparent anger. "It's not meant for humans. It's used in experiments, research and so forth."

"What kind of experiments?"

"Mr. Adams," she said. Then she paused and gazed out the window at the traffic down on Brookline Avenue. "Animal research." Turning back to me, she seemed renewed for attack. "You don't have any idea how it got in her?"

I thought about Petra Mouzakis in the fluorescent white corridor up on the sixth floor, telling me that she had seen my father enter my mother's room. "No," I said. "Do you have any idea when it might have been administered?"

This question seemed to surprise Dr. Ault. I gathered from her accent that she had been raised in the Caribbean, and I imagined her in a school uniform, taught by teachers with precise British accents. "When?" She sighed. "I don't know, sometime before she died."

"Can you tell if it was days? Weeks?"

She hesitated. "Days, I think."

"What are its effects?"

"Its effects." She folded her hands on the open folder and something crossed her face—I suspect some realization that it was she who must be careful about what she said. Certainly medical institutions and personnel are being sued all the time. "Well, we're not sure—as I said, RSP is only used in experiments at this point."

"But why? What will it do to or for someone?"

She pulled her lips in, ran a bright pink tongue over them, and then relaxed her mouth. "I'm not sure, except that it seems to have some effect on the cerebral functions."

"The brain."

"Yes."

"What's it do to the brain? In animals?"

She refolded her hands on her desk. "Damage. It does extreme damage."

"So, you're saying that this drug was introduced into my mother while she was here, it probably did serious damage to her brain, and then she died."

"No, I'm not saying that, Mr. Adams. I'm saying that we have found traces—"

"Could it have caused her death?"

"No. She died of failure of the pancreas, which was a result of her cancer."

"I see. Was she a part of an experiment?"

"*No.*" After a moment, she added, "Not to my knowledge, Mr. Adams. Not to anyone's knowledge—anyone here on the staff."

"Then it seems likely that someone, someone other than hospital staff, went into her room and—what?—injected her with the RSP."

"Yes," she said. "That seems most likely."

"What do you think it did to her, to her brain?"

She ran a finger along one eyebrow. "Oh, total memory loss, and I gather the loss of control over primary functions. From that point on she would essentially be comatose."

"Unable to speak?"

"Definitely."

"Inability to communicate—through sign language, eye movement, a nod?"

"Yes." She leaned back in her chair, which squeaked beneath her. "The nurses on her floor, they tell me that you were up there with your mother almost constantly. For days." She glanced at the folder. "She was here for ten days."

"I was with her as much as possible."

"You slept on a cot in her room."

"I did."

"You must have left at times."

"Occasionally," I said. "For a meal. For a walk outside. She insisted on that. Until she stopped insisting on anything at all."

"And at those times she was left alone—other than the ordinary care of the floor staff," Dr. Ault said. She wasn't asking me so much as contributing this to what had become our joint effort to determine what had happened to my mother's brain. "You know of no one else who was alone with her? Family? Friends?"

I thought of my father. I thought of Petra Mouzakis. I shook my head.

"Surely she had visitors."

"She did," I said. "Aunts, uncles, cousins. Lots of them. But they were good about calling ahead. They came in groups and stayed for a short time. I was always there when they arrived."

Now Dr. Ault seemed to have run out of ideas, and we didn't speak for quite some time.

Suddenly she seemed curious, embarrassed. "What do you do, Mr. Adams?"

"I'm a journalist," I said. I felt she deserved a more precise answer than that. "I don't have a specific association these days. When I work now it's on freelance jobs. Haven't been many lately."

She closed the folder. "Someone said you wrote a book. About your father."

"Guilty," I said. "What happens now?"

"I don't know," she said. "A report has to be sent up to the director of pathology. I'm not sure how he'll view this. It may be considered a criminal matter. RSP isn't something that just anybody can get their hands on."

"Whatever happens," I said, standing, "I want to be kept informed."

She didn't look up. "Of course."

"Why does the bag have my name on it?"

She looked at the grocery bag on her desk. "Oh, yes. The floor staff sent this down for me to give to you. It's your mother's clothes, her belongings that were left in her room." She picked up the bag and handed it to me.

"I feel stupid," I said, rolling the top of the bag in my hands. "It seems thoughtless, like I couldn't wait to get out of there after she died. I can't believe I'd forget—"

For the first time there was sympathy in her eyes. "Relatives do it all the time, Mr. Adams. They're in such a state that they leave without collecting things from the closet and drawers, and the nurses send it to the families or, in this case, down to us. It's really all right. Nothing unusual at all."

"You're just saying that."

"Believe that, if you want, Mr. Adams." For the first time she smiled, if only briefly. "As a physician, my job here is often an attempt to understand why people die. What I can never understand is why so many of us punish ourselves for the death of a loved one."

I WENT OUT on Brookline Avenue, the paper bag tucked under my arm. It was a cold afternoon and leaves rattled along the sidewalk in the wind. Across the street was a row of shops, a newspaper stand, a restaurant, a liquor store. I went into the restaurant, which served Greek dishes. When my mother was up on the sixth floor, I'd come over here to eat sometimes instead of going into the hospital cafeteria. Their spinach pie was good, but now when the waitress came to my booth I ordered coffee.

It was about three-thirty and the place was nearly empty. I opened the bag and took out my mother's white cardigan. That was enough. I drank my coffee with the sweater in my lap, one hand squeezing the familiar wool. When the cup was empty, I managed to put the sweater back in the bag. I got up to leave, but instead went to the phone booth at the back of the restaurant. At some point during the past week Petra Mouzakis had given me her card, which I still had in my wallet.

"I'm reasonably sober now," I said when she answered. She didn't say anything and I could hear the sound of an office in the background—journalists who put in a day's work. Phones rang, a computer printer buzzed. "I know why my mother couldn't finish telling you what she knew," I said.

"Can you hold for a minute." She muffled the phone and spoke to someone else. When she came on again, she said, "Sorry, we're running up to deadline now."

"I understand."

"Can I call you later?"

"Ever hear of RSP?"

"RSP," she said. "Where are you going to be, say, at nine?"

"I'm a man of relative leisure these days. You name it."

"I have to go over to Beacon Hill later. How about Charlie's Grill." She hung up and the familiar sounds of a deadline were replaced by silence.

MOST PEOPLE DON'T realize what it takes to get a quote in print. How many calls, how many conversations, how many interviews, how many press conferences, how many sources have to be nailed down. Fourteen-, sixteen-hour days, one after another, until your eyes can't look at the screen any longer. And I'm a part of the transition generation—when I started we still wrote copy on typewriters and submitted it, walked it over to the editor, a guy named Ed Nichols, who really smoked a cigar and wore suspenders. When your story came out you'd see Nichols's hand at work, the tiny incisions, the additional comma. You'd wonder what happened to that adjective in the third graph. He was ruthless when it came to adjectives. Called them mortal sins. At first I felt resentment, but it was really based on the fact that he was right. In print, the adjectives were seldom missed; without them the story was clean and tight.

When I wrote my book, *One True Assassin,* I could use all the adjectives I wanted. My editor loved them. And she's responsible for the title. She wasn't concerned with taut sentences and reliable sources, only sales. Conspiracy theories sell in America because we're all conspiracy theorists. We love conspiracies, at home, at school, at work, in the news. Without a conspiracy, we're bored. So we make them up. Give them a name—*Somethingate*—and your editor will buy lunch, get you on radio talk shows, TV spots. Rather than doing the interviews, they'll interview you. They'll quote you, and sometimes they won't get it right. More often, they'll take what you said *verbatim* and place it in a context that will completely alter the meaning. I knew how that works, though of course I never did that myself when I was writing stories. No, I prided myself on my objectivity, my ability to maintain *distance*. A few politicians on Beacon Hill who hated my guts had to admit that I was fair.

But then I got this theory in my head, a conspiracy theory. It's like religion. With conspiracy theories people either buy it or they don't. You're either a genius or a nutcase. Either way, when your conspiracy theory involves dead presidents, people will read you, they'll call in to talk to you on the radio, they'll tell you they think you're brave for speaking out or they'll tell you you're full of shit. They'll use adjectives that would never get by Ed Nichols.

4

I kept thinking about home. *Home.* What the word meant to my family. It's safe to say that Abby and I were moved around so much during our "formative years" that our concept of home wasn't a sense of place, one specific address, with bedrooms and a kitchen, with wallpaper and views out of windows. Instead we had our mother. She was the center. She was the constant. I realize now—too late—just how difficult it must have been for her. Alone most of the time with two young children. When I hear the term *single parent,* something toxic and jittery sets loose in my blood. Technically, my mother was married; she had a husband who supported us, who was, indeed, at times a participant in (as opposed to being a part of) our daily lives. As kids often say today, our mother was always there for us. (Ed Nichols marginalia would ask "Where's there?")

Most remarkable was my mother's ability to maintain the charade that this was all perfectly normal. Like everyone had a father who was gone for months at a time without any word. A father who would then suddenly appear, pull into the driveway in a strange car, or call from the airport, saying he had just flown in. We wanted to believe our mother, and pretended that it was normal. When our father did appear, he often brought us presents from places he said he'd been on business. Europe, Africa, South America, Cuba. My middle name, Xavier, is the result of my father's Cuban connections. Once, in my early teens, I asked what side of the family it came from and he said it didn't—it came from a friend in the war. I asked who and my father said someone who had saved his life, someone who died because Castro took power.

When we moved to Salem in the fall of 1963, things changed. Abby and I weren't willing to pretend anymore, and our mother had given up trying to pretend everything was normal. Her moving us back to her native Massachusetts was an act of both desperation and determination—two words that can be used in describing most of my mother's actions. She realized that we lacked a sense of *home,* and she thought the only solution was to take us to her family, to the place she knew—the New England coast. On the other hand, over the next few years it became clear to Abby and me that our moving to Salem was a kind of ultimatum: Our mother was not going to let our father drag us around the country any longer. We would stay put in one place and he could follow us if he wanted.

But he didn't, not at first. His visits to our house on Andrew Street were fleeting, two or three days usually. We wouldn't know he was coming until he called from Logan Airport. Sometimes he would simply show up at the front door.

That fall of '63, when we were once again new kids in a new school, I was sick in love with a blond girl named Jennifer Tyng. I called her and hung up because I was too nervous to speak. I walked by her house day and night. As we moved into the month of November—our first New England fall, which was in itself a dark revelation of seasonal change—it seemed everything was spiraling toward a terrible unknown. Abby liked the notion of being a witch so much that she continued to be one after Halloween had passed. She rarely wore anything but black. Painted her fingernails and toenails black. Painted her eyes with broad strokes of black eyeliner, which on the day she was sent home from school (the day she'd finally painted her lips black, too—it took some doing, finding black lipstick in 1963) were streaked from tears. The day the vice-principal, Mrs. Blount, told Abby she could no longer come to junior high dressed as a witch was the worst day of my sister's young life. She announced this at the top of the stairs: *This is the worst day of my life.* My efforts to gain Jennifer's attention culminated in mid-November, with her agreeing to accompany me to the homecoming dance in the school gymnasium. For the event my mother took me out to Robert Hall's on Route 1 and had me fitted for a charcoal wool suit. I protested vigorously that none of the other boys were going to wear suits to the dance, just sport coats, but my mother was insistent. So my nervous anticipation was doubled—the anxiety of impressing Jennifer on our first "date," and realizing that I'd be the dopey kid whose mother made him wear a suit to the dance.

That Friday afternoon it was a perfect autumn day. The sky was the deepest blue, and the air was warm in the sunlight, though chilly in the shade. After seventh period we all returned to our homerooms. Mrs. Slavin's math class on the first floor consisted of all the names that began with A, B, and some of the C's. Adams (there were three of us, Abby, me, and a hefty girl named Jannine) through to Dante Carnacelli, whose father owned a fish market down near Pickering Wharf. I sat in the back of the class between Dante, who was the center on the football team, and a girl named Becky Bates, who had a withered arm, which she used expertly when handling her schoolbooks. It was 2:25, and we were all anticipating the bell that would allow us to break for the door, the corridor, the weekend, the freedom of getting out of school on Friday afternoon.

But the bell didn't ring and the big hand on the clock above the chalkboard inched toward the six. Some kids up front, including my sister, began grumbling, trying to point out to Mrs. Slavin that the bell should have rung and that we were being detained beyond the appointed time. She would have none of it, of course, and ignored us by turning around and erasing math equations from the chalkboard. I remember watching Mrs. Slavin's rump (she was in her forties and you couldn't miss it in the yellow-and-orange-flowered dress that she wore every other week), not realizing that something was about to happen that would cleave all of our lives, that we were about to experience a moment that we would always remember with remarkable clarity, that we were all about to step into a new time, a new era.

When the principal's voice came over the PA system, Mrs. Slavin stopped erasing, which in turn stopped the jiggle in her rump, but she did not turn from the chalkboard. Mr. Ballenger cleared his throat, as usual, and said he had two brief announcements. First, the homecoming dance planned for that evening was canceled. I glanced at Dante, who winced dramatically, exposing his chipped front tooth. And then I looked forward again as Mr. Ballenger cleared his throat and made his second announcement: President Kennedy had been assassinated in Dallas, Texas.

The room was still for a long moment. Only out of the corner of my eye did I notice Becky's withered arm, her tiny, curled fingers twitching, as though trying to tap out some code. Then Mrs. Slavin carefully put her eraser on the chalkboard ledge and time began again.

AT CHARLIE'S GRILL Petra ordered ouzo, so I went with that. We sat at a table that wobbled badly. Charlie's had a reputation for being a "literary" bar, and for some reason cheap furniture was supposed to reinforce that perception. But you were just as likely to sit next to a state senator or a surgeon from Mass General. The Harvard or MIT professors could be mistaken for street people, and vice versa.

I said, "You made deadline?"

"We made deadline." She had asked for rocks on the side and, taking a few cubes from the glass, she dropped them into her ouzo. As if by magic the clear liquid turned milky white. I did the same.

"It's been years," I said and took a sip. "Licorice. I loved licorice as a kid."

"Me, too. My family has a restaurant up in Haverhill, and this is usually what they drink. It always made my father want to dance. By midnight when the dining room was closing down, he'd be back in the kitchen looking like Zorba." She spread her arms out, dropped her head back, and closed her eyes.

"Your whole family, they all live there in Haverhill?"

She nodded. "Since my grandparents came over from Greece. Crete, actually. My father was fourteen. My mother's parents came from Athens, and she came over as a baby." She took out a pack of Winstons. "You mind?"

"No."

"He dropped dead dancing," she said.

"Your father?"

"My mother had been telling him for years that's what would happen, and it did." She inhaled, lifted her head, turned away, and blew smoke toward the ceiling. "And it did. Cigarettes, ouzo, dancing—and too much lamb. When I was a sophomore at BC, I went home one Christmas and said I was a vegetarian, and he just laughed. He said that's no way to live. I resisted, of course. I lived such a clean, tidy little life. No cigarettes, no lamb, and very little dancing." She raised her hand and got the waiter's attention. "Two years later my father was dead, and since then I live in his honor."

"I'm envious," I said.

"Don't be." She picked up her glass and said, "Let's drink to him."

The second round came, and then the third, and several hours later we had eaten lamb at a Greek restaurant off Mass Ave and were in another bar, a dark pub with a folksinger who had a gold stud in her nose. When the next round of ouzo arrived at our table, Petra raised her glass in a toast. "To deadlines and dead fathers." We were in a semicircular booth and she was sitting close beside me. It had been a while since I'd felt a woman's shoulder and hip lean into me that way. And then she raised her free hand to touch my face. "And to dead mothers," she whispered.

My place was closer. She lived out in Arlington near Spy Pond, so we left her car downtown and drove across the river to Charlestown. We never even turned the lights on in the apartment, undressing each other as we crossed the living room and collapsing together onto the unmade bed. Downstairs Mrs. Hennesey coughed.

"THIS IS THE second time I've been hung over since my mother died," I said as I handed her the coffee mug without the chipped rim.

While I'd been in the kitchen, she'd opened the curtains to admit a wedge of morning light. She now wore my blue shirt, unbuttoned. "I hope I haven't led you astray."

"I'm at least ten years older." I got back into bed. "I'm supposed to take care of myself."

"It's a wonder you can still get it up." Sliding one hand beneath the blankets, she laughed. "I know guys *my* age who can't."

"It's your profession. Does strange things to the body, mind, and soul."

She settled back on the pillows, the blue shirt parting. I put my coffee mug on the nightstand. As I leaned toward her, a bar of sunlight struck through the window, dividing the bed diagonally.

WHEN I AWOKE I watched her come out of the shower and dress. The sway of her breasts, the arch of her hips. There was an anxious click to her boots as she walked about the bedroom, collecting her things.

"Did you know there's a gun on the coffee table out in the living room?" she asked.

"How did that get there?"

"Planning a crime? The perfect murder?"

"Can't remember now. This is Charlestown—maybe I'm going to knock over a bank. Or I might have been feeling suicidal."

"You? I don't think so."

When she sat on the bed and leaned down to me, there was the smell of shampoo. "Now that you've plied me with drink," I whispered into her damp hair, "tell me what you know about my father."

"Yes, that was our intention, wasn't it? To talk about your father. Disappointed?"

"No." I nibbled her ear until she pulled away, smiling. "But you were the one who called the other night—the first time I'd been drunk in a long time—and you had something to tell me."

Her brown eyes studied me a long moment. "You mentioned some chemical."

"They found it in my mother, RSP. Affects the brain."

"And your father did that?"

"Perhaps. You said you saw him go into her room while I was down in the cafeteria. How long was he in there?"

"Minutes. Only a few minutes," she said. "But long enough to inject your mother with this RSP. After that your mother couldn't finish her story, couldn't tell me anything. She was just—gone."

"I know. Before that, how much did she tell you?"

"About your father? Little that I didn't already know. She merely confirmed what I had suspected." She lowered her head and fastened a button on her blouse. "She had more to say. I could tell. She was still unsure. I don't know whether it was *me,* whether I was the person she wanted to tell it to, or whether she still couldn't bring herself to tell it. But there was, you know, this burden, a *weight* on her, and I felt she'd been carrying it a very long time."

I nodded. I knew this burden. "I'm supposed to go see her lawyer this morning."

"She talked a lot about you, Sam, and about your sister."

"Any idea how my father knew she was talking—to you?"

"No. Good question." Petra stood up, one hand brushing her hair back over her shoulder. "Listen, I'm late."

"The new deadline beckons."

"I have eighteen things to do at the office before I go to the statehouse to Senator Hume's press conference at one."

"It's a habit, deadlines, hard to kick. I'm clean."

"I really have to go."

"He has her ashes." Petra was pulling on her coat, a long black wool overcoat with a high collar, and she paused, one arm halfway up a sleeve. "He's taking her home," I said. "And I don't know where that is."

5

Several days after the drama of President Kennedy's assassination played out on our black-and-white television, my father called. It was only the second time my mother had heard from him since we'd moved back to Massachusetts. She was on the phone in the front vestibule, and her voice was both frightened and angry. When she began to cry, Abby and I, sitting at the kitchen table, stared into our chicken potpies.

Toward the end of the conversation my mother seemed to have agreed to something and her voice became calmer. After hanging up she returned to the kitchen, wiping her eyes. "Tomorrow I'm going in to talk to your principal," she said, attempting a smile. "You're getting out of school early for the Christmas break." My sister and I exchanged glances. "We're joining your father for the holidays. In Mexico."

While I was writing *One True Assassin*, I returned to Mexico. I wanted to see the hacienda we had stayed in that Christmas of 1963. It was in the hills above Ensenada, a fishing port about a hundred miles down the Baja coast from the border. I flew from Boston to San Diego, rented a car, and crossed into Tijuana. The road down the coast (vastly improved over what I remembered from the sixties) was still carved out of steep hills that fell into the Pacific. Not too far north of Ensenada, as I approached a small village called Popotla, I rounded a bend and a giant ship came into view. Actually, it was only part of a ship, an ocean liner, which sat on the beach, supported by an enormous system of struts, scaffolding, and hydraulic lifts. During lunch in the village I learned that the ship was a replica of the *Titanic*, which had been built for a film that was being shot. I continued south, thinking only a lunatic would make another movie about the *Titanic*.

Ensenada was far bigger than I remembered. The hills surrounding the town were now dotted with houses, most with orange tile roofs. I stayed three days but couldn't find the hacienda, which had been perched on a hill overlooking the harbor. I was told that it was not uncommon now for the wealthy to tear the old places down and build newer, bigger houses. The fact that the hacienda no longer existed seemed to call the memory of our Christmas there into question. In my mind I could see its stucco walls and the wide terrace that had a view of the entire bay. But I began to doubt whether any of it really happened. Since the president's assassination my mother had been extremely agitated. My sister awoke from nightmares, screaming. When we joined our father in Ensenada, he tried to be consoling, but it somehow didn't feel convincing. He took long walks in the hills each day. He was on the phone a lot, usually speaking Spanish. I had the distinct feeling that he was hiding out.

One night he and my mother argued at dinner. We were sitting out on the terrace, being waited on by the caretakers who came with the hacienda, an elderly couple named Roberto and Consuela. My mother was talking about Massachusetts, about the house on Andrew Street in Salem, the excellent school, about being near her family again. It was clear that my father didn't want to hear any of this. He had pushed away his plate of beans, rice, and enchiladas. Finally he said, "It was a mistake. You should never have left San Diego." He turned his head and stared out at the sea. The sun had set, and the sky and water were remarkable deep colors of blue, rose, and purple. "Look at it here," he said. "*Look* at this place. Back there it's cold and dark."

"It's home," my mother said.

"You can't go back there."

She was silent and, I could tell, angry. "We're flying out after New Year's."

"You can't."

"We will, Jack."

He continued to look at the fading light on the Pacific.

"You can come, too, Daddy," Abby said.

My father lit a cigarette, a Chesterfield, and snapped shut his lighter. I listened to the tobacco and paper burn. It was an appealing yet cruel sound. "I can't, sweetheart," he said. "Not now."

"How come?" I asked.

After a moment, my mother said, "Your father and I need to discuss this. I want you children to take your plates in to Consuela."

Abby and I left the terrace, the tiles still warm beneath our bare feet.

The night before we were to make the trip up to San Diego for the flight to Boston, I was squatting on a rock, watching a tarantula walk across the dirt. Desert wildlife fascinated me: tarantulas, snakes, lizards, coyote that frequently howled and yelped in the surrounding hills. It was almost dark when I heard footsteps coming down from the terrace above me. Keeping still I watched my father walk by on the path that wound down through the arroyo. I waited a bit and followed. Below me, I could see the occasional glow of cigarette.

At the bottom of the arroyo he crossed the dirt switchback that wound up the hill and entered a cantina. Staying in the mesquite, I circled around to the back of the cantina until I could see my father sitting on the patio with a man in a white suit. The waitress came with their drinks. They both smoked, my father his Chesterfields, the man a pipe with a crooked stem. I couldn't hear them clearly, except that the man had an accent that suggested that Spanish was his native tongue. My father spoke several languages—it was part of his work for the government to negotiate with representatives from other countries. My father's voice was quiet but emphatic. The man in the white suit gestured a lot with his hands, his arms, and he was clearly trying to console my father. I had the distinct impression that there had been some breach of confidence, some promise broken. Finally this man said in English, "It's too dangerous right now, John."

A few minutes later the waitress came out and she must have seen me. Waving her flabby arms, she shouted, *"No dinero aqui! Vamos!"* She was apparently accustomed to shooing away boys who came to beg from customers. I started to back up and it was then that my father caught sight of me. He rose from his chair and called my name. I stood still, peering through mesquite branches. He called again, angrily, and he began to walk off the patio toward me. I turned and ran, scrambling up the hill on my hands and bare knees. I never looked back, and by the time I reached the hacienda, it was dark and I was bathed in sweat. I went right to bed.

In the morning we left early for San Diego. I avoided my father while we loaded Roberto's old car (running boards and chrome headlights that jutted up from high, rounded fenders). When we were ready to leave, my father kissed and hugged my mother and Abby. I climbed in the backseat and shut the door. Eventually he came around to my side of the car. He was in his green striped bathrobe, both hands in the front pockets. He said good-bye but I would not look up at him. He rubbed my head for a moment, then stepped back as Roberto put the car into gear. As we descended the switchback, periodically I could see up the hill. My father remained standing at the edge of the terrace. I believed I would never see him again. I didn't think I wanted to.

BOSTON MORNING: a walk up the hill to Monument Square. Tour buses unloaded schoolchildren and retirees who were to be herded around the concrete Bunker Hill Monument, a granite obelisk that dominates the bow-front brick town houses surrounding the square. A park ranger pointed east toward the harbor, where on the hot morning of June 6, 1775, British troops had rowed across from Boston. I could hear the ranger say "redoubt."

I continued down the other side of the hill to Bunker Hill Avenue, which has never been on anyone's tour route. The Bunker Hill Projects are across the street—brick buildings marred with graffiti, broken windows, and battered metal doors. I went into Billy's Spa on the corner, where four men stood at the window counter, steam rising from their cups of coffee. At the cash register I paid Billy for my coffee and the morning *Globe,* and found a space among the men. Regular coffee with a whiff of cunnilingus.

Watch this. The Boston Police patrol car double-parks at the corner, and an officer climbs out of the passenger seat, while his partner remains behind the wheel, smoking a cigarette. The officer, face ruddy from the cold, walks into the spa, greets several of the men at the window by name, and then approaches the cash register. Billy takes a copy of the *Herald* from beneath the register and hands it to the cop. Rolling the newspaper into a tight cone and tucking it under his arm, he strolls out to the curb. As he gets back in the cruiser, nobody at the window says a word. A few smile and one nods, as though witnessing an honored ritual. The weekly pickup.

After my second cup I walked downhill and took the bridge across the Charles to the North End. There was the sound of traffic and construction everywhere. The new Zakam Bunker Hill Bridge above and to my right (its two obelisks mimicking the Bunker Hill Monument), and, as I turned down Causeway Street, the Big Dig belowground. There used to be the delicious smell of bread coming from the bakery on this block, but it was gone now. So was Boston Garden. Where it was once dark and mysterious beneath the elevated tracks, there's now an open plaza, full of light, presenting the bland, sleek facade of the new Fleet Center, where the Bruins and Celtics play. The history of Boston is largely a matter of moving dirt: Centuries ago this part of the city used to be a millpond. I turned down Canal Street, walked past Haymarket Square, and climbed Beacon Hill until I was in the cool shadows of the Saltonstall Building. Shortly before eleven I took the elevator up to the offices of Everett, Hanrahan, and Threadgold, Attorneys at Law.

We sat in Miles Threadgold's office, which had a view down on the Charles and Cambridge. My mother's oldest surviving brother, James Byrne, sat in the leather chair next to me. Uncle James was in his late seventies and for years had been the one to represent the entire clan. It was probably because he was the oldest, but he liked to say, when drinking in the company of his male relatives, that it was because he still had the firmest yard.

"There's no surprises, of course," Miles Threadgold said. A document—my mother's will—was spread out on his desk. With the light behind him, his bald head was exactly the shape of an egg. His facial features were difficult to see against the light. He read the entire will and at one point Uncle Jimmy's breathing began to lengthen; I reached over, touched the sleeve of his suit coat, and he lifted his double chin off of his gold silk Windsor knot and said, "Yes, that's very good."

A little before noon we were back down on the sidewalk, the wind coming up Beacon Street. The air seemed to revive my uncle. "I hear the bar at the Parker House now serves the Irish," he said, his blue eyes gazing down toward King's Chapel and the hotel on the corner of Tremont and Beacon.

"Thanks, Uncle James, but it's a little early."

"You're not disappointed?"

"In the acceptance of the Irish?"

"In your mother's will. I mean your share. There's a lot of family to cover and Agnes was always a generous woman. You knew she'd spread it around. There'll be something more for you if we can ever get that house in Salem sold. Been on the market over a year and no serious offers." Over a drink Uncle James would always oblige you with the story of how he had gone from being a day laborer on the docks of South Boston to pharmaceutical sales rep covering the six New England states. Since retiring, his dominant theme was that America was losing its greatness because it no longer valued the attributes of the salesman. "We should switch real-estate agents," he said.

"Let's wait a bit."

He sighed, meaning he was no closer to that first drink at the Parker House. "Suppose you're right, boyo. They're all the same now. They all have computers and cell phones and those stupid little beepers that vibrate on your belt, but not *one* of them can walk up to a customer, shake his hand, look him in the *eye,* and say, 'I have *the* piece of property for *you.*'"

If I didn't make my getaway soon, he'd be telling me about how he could sell thin air.

"Uncle Jimmy," I said, "there's a problem. It's about Mom's ashes." This cut through and he squinted at me. "Dad picked them up from the crematorium."

"The *bastid.* Where'd he take 'em?"

"He said 'home.' He was going to take them 'home.'"

I watched my uncle's puffy face carefully. He was a salesman indeed, and he could conceal and dissemble. But this caught him off his guard for a moment—a weariness came to his eyes and his mouth opened in wonder. "Your father never *had* any sense of 'home,'" he whispered.

"What about Mom? I'm sure it's not the Salem house, not since she closed it up after moving into assisted living. I thought it might be Grandma's house."

"Dorchester? No, your mother wanted no part of where we grew up, not the way it is now. Home? If you ask me, the great agony of my sister's life was that she was always searching for *home* and she never found it."

I nodded.

And we parted, he to the Parker House, I to walk with no clear destination in mind.

I MUST HAVE done the back streets of Beacon Hill for the better part of an hour when I found myself on Mount Vernon, behind the statehouse. But I couldn't see much of the building, because in Boston construction, renovation, and restoration are everywhere always. The building appeared to be a gigantic present, wrapped in a cheap, off-white paper, behind which workers on scaffolding ground and drilled away at brick and mortar. Only the massive gold dome rose above the wrapping, Bullfinch's contribution to the Commonwealth's perception that it was "the City upon a Hill."

Petra had mentioned going to Marshall Hume's press conference at one, so I thought I'd look in and see if she was interested in lunch afterward. It had been a while since I'd prowled the corridors of the statehouse, and the echo of my footsteps was as comforting as an old familiar song on the radio. Beneath the high glass rotunda the former senator from Massachusetts stood at a podium in front of a display case exhibiting a war-tattered Old Glory. Cameras flashed as he fielded questions. People came and went as though it were a slow fifth inning at Fenway. There might have been fifty or sixty people gathered on the marble floor beneath the rotunda; I couldn't see Petra anywhere. I did see Dirk Czlenko, who also wrote for the *Beacon,* and I made my way around the edge of the crowd and came up behind him. He was fingering a black walrus mustache and his charcoal suit coat was dusted with dandruff.

"Dirk," I said.

He looked around. "Hey. If it isn't the author. Don't tell me you're *working?*"

I shook my head.

He turned back and watched Hume. "Didn't think so."

"Why are you covering this?" I asked.

"There hasn't been a serial killer or a mass rapist on the loose for days, so they don't know what to do with me. Besides, this guy's so dirty they probably thought I'd *enjoy* this."

"I thought Petra was covering Hume."

"Guess I'm filling in."

"How come?"

"She didn't come to work is how come."

I waited a moment and tried to frame this right. "She wanted me to help her with some background on Hume. Said she had about eighteen things to do and to meet her here. I thought she was in the office."

"This morning? No."

I didn't want to appear anxious, as if I was really looking for Petra, so I studied Marshall Hume for a moment. He was almost fifty, but his hair was dazzling silver under the lights. He was talking about cleaning up the streets of Boston, making them safe for our children, for the elderly, for the woman who wants to walk her dog at night. He was making it easy for the TV crews, every sentence a pithy sound bite. Take your pick. Uncle James could boast that he could sell thin air, but he couldn't beat this guy. When he was a young state congressman from Essex County, I thought he was too rough to get south of Beacon Hill. I was wrong. Marshall Hume had become a real good package. He knew people, and he knew how to work them. After Senator Joseph Bataglia died in an airplane crash in 1986, the governor was persuaded to appoint Hume senator. He would have to run for the seat in 1988, so Hume quickly finagled his way onto a subcommittee that was gathering, yet again, information on the assassinations of John Kennedy, Bobby Kennedy, and Dr. Martin Luther King. To some degree, it was because of Hume's subcommittee that my book, *One True Assassin,* was suddenly relegated to the remainder table. He was going to crack the assassinations, particularly JFK's, or so it was suggested in the media, in the newsroom, in some of the finer hotel bars between Boston and Washington, where people of power and influence congregate. But then Hume ran into trouble over campaign financing and was forced to withdraw from the race in '88. However, now, after nearly a decade in which he had established a lucrative private practice, Marhsall Hume appeared to be gearing up for a run for the attorney general's office next fall. He was a long shot, but he was always good copy.

Without turning to Czlenko, I asked, "You sure she wasn't in the office?"

He shook his head. "Guess her eighteen things weren't so important." And then a grin beneath his whiskers. "I have a theory: Nothing fogs the mind and makes one forgetful of one's responsibilities quite like the end result of fellatio."

I grabbed Czlenko by the arm, pulled him back away from the crowd and through the nearest door. When I shoved him against the wall, the sound of his head against plaster echoed down the corridor. "Now pay attention," I said. His eyes were stunned and there was a little fear there. "You *sure* Petra wasn't in the office this morning?"

"Yes." His voice was high, like a teenager. *"Told* you, they sent *me* instead."

"She call in? Say *why* she wasn't going to make it?"

"No, and that doesn't sit well with the brass. They're *women,* you know." He blinked and decided not to take that idea any further.

"You have no clue where she is?"

"No one does." Czlenko stared down at me a moment. He was perhaps six-foot-two, and I wasn't accustomed to looking up at people. He smiled as though he understood that. "You're, like, *really* looking for her? *That's* why you're here."

"I told you—"

"No, *sir."* He had it now and he reached up and rubbed the back of his head. *"This* ain't no professional inquiry or a matter of source material."

I suddenly had the urge to plead, to bargain with him. But I had nothing and he knew it. When you're not working, you don't have much in the way of trade.

"You want, you can give me the info you had for her." He grinned broadly now, knowing that I had nothing.

"Look," I said, "I need to talk to her. If you see her, tell her I was here."

As I walked down the corridor, the sound of applause for Marshall Hume echoed from the rotunda.

6

The few years following our Christmas in Ensenada, we only received letters and phone calls from our father. My mother claimed that this period was when I changed so. As I approached my fifteenth birthday, my hormones went berserk, my voice dropped, I began shaving, I put on about thirty pounds and came to my adult height of six feet. Boys at that age tend to get into fights and I got into a few, always with the other boys who were physically lurking near the top of the food chain. In the spring I went out for the tennis team and played number one singles. My advantage over my teammates, aside from my height, was that having spent so many years in California, I had developed consistent strokes and a serve that I could hit flat or slice. With my added weight I was beginning to pound the ball. My mother would probably say that the endless hours of hitting white Wilson tennis balls with my Jack Kramer wood racket helped me to vent my anger toward my father, who was never there. At the time I just wanted to beat every kid who stood across the net from me, but now I think she was probably right.

In the next couple of years I also saw dangerous things happening to my mother and sister. Occasionally a man would take an interest in my mother. It was all very clean and social; he would accompany her to a dinner or a cocktail party, but in a few instances he'd stay late down in the living room. I'm not sure what transpired, though I know that none of them ever made it upstairs to her bedroom. One man, a Bill Suskind, who was "in life insurance," was particularly persistent, and it may have been that the few weekends that my mother went off to visit relatives really were trysts with him in the Green Mountains or perhaps up the coast in Maine. She was a woman in her early forties, still attractive (the operative word used at the time), and despite her two children and her extended family, it was clear that she was lonely. But she never admitted to it; she always tried to remain busy and cheerful, as though our situation were perfectly normal. Though I was suspicious of Bill Suskind, and the other men who escorted her to and from our front door, it only fueled my anger at my father, whose calls, cards, and letters usually came infrequently from other countries, other continents.

Abigail (around the age of fourteen she began to insist on not being called Abby, although I was always an exception) developed hips and breasts, and her face turned remarkable—frail, full-lipped, her eyes large, dark, and complicated. Boys called all the time. At first she didn't want anything to do with them, or perhaps she didn't want to admit to any interest. The witch thing—subtler now—more or less sustained her through high school. She was the hauntingly beautiful girl in black. In the mid- and late sixties high-school kids were easily grouped. There were still the clean-cut jock types, and their female counterparts wearing sweaters and kilt skirts to the games. But other kids were smoking pot and listening to Hendrix, Cream, the Fugs, Tim Hardin, the Paul Butterfield Blues Band, and on and on, and their behavior was a welcomed challenge, if not an outright threat, to the preppy set. Abigail and her group of girlfriends were outside both groups. They became known as the Witches. They kept poppets in their lockers, they put hexes and curses on people they didn't like; stoned, they danced naked in the woods. Mother felt I could always handle myself, but she was genuinely worried about Abigail, and her reaction to her daughter's descent into the Invisible World was anger and frustration. They fought constantly.

Then, in the winter of 1967, my father suddenly returned.

WHEN I GOT back to Charlestown I found Mrs. Hennesey sweeping leaves off her front stoop and onto the sidewalk, where they rattled downhill on the wind. As was often the case, she was talking to herself, her head bent to her task. She hardly stood five feet tall and I could see down through her thin white hair to the mole on her skull. I took the broom from her and continued the job.

"When my husband died," she said, "I prayed to join him soon. Twelve years later I'm still here." I'd been her tenant for almost seven years and it always seemed we'd only had one conversation, with occasional pauses that could last days. "But a mother," she said, "a mother is a different thing."

I kept sweeping maple leaves.

"The girl is very pretty." A typical abrupt segue. Mornings she sat at her front window drinking tea. "All that dark hair and those eyebrows. Spanish maybe?"

"Greek," I said. "From up in Haverhill."

"And the man?"

I stopped sweeping and turned to her. "What man?"

"In the car."

I looked out at the narrow street a moment. "He picked her up here?"

"A nice car. Big. Not one of those Japanese things."

"Did you see the man?" I turned to her now. "Did he get out?"

"No. She walked up to the car, spoke to him for a moment, and got in."

"Did you get a look at him?"

"Jealous?" she said, smiling. One eye was nearly closed and perpetually moist. Taking a crumpled tissue from her sleeve, she daubed at her wet cheek. "Not well," she said. "He only cracked his window, and the reflection, you know."

"Just one man, or were there others in the car?"

"No, only one, I think."

I resumed sweeping brown leaves off the stoop. Most of them blew down only as far as the next house, where they were collecting against the Aherns' stoop. I've long suspected that this was the reason that old Mr. Ahern never acknowledged Mrs. Hennesy, though she would always greet him cheerfully.

"You shouldn't be jealous, Sam."

"You don't think so?"

"I could tell that he was much too old for her."

THE PHONE WAS ringing when I got upstairs to my apartment. It was my aunt Kathleen, James's wife. I should have known, and I braced myself.

"Sam, what in *God's* name is this about your poor mother's *ashes?*" Her voice was very nasal and loud. Furthermore, it sounded like a gross parody of the Boston accent, the one employed by comedians who come from anywhere but eastern Massachusetts—full of long *a*'s and dropped *r*'s. "Where *are* they—Jim said something about your *father?*"

"'Fraid so."

"This is just great. How are we supposed to have a decent memorial for her? It's bad enough that she wanted to be *cremated*—you know the Vatican used to have very clear views on that—I mean, if there was a *body,* we could have a funeral and bury her in the ground like a respectable Christian. Of course, knowing your *father*—though I suppose I can't say that I really *do,* considering that I saw the man so seldom all these years—he probably would have stolen her *body,* too."

She was just getting warmed up. I put the phone down on the kitchen counter, went to the refrigerator, and took out the carton of Tropicana. I picked up the phone again and she hadn't missed a beat.

"Well, you have to *find* him and get them *back,*" she said. "But *how* are you going to *do* that? Nobody knows where the man *is.* Nobody's *ever* known where he is." I took a long drink of orange juice. With Aunt Kathleen you could eat a full meal at Locke-Obers and never have to say anything. "But then you might come up with one of your *theories* and figure out where your father *is,* but this time just try *not* to embarrass the entire family. Your branch has been so *strange* so long. You're like the limb that's dying and about to fall *off,* and poor Agnes, rest her soul, she had to *endure* it all these years, but *you* seem to thrive on it."

I put the carton of Tropicana on the counter. "What do you mean by that, Kathleen?" I knew it was a mistake to ask, but I couldn't help myself.

"Well, it gives you something to *write* about, your father. If you had a *nor*mal father who lived with his family, who went to *work* every morning and came *home* for his dinner at night, you wouldn't have grown up to write that *book,* now would you? No, you'd have gone into some re*spec*table business."

"Sales probably."

"Yes, sales would be *good.* Though frankly, Sam, you couldn't sell *water* in the *desert.* And if your father had been *around* more, you might have grown up and gotten married and had *child*ren, too. You know, with your sister dead, you're the only one to carry on the family *line,* and it's pretty late in the hockey game for *that!* And your *father,* he can run but he can't live *forever,* so there'll only be you. And when *you* go, the family's going to say wasn't *that* a strange branch, cut itself off, fell down on the ground there, and *died.*"

"How do you *know,* Kathleen?"

"How do I know *what?*"

"How the family's going to think." She didn't answer. "How do you know? You're not even a member of the family. You've *never* known how we think."

"What?" She was getting shrill. "I am *too* a member—"

"No, Kathleen, you just married into the family."

"We have five children and twelve grandchildren and—"

"So you've served your purpose."

"What! I don't believe—James! *James!* Come *here!*"

"Kathleen." I waited. "Kath*leen.*"

"What?" She sounded frightened now.

"My mother's ashes are of no concern to you, and don't *ever* mention my sister to me again." I hung up.

A YEAR BEFORE President Kennedy was assassinated, I witnessed Abigail's fear for the first time. We were still living in San Diego. In October the Cuban missile crisis played out over the course of a couple of weeks, and it was the first time that either of us was truly aware of world events. Suddenly all the bomb drills we had been doing in school made sense. Every so often the teachers instructed us to get up from our desks and walk single-file out into the corridor, where we would sit along the walls and place our heads between our knees and our hands on our skulls. The common wisdom was that if you kept your eyes shut, the flash wouldn't blind you.

Then there was President Kennedy's speech, which we listened to on the radio. My father wasn't home; he was away at "work." As the president explained how the embargo would go into effect the next morning, my mother chain-smoked, and I remember how her fingers kept toying with the cellophane on her pack of Chesterfields. I thought it was odd that we couldn't watch the president on television, a small black-and-white Sylvania in the living room. Long after we were put to bed, the phone rang. It was my father, and my mother's voice was tight with anger and fear as she berated him for being in Miami at a time like this.

The next morning my sister didn't come into the kitchen for breakfast. Mom told me to go get her. I went down the hall to her room, but she wasn't in her bed. I opened the closet door and found Abby sitting in the dark, her head tucked between her knees, her hands on her skull. When she raised her head, her eyes were enormous.

AT FIRST it was Abigail's theory really. The first time she went into a rehab clinic, she told me where our father had been on November 22, 1963. She was thirty. She'd lost a great deal of weight, and suddenly she was no longer "a young woman with no mean share of beauty," as Hawthorne said of Hester Prynne. However, my sister's eyes were still enormous and beautiful.

"He was there," she said.

"He was where?"

"Dallas."

The clinic was in Newton and it was snowing out. There were Christmas lights on the old houses lining the avenue. "What makes you think that?" I was sitting in a creaky wooden chair that was very uncomfortable.

"Because Mom knew, she said so." Abby was fighting a cold and she wiped her nose on the sleeve of her pajamas. "I heard her, on the phone."

"You heard her?"

"Yes, she was talking to Daddy. You were out playing tennis or something. She was really upset and she was on the phone in her bedroom with the door shut. I was sitting out in the hall and I could tell by her voice that she was talking to him. She said, 'I know you were in Dallas. Don't give me New Orleans, Jack. You were in Dallas.'" Leaning back into her pillows, Abigail closed her eyes. The treatment had gotten her clean for the time being, but it had exhausted her. They had been encouraging her to get out of bed and walk, take regular exercise, but she seldom did—and I knew that once they let her out of there, she'd be right back on the street.

What they said about pot when we were in high school wasn't true—it didn't mean you'd become a dope fiend. Only sometimes. Unfortunately, Abigail was one of the few who went from smoking to pills to shooting horse, and I would lose contact with her for months. Usually she'd turn up in New York; once I had to drive down to Philadelphia to get her. She must have learned how to disappear from our father. The need to escape was something she shared with him.

"Even if he was in Dallas," I said finally, "what's that supposed to mean?" I think now I was too accommodating. Somehow I always believed Abigail would eventually pull herself out of it. I thought she was strong enough.

"It means he was *there*. Don't you get it?"

"Okay, Abby, what if he *was*? He works for the government. A lot of them were there that day."

Disgusted, she looked out the window at the Christmas lights.

I sat on my living-room couch with the carton of Tropicana. There was a tennis match being rerun on the ESPN Classic channel: Borg and McEnroe at Wimbledon in the 1980 match with the incredible tiebreaker. I had the sound off and just watched them move about the worn grass court. Borg's big, looping topspin strokes from the baseline; McEnroe's hands at net; the meticulous, slow turn of his body as he tosses the ball up to serve. It was Prince Valiant in a headband versus Richard III. The Nordic god and the Gnome of New York. They were playing with white balls and wood rackets. McEnroe won the tiebreaker, 18–16, but Borg took the championship match in five sets. By the time I finished the orange juice, I found myself crying like I hadn't since I lost Abby.

WHEN YOU DEVELOP a conspiracy theory, you tend to look for linkage. Cause and effect becomes the gaping abyss that must be traversed—everything is connected to everything else. My sister was convinced that my mother knew my father had been in Dallas. On her deathbed in Dana Farber my mother was insistent on talking to Petra alone. Petra climbed into a car and, apparently, disappeared. If she had been taken away, was it because of something my mother had told her? If my father did administer RSP to my mother, was it in an effort to erase all memory of his being in Dallas? If so, it made sense that he'd want Petra as well. His profession required that he be thorough and tidy.

But why the ashes? Why did he want them? After evading my mother most of their married life, could he really now hold such sentiment? Did he love her so?

This I could not accept.

As Borg hoisted the gold cup above his head and smiled at the Wimbledon crowd, I picked up the wire brush that came in the cleaning kit for my .38. The gun and the kit were still spread out on my coffee table and I began to put the brush and the oil back in the cardboard box. I'd never owned a weapon until after my book had come out and I'd received some crank calls. I'd practiced firing the gun once, years ago. When I acquired my father's military records, I learned that he had always been an expert shot. His fine marksmanship was documented all the way back to boot camp. When I was a boy there were never any guns in the house—that I was aware of—and I was never encouraged to take up firearms. The closest thing to a weapon in my last apartment was my Carl Yastrzemski Louisville Slugger, which I kept by the front door with the umbrellas.

At first *One True Assassin* sold well. My conspiracy theory appeared sound. People who called in to talk shows told me they were convinced. But others called me at home—some even after I got an unlisted number. They usually told me I was full of shit. Some said they'd get me; a few sounded like they meant it. My friend on the Boston Police force, Ike Santori, gave me the .38 Smith & Wesson. But I never really needed it. A few months after the book had been out, the newspapers were full of information that had leaked out of Senator Marshall Hume's subcommittee, information that refuted essential facts that I had claimed supported my theory. There were government sources; there was new testimony, which strongly suggested that the JFK assassination couldn't have happened the way I described it. My father wasn't on the grassy knoll. Columnists and people who called in to talk shows began to ask what kind of a man accuses his own father of being a president's assassin? I was just another nutcase. Sales went flat and my book was remaindered.

7

When my father showed up in the winter of 1967, he stayed put for nearly half a year, longer than any time in my memory. I was seventeen, a junior in high school, and at first I was resentful. He acted as if his return were the most natural thing in the world. My mother, too, tried to make it seem like nothing extraordinary. Meanwhile, my sister was out dancing stoned and naked in the woods, and jabbing needles into poppets, while I was trying to pound tennis balls down my opponent's throat.

That spring my father did what any sensible man of leisure on Boston's North Shore would do: He bought a sailboat, a twenty-six-foot Pearson, which he moored off the wedge of land known as the Willows. I soon found that next to the tennis court there was nowhere I was more comfortable than on the deck of a boat. Together we sanded and varnished teak, polished brightwork, tuned the rigging. *Shallop* was my father's attempt at making amends. Though he'd served in the navy, I didn't know he was an experienced sailor; he proved to be an excellent teacher. I soon learned how to handle lines, tie a boland, reef the main, and navigate in and around Cape Ann's rocky coastline.

One afternoon when we were reaching nicely on a fresh southwest breeze, he asked me what my plans were, meaning college. At first I shrugged and said something about applying to a few schools senior year.

"Any idea what you'd like to study?"

"Journalism, maybe."

He was at the tiller and he didn't speak right away. Squinting up at the wind vane at the top of the mast, he kept his free hand in the pocket of his khaki trousers. His nose, which was rather long and pointed, was coated with white cream. "You might consider reading history first." Removing his hand from his pocket, he hauled in the mainsheet. "Journalism is the inspection of what *is*. History, what *was*. Too many journalists these days fail to take the relationship between the two into account."

We were heeling well to port and I sat out on the coaming to help trim. We were doing seven knots and heaving through long three-foot swells. "Some guys don't plan on going to college after they graduate," I said.

"Sure," he said. "They'll stay here in Salem and work a trade if they're lucky, marry young, and raise a brood of kids. If they're not, they'll be pumping gas at the Gulf station."

"Maybe," I said. "Or they'll enlist."

"You interested in a military career?" He sounded genuinely surprised.

I kept my face to the wind. "I don't know. Some guys really want to go to Vietnam."

"You'd need to take the right approach," he said. "I could get you a nomination." I turned to him. "To Annapolis—unless you were thinking more about West Point," he said. "In either case you need to be nominated by someone in office. This could be arranged, probably through Ed Brooke."

Now I was genuinely surprised. "Senator Brooke?"

He nodded.

"You know him?"

"These things can be arranged, Sam."

"I see. After a military career, people often go into government."

He hesitated. "Some do."

"You did."

I looked back off the starboard bow and he didn't pursue it further. Thinking about my future was difficult enough; planning seemed impossible. We sailed five miles out, came about, and ran for home with the spinnaker flying. My father loved to sail with the spinnaker up; he never actually said so, but I could see the way he stared up at the loose triangle of silky canvas as it swelled out over the bow. *Shallop*'s spinnaker was midnight blue, with a large white navy ensign, and it was something to see against a clear sky.

Senior year everything seemed to come apart. There was the Tet Offensive. In the spring first Dr. Martin Luther King was assassinated, then Bobby Kennedy. Guys who a year before had been gung-ho on the marines were now wearing headbands and bell-bottoms. Kids were getting busted for pot everywhere. There was no more talk of nominations to military academies. We lost both of our cats: After Twist got run over, Shout died of cancer. I was accepted at Boston University. Abigail didn't graduate in the spring, though they let her walk in the ceremony.

THE PHONE WOKE me sometime in the middle of the night. The television was still on, with the sound off. After my crying jag I had walked down to the package store in Thompson Square and bought a bottle of Johnnie Walker Black, telling myself that it was in honor of the brilliance of Bjorn Borg and John McEnroe; besides, my mother had just died and I needed to work through it. That's what I *told* myself as I climbed up the hill, the bottle in the paper bag under my arm. What I *knew* was that I was slipping.

But I was sitting at the kitchen table, and the only light in the apartment came from the television. I'd just awakened from a dream I couldn't remember, although I was sure my father had been in it.

It was a man's voice on the phone, grave, direct, unfamiliar. "Adams."

I had a stiff neck from sleeping in the chair. "Yeah?"

"Listen. You want to see your lady friend, be at the corner of Clarendon and Newbury in the morning. Eleven o'clock." He hung up.

On TV Pele was in some World Cup soccer match and he'd just scored. He ran across the field, waving both arms above his head, until his ecstatic teammates piled on him. The camera switched to the goalie, kneeling in the grass, his hands on his head, his eyes raised to the sky. If I hadn't spent my first thirteen years zigzagging around the country, if, instead, I had grown up in Salem, where a kid starts playing pond hockey at four, I would have been a goalie. Don't ask me why. They eventually end up on their knees in the goal crease, in agony.

IN THE MORNING I was just getting out of the shower when there was a knock on the door. "Who is it?" I yelled.

"Czlenko."

I walked through the apartment, dripping wet, a towel held around my waist. Opening the door, I said, "What the fuck?"

He looked contrite, something I didn't think he was capable of, but then he was probably Boston's sleaziest journalist and he had gotten some of his confessional stories through such mutations of sympathy and charm. "Have you heard from Petra?" he asked.

"No."

"Look, the brass down at the office is getting pissed off."

"What do you want me to do about it?" Cold air came up the narrow stairwell. He was standing there in a suit, tie, and a black overcoat—at least eight hundred dollars of expensively tailored worsted wool. I turned around and walked back through the apartment, toweling.

"They're going to have to call the police if she doesn't show up soon." He followed me as far as the living room. "You know how that's going to look in the news, one of our reporters just disappears?"

"It'll look like you guys don't know shit. So?" I began to pull on my clothes. "I'm in a hurry here."

"Something's up," he said. I concentrated on turning a sock inside out. "Come on, Adams, I know it is. I can smell this sort of thing." I got up off the bed and went to the closet for a shirt. "Where are you going?"

"Out."

"All right. Do this on your own—whatever it is—but I'll tell you these two women running the paper now, they're a couple of real suits. If Petra doesn't show up soon, they're going to call the cops and tell them that you're the last one to see her alive."

"Jesus, you talk like you write, Dirk. You mean you fucking *told* them I was the last one to see her?"

He glanced around the living room. My .38 was lying under a section of the newspaper on the coffee table. "You want the Boston Police to come around?" he said. "They'd have a field day with the city's former celebrity conspiracy theorist."

He had a point. I buttoned up my flannel shirt. "Listen, Dirk. I can't talk about this right now. I've got to get going."

"I can see that." He glanced at my shirt. "Back to Filene's Basement?" I walked past him through the living room. "Come on, give me something," he said.

I took my coat off the back of the stool in the kitchen. "Give me today," I said, opening the door. "If something doesn't turn up today, I'll call you. All right?"

"Can I use your bathroom?"

"No."

"I gotta take a piss."

"I'm leaving." Then I said, "All right. Hurry up."

When he'd shut the bathroom door, I picked up the gun from under the newspaper. I stuck it in my coat pocket. But then I took it out and put it on the shelf behind some books. A concealed-weapon charge in Massachusetts brings a mandatory jail sentence. When I heard the toilet flush, I went to the front door and waited.

"I can tail you," he said.

"No you can't, and you know it."

We started down the stairs. It was cold outside. There were more leaves on Mrs. Hennesey's stoop. Something depressing about relentless maple leaves in the fall. He said, "What is this between you and Petra? I didn't know you guys were, you know . . ."

"You sound jealous."

He looked up the hill toward Bunker Hill Monument. "That's very phallic," he said. "Yes, actually, I am jealous." Turning to me, he said, "Look, I like Petra, okay? I'd jump her if she gave me half a chance, but she really is a good friend at work."

For a moment I almost bought it, then I said, "You're really good."

"I mean it."

"Dirk, you don't *have* any friends. Neither do I." I went down the steps to the sidewalk. "You two are pals only as long as it helps you. Now I told you, if I don't find something out today, I'll call you."

As I started downhill, Czlenko said, "Thanks, pal."

In the last thirty years or so Newbury Street has gone from Back Bay decadent to upscale pricey to world-class chic. When I was at BU I knew students who lived in apartments in the Back Bay that didn't cost a hundred dollars a month. Now those same dumps, with sanded and varnished floors and high-end kitchen appliances, are condos that go for big bucks. The only thing crazier than Boston's streets is its real estate. This is why I rent in Charlestown.

I stood on the corner of Newbury and Clarendon from exactly 10:42 until 11:20. The sidewalk traffic was starting to build appreciably toward lunchtime. There was a restaurant, Pho Pasteur, down the block that had tables out, despite the cold. People were going inside, people with big shopping bags, people who walked with an urgency that passed for style and grace. Stunning women of apparent leisure. A black-and-white Town Taxi pulled up next to me and two women speaking German got out. The cabbie, a guy with a stubble beard, had his window down. He sat there at the corner for a few minutes, playing jazz on his saxophone. When his next fare got in, he put the sax aside; as he drove away, people who had gathered at the corner applauded. It was a Boston Moment.

I was getting close to giving up when a gray car, American, one of the luxury models that I can't tell apart anymore, pulled up to the intersection. An older man wearing a lid was behind the wheel. Then I saw Petra sitting alone in the backseat. Her window was up and she was staring out at me. She seemed confused, as though she'd just awakened from a long, heavy sleep. Her hair was tangled, her lipstick askew.

As I stepped toward the curb, the car began to pull out into traffic. *"Wait!"* I shouted.

The son of a bitch sped up. I began jogging down the sidewalk after him, dodging pedestrians. He maintained a speed that kept him just ahead of me for almost half a block, then he saw an opening in the traffic and took off.

I slowed down, winded. I was now standing in front of Pho Pasteur. A man sat at one of the tables, watching me. He was perhaps seventy but very fit. Short gray hair in tight kinky rows. A blunt nose and skin that looked as though it had recently been stretched and roasted in sunlight. A good topcoat, with the collar up, silk tie, and a crisp white shirt. He nodded and I sat down across from him. He stirred his cup of coffee.

"You want anything?" he asked pleasantly.

I shook my head.

"As you can see, your girlfriend is all right." He had a problem with one eye; it was closed partway and I wondered if it was blind or perhaps false. It was clearly his left eye that engaged me. "She can be returned to your apartment soon—today, perhaps." He paused and scanned the sidewalk a moment. "But we need to know something first."

"What?"

"Your father. Where is he?" I didn't answer. "He came to see you and your mother before she died."

"I didn't see him."

"You didn't see your father when he visited—"

"I haven't seen him in years."

"That's what your girlfriend said. At least you're consistent. Getting your stories straight is a sign of real love."

"You're wasting your time," I said. He studied me with his eye. "And she's not my 'girlfriend.' I'm too old for the term."

"But then why are you here?"

I leaned forward and placed my arms on the wrought-iron table. "I don't know where he is. I'm telling you I haven't seen him in a long time."

"Have you heard from him?" I leaned back. "I thought so," he said.

"Look, he called and left a message about my mother.

He waited. After a moment, he said, "And?"

I thought about her ashes. "And that's all, I'm telling you. He just left a message on my answering machine. I have no idea where the fuck he is, and there's no point in your taking Petra—" I stood up suddenly. Then I realized that I probably wasn't playing this right and I sat down again. "I really don't know anything about my father. I haven't my whole fucking life. He was gone most of the time, and when he showed up, it was usually brief and all of a sudden."

"You know, I think I believe you." He raised his arm above his head. There was something about the skin on the back of his hand—it looked mottled and it wasn't tanned like the rest of him, but very pink. As though he'd suffered some kind of burn, or perhaps he'd had a skin graft.

Behind me I heard the squeal of tires as a car braked. He stood up, walked over to the curb, and got in the front seat of a silver sedan, which immediately sped down Newbury Street.

8

I was stretched out on the couch, drinking Canada Dry, trying not to slip. The Bruins were playing in Toronto. J. P. Proulx was taking a regular shift. He skated with his head up and wasn't afraid to go into the corners. Early in the third period, with the Bruins down 2–1, he took a pass on the backhand, broke in over the blue line, and let go a wrist shot that beat the goalie over the inside shoulder. He had the good shot.

The episode on Newbury Street meant that I wasn't the only one looking for my father. My guess was that the people who had Petra were government. Or perhaps, considering the ringleader's age, ex-government, which I presumed my father was by now. But you don't know—those guys probably never really get out of it. They don't just get old, retire, and take up golf. They've invested too much. They know too much. They must be kept in the game somehow.

When I was researching *One True Assassin,* I tried to get as much info on Secret Operations Service as possible. SOS had been a small branch of the CIA, but at some point back in the seventies it apparently was disbanded. Officially, at least. It was very difficult to get anything that could be corroborated. I had managed to find a few sources that seemed reliable, but they would go only so far. Then I got a call from a man in Florida, who said his name was Trini Lopez. Right. After a twenty-minute conversation, however, I was convinced that he knew what he was talking about, so I flew down to Orlando, where he had agreed to meet me at Disney World. We spent several hours at Epcot Center, moving from bench to bench, avoiding the people standing in lines. He was in his late seventies then, and it was clear that his health was failing. Periodically he pumped an inhaler into his mouth. It was a gesture he did with his arms that made me realize that this was the man in the white suit I had seen with my father outside the Mexican cantina in 1963.

I stayed in Orlando a week and we met three times, always at Disney World. Through other sources I had located my father in New Orleans on November 20, 1963, and Lopez confirmed it. "We drove over to Dallas together," he said. "In this navy blue Olds 88. *That* was a car. Detroit really put some chrome on them back then."

"Why'd you go to Dallas?"

He wore a light tropical suit, and his cuff links glinted in the Florida sun. After watching a crowd of schoolchildren who were getting in line for a restaurant, he held both palms up, a graceful gesture. "Everyone else did. There was no stopping it. It was going to happen. There were plans for Chicago and Miami, but it just came together in Dallas. It had been a long time in the making. You have to realize that those brothers brought it on themselves."

"The Kennedys?"

He made the gesture with his shoulders, a shrug and a lifting of the arms, as though I had stated the obvious.

According to Lopez, there had been one shooter behind the fence above the grassy knoll and another in the book depository. My father was one of them. "It was a textbook crossfire setup," he said. "Of course, there's no telling whose bullet really killed JFK. Your father may have been one of the ones who missed." He got up slowly from the bench. "They were all good shots, and still some of them missed."

"What was your role?"

"I just drove the car. Got him in, got him out. And afterwards I was responsible for getting him *out,* out of the country. They had their fall guy."

"Oswald," I said. "All those reports of Oswald incidents before the assassination—at the car dealership, at the Russian embassy—they were just setups, right?"

"Listen, the man was born for the part. He told it like it was—he was the patsy, and he didn't even know it until the deed was done."

"What about the theory that the real shooters were a couple of guys imported from Italy?"

Lopez shrugged. "Sounds good to me, if you like that stuff. Make a nice movie."

"My father, behind that stockade fence." He wouldn't look at me, but there was patience in his eyes as he watched lines of schoolchildren shuffle by. I was to understand that he was doing me a great favor. "And you got him in and out of there so clean nobody ever had a clue."

One eyebrow arched in a salute of appreciation. "No clue until now, amigo. And his own son, wouldn't you know. It was my job to get him out of the way. I wanted to take your father to Mexico City, but he insisted on Baja. He wanted to be near the Pacific, near San Diego. Your mother and you kids lived there before you moved up to Boston, right? He thought he could talk her into bringing you back to San Diego. I had great respect for the man. He was always thinking of his family."

"Was he?"

"*Si.*"

We walked out of Disney World, to the large parking lot where hundreds of cars simmered in the Florida heat. I told Lopez I had seen him that Christmas in Ensenada with my father. He didn't remember the occasion, but after a moment he said, "Oh, yes. Several times your father wanted to just go to Boston. I had to keep convincing him that he couldn't do that. So he had you come out to visit. I didn't think even that was a very good idea."

"How long have you known my father?"

He looked at the asphalt a moment, pursing his lips. "Long time."

"Bay of Pigs?"

He nodded.

"Did you know Xavier?"

This seemed to surprise him. "You know about Xavier?"

"It's my middle name."

"*Ah.*" He smiled and whispered something in Spanish. "Your father always had a strong sense of loyalty. Xavier and your father and I go back to the war, but Xavier died in Cuba. He did things that saved a lot of lives, including your father's. Like your father, Xavier believed deeply in freedom. They're the kind of men who live for a principle. Such great men are hard to find now."

I offered Lopez a ride in my rented Chevrolet, but he declined and said that we wouldn't be able to meet again because he was leaving the country soon. When I asked where he was going, he said, "Somewhere where it will be hard for them to find me. I'll be dead soon anyway, so I don't think they're too concerned anymore." I asked who was looking for him, but he simply shook my hand and walked away slowly. He moved like a man who didn't have long.

The Bruins and the Leafs went into overtime tied at two. Each team really opened up and had several scoring chances, but the goaltending at both ends was outstanding. With just over a minute to go, I heard the repeated clank on my radiator, which was how Mrs. Hennesey often communicated with me—she kept a wrench in her living room for that purpose. I got up off the couch and went to the door. She stood outside her apartment, looking up the staircase.

"It's her," she said, almost breathless. "Out there on the stoop."

I clambered down the stairs and went out the front door into the rain. Petra was sitting on the top step, her arms folded, shivering. Her overcoat was soiled and torn at the shoulder and I suspected she'd been pushed out of a car.

"I'm very thirsty," she whispered.

I helped her to her feet. Mrs. Hennesey held open the front door as I took her inside and up the stairs.

I GOT HER INTO a clean pair of my pajamas and into bed. She drank several glasses of water. She kept her eyes closed most of the time and she seemed to come in and out of it. I assumed she'd been drugged. Sitting on the edge of the bed, I gently washed her face with a damp towel. She had a swollen right cheek and there was a small cut on her lower lip. Her breathing had been irregular at first, but now it was beginning to even out, and I expected her to drop into sleep at any moment.

About fifteen minutes after I got her into bed, someone climbed the stairs to my apartment. I left the bedroom, closing the door behind me, and went into the kitchen. Dirk Czlenko was standing out on the landing, soaking wet.

"It's really starting to come down," he said.

"You here to give me the weather report?"

"No." He looked past me but I didn't move to let him in. "My bosses are getting extremely cranky about Petra. They think they have to do something soon or it will appear they were negligent—or worse, responsible."

"For what?"

"We don't know. But of course in this business you always think the worst." His short black hair was soaking wet and he sniffled loudly. "I suggested she got knocked up and is off having an abortion someplace like Vermont, where the Christian Right are less likely to blow her and the doctor to smithereens."

He stared past me as the door to my bedroom opened. I turned and saw Petra, leaning against the doorjamb. "That's pretty good," she said weakly.

"I thought so, too," Czlenko said. "It should buy a little time before they call the police."

I stepped back into the kitchen and he followed, peeling off his wet overcoat. He took a dish towel from the kitchen counter and began wiping his hair and face. I went into the living room and helped Petra, who was trying to lie down on the couch. "How did you know she was here?" I asked, putting a blanket over her.

"People don't give Dirk enough credit," Petra said slowly. "He has good instincts."

"I do," Czlenko said, "but the fact is I've had a thing for Petra for a long time and, as I told you, I'm just plain jealous. Can't figure what she sees in you older guys." He was standing in the kitchen doorway now, staring at the TV. "Hey, how'd the Bruins do?"

"I don't *know*," I said. "Think they tied."

"That new kid, Proulx, he looks pretty good."

On the couch Petra was sound asleep, the blue blanket pulled up to her chin.

IN 1690 AMERICA's first newspaper was published in Boston. *Publick Occurrences Both Foreign and Domestic,* which consisted of three seven-by-eleven-inch pages, was unlicensed, and the Puritan authorities, who feared any challenge to the theocracy, shut it down after one day. Fourteen years later the Postmaster of Boston, John Campbell, published the *Boston News-Letter,* which was a sensation throughout the colony, and it appeared regularly until 1776.

When I began to study journalism at Boston University in 1968, there was a sudden emergence of all things alternative—alternative newspapers, alternative radio stations, and something known as alternative "lifestyles." WBCN, the first FM radio station to play rock, came on the air at the time, and it's still at 104.1 on the dial. There was the *Boston Phoenix,* which still exists, and there was the *Boston Beacon,* which, along with a bunch of other alternative weeklies, folded after a few years. When I began writing for the *Beacon,* while still an undergrad at BU, the paper was analogous to a Red Sox team in a year when they were desperately trying to play .500 ball and achieve respectability. The writing staff consisted of a few veteran sluggers, refugees from places like the *Record-American,* plus there were a lot of us rookies, desperate to get anything into print. My first pieces had to do with city events, which at the time were referred to as "culture": I reviewed a gazillion rock concerts, from the Boston Tea Party to the Common to the Garden, and at times I covered various protests—marches, sit-ins, draft-card and bra burnings. The first piece I wrote that got some notice was about an army deserter who had sought sanctuary in the chapel at BU. Hundreds of kids surrounded the building and supported the chaplain, who would not give the police permission to enter his house of worship. I managed to sneak in a basement window and spend an afternoon eating cold pizza with the draftee, a kid from New Hampshire who just wanted to go home to his family's dairy farm and milk cows.

The *Boston Beacon* deserved to go under; it was simply a product of the times. It became a trivia question. Which was exactly why a group of Yuppies with money to burn revived it a few years ago. There was nothing *alternative* about it now. Most of the advertising came from high-tech companies and clothing designed to portray what has become known as a "lifestyle" with an "attitude." A lot of the pieces simply promoted celebrities, movies, and products. However, giving ballast to so much fluff were some very good longish stories written by their few stars—Petra Mouzakis, who covered the statehouse as well as anyone, and Dirk Czlenko, who had a talent for being on the street when graft, grizzle, and gore happen. The fact that Petra had been looking into my father for some time was a source of worry and jealousy for me. Worry, because I was afraid she'd find out something new or, at the very least, *find him.* Jealousy, because she might not blow the story, as I had. And having Dirk snooping around was bound to give you the creeps. It's like you're marked for tragedy, a pool of blood waiting to happen.

But I believed Petra when she said that Czlenko deserved credit for having instinct. With all the cyber-noise in this profession, you don't see that much anymore. And I believed Czlenko when he said he was jealous. Scratch his streetwise veneer and you'd find a lust for the lurid, but below that festered the old-fashioned dream of finding the Right Girl. So while Petra slept on the couch I took Dirk into the kitchen and got out what was left of the bottle of Johnnie Walker Black.

"I covered for her—and you—at the office," he said, "so the least you can do is clue me in." We were both drinking Scotch neat out of glasses I'd picked up at a yard sale; his had an image of Old Ironsides and mine Bullfinch's gold dome atop the statehouse on Beacon Hill. "She hovered around your mother while she was dying. Why—something to do with your father?"

I nodded.

"She thinks there's something to your father's involvement in the JFK thing."

I shrugged. "What do you think?"

He actually seemed embarrassed, which surprised me. "I think you messed that story up good," he said.

I finished my drink.

"But then you were never the one to do the story."

I reached for the Scotch and replenished our glasses. "Be kind. I'm buying."

Dirk wiped his long face and fingered his mustache a moment. Like Petra, he was in his late thirties, but you could already see the older man coming through in his sagging jawline, the pouches beneath his tired eyes. Too many deadlines. "Look, you were the man's son. You're the last one who should ever have taken the story on. It's like a doctor providing medical care for his own family—you can't be objective, you can't make the hard prognosis." He threw back his shot. "You know, a lot of that book you wrote held up. It was just that all that new shit came out of Senator Hume's subcommittee, contradicting your story, and the papers had a field day." He smiled at me as he glanced around my cramped kitchen. "You really took it on the chin. Just beginning to be a big deal. And then whammo, somebody jerks the chain. Maybe you were set up? My nose tells me you might have been too close to the truth."

"Maybe," I said. "But prove it."

"Maybe Petra wanted to?" He put his glass on the counter and picked up his soggy overcoat. "I think she got some good stuff from your mother. But the condition she's in, she can hardly remember her own name."

"It'll wear off," I said. "Just give it a few days."

"Why do I get the sense you're fighting time?"

This surprised me. "It's a personal thing. My father, he has my mother's ashes."

"No shit?" His silence for a moment was his best attempt at being respectful. Then he whispered, "The bastard." He began to pull on his overcoat but stopped, his face animated by a sudden idea. "Her notes," he said. "They're in her desk at work. After she came back from seeing your mother, I saw her put them in a drawer and lock it. I thought that was strange at the time." He grinned. "With the key and a little help, I could get them."

"Maybe it won't be necessary," I said.

"Sure, she'll be fine in the morning and remember everything like it was yesterday." Glancing back at me, he said, "I'll call tomorrow and see how she's doing?"

I nodded. For a moment I almost wanted to put my hand on his shoulder—some gesture of friendship and appreciation. I wanted to apologize for slamming his head against the wall in the statehouse. I think he understood all that. As Petra said, he had good instincts.

Instead I took one of my coats off the rack and handed it to him. "Here, take a dry one."

"You sure?" Looking at the rack, he said, "Guess you have a few to spare." He pulled mine on and zipped it up to his throat. "Nice," he said as he opened the door.

I hung up his wet raincoat. "One thing I still believe in is a really good coat."

I CARRIED PETRA back to bed and sat up with her most of the night. Periodically she awoke, groggy and always thirsty. Once she started crying in her sleep. Toward daylight I dozed awhile in the chair by the bedroom window, and when I awoke she was staring at the ceiling. I went over, sat on the bed, and smiled down at her. Her eyes seemed more focused. "How you doing?"

"All right, I think."

"You remember any of it? Where you were? Who took you?"

Her thick eyebrows moved toward each other, creating a small ridge of concentration in her forehead. "I remember it was dark."

"Of course."

"The sound of water."

"What kind? Running—like from a faucet?"

"No. Like the ocean because there was the smell of salt water and low tide." Her eyes scanned my face, as though I had the answer. "Rocking," she said. "The boat was rocking."

"You were on a boat, like it was tied up or moored."

"Yes." Suddenly she raised one arm, turned her head, and took a deep breath. "*Phew.* Do I need a *bath!*"

"I'll help you into the bathroom."

"You going to bathe me?"

"Every inch, if you want."

"Can I take a rain check on that?"

"Definitely."

I helped her out of bed and into the bathroom, where I began to draw water in the tub. Then I went into the kitchen to begin breakfast: scrambled eggs, veggie sausage, sourdough toast, Cape Cod cranberry jam, orange juice, and real coffee. I felt good for the activity. It reminded me of days when my mother would finally get over the nausea from the last bout of chemotherapy or radiation, and of all the times when Abigail tried to get clean in my apartment. When we were in our twenties, she was like my shadow. I lived in a succession of apartments—in Brighton, Alston, along Commonwealth Avenue, in the South End, and over here in Charlestown. Abby would disappear for weeks, months at a time. At first she'd come back drunk and stoned; but over the years it spiraled down into pills and cocaine and heroin addiction. There were numerous occasions when, after days of sweat-soaked, feverish sleep, she would finally make it into the bathroom not just to throw up but also to clean up, and that's when I would make breakfast.

I went to the bathroom door. "Finding everything all right?"

"I'm still in one piece."

"That's a relief. Coffee?"

"Bring it in. I found the bubble bath." I opened the door and her arm came up out of the suds. "I'm going to smell good for you, you'll see."

I sat on the edge of the tub. "Do you remember visiting my mother in the hospital?"

"Barely. I remember what a sweet lady she was."

"Dirk tells me your notebooks are locked up in your desk."

"Guess I didn't want anyone else to see them." She sipped her coffee.

"Or maybe to take them," I said. "You suppose seeing the notes would help?"

"Might."

I went and took her overcoat off the hook by the front door. In the pocket was a wallet. Petra got out of the tub and came into the kitchen wearing my green terry-cloth bathrobe and slippers. Her wet hair was slicked back against her scalp.

"Mind?" I asked.

"No."

I emptied the contents of the wallet on the kitchen table. License, credit cards, a ticket to the Boston Aquarium, a photo of her standing on the statehouse steps with several politicians and reporters. I unsnapped the coin purse and among the change was a small silver key, the kind used to open the flimsy locks built into cheap metal desks.

She sat at the table, seeming exhausted from the effort of bathing. "I can't go in there," she said. "I'm not ready for the office yet."

"All right," I said. "Mind if I try?"

"No."

"But first, you must be hungry."

"Starved."

9

After breakfast Petra went back to bed. I got the *Globe* off the bottom of the stairs—Mrs. Hennesey reads it first, then puts it out for me. The Bruins and the Leafs game ended in a tie, as I suspected. The NHL used to consist of just six teams, still referred to as the Old Six, and there was no overtime. There were no helmets. There were no curved sticks—which meant a lot of backhand shots. If the goalie's face was cut, which was not uncommon before Jacques Plante began wearing a fiberglass mask, the game was delayed while the wound was stitched. On the road a tie was as good as a win.

Then I read my mother's obituary. It was short, factual, and accurate, except for its deletions: It said that she was survived by her son, Samuel Adams; there was no mention of my father. Uncle James's doing, no doubt.

I poured another cup of coffee and looked at the front page. Senator Marshall Hume was pictured standing on a neighborhood street corner, with the Boston skyline behind him. He wouldn't confirm that he planned to run for attorney general next year, but he was already starting the campaign—the first step being to get some press that was *not* about his difficulties in the past.

Then I remembered the photo in Petra's wallet. I went back into the kitchen, where its contents were still spread out on the table. The photo showed about a dozen people grouped on the front steps of the statehouse. Several state reps (all Democrats), several news reporters, and a few people I didn't recognize. Staffers, most likely. Marshall Hume stands in back, and Petra's in front of him, one step down. Everyone's smiling for the camera.

They all look at least ten years younger. Petra's face is fuller, her hair longer; she has what my mother would call a good carriage.

Hume once gave me credit for helping him get appointed to that Senate seat; but, of course, he undercut the compliment by claiming to have tanked a tennis match to get me to do so. I did an exclusive interview with Hume for *Northeast Journal*. Over the phone his staffer said that Hume heard I played a pretty good game of tennis. I said I still had my racket. She said to bring it to the Longwood Cricket Club.

This meant playing on grass, something I had never done. When I was in my teens, I used to go to Longwood and watch the likes of Rod Laver, Roy Emerson, Pancho Gonzales, and, later, Arthur Ashe play brilliantly on those elegant lawn courts. So finally, in my late thirties, I was sliding across the manicured grass into forehands and backhands, playing the next senator from the Commonwealth of Massachusetts. Hume had a good, consistent game, the kind that always gave me trouble, as my tendency was to rely on a big slice serve and quick points finished off by winners. He just kept sending everything back, like a good politician. I overpowered him in the first set, 6–2. The speed of the ball coming up off the grass was remarkable. The second set became a long, grueling ordeal; it was late September— Indian summer—and the heat and humidity took it out of both of us. When he won, 9–7, I expected that he would suggest we call it a draw and cool off in the clubhouse. Furthermore, his redheaded staffer, the one who had contacted me by phone, who was in her mid-twenties and had very long legs, kept walking out from the shade of the clubhouse to tell him who was on the phone. In every instance, Hume said he'd call back. But after the second set he went and took a call, and was gone for at least ten minutes. I sat out there in the sun, nursing a small bottle of warm water, knowing he was in the clubhouse getting revived for a third set. Which we played, and which I won, 6–4.

Then we retreated to the cool interior of the clubhouse, where for nearly an hour Marshall Hume explained why it was imperative that he represent the Commonwealth of Massachusetts in the United States Senate. My piece in *Northeast Journal* attempted to be evenhanded, though I heard through several sources that he was displeased with how I portrayed him, and there was always the suggestion that I had not been gracious enough to accept his gift of a tennis victory. There were no gifts—neither the match nor the magazine article. Needless to say, I was never invited back to play on the lawn courts of Longwood.

Petra awoke midafternoon, and I made her a bowl of Campbell's chicken noodle soup. She looked much better and she ate sitting up in bed.

"That photo in your wallet," I said, "when was that, about ten years ago?"

She nodded.

"You weren't writing for the *Beacon* yet. Some local paper?"

She slurped up the last of her noodles.

I studied the part in her hair a moment. "You were a staffer."

"I started out as an intern when I was at BC, and one thing led to another after that."

"Hume?"

She wouldn't look up from her bowl. "That was near the end of it," she said. "When he was appointed to the Senate, I quit and found work across the street. I didn't want to leave Boston."

"I'll bet you haven't been to Longwood since then."

She lifted her head then and it was clear she was a long way back from where she'd been last night. The swelling in her cheek had gone down, too. "Marshall had certain expectations of his staff, particularly the females, of course. Staff loyalty knew no bounds. I goofed, that's all. I was coming off my divorce and I was vulnerable, as they say. Guys like Hume, Jesus. They just can't understand that we are not *all* easy blowjobs." She handed the empty soup bowl to me. "Is there any more?"

"I'll have to go out and do some shopping this afternoon. I wasn't expecting company. You look much better, but you should stay quiet."

"Okay, Dad." She slid down beneath the covers. "My head feels clearer. I've been thinking about this floating sensation on the boat. There were sounds, too—the boat moved because I could feel the throb of the engine. And then there were jets taking off nearby, regularly—I mean, like every minute or so." She closed her eyes a moment. "Hume, he didn't care for you," she said. "Something about a tennis match?"

As I was walking down the front steps to the sidewalk, a black Cadillac was coming slowly up the hill. It looked like it could hardly fit in the narrow street, parked cars all lined up on one side, and the row of brick and asbestos-sided houses seeming to lean out over the curb. The kind of street that sees direct sunlight maybe two hours a day tops. As the car came alongside, the driver's window slid down, and a trail of blue smoke escaped into the fall air.

"Hi there," Uncle James said. He took the cigar from his mouth.

"Figured I'd hear from you soon enough," I said, "though I didn't think you'd actually come by. Aunt Kathleen must really be giving you an earful."

He hung his large head out the window and dropped a wad of saliva on the pavement. "Don't worry about her. She's always gotta be exercised about this or that. We want you to come out for Sunday dinner." Before I could respond, he raised his head and said, "Look, your mother just died. You don't have to go through this alone, Sam. You come out to the house and eat a meal with everybody else. You have a family, you know."

"Jimmy, they're all going to ask the same thing. *Where are her ashes?*"

He sighed and studied Mrs. Hennesey's house for a moment. "Hey, come on—get in. Let's go for a belt. How 'bout we go down to the harbor and get ourselves a bucket of steamers?"

When I was a kid, it was always Uncle James who came out to the house in Salem, usually spur of the moment, and took me somewhere. Often Abby would come, too, if it was for ice cream or something. But there were also times when he'd have a couple tickets to Fenway Park or Boston Garden, and it was just the two of us. Every boy growing up in New England, if he's lucky, is supposed to see his first Red Sox game with his father. For me, it was Uncle James, and I loved him for it. And I could never turn him down.

"Jimmy, I just can't," I said, nearly pleading. "Not right now."

He took a puff on his cigar and tapped the ash. "Well, I'd invite myself up, but I guess you don't keep much booze around anymore."

"I know what you're trying to do—and I appreciate your handling Mom's obit. But I'd rather not come out and see the family until, you know, this thing gets resolved."

"Sammy," he said—and he's the only person who ever called me that, "it's really just ashes. It's no big deal. We can have a memorial Mass and then all go back to our house and eat and drink ourselves through it. Don't take it all on yourself alone."

I put one hand on the roof of his car. It was spotless. Since he'd retired I think he had his Caddy washed and waxed about every other day. Though they lived out in Wellesley now, I also suspected that he still drove into town most days and just hung around, stopping in on old customers, or finding a corner table in some of the bars he hung out in when he was starting out in Dorchester. A guy in a black Caddy in Wellesley is invisible. But James Byrne parking his Caddy out front of some neighborhood pub is somebody, a man with a history, a life. "Jimmy, thanks. Really. I'm all right. Tell them I'm all right, and tell Aunt Kathleen I'm sorry—I didn't mean to sound the way I did on the phone. I'll get out and see everyone soon." He was watching me closely, his blue eyes one of the few things I've ever really trusted since I was a kid. I leaned down to him, inhaling cigar smoke. "I can't just let this go, Jimmy. I've got to find those ashes, and you know it."

I DROVE THROUGH East Boston and parked on Bayswater Street, where I could look across an inlet toward Logan Airport. The wind was coming off the Atlantic, so the planes were lining up at the near end of the runway, about a quarter of a mile across water. Every minute or two the thrust of jet engines would transform the air so it sounded as though someone had poked a hole in this life and let in a blast straight out of hell. Across the street these neat, older homes looked like they'd spent decades braced for this daily barrage. Modern transportation has not set well with Boston, which was originally built around a pasture and whose first streets were sinuous cow paths.

I walked for several blocks looking at the boats moored in the inlet. Some were skiffs with outboard engines; some were powerboats that had all the grace and buoyancy of empty Clorox bottles. There were a few sail-boats. Nothing exotic. One was a Catalina, which is designed for family sailing—sort of a Winnebago that floats. Down near where the inlet feeds into the harbor there were two larger sailboats, *Boston Light,* Winthrop, which was about thirty-five feet and covered with seagull droppings, and a ketch, *Simple Truth,* Nahant. A couple of dinghies were hauled up on the beach and I considered taking one and rowing out, but in East Boston that could get you shot. So I stood on the shore and watched the sailboats for a while, then drove back into the city, taking the Sumner Tunnel under the harbor, coming up out of the dark into the splendid confusion that is down-town Boston.

A LITTLE AFTER dark I met Czlenko on the sidewalk outside the office of the *Boston Beacon,* an old brick building in the Fens. We climbed the steep flight of stairs to the second floor and entered through a steel fire door. The open loft was filled with a couple of dozen computer terminals beneath long panels of fluorescent light. Phones rang constantly and staffers, few older than thirty, bustled around with that quick, harried step I used to know so well. There wasn't an Ed Nichols in sight.

The place wasn't going full tilt, either; it was the end of the day. Many desks were already empty. People were packing up to go home. But for every staffer who can't wait to get out the door, there's usually one who finds it hard to leave, who hangs around, tinkering with a story on the com-puter, talking on the phone, or just sitting there looking like a trained dog awaiting the next command. I used to be one of those people.

Czlenko and I hung around his desk for about twenty minutes while the place really emptied out. Phones stopped ringing; printers were shut off; computer screen savers swirled and drifted. Someone switched off sev-eral lights on their way out, and that was when Dirk took the bottle of vodka from his desk drawer and poured some in two Styrofoam cups.

"Which one's Petra's desk?" I asked quietly.

He nodded toward the wall of windows that overlooked the street. A neat desk—no surprise there—with paperwork stacked in squared piles.

No stuffed animals, no crude cartoons taped to the sides of the gray metal desk. A young woman sat at the adjacent desk, working at her computer, oblivious to the fact that there were now only the three of us left in the office.

"Celeste," Dirk said, finally, "take a fucking break and come over for a drink."

She looked up, needing a moment to focus her eyes, and then pushed back her chair. She was in her early thirties, had short spiky blond hair and a small gold nose stud. Her skin wasn't pale; it was white. Certain Bostonians are capable of achieving such pallor; it's as though they have never been out in the sun. She sat down at the desk next to Dirk's and accepted his offer of a Styrofoam cup. She was wearing a very short black skirt and she had the legs for it.

"Celeste Lapierre, this is an old alum from the original *Beacon,* Samuel Adams."

"I recognize you," she said. "I liked your book."

"Thanks," I said. "That practically makes you family." She smiled and there was the glint of a gold stud back on her tongue.

"Celeste is our new Metro editor," Dirk said. His voice was approaching charm, which on him sounded downright salacious.

"Congratulations," I said, raising my Styrofoam cup. "Now you'll never know who your friends really are."

"I know," she said. "I've lost most of the ones I thought I had, and I've gained *so* many who want something from me, some story."

"She's doing *fine,*" Czlenko said. "How 'bout we go down to the Cask and Flagon?"

Celeste glanced at her watch and said, "Sure."

Five minutes later we were walking toward Fenway Park. The bar was on the corner, just across the street from the left-field foul pole. We went inside and Czlenko insisted on ordering a round of Sam Adams, of course. Then he thrust his hands in the pockets of his coat—my coat, the tan-and-green North Face shell that I had lent him the night before—and said, "Fuck if I left my wallet in my desk." This sounded more convincing than his charm act.

"What people will do to get out of buying a round," I said as I put a twenty on the bar.

"I'll be back for the next one," Dirk said, and he hustled out the door.

Celeste lit a cigarette. She sat on the stool with her legs crossed and it was hard to keep myself from looking down. I studied the walls, which were covered with old photos of Fenway Park and Red Sox players. "So, you working?" she asked.

"Not much lately. Freelance projects here and there."

She drank down a good portion of her sixteen-ounce beer. "Samuel Adams," she said. "I suppose these days a lot of people—people *my* age—only think you're named after the beer."

"A lot of people *my* age are halfway to Alzheimer's, so they don't know pilsners from patriots. It was funny, though, when the beer first came out, people kept giving me T-shirts, mugs, ball caps, and stuff. Most people don't know that Sam Adams inherited a brewery from his old man but it went bankrupt. And he was Cambridge's tax collector—he was so bad at it, they kept reelecting him."

"Another mediocre life saved by revolution." She finished her beer.

I ordered another round.

"You're not working much because you don't want to, or because people aren't returning your calls?" I put an elbow on the bar and squared myself to her. "You still have this stigma, I suppose," she said. "It's too bad. In this business people have long memories, particularly for the deep shit." I nodded. "I have to tell you that when I read your book, my first reaction was, *Oh, come on.* But finally I was convinced. And I realized it must have been a bitch for you to write."

"Assassination theories are a dime a dozen."

"I know, but to lay all that stuff out about your father—where he was on such and such a day, who he'd been in contact with, what memos, phone calls, and letters went back and forth—it must have been really hard. I mean it's your *father.*"

"In some ways I felt I was really getting to know him for the first time."

"Yes, and *that's* why the book *worked.* It was written by a journalist doing his job, *and* by a son who was just trying to understand. Later when

Hume and the press started tearing the whole thing apart, it almost seemed to be with a vengeance—like you had struck *too* close to a nerve." She watched me for a moment and I glanced toward the door, hoping that Czlenko would be quick about unlocking Petra's desk, getting her notebooks, and returning so this wouldn't go another round. "Now that I'm doing the Metro section, I'd like to do some new things." Celeste was staring up at me, all business. "If you're interested in some work, pitch me an idea."

"Nothing comes to mind at the moment, but thanks," I said. "Really."

"I'm not talking about an interview with some new starlet in town to pump her movie, you know. I want to take the section somewhere else." Her glass was already empty and I was only half done with mine.

"Celeste, I think you have a future in this business."

She smiled, gold glinting. "How 'bout if I get this round." She raised her arm to get the bartender's attention. "And let's punch it up with a couple of shots of Stoly."

I nodded. "Yep, definitely there's a future here."

AFTER WE FINISHED the second shot of Stoly, I said, "What's keeping Czlenko?"

"The man doesn't move in a straight line. He zigzags."

"I'm going to walk back to the office. You can wait here, if you'd like."

"No," she said. "If I don't get out of here now, I won't leave till last call."

We went out into the Boston night. The backside of the Green Monster loomed above us. The lights of Fenway Park were dark, now in hibernation until the coming spring. As we hustled down the sidewalk, we talked about how there were plans to tear Fenway down; it was still hard to believe. Celeste said she was from Waterbury, Connecticut, and that she'd grown up in a divided house—her mother, a New Yorker, was a Yankees fan, while her father, from Warwick, Rhode Island, was a Sox fan. Celeste, an only child, sided with Daddy. We talked about John Updike's piece on Ted Williams's last game. I told her about WMEX, which back in the fifties and sixties was *the* station kids listened to and one of the DJs was named Fenway.

And I told her about the Boston Tea Party. "It was originally on Berkeley Street in the South End, in this old church," I said. "We'd go and see new acts like Jeff Beck and Rod Stewart. The house band was J. Geils before they went national. Then the club moved to one of the buildings on Lansdowne Street, right across from the wall outside center field. On a summer night you'd come out of the Tea Party after listening to a set by B. B. King or something like Ginger Baker's Air Force, and the lights would be on above the park—and suddenly there'd be this incredible roar of the crowd."

"You used to cover concerts for the *Beacon,* right?"

"Concerts and protests mostly."

"Not much of either now."

"Yeah, I'm a real dinosaur."

At the next intersection we turned down the street to our right and leaned into the cold wind. The block was dark—one of the street lamps was out—but I could see Czlenko step out of the entrance to the *Beacon* offices. As he came toward us, passing in and out of shadows, I noticed movement in the street—a car without its headlights on cruised up slowly, and when it was alongside Dirk, three shots were fired. Czlenko's head snapped to the left and then he sprawled forward onto the sidewalk. Celeste screamed and grabbed my arm. The car speeded up and raced by us—a luxury sedan, though it was too dark to tell its color or make—and its tires squealed as it turned the corner.

We both ran to Czlenko. I remember drawing cold night air into my lungs, and suddenly feeling terribly sober. Behind me Celeste was crying, and within moments there was the sound of people running toward us from the buildings across the street. Overhead, a window opened and a woman shouted out that she'd called the police. I reached Czlenko first. The right side of his head was exploded and raw flesh trailed out onto the bricks. There was already a tremendous pool of blood beneath his face. Suddenly I knelt down and reached into his coat pockets and took out two reporter's notebooks.

"What are you doing?" Celeste said behind me.

"It's *my* coat," I said. "Don't you understand? He's wearing *my* coat."

And then it became something else. A public event. The police arrived first, followed minutes later by the ambulance. A crowd gathered around the body. There was confusion, panic, bold curiosity. It became a public event on a Boston street. A brutal slaying. Blood and brains on the sidewalk bricks. It became the kind of event Dirk Czlenko covered like no one else.

Part II

Spectral Evidence

10

The police investigation took hours. Celeste and I were questioned together by a cop on the beat, then separately by a detective. I didn't get back to Charlestown until nearly two in the morning. By then a cold mist had blown in off the Atlantic. The apartment was dark and the bedroom door ajar, so I undressed in the living room. As I started to settle into the couch, Petra came out of the bedroom.

"You heard about Czlenko?" she said.

"Yes. I was there."

"Oh, God," she whispered. "Sam, I didn't know. I just caught the end of the news on TV." She sat next to me on the couch.

"He was wearing my coat."

She took my hand. "Come to bed."

"He was wearing my coat."

"It's not what you think, Sam."

"How do you know?"

"No one would mistake Dirk for you."

"We're both tall," I said. "It was dark—a street lamp was out and—"

"Please, just come to bed."

She took my arm and we stood up. Without turning on a light, we lay down in the bed. She pulled the blankets over us. I started to speak but she whispered, "Shhh," and we held each other until exhaustion gave way to sleep.

———

AT SOME POINT near dawn we awoke. Though I don't remember really opening my eyes, I realized that we were making love. It was as though we were still half asleep. Both of us sobbed. Neither of us spoke. And when it was over, we slept again.

WE AWOKE TO the dull gray light of an overcast day. I got up and went down to the bottom of the stairs for Mrs. Hennesey's *Globe*. I looked at the front page before the sports section. There was nothing about Czlenko's murder—it happened too late to get into the morning edition. When I got back up to the kitchen, I nearly stumbled on an old pair of my boots lying on the floor by the coatrack.

Petra was at the counter making coffee. She saw me looking at the boots and said, "When you didn't come back by about ten, I walked down to that corner store and picked up a few things for dinner." She brought two mugs of coffee to the kitchen table. "You want something? Eggs?"

I shook my head and sat down. We drank coffee, looking out the front window.

"It's ironic, I suppose," she said finally. "A guy who makes a career out of writing about street crime—the senseless slayings that we come to take for granted—"

"This wasn't random violence," I said. "They thought it was me."

Petra ran her finger around the handle of her mug. She was trying to be careful not to resist in a way that would only further solidify my supposition. "What did the police say?"

"They asked a lot of questions. That's their job. What *could* they say? They didn't know it was my coat."

"You didn't tell them."

"No, I didn't tell them."

I went to the coatrack and brought the two reporter's notebooks back to the table.

"Have you read them?" she asked.

I shook my head. "They're yours. Shouldn't I have permission first?"

She considered this for a long moment. Her eyes were clear now, but they were guarded. Looking down into the street, she said, "Your mother told me a lot of things—things about you, your father—your sister. Some of it's . . . personal."

"Everything's personal. Only the idiots in our profession pretend it can be made into something else."

She tilted her head and put her hand up under her hair, then ran her fingers out through the ends. A momentary look of disgust crossed her face. "I can't do this." Picking up the notebooks, she pushed back her chair. "Not now. I'm not ready." She went into the bedroom and closed the door.

I REMAINED AT the kitchen table. My street, like all of Bunker Hill, is centuries old. How many people have inhabited this hill across the harbor from Boston? I like living in old places. I feel that I'm a part of something larger than my own life—the slow accumulation of small events that comprise history. It seems appropriate, even necessary, to remain watchful of the street. It's an American tradition.

Finally, I went into the living room and stretched out on the couch. I must have slept until around noon, when I was awakened by Petra, naked, and we made love again. As I lay on my back, I could look out the bay windows behind the couch at swift clouds racing in off the Atlantic. When Petra knelt above me, fleeting sunlight cut across her breasts. As she leaned forward, her hair spilled over her face, and I could only see her open mouth. Downstairs Mrs. Hennesey was watching an old movie and Jimmy Stewart's stammering echoed up through the floor. He was cross-examining Lee Remick, and when we came noisily, Mrs. Hennesey turned her TV down. Petra settled on top of me, our skin damp with sweat, and I pulled the blanket over us. She looked at me, curious, baffled, exhausted. "One of my favorites," I said. *"Anatomy of a Murder."* There was a hint of a smile as she closed her eyes.

WHEN I AWOKE, Petra was running water in the bathtub. I went into the kitchen and saw a red *4* blinking on the answering machine. Turning up the sound, I played back the messages. Two were from reporters, one from the *Herald* and one from Channel 5, who wanted to interview me about Czlenko's death.

One was from Ike Santori, up in Salem. His voice was deeper than usual; he sounded like he was getting over a sore throat. "Hey, I just got in from a week on Georges Bank. I'm sorry about your mother, Sam, real sorry. This other thing, the reporter being shot—we have to talk. Soon. And remember, if the city gets too hot, you can always go fishing. It's another world out there on the water. Okay, man, you hang in there."

The fourth message was from my father. "Sam, you have every right to be upset, but I had to do this. Now I just heard on the news that you were there when this reporter was shot. I hope your not answering means that you've already gotten out of there. If not, go somewhere where they can't follow you, Sam. I'm hoping you've figured this out enough at least to realize that you're not safe at the moment. But if you do get this message, you'll have to think fast, son. You always could." He hung up.

"That your father?" Petra was standing in the living room, wearing one of my shirts. Her hair was pinned up in back and her head looked small and delicate, her lips fuller, if possible.

"That sound in the background," I said. "Seagulls? The cawing of seagulls?"

After a moment, she nodded. "He's saying you're in danger?"

"He's near water, salt water," I said. "Before anything else, he was a navy man. He loves the ocean."

"What are you going to do?" She looked and sounded frightened suddenly.

"You're drawing a bath," I said. "That seems like the next logical step."

So we sat in the tub, our heads just above the suds at opposite ends. As kids Abby and I often bathed together. Mom let us until I was about nine or ten. My sister's frail young body was as familiar to me as my own. When we got older and she developed hips and breasts, I still thought of her as the skinny girl who played in the tub. Later, when the cocaine and the heroin and the booze—and the men—had taken their toll, I sometimes bathed Abby. She would come to me, helpless, and after several days of sweating it out of her system in my bed, I would finally get her into the tub and bathe her. She was still young and she should have been beautiful, but there were the tracks, on her arms, her thighs, and there was something about her hips and breasts, though still profoundly sensuous, that seemed shamefully worn and used. When she died she was thirty-five, nearly the same age as Petra, but by then my sister's body seemed hopelessly eroded. Years later I helped my mother in and out of the bathtub when she was particularly weak during the chemotherapy or radiation treatments. Though her skin was mottled and wrinkled, she was still beautiful. We often say that someone is "possessed of beauty." That was so in my mother's case, and it was a sense of possession that she had throughout her life. Abby was meant to have that possession, too. She should still have it; she should be approaching fifty, matronly, and handsome. Instead she became *possessed*. Or perhaps her body should never have been transformed from that of the child I knew in the tub, the one with skinny, flailing arms, splashing me, splashing Mom, delighting in the warm, soapy water, the bobbing ducks and boats, the festivity of getting clean.

"You say my mother told you personal things. What kind?"

Petra ran the sponge along her shoulder and down her arm. She wouldn't look at me.

"Did she tell you about senior year, how Abby didn't graduate because she was stoned all the time and hardly ever went to class? That was the year she became possessed. I mean a lot of people in Salem didn't think it was some kids' prank—they really thought she was a witch. We had a home economics teacher—we still had those back then—who called my mother and said she was certain that Abby was the reincarnation of Abigail Williams." Petra looked fiercely at me across the lumpy plain of bubbles. "You know, the girl who danced in the woods and accused others of witchcraft."

"When was that, Sam, 1690s?"

"It had been going on for years, but the worst of the trials took place in 1692."

"Over three hundred years ago," Petra said, nodding. "Your mother said you rely on this cockeyed sense of history. That was her term, *cockeyed*. It's somewhere in my notes, if you want to look it up."

"My father believes journalists have no sense of history, that we're only concerned with what *is,* not what *was.*"

"That sounds like an accusation." She started to get out of the tub. I grabbed her ankle, and she sat down hard and glared at me.

"Let's look at the history for a minute," I said. "Let's go back to the beginning. What first prompted you to go see my mother while she was dying?"

"I—" She settled back into the suds and exhaled slowly. "All right, Sam. I thought—I *think*—that you were right, or close to right. I have thought so ever since I read your book. Despite all the stuff that's come out since, I think it's quite possible that your father played a role in Kennedy's assassination." I let go of her foot under the water. "I thought that if I could find him, I could—I could do what *you* never did. I could *ask* him." She stared hard at me. "You built this whole case in your book and it all added up, but it was circumstantial. You had eyewitnesses who placed him in Dallas, who placed him in Dealey Plaza prior to the president's motorcade, who placed him in a car going into that parking lot between the railroad tracks and the stockade fence up on the knoll. And you had the photos of a man with a rifle. Fine—but you never found your father, Sam. You never asked him."

"Finding him has never been easy."

"Maybe you haven't *tried.* Maybe you haven't tried *hard* enough, Sam." She was almost yelling now. "Maybe you're afraid to hear it from him. After all, he *is* your father."

"You think I'm afraid of him? You think I never confronted him?"

She just looked at me.

I splashed her. Her face froze into shock, even alarm. As I splashed her again, bubbles drifted down on her hair. And then she began flailing her arms and I closed my eyes against the soapy water. She was screaming, swearing, and this, too, for a moment reminded me of times when I would be trying to help Abby—when she would curse me, spit at me, strike out with her arms and feet.

Finally I got hold of Petra's wrists and held tightly until she became still. We were both winded and our breathing echoed off the bathroom tiles. "You went snooping around my mother while she was dying," I said quietly.

"She *wanted* to talk to me. She kept telling me to come back."

"So? And *then* what? If she helped you, if you *found* him, *then what?*" She tried to pull her arms free. "You'd open this whole thing up again? I'd have to live through it again? That's what all this is? The ouzo. This sudden intimacy? All for the story. *Right?* All for a fucking *story!*"

"You think that, Sam? You really think *that?*"

"Was Czlenko a part of it, too?"

She shook her head. Hard.

"But *this*—*this* is all to get to my father." She leaned back and closed her eyes. I let go of her wrists. "Or maybe you just like fucking older guys?" She was shaking her head slowly and tears formed at the corners of her eyes. I got up out of the tub, wrapped a towel around my waist, and left the bathroom.

AFTER DRESSING I went into the kitchen and looked for something to eat. There wasn't much in the refrigerator other than some sliced turkey that I'd bought maybe a week earlier. I tore away the hardened edges and put what was left between two pieces of stale sourdough bread. After taking a bite, I opened the sandwich up and added mustard. As I chewed I stared at my boots on the floor beneath the coatrack. Finally I tossed the sandwich in the trash and picked up one of the boots. Dexters, a good, sturdy walking shoe made in Maine; I'd had them for years. The sole, worn and rounded at the heel, was encrusted with sand.

Petra came into the kitchen, dressed; she pulled on her torn overcoat and went straight to the door. "I'm sorry, Sam. I won't interfere with your *personal* life any longer."

I leaned over the trash basket and brushed the sand off the boot. "When you went out for food last night, what did you get?" She had her hand on the doorknob but she didn't move. "You said you went down to the corner." I put the boot on the radiator. "There a beach between here and there?"

"*What?*"

"You follow me over to East Boston yesterday? That where this sand came from?" I went over and pushed the door shut. "Sit down." Her eyes were hurt and hateful. "Sit *down,*" I said. After a moment she moved to the kitchen table and dropped into a chair.

"How'd you follow me? You don't have a car here."

After a moment, she said, "There was a cab down in Thompson Square. I was lucky to find one so quickly. Actually, I was going to go back to my place and get some things, a change of clothes. But when I saw your car ahead of me in traffic, I told the cabbie to follow you." She shrugged. "Sorry. I'm a reporter, Sam. I was curious."

I picked up the other boot, brushed the sand off into the trash basket, and placed it on the radiator next to its mate. Out the window I could see a flock of seagulls lined up on the roof peaks across the street. When they come this far in from the harbor, it usually means we're going to get weather.

"You want this story," I said, sitting across from her. "You want *this* story *that* bad, then you're going to have to stick with me—*real* close. We need each other. You want my father. I want my mother's ashes. Fine." Petra looked down into the street a moment, then back at me. "Now get out those notebooks," I said, "and let's see what's in them."

11

My sister became possessed our senior year in high school. I knew she was using pot and hash and speed and, by springtime, LSD, but Salem began to believe that she was truly in congress with the devil, that she was the leader of a group of girls who were, much like their seventeenth-century predecessors, dancing naked in the woods.

I also knew she was involved with various boys, although who was in possession of whom is debatable. And then there was our beloved Mr. Frye, who taught music and voice, and was the indisputable heartthrob of the school's female population. Abigail was a sweet, clear soprano, and she sang in the school chorale. Mr. Justin Frye was in his late twenties, recently divorced, and he was one of the first members of the faculty to grow sideburns. He was giving private lessons to my sister in the small, soundproofed practice rooms off the band room. When she told me this—while stoned, of course—she said that Mr. Frye admired how she could hit F-sharp when she came. I didn't get a chance to take this up with Mr. Frye because he disappeared a few weeks before graduation. Some of our classmates believed it was the result of my sister's witchcraft, some hex, some spell she had cast. I suspected my father, but I couldn't prove it. Part of me wanted to believe that my father had taken care of Mr. Frye. But, of course, my father hadn't been in Salem since the previous summer. (I even entertained suspicions that he had farmed the job out.) Most likely, the truth was that Frye disappeared because the school administration had caught wind of his dalliances—or maybe he just couldn't take another day of teaching music.

When my father returned to live with us in Salem, it was clear that he was uncomfortable in the role of father. He'd had little practice. He was restless, and he devoted much of his time and energy to seeing that *Shallop* was seaworthy. Several times he and I cruised the coast, mooring as far down east as Mount Desert Island in Maine. They were the best times we'd ever had together—perhaps the only real father-son times we'd had; often, though, he single-handed, sailing away for days, and then suddenly calling to say he'd be returning to Salem the following evening.

I think now that tacitly we conspired to drive him out. The domestic ruckus of our daily lives was wielded as a form of retribution for all the years he had abandoned us. When he was home he was frequently the designated chauffeur (I had my license, Abby did not), driving his daughter to school functions, musical events, friends' houses, dentist appointments. While most of our classmates' fathers quietly submitted to this subservient role, our father always seemed anxious, impatient. And oblivious. For a man who apparently had performed complex, secret missions for the government, when it came to his own family, he was often just plain dense. Abigail seldom wore anything but black. She had a perpetual dazed expression, or she was so high that she was acutely energetic. Our mother, though unaware of the real causes, understood that Abby was going through what was then called "a difficult phase." Nowadays, American parents expect their children to encounter drugs by the time they're in their teens; in the late sixties, that was hardly a foregone conclusion. Mom simply tried to stay in touch with Abby. She did not, like so many parents, want to suffocate her daughter. She assumed, as she always had, that we possessed the responsibility to do what was right for ourselves. But Abby was possessed by something other than responsibility. And once it took hold, it never really left her.

Opening one of the notebooks on the kitchen table, Petra said, "Your mother talked about your sister a lot."

"She always did."

"She blamed your father for what happened to her."

"No surprise there."

"She blamed herself for what happened to you."

After a moment, I said, "What, in my mother's estimation, happened to me?"

"It's more a matter of what *didn't* happen. You never married. You never had children and—"

"I never had a family," I said.

Petra started to look up but instead flipped the pages of her notebook. "She said you took on your father's responsibility—for her, for your sister—and to get married would have been akin to abandoning them."

"Really? And I thought it was because I just hadn't met the right girl. You know, one my mother would approve of."

"She told me you were right—your father *was* in Dallas. She didn't say if he had anything to do with the assassination, but I don't think she'd be surprised if he had. It was as though that was something she'd been avoiding for years. When I'd bring up Dallas, she'd change the subject, but then she'd inch back toward it in her own fashion. It was as though she were trying to develop a defense for your father." She tapped a finger on the pages of her notebook. "Your mother covered so much ground it's hard for me—I really need to sit down and type this stuff up."

"My father," I said. "Did she have any idea where he's been in recent years? Had he been in touch at all? Sometimes I thought so, though it was hard to tell with her. She was too forgiving."

Petra opened the second notebook and thumbed through the pages.

"Look," I said. "There's someone else who wants to get to my father, right?"

"Yes. They had me doped up on a boat. And I think that place across the harbor is a good guess. The jets were loud."

"Uh-huh."

"It's the truth, Sam."

I smiled. "Okay, you're a reporter. What do you know about the truth?"

"It really happened," she said. "All of it."

"Maybe," I said. "But it *is* true that someone's after my father—I met them on Newbury Street. But it's *also* possible—if somebody *did* think Czlenko was me—they want to stop me from finding him. So which is it?"

"Or is it both?" she said. I hadn't considered this and she could see that. "Is it someone who's trying to get to your father, or someone who's trying to keep you from getting to him? Or both?"

"Good question," I said.

"I'm a journalist. We're supposed to ask them." She leaned forward slightly. "Sam, in that phone message your father said you're in danger and you should get out of here."

"He did," I said, closing up the notebooks and handing them to her. "And when you're in danger, what do you do? Who do you go to?"

"The police?" I nodded. "But not you?"

"Ike Santori isn't any ordinary cop." I took my boots off the radiator and handed them to her. "You might need these."

She started to unbutton her shirt as she walked into the bedroom. "I'll be a minute."

When I heard the bathroom door close, I went to the bookcase in the living room. I pulled out several novels I'd had since college—*Portrait of a Lady, The Castle,* and *The Late George Appley.* I put the .38 Smith & Wesson in my coat pocket, blew dust off the tops of the volumes, and put them back on the shelf.

ROUTE 1 WINDS north out of the city, taking you past discount stores, home-supply centers, motels, restaurants, and not a few adult bookstores and strip joints, classic American eyesores crammed together in competition for the unsuspecting motorist's buck. Things start to thin out as you approach Danvers, which in the 1690s was the Salem Village of witch trial fame. As the monolithic theocracy eroded, breakaway parishes formed new towns, so the contemporary map of eastern Massachusetts is the product of subdivisions that multiplied and spread much like rampant cancer cells. Thus old Salem is now Salem and Danvers, Newbury is now Newbury, Newburyport, and West Newbury, Dedham is now Dedham, Needham, and Wellesley, and so on. The old seaport of Salem, like Breed's Hill, has in modern times taken credit—or blame, depending on how you look at it—for events that took place nearby.

Salem is less than twenty miles from the Mystic River Bridge, which takes one north out of Boston, but it feels like two centuries. It's a town that suffered its worst episode, the witch trials, three hundred years ago, and it has been in gentile economic decline since the second war with Britain, which ended in 1815. The international shipping trade prior to the British blockades and Jefferson's embargoes resulted in enormous Federalist houses that still dominate the narrow streets; some Colonials have also survived, such as the Turner-Ingersoll House, dubbed the House of the Seven Gables by Nathaniel Hawthorne. The city's biggest industry now is tourism, based on the desire to look at historical remnants of the Puritan age, when fear of witches was as powerful and real as the present-day fear of the atomic bomb.

I turned my battered '88 Volvo into the parking lot above the dock near Pickering Wharf, where the small fleet of commercial fishing boats was tied up. Ike Santori waved from the pilothouse of his trawler, *Madonna,* and we climbed aboard. Two of his crewmen had tools and engine parts laid out on the stern deck. Petra and I went into the pilothouse, where Ike was on his cell phone arguing over the price of cod and haddock. He pointed at an open bottle of red wine on the chart table and then raised a finger to indicate that he'd be right back. He went outside and limped astern, still talking on the cell phone.

"Ike?" Petra said. "Dwight Santori?"

I poured wine into three coffee mugs on the chart table and handed one to her. "His father fought in the Normandy Invasion and believed Eisenhower was the greatest soldier who ever lived. So he named his son after him. Ike was a Boston cop and we go back to the days when we both had beats to cover—sometimes the same protest or concert. We used to drink together, and if he heard something interesting, he'd pass it along. About six years ago some kids were knocking over a warehouse in Mattapan and Ike took a bullet in the hip. He's been fishing out of Salem ever since."

Ike returned and gave me a big hug. "Sorry, man. When's the—"

"No memorial service set yet," I said. "There's a bit of a snag." His sad eyes regarded me a moment, then he smiled at Petra. "Petra Mouzakis," I said.

"I'd give you a hug, too," Ike said, "but I reek of fish. Why is your name familiar?"

"I write for the *Boston Beacon.*"

"The new one." He shook his large head and smiled. "Never read it."

I said, "Then maybe you remember her as an aide to one of our state reps, who went on to become U.S. senator."

"Ah, yes," Ike said. "When I was on the force, there were jobs Mr. Hume needed done. We escorted him all over the city." Raising his mug of wine, he said, "I *never* forget a beautiful woman. You don't have anything to do with Hume now?"

"Not in a long time," Petra said.

Ike leaned against the wheel and sipped his wine. His other hand stroked his black stubble goatee. Ike was the closest thing to a brother I'd ever had, and I knew he was waiting for me to ask him to speak his mind. When he hesitated like this, it was never a good sign. Finally I said, "Okay, tell me."

"I hear things, you know? Fish talk to me. The seagulls come to my window at night and whisper. I get phone calls from people in Boston who, I don't understand it, but they feel this need to unburden themselves." His arms and shoulders were working hard, and this was all for the benefit of the beautiful woman in our presence. I glanced at Petra and she was loving it. I'd seen variations on it for over twenty years—in bars, restaurants, at parties, simply out on the sidewalk in Back Bay.

"Yes, yes," I said to Petra. "He's always had this powerful connection with our city on the hill."

"This Hume," Ike said, "I'm hearing whisperings, murmurs. Now that he's been booted out of Washington, he wants to come back home and prove them all wrong."

"You mean by running against Pauline Wainwright for attorney general," I said.

Ike nodded. "Wainwright's very popular, even if she *is* practically the last breathing Brahman in public life. The *Herald* calls her 'the Yuppie Yankee.' You see the wisdom of his strategy? It's just like a guy like Hume to go after the toughest spot. Put himself right where he isn't needed. Wainwright's good—at the rate she's going, she could become governor of the Commonwealth, if she doesn't get lured down to Washington first. It would take something extraordinary for anyone to beat her—especially someone who left Washington under the veil of scandal. So he needs a plan, a most diabolical plan."

"And this is what the seagulls have brought to your window?" Petra asked.

"Of course—and you should never doubt seagulls, the best fishermen in the world!" Ike put his mug on the chart table. "So to win, Hume needs to clear the Green Monster. A grand slam, even."

"I've seen Hume play tennis," I said. "He doesn't have that kind of power."

Ike tugged on an earlobe as he studied the harbor a moment. "Sometimes I don't want to believe the things I hear." He still wasn't looking at me, and I was worried. "You know the last thing I'd want to do is to say something that might suggest disrespect for one's family."

"I know, Ike." Since I had to move my mother into assisted living, Ike had been looking after her house up here. "You're the closest thing to family I've got now."

He looked at me. "It's about your father, Sam. Hume is running his 'clean' platform. He's going to clean up the harbor, clean up the river, clean up the streets of Boston. *Right.* But he knows that *every*one knows that's never going to happen—it's just something politicians say at election time. So, where's the grand slam?" He picked up his mug of wine. "He thinks he's going to steal the election by solving the biggest mystery of our generation once and for all—do what all those assassination committees and commissions failed to do. He's going to pull your father in and prove he was the one, the real one who pulled the trigger."

I went to the starboard windows and looked up toward the old customshouse. I had to let Salem back in slowly, and I always tried to first see it from the water, before I went down its narrow, crooked streets, its buckled brick sidewalks. "I knew someone was looking for him—someone besides me," I said. "I just didn't know who or why."

"You going up to the house?" he asked.

I nodded.

We were silent a moment. When I turned around, tears were streaming from his big brown eyes. There was no flair now, no bravado for old times' sake. "When I got shot," he said to Petra, "my mother had been dead less than a year. The doctors replaced my hip with this plastic gizmo held together by a couple of nuts and bolts they picked up at Ace Hardware. The day I'm going to be released from the hospital, Sam and his mother come into the room and she says, 'You're coming home to Salem with me.' And she took care of me all those weeks while I learned to walk again."

I put my hand on Ike's shoulder and squeezed hard. My mother had been dead only a few days and it hadn't been something I'd had to come to terms with yet, which was really how I preferred it. I wanted to find her ashes in the worst way, but I wasn't looking forward to the occasions with my relatives—the memorial Mass, the meals, the drinks, the *event* of it. In this I think I understood my father.

PETRA AND I drove up to my mother's house, which was on Andrew Street, a few houses off the Common. White paint was peeling from the nail-sprung clapboards.

"How long since your mother lived here?" she asked as I unlocked the front door.

"More than a year," I said. "She always said she'd come home again, so I tried to keep it as it was—but I think she knew she wouldn't." We went into the front vestibule; to the right, the living-room furniture was covered with sheets. The house was cold and damp. I turned the thermostat dial and the furnace rumbled down in the cellar. "My father said he was going to 'take her home.' This was her home—our home—but he never considered it 'home.' I don't know where else to look."

In the kitchen Petra opened the refrigerator, which was empty except for a can of coffee and several bottles of beer. We split one of the beers. It was late afternoon and we were both exhausted. We went upstairs and got into my mother's bed, still wearing our clothes, and fell asleep in minutes.

12

Returning to Salem had never been easy for me after Abigail's death, and there were times when my mother talked about living elsewhere. But she had spent so many years moving around with my father that she was afraid to leave Andrew Street. My father said he was going to take my mother's ashes home. But I found no sign of him in her Salem house. I had missed something.

When people ask me where I grew up and I tell them Salem, they often get this skeptical look. There are so many stories about the supernatural associated with this town that one never thinks of people living conventional lives here, playing tennis here. My mother was remarkably down-to-earth, yet she was absolutely certain that she had seen Abby after her death. Once she saw her float across the ceiling above her bed, and several weeks later she saw her walk down to her room at the opposite end of the hallway. My mother wasn't frightened by these experiences; in fact, she seemed to cherish them, though she was concerned that it meant that Abby's soul was disconcerted and restless. I have always wanted to see Abby again but have not. I would much prefer some sign of her presence; it's memory that truly haunts.

When she was alive my sister often spoke of her death. She liked to joke that she was living just to die—it was the only way to live. It was her rationalization for everything: addictions, men, the constant search for that which is both degrading and splendid. The year before she died she talked about how she wanted to be cremated, and how she wanted her ashes spread on the ocean. After she died I found a tape she'd made, which was labeled "My Memorial Soundtrack, Vol. 1" (I never found a Vol. 2). We went outside Salem Harbor aboard a rented fishing boat, a sixty-foot trawler much like Ike's *Madonna*. I played the tape on a boom box and my relatives took it as her last affront. Watching Aunt Kathleen enduring the Velvet Underground's "Sweet Jane" was, as Abby had expected, almost worth the price of admission.

IF I HAVE been haunted by anything other than memory, it's a deep sense of regret. Regret over my neglect. Though I took Abby in, fed and clothed her, gave her money, chased off some of those who used and abused her, I knew that there was more I could have done. She prided herself on her ability to go down deeper than anyone else, to dig into the darkness where no one could find her. It had been that way since we were small. She would get quiet and sad. If I tried to talk to her, she'd say I couldn't find her. And I'd say, But you're right here. To which she'd reply, *But you're not really looking.*

WE NAMED OUR cats Twist and Shout. Shout was born mute; she would open her mouth and no sound would come out. Twist would never shut up, purring, crying, howling—we swore he was speaking in tongues, and we pretended to interpret him. Twist bought it under the wheels of a car out on Andrew Street. Shout grew thin, listless, and wouldn't eat. We knew she was lonely; the vet said she had cancer. We nursed her for months, until the day we came home and found her in the den hanging by her claws from the back of an upholstered chair. She had gotten caught and didn't have the strength to get loose; she had probably hung there for hours. She looked up at us, opened her mouth, and nothing would come out, but we knew she was screaming. Horrified, we took her to the vet's and stood around the stainless-steel table while he put her to sleep.

Sometimes when I'd ask Abby how she was doing, she'd simply raise her arms, curl her fingers as though they were claws, open her mouth, and look like she was screaming.

I AWOKE BEFORE dawn and found myself staring at the shadows on the ceiling above my mother's bed. Those shadows, cast by the street lamp at the corner, had hardly changed since we moved into the house in 1963. Only the maple in the side yard had grown fuller. My mother was a light sleeper and often, if I got up in the middle of the night to go to the bathroom, she'd be sitting in bed reading. She always explained that she was tired of staring at the shadows of the maple's branches on the ceiling, worrying about things.

Petra was sound asleep, so I made my way downstairs in the dark. The creaking floorboards were all familiar to me, but it was as though I were hearing them for the first time. I went out the front door and began walking toward the Common. Something else I'd missed seemed to be pulling at my mind, and then I realized what it was: The Bruins had played in Detroit and I didn't know how they'd done.

I crossed the Common and went down Essex to Central Street. Red's Sandwich Shop opened at five A.M. It's in a small Colonial house with red clapboards; outside, the sign reads WHERE PATRIOTS MET BEFORE THE REVOLUTION. Inside, the smell of bacon, sausage, and potatoes cooking on one of the two large grills. There were a few customers, fishermen and tradesmen, and two state troopers. I sat at a table in front and ordered coffee. The cops seated at the counter were both beefy young guys not yet thirty.

"How'd the B's do?" I asked.

"Lost, four-two," the one with the bristle cut said. "Empty netter at the end."

As I took my first sip of coffee, I stuck my other hand in my coat pocket and felt the handle of my .38—to make sure it wasn't visible.

The cops finished their breakfast and left. The girl who was waiting on us wore black pants and a white blouse, and a tiny silver ring was embedded in her eyebrow. When she poured my refill, she said, "Proulx was injured."

"How?"

"High stick to the mouth. Ref didn't even call the penalty."

After she went around the counter, a man and a woman walked in and sat across from me at the table. I was certain I'd never seen either of these people before.

The woman was perhaps thirty-five. "You're not having any luck, are you?"

I sipped my coffee.

The guy, who was closer to my age and very fit, leaned forward. "That was a question."

"We didn't go to high school together, did we?" I asked. He leaned back. "I didn't think so. She's too young and you're too naive." Both stared at me, disappointed. "Perhaps, then, we should begin with introductions."

She put her elbows on the table. There was a hard efficiency to her mouth, her short brown hair, the business suit beneath the wool overcoat. She seemed in charge. "Names are not important. What is important is trying to help your father."

"I see."

"Do you?" the guy said. He was clearly accustomed to the fill-in lines that are intended to be vaguely threatening. He had the dead-on stare down.

"Hume sent you," I said.

Though they maintained their blank expressions, I could see surprise in their eyes. She leaned back as the waitress approached. "Wrong," she said. Then looking up, she said pleasantly, "We came to pick him up and we're late as it is. Could we have three coffees to go?" The waitress nodded and went back behind the counter. "No, Sam, we're trying to help your father keep away from Hume."

"Ah. You want to protect him."

"Basically, yes."

"He's done pretty well on his own for a long time," I said to her.

"Not anymore." She nudged her partner, and they pushed back their chairs. After a moment I stood up, too, and put my hands in my coat pockets.

We got the coffees and went out to a dark blue sedan. The guy opened the back door for me and I got in. He drove and she turned and offered me one of the Styrofoam cups of coffee. I shook my head. "We just want to show you something," she said.

"You're with the government?" I said. She almost smiled as she peeled the lid off the cup. "I really wish we could get on a first-name basis," I said.

"Call us what you want," she said as she tipped the cup to her lips.

"Okay, how about . . . George and Gracie?" I don't think she got it—too young—but the guy glanced up at me in the mirror.

Gracie only blew on her steaming cup of coffee. George was driving down Derby Street. It was just getting light out. In five minutes we reached the Willows, stopped in the parking lot in front of the arcade, and got out. We walked across the grass toward the water. There weren't many boats left moored. To the east the sun was coming up and the pink sky was reflected in the ink-blue water.

"This is really beautiful," I said. "I've always loved fall mornings here."

Neither spoke; she sipped her coffee and they both seemed to be waiting for something to happen. The day brightened seemingly by the moment and I studied the boats. Most were fishing skiffs. Only a few had masts.

And then I saw it, the ketch *Simple Truth*.

I turned to Gracie. "Look familiar?" she asked.

"What do you know about it?"

George didn't look away from the sunrise. "We thought you could tell us."

"I'm not sure," I said. "I'd need a closer look."

Gracie poured her coffee out on the grass. "Good idea." Pulling her coat tighter around her throat, she started back to the car.

"I gather I've disappointed her," I said. "George, tell me how to get in touch with you and then leave me alone until I call."

His face was flushed pink by sunrise. "And I suppose you want me to write a number down inside a matchbook cover?" I smiled. "How's your memory?" he asked.

13

As early-morning sunlight angled down Salem streets, I walked back to my mother's house. I picked up the *Globe* on the way, and there was a photo of Czlenko on the front page. I saw it again, Dirk coming toward us on the dark sidewalk, the slowly approaching car, the three shots. The snap of his head.

We all know that snap. We all have the film in our minds, the president's motorcade turning into Dealey Plaza, approaching the street sign in the foreground. We watch him and no one else. His head. His hair. His eyes—bright yet already a touch weary, even sad. As though he knew that he would never have time to do everything he wanted. Abigail was convinced that he knew he wouldn't live to serve out his term. Then we watch as he emerges from behind the sign, his hands raised to his throat, as though he were choking on something. An awkward gesture: elbows out. And we wait through that long moment, watching, watching his head, knowing now that the bullet is on its way, and then there's that swift, powerful explosion of blood, bone, and tissue. Even in extreme slow motion the snap of his head is ruthlessly forceful and definitive.

The perfect shot.

I wonder how the gunman behind the fence on the grassy knoll must have felt at that moment. Beneath the adrenaline there must have been pride and satisfaction. He saw it first, before any of us, the terrible, beautiful perfection of it. He was the perpetrator of history; we are merely its repeat witnesses.

WHILE RESEARCHING the book I went to Dallas. Dealey Plaza was already so familiar, though it seemed more compact than in the photographs and on film. The distances were closer. The schoolbook depository has been turned into a museum. I took the elevator up to the sixth floor and spent an hour walking through. There were exhibits, short films, assassination memorabilia—it all had the same blandness that you get if you do the tour on Bunker Hill or walk the Liberty Trail through Boston. Homogenized history, designed for the seniors' tour from Akron and the schoolchildren bused down for the day from Bangor. The corner where Oswald is said to have fired three rounds was enclosed in Plexiglas: Wood crates were still stacked by the opened window, with shells strewn on the floor.

After leaving the depository I walked around the grassy knoll and the parking lot. The wood fence is so close to the street. It seems that anyone could have made the shot. I stood there behind the fence and just looked down the knoll at the plaza for a long time. How many of us have stood there and done the same thing? I was there in December; it was seventy degrees and I wasn't used to such heat. In my book I have the photograph and I quote several eyewitnesses who saw the man in a white short-sleeve shirt and chinos get a rifle from the back of a two-toned car. The man, in his early forties, had thinning hair and was lean almost to the point of skinny. He took a drag on his cigarette, then crushed it out under his shoe as he walked from the sunlight into the shadows of the trees above the wood fence. It could have been anyone. But it wasn't just anyone.

WHEN I REACHED my mother's house, Petra was up; she had showered and she'd put on her overcoat as a bathrobe to make coffee in the kitchen.

"You couldn't sleep?" she asked.

"I seldom sleep the night through."

Her hair was wet and she looked petulant, anxious; then, briefly, something passed across her face—a recognition, I think. Small details about our daily habits, phobias, and quirks accumulate slowly, resulting in a knowledge that often passes for intimacy. "I can't put my clothes on again," she said. "I've worn them how many days now." Placing both hands on the tile counter, she arched her back until I could hear vertebrae crack.

"Come with me."

I led her up the back stairs to Abby's room at the end of the hall. Opening the closet and one of the bureau drawers, I said, "Mom could never bring herself to get rid of my sister's stuff. I think you'll find something that fits. Everything's clean because my mother used to take it out and wash it periodically. I think she half-expected Abby to walk in the door someday."

I went down to the kitchen, poured myself a cup of coffee, and read about how it took twenty stitches to sew up J. P. Proulx's mouth. The NHL was reviewing film of the high-stick incident to determine whether some disciplinary action should be taken against the Red Wings player who injured Proulx. This meant that word about the Bruins rookie was going around the league. They hit you like that, they want to take you out of the game, and they do that because they fear you.

It could have been any number of Salem mornings, sitting by the window that looked out on the backyard. But this morning happened to be at a point in time when my sister had been dead for a decade and my mother had just died. This was not history; it was people's lives, the knowledge of them, beginning to end. I felt something I'd never felt there in that kitchen. Alone.

THE YEAR THAT the *Boston Beacon* went under I couldn't find work. I was living in an apartment on Gainsborough Street near Symphony Hall, a raucous neighborhood full of college students (Northeastern, BU, the Berkeley School of Music, the New England School of Music are all within walking distance). Laura, my girlfriend at the time, was a paralegal who was going to Suffolk Law School nights, and she covered our rent for a while, which didn't sit well with her. I couldn't find anything, and finally it was Abby who helped me out. The guy she was with then, a guy who called himself Stick, drove a taxi and he got me in at Boston Cab. So that winter I did twelve-hour shifts in the brown-and-white Checkers, arriving and leaving the garage on Kilmarnock Street in the dark. At the time the Hancock Tower was under construction and they were having trouble with the large glass windows, which due to some design flaw kept blowing out and raining down in shards on the streets. I was not a very aggressive cabbie and

I spent a lot of time reading while waiting in line at cabstands. I may be the only person to have ever read all of Albert Speer's *Inside the Third Reich* inside a taxicab.

After cruising the streets of Boston all day, my right leg would ache from working the pedals. Some cars had little or no heat, which would mean I'd be chilled to the bone, and some cars had shitty brakes, which would mean I was lucky to be alive. Everything they say about Boston drivers is an understatement. Before going back to my apartment, I'd often meet Abby and Stick at the Linwood Pub, which was across the street from the garage. One night she was late and he didn't show up, which was fine with me.

"What's going on?" I asked.

She kept rubbing her hands together. "They picked him up."

"Stick? Who picked him up?"

"The *cops*."

"Why?"

"He was doing a job."

"A job. Wasn't he out on the street today?"

"No, Sam." Her eyes were remarkably angry. "He had a *job*. He was caught in someone's apartment in Back Bay." We were drinking shots of tequila and I watched as she tried to shake salt on her wrist, which wouldn't hold still.

"A job," I whispered. "Like a robbery job?"

She licked salt from her wrist, then raised the full shot glass. It dripped as she brought it to her mouth. She tossed the whole thing back.

"It's going to get bad in a few hours, right?"

She put the glass down and picked up the lemon wedge. "It's bad right now. But, yeah, it's going to get a lot worse. This guy, our supplier, he won't help me out unless I have cash." She bit into the lemon and winced.

"Abby, I'm broke, you know that."

"I'm not asking."

"You could stop." She stared at me as though I'd said the stupidest thing in the world. My sister got that look down when she was about four and she'd been nailing me with it ever since. "I'll help you," I said.

There was something new in her face, something concealed. After getting the bartender's attention and pointing at our glasses, she said, "I'll manage it."

"How? If he won't take anything but cash, how?"

She rubbed her hands together. "How do you think, Sam? How the fuck do you *think*? What else do I have?"

The bartender came down and poured us two more shots and then drew our beer chasers. Abby tried to light a cigarette, but her hand was so unsteady the match waved out.

I took the matchbook and lit the cigarette for her. When the bartender left, I said quietly, "Hooking? You're *not* doing it, understand?"

"*What,* you think I haven't *done* it before? You think I haven't done a guy to get what I *need? Jesus.*" But her eyes were frightened and I gathered that this was something altogether different.

"Listen," I said, "we finish these shots, then go back to my place. I'll stay with you through it. We'll get you clean."

And we did. It was the last straw for my paralegal girlfriend. I bring my junkie sister home and she stinks up the apartment for days, puking, shitting, sweating—it drove Laura right out, which was inevitable, I guess. When we had started seeing each other, she thought she was going with a guy who wrote for one of the city's newspapers, who wouldn't end up driving a cab and bringing his sister home for cold turkey.

Abby got stronger after about a week. She looked better and she ate well. The rest of the winter we stayed together in that crappy little apartment, the kids elsewhere in the building playing stereos constantly. Abby and I liked The Band. They weren't psychedelic. Their songs combined everything from Delta blues to R&B to Dixieland to honky-tonk to gospel; their harmonies were rough as tree bark and Garth Hudson's keyboards were, in Abby's words, right out of the Invisible World. We listened to The Band all winter, playing them loud enough to drown out the stuff coming from stereos downstairs, upstairs, across the alley out back.

This was the winter that the conspiracy theory was born. One night, while returning from the Laundromat on Hemenway Street, we were talking about our father, speculating about what significant historical events he might have participated in—it was a game we played: He certainly might have been a player in the Red Scare, getting the dirt on people for Joe McCarthy's hearings; he probably was involved in the Cold War spy games (Abby: "You think he's high up enough to run agents, or is he out there being run?" Me: "Run. Dad likes the action." Abby: "Definitely"); he might have been involved in Nixon's dirty tricks (though we wanted to believe that even *he* was above that); and we were certain that he was in and out of Southeast Asia on secret intelligence missions. We were romanticizing the man we hardly knew. But we also knew things because our mother would at times let them slip. *Your father called from Laos. I got a letter from West Berlin.* After I went to BU, Abby, who never actually received a diploma from Salem High, more or less tagged along and got caught up in the street life of Boston. Our father was long gone, and Mom went into what seemed a period of mourning. In fact, there were times when I really believed that she'd learned that he'd been killed but didn't want to (or perhaps, for security reasons, couldn't) tell us because it was somehow connected to secret activity. The war in Southeast Asia was out of control, and I'm certain he was over there trying to help bring it to some kind of "peace with dignity" before it tore America apart.

But as we walked down Hemenway, Abby suddenly said, "He was there."

It was snowing, and the wind was cold and damp. Almost as consolation I had a duffel bag of clean clothes slung over my shoulder, still warm from the dryer. "He was where?"

"Dallas, stupid."

"So? He was there. We've been through this before."

"It's not just that he was there—Sam, come *on*."

"Come on, what? What are you saying? He pulled the trigger?"

"I just know it. And you do, too. Think about how Mom acted when Kennedy was shot. Think about how everything was when we went down to Mexico that Christmas. We know it, Sam. We just have to prove it. *You* do—that's your *job*. You're the journalist."

We let it drop then.

The one thing about driving a cab is you got tips, which meant you always had some money in your pocket. That night we sat in the kitchen eating spaghetti and sharing a cheap bottle of red wine, listening to *Music from Big Pink*. In some ways my sister and I had never been happier. When she disappeared that spring, leaving me a note that she'd gone to New York City, I think it was because she needed to be alone. And she knew I did, too.

I was at the counter pouring another cup of coffee when Petra came down to the kitchen, wearing a pair of Abby's jeans and the black turtleneck sweater that I had given her for Christmas the year before she died. "You look like you've just seen a ghost," Petra said. "Is this, you know, too much?"

"No, it's all right."

She came over and kissed me. "I'm not so sure."

"Really, it's all right," I said. "The sweater looks good on you. Keep it, okay?"

She playfully tugged at my belt buckle. "Perhaps there's something I can do for you to confirm that?" I took hold of her hand and she regarded me seriously. "What?"

"I need to show you something."

"Right here in the kitchen?" She smiled. "Okay."

"Get your coat."

We drove out to the Willows. It was a cool, sunny morning and there were few people in the park, just dog walkers and joggers. To the east were small, low islands, and the open Atlantic beyond; to the north, across the river, Beverly. Dinghies were tied up to the pier and I climbed down into one.

"Whose boat is this?" she asked.

"I have no idea. When we were kids, Abby and I used to come down here and row all the time. We'd just take a dinghy. No one ever said anything. That was Salem then and I don't think it's changed that much."

She got in, and I began to pull us away from the pier. I didn't row directly toward the ketch; instead I did a slow loop around the moored boats, coming up on her portside. The tide was falling and her bow was to the west; she had a long pulpit of teak and chrome, and the hull was reassuringly beamy. As I worked the oars, Petra gazed about, but when we passed below, she stared at the transom and whispered, *"Simple Truth."*

"Recognize it?"

"I'm not sure. Kinda."

"Let's go aboard and have a look."

I wiggled the dinghy up to the stern of the ketch, and Petra stepped onto the ladder. After tying the dinghy off, I climbed up into the cockpit.

Petra stared at the cabin hatch, which was locked. "I think this is it. But it was dark."

I led her up along the starboard deck. She got down on her knees, cupped her hands around her face, and peered into a porthole. "Yes," she said. Crawling forward, she looked down through a Plexiglas hatch over the forepeak. "They kept me in there, where my feet fit right into the bow."

"V-berth," I said. I studied the running rigging a moment. "You sure?"

Getting to her feet. "See that?" She pointed down through the hatch at a map on the bulkhead. I couldn't read it through the smoky Plexiglas. "It's a map of Boston Harbor. And over on this wall beneath us there's one of the entire New England coast with places circled. They didn't let me out except to use the toilet—it was really tight in there."

"Heads usually are." I led her back to the cockpit. "You said 'they.'"

"Two men."

"Any idea of age? Anything?"

Petra shrugged. "They had me pretty whacked out, Sam." She looked at me, squinting in the sun. "You think your father was one of them?"

I studied the rigging one more time. "I know this: My father never sailed this boat."

"You can tell?"

"The knots. Look at this mainsheet, the way it's coiled and hung from the boom—sloppy. And up on the deck there's all kinds of loose line underfoot. He'd never have it."

"You're sure?"

"Absolutely. It's like a sailor's fingerprint."

We got back in the dinghy and I rowed some more. I simply liked the effort. It's usually your first connection with boats, pulling on oars, and I have always loved the lengthening and tightening of muscle, the even strain that develops from the legs up through the back and out the extended arms.

"Sam, how'd you find *Simple Truth* up here?"

"Good question. You must be a journalist." I leaned toward her, dipped the oars, and pulled back slowly. The breeze hadn't yet come up and the water was glassine, pastel blue. "Early this morning I couldn't sleep, so I took a walk and I met the other side. They joined me while I was sitting in Red's having coffee. Ike told us that former Senator Hume has changed his tune since he chaired that subcommittee; now he wants to find my father and pin the JFK thing on him—make a big splash that'll win him an election. I tend to buy that."

"I do, too."

"But someone else is looking for my father," I said. "I think they're government—I don't know who or what branch. In fact, I wonder if there aren't two groups from the government. One's the people who grabbed you. I wouldn't be surprised if they were really trying to find my father and help him. When they realized I really didn't know where he was, they gave you back. A little doped up, but there was nothing they could do about that."

She nodded. "And the other group?"

"This morning there were two people who walked into Red's—a man and a woman—and they brought me out here to see that sailboat. They wanted me to believe they were trying to help my father, perhaps protect him from the senator."

"You believe that?"

"I don't know. Maybe. On the other hand, if they believe that the tarnished former senator really *can* stick it to my father, these 'friends' might prefer that he not be found at all."

Petra leaned over and trailed a hand in the water. After a moment, she pulled her arm in and put a wet finger to her tongue to taste the salt. "God, Sam. You really think they'd kill him?"

I pulled a couple of strokes. "I think we need to have another look at your notebooks. My mother must have had some idea of 'home' that she shared only with my father. Something Abby and I never knew about. That's where he's taking her ashes."

We were nearing the pier. Petra looked back toward *Simple Truth.* "That's why they sailed up here from Boston—thinking that he'd come to your mother's house."

I nodded as I shipped oars and the dinghy bumped gently against the piling.

14

We stopped at the grocery, then went back to my mother's house and made breakfast. Fresh salt air always affects the appetite, and we had poached eggs on English muffins. When we finished, Petra got the notebooks from her coat pocket and came to the table. I had washed off our plates and when I shut off the faucet I heard it—the creak of a floorboard upstairs.

Petra was sitting at the table, talking about my mother's eyes. I went to the table and took the pencil from her hand—she had already begun to jot ideas down on fresh pages torn from the notebooks—and I wrote, *Keep talking*.

She stared up at me, confused. I pointed toward the ceiling. After a moment, she said, "Well, you know your mother, how beautiful her eyes were. They were so—I don't know—honest and direct."

Nodding for her to continue, I went back to the sink and turned on the faucet again, a full blast of water. I walked carefully from the kitchen to the front hall and got my .38 from my coat pocket. Then I climbed the front stairs slowly. My mother's house was built in 1802, and it's impossible to walk through a house that old without the creak and groan of floorboards and stair treads announcing your movement. By the time I was halfway to the landing, whoever was on the second floor knew I was coming, and I heard the sound of feet, moving down the hall toward the back of the house.

Quickly I took the rest of the stairs two at a time—something I used to do with ease. There was no one in the hall and it was quiet now, except for the sound of running water and Petra's voice coming up from the kitchen. As I looked toward the back of the house, there were four doors: my room on the left, with the door half opened; a linen closet on the right, which was closed; the bathroom next to that, which was wide open; and at the end of the hall the door to Abby's room, which was opened slightly. To the left of Abby's door were the back stairs, which went down to the den, adjacent to the kitchen.

I cocked the hammer and the precise click seemed remarkably loud. Then I walked slowly down the hall and pushed the door to my room open. It was empty and the closet was open, full of clothes I hadn't worn in years. I continued on until I reached the bathroom door. Peering in, I could see the shower stall in the mirror; no one was there.

Then I heard something move in Abby's room, and I quickly stepped across the hall and into the bathroom. "What do you want?" I said. There was no answer.

I heard the bedroom door groan on a dry hinge. Peering around the bathroom doorjamb, I watched a man step out of Abby's room. He wore jeans, a leather jacket, and a Red Sox cap. One hand was in his coat pocket.

"I'm armed," I said.

He had a thick black mustache, and I think at that point he smiled, as though to say, *Who are you kidding?* I realized I should have turned so I could point the gun at him, but I didn't move. We simply gazed at each other. He didn't appear threatening, nor did he seem concerned by his predicament. He looked remarkably calm and I kept expecting him to speak, to explain why he was in my mother's house. Actually, there was something about the guy that I liked.

And suddenly he moved. He had been so still, standing outside my sister's door, that when he turned and jogged down the back stairs, it was as if it hadn't happened, he hadn't even been there. But his footsteps, pounding down the narrow stairway, were loud, and when he ran through the den and into the kitchen, a chair was knocked over, clattering on the tile floor, and Petra screamed.

I ran down the hall, took the stairs in twos, and landed in the den. Through the door I could see Petra standing, both hands on the kitchen table, her chair lying on its side on the floor, as she stared out the window. Beyond her the back door was open. I ran into the kitchen, out the door, and into the yard. It was tiny and surrounded by a high wood fence that was covered with vines. I caught sight of his hands on the top of the fence as he let himself down on the other side, and then there was the sound of his running through Mrs. Fanshaw's yard toward Briggs Street. Stupidly, I looked about at my mother's overgrown, untended garden for a minute, catching my breath.

When I went back into the kitchen, Petra was still leaning on the kitchen table. She turned toward me and looked at the gun in my hand— I didn't think she could be so pale. She said something, but the running faucet, which had been on all this time, was too loud for me to hear.

I eased off the hammer with my thumb, laid the .38 on the counter, and turned the water off. The silence was a relief.

AFTER RIGHTING HER CHAIR, I had put some bourbon in Petra's coffee, and it was bringing the color back to her face. "Are you all right?"

She nodded, using both hands to get the mug to her lips. "He works for Hume, and I need a cigarette."

"Any in your coat, your purse?"

"I try not to keep them on me." She had trouble setting the mug on the table. "And then I go to a bar and totally cave in—buy a whole pack and smoke it in no time."

"Any idea what his name is?"

"No."

I went to the counter and opened drawers. My mother used to be a smoker, quit years ago, but I know occasionally, especially after she learned she had cancer, she caved in herself. I found a pack of Marlboros and brought them to the table. "What's he *do* for Hume?"

"I don't know." She worked the book of matches out from under the cellophane. "But I've seen him at press conferences and meetings that Hume has attended. My guess is the guy isn't an official aide or anything. He doesn't push paper for Hume. He does, you know, *stuff*. Everything from drive the car to the dirty little jobs. Why else would he be here?" She lit a cigarette and inhaled deeply.

My coffee wasn't spiked but I was considering it. Instead I got up from the table and went up the back stairs. I walked down the hall toward my mother's room and pushed the door open: The contents of her bureau, her closet, her nightstands had been dumped on the floor.

"*God,*" Petra whispered as she came up behind me.

I sat down on the bed, feeling as though someone had knocked the wind out of me.

"Are *you* all right?" she asked.

"Think so."

"Want me to do anything?" She put a hand on my shoulder.

"No."

"I recommend the spiked coffee."

"All right. And find Hume's phone number."

"You got it."

Petra went downstairs, and I lay back on my mother's bed. The smell of her—her clothing, her perfume—was suddenly overwhelming. I began to close my eyes, but I was afraid of what I might see. A knot of pain descended through my intestines.

Getting up, I went down to the kitchen, where Petra was hanging up the phone and writing a number in her notebook. "That's his office," she said.

The bottle of Jim Beam was on the table. I never liked bourbon, but I poured some into my coffee mug and took a big swallow. My stomach tightened and my legs felt weak. I sat down, exhausted. After a moment the shooting pain in my intestines subsided, and I took another sip from the mug. "You know, maybe this stuff will work."

She almost smiled, but her eyes were still nervous, spooked.

I took the phone off the wall and dialed the number she'd written in the notebook. It took a good dose of automated voice menus and a second shot of Jim Beam to get a Ms. Cluff on the line. She had some title like Associate Aide, and she made it clear that the senator's schedule was such that he was unable to take calls directly.

"Ms. Cluff, you and I know that the senator is never really far from a telephone."

After a moment she said, "Who's calling, please?"

"This is Samuel Adams, not John Adams. That's an important distinction, as far as the senator is concerned."

"What is it you wish to discuss—"

"Ms. Cluff. Get the senator on his cell phone—or on his *aide's* cell phone, which can be handed to the senator—and tell him that I found his *guy* ransacking my mother's house, and my next phone call is to the Salem Police and several Boston newspaper reporters." She didn't say anything. "Now, I'm going to give you my phone number so the senator can call back. *Got it?*"

"I'll see what I can do, sir."

Because I'd once played tennis with Hume, I knew he'd call back, but he'd give it a while. On the court he was a patient player. He didn't have a lot of passing shots in his game, just consistent ground strokes that kept the ball in play. He was the kind of player who seldom hit an outright winner; instead he waited until his opponent blew a shot and lost the point. He understood the concept of the unforced error.

So I poured more bourbon in my now-empty coffee mug and said, "What I need is a hot shower."

I went up the back stairs again, peeling off clothes, which I dropped on the hall floor on the way to the bathroom. The shower, coupled with the bourbon, worked wonders. When I returned to my room, a towel about my waist, my clothes were piled on the chair by the closet. Petra was lying on her side in my bed, the blankets up to her bare shoulder.

"This must be your room. There're still photos of Red Sox and Bruins players on the walls, and who's that tall, skinny boy with the wood racket?"

"High-school tennis team."

"Nice legs. Looks like a good backhand," she said. "So this must be the room where he had all those nasty adolescent fantasies."

"It was so long ago, I hardly remember."

"Ever have more than a fantasy in this single bed?"

"Nope. Just the occasional nightmare."

She slowly raised her arm. Her olive skin seemed so dark against the white linen. I climbed in beside her, and she brought the blankets and sheet down over us, capturing the warmth of our bodies.

Something about sex right after you've gotten out of the shower. Your flesh feels new. I was still damp, still warm, and Petra wrapped her legs and arms around me tightly, as though trying to draw the heat from my skin. My water-shriveled fingers lingered over each nipple. We threw the blankets off and the cooler air raised goose bumps on her thighs. When I knelt behind her, the box spring groaned in a familiar, almost musical way. As I ran my palm up her neck, spreading her thick dark hair and kneading the base of her skull, she buried her face between her forearms. This was not as I had imagined it in my adolescent fantasies; to be looking down at Petra's arched spine, to be listening to her breath quicken in the daylight, was something I could never have imagined as an adolescent—it was too real for a fantasy. Extending her arms, she braced her hands against the headboard and held her hips so firmly that there was the repeated slap of flesh. We were alone in my mother's house, and it meant we could make all the noise we wanted—it was as though we were suddenly engaged in a ritualistic prayer. If my younger self could have heard us, he might at first have thought that we were in pain; but afterward, as we settled together on the mattress, our breathing protracted and labored, he would have realized that this was all any of us ever really sought.

"It frightened me," she whispered. "The guy came running down the back stairs and bolted through the kitchen." With a smile, she drew hair off her face. "Nothing like an orgasm to ward off fear. It's a form of exorcism."

"Hume's guy," I said, lying on my back, "he was looking for some *thing*."

"A phone number? An address?"

"Maybe."

"What else could lead them to him?" She sat up and leaned back against the headboard. "I mean they must think she could draw them a map?"

I closed my eyes. I couldn't think of anything. I didn't want to think of anything.

I must have dozed, because when the phone rang, I was alone in the bed and I could hear the shower down the hall. I got up, pulled on an old bathrobe, and went down to my mother's room.

"Hello?"

"Still have that big slice serve?" Hume asked.

"Haven't played much lately," I said.

"We should get out sometime. I'm ready for a rematch." I didn't say anything. "I'm sorry about your mother, Sam."

"Funny way to send condolences."

He didn't answer right away. "Look, when I first read that book of yours, I felt in my gut that you were right."

"Enough that you set up your own subcommittee on the assassination."

"I know you think that somehow that committee wrecked your book, your *moment*. But JFK's assassination is a very complex matter."

"Right," I said. "And everybody is entitled to their theory."

"It would seem so, Sam. This is America and we have a lot of rights."

"Enough with the civics lesson," I said. "What do you want now?"

"Oh, I don't know. Over the past few years I've heard a few things between Beacon Hill and Washington that suggest that your theory wasn't so harebrained after all."

"In other words, you've suddenly discovered it might be useful."

"We all just want the truth, Sam."

"Right. What kind of things have you heard?"

"Things, Sam. Mentioned over drinks, after dinner. Most of it's specu-lation, everything's circumspect, but they accumulate, they make an impression."

"Hume, I'm sitting in my mother's bedroom, looking at what your guy did, and it's pissing me *off*. What was he looking for?"

"You don't know?" I didn't answer. "Come on."

"Come on *what?*"

"You need to get out on the court more, Sam."

"I think I need to make some phone calls, is what I think. I'm *that* fucking close."

"Calls where—to your old friends in the newsrooms? You think they're going to listen to you? You think they're going to buy what *you* have to say? Sam, you need to take a hard look at your credibility."

"You're one to talk about credibility," I said. "A guy broke into my mother's house and tore it apart. The guy works for you."

"You don't know that."

"But I do, *Senator.* I have a witness who can identify him."

There was a long pause and the sound was muffled—I assumed he was holding the phone against his chest and talking with someone, an aide, perhaps even the guy. Down the hall Petra turned off the shower.

Hume cleared his throat before he spoke again. "All right. Look, we can work this out." His voice was conciliatory. In his profession he had learned how to concede a point—but I knew he was also quickly trying to calculate how to play his next shot. "What do you want, Sam?"

I wanted my mother's ashes. It was a pure, simple need—a desire, really—but it had turned convoluted and difficult. Complex, like JFK's assassination. "A meeting," I said. "I want a meeting."

"Where? Longwood, perhaps? I believe the grass courts are closed for the season."

"I'm not coming back to Boston just yet."

"All right. Where?"

"Salem Common. It's just down the street from my mother's house. Think your driver can find it? Or do I need to draw you a map?"

"No," he said. "All right. Six o'clock." And he hung up quickly.

As I put the phone down, I saw Petra step out of the bathroom, wrapped in a towel, her hair tied back behind her head. Down at the end of the hall the afternoon sun was streaming into Abby's room and it seemed to cast an aura around Petra, making it difficult to see her face. But her legs, her arms, and her bare shoulders were delicate and graceful. She might have been an apparition.

15

There was no hiding it any longer. By the winter of 1984, Abigail weighed about ninety pounds and the whites of her eyes had the dull sheen of a hard-boiled egg. Her hair was short dark spikes. My mother, who had been so rock solid through all the years of our father's absence, was shattered by the realization that her daughter was a flat-out drug addict. We admitted her to the Ferguson-Duval Clinic in Wenham.

In June, Abby was released and she reluctantly moved in with Mom. I was working again in Boston, freelancing enough to get by, plus I had begun research on the book and had found an editor at Wallace Stapleton who was very encouraging. They were strange, frantic months. I traveled and wrote constantly, doing pieces for various New England newspapers and magazines, and then I'd return to Salem to find two women quietly driving each other nuts, something that had been happening for generations in the old houses of that seaport. For centuries Salem men went to sea, to fish, to trade, to do battle, and they left behind women who paced rooms and widow's walks, constantly looking toward the Atlantic.

But, of course, men, whether they return or not, are a paltry form of salvation. I proved to be virtually useless. I was unable to penetrate the taut silences that had developed between my mother and sister. I was aware of the layers of resentment that separated them, but I could do little more than speak when spoken to and eat what was put in front of me. At best I provided mild comic relief. None of us had heard from my father for several years—it was the first time that he'd consistently kept out of contact with my mother and that, coupled with Abby's "condition," as she called it, was what pained her most.

Abby knew about the book I was writing; my mother did not—we didn't have the heart to tell her. So it became the dark, unwholesome secret Abby and I shared, and if nothing else, it served its purpose in that it kept my sister engaged: It gave her something to look forward to, other than the next session with Dr. Norman Metz at Ferguson-Duval. I would take her for drives or, in decent weather, we'd row a dinghy out into the harbor—anything to get her out of the house.

One humid afternoon in July we drove north and went to a place we liked called Brown's, a seafood shack out on the marshes behind Salisbury beach. At Brown's you sat at picnic tables on a big screened-in porch and ate off paper plates and drank from plastic cups. The place was noisy with families that had spent the day at the beach, and there was the constant squawk of the PA system, calling out order numbers. Abby loved it.

This day she seemed particularly excited, to the point where it made me nervous.

"What's up?" I asked finally.

"Lots," she said as she pulled a steamer from its shell. "I'm moving out."

"You think you're ready to go it alone?"

"I won't be alone." She expertly pinched the skin off the neck of the clam, which she then dunked first in the broth, then the drawn butter, and ate. I could hear the crunch of sand in her mouth. "Stick and I are getting back together."

"Bad idea, Abby."

"He's clean, too."

I just looked at her.

"I've been seeing him for a couple of months," she said. "I'm not exactly a prisoner, you know. He drives up from Boston and we meet for a while."

"Great. What would you two do? Where would you live?"

"Belize."

"Belize. Like in Central America."

She picked up an onion ring and bit half, drawing the whole soft white strand out of the half moon of breading and sucking it into her mouth.

"What's in Belize?"

"Stick knows a guy, a relative, actually."

"I'll bet he does."

"He's starting a resort down there and we're going to live and work there."

"You and the iguanas."

After eating another clam, she said, "I'm going, Sam, and I'm going to help you, too."

"How?"

"With the book."

"From Belize?"

She nodded and drank from her Diet Coke. I hadn't seen her this wired in a long time. It was frightening. Her eyes were glossy, black, and absolutely impenetrable. "He's down there."

I put my clamshell down. "Dad? How do you know?"

Abby smiled, her lips slick with drawn butter. "You have to help me, Sam. I *have* to get out of that house. It isn't any good for me or for Mom— you *know* that. And Dr. Norman Metz, he's done what he can, and I can't do any more for him."

"What's *that* mean?"

"Oh, come on, grow up. He's been out to ball me since I first walked in that place. So finally I let him, and now he has to cure me and get me out of there for good. Otherwise, I'll sue his ass."

"If I don't kill him first."

"Sam, you're missing the point."

"What *is* the point?"

"*Dad.* I've found him." She stopped grinding sand in her teeth for a moment and gazed out at the salt marsh. "Well, I think I have—I'm pretty sure."

"How?"

She shrugged. "Calls. And luck. I found someone in the State Department."

"You ball him, too?"

"It's a woman. I'll let you do her, if you want." She pushed her empty tray aside and wiped her fingers on a paper napkin. "He's down in Mexico and I think I can find him." She shook her head. "No, Sam. You help me get out of Salem, and when I get to Belize, then we'll talk. Right now I don't exactly trust anyone, including you." She leaned forward and put her hand on my wrist. "Listen, you *have* to finish that book and you *have* to get it right. If you go looking for Dad, you won't even get close. I *can*. He'll see *me*. You know it."

I tossed my napkin on the table with all the others. "I don't like it." But I didn't have the heart to pull my wrist away from her hand.

THAT SEPTEMBER I put her on a plane for Belize. Stick was already down there, and just before she got on the plane, she took off her jacket and gave it to me, saying she wouldn't be needing it anymore. When she hugged me and went through the gate door, I was sure I'd never see her alive again. I was off by a few years.

For months I heard little, an occasional card, one or two calls that were always poor connections. Midwinter I got a collect call from Stick; he wanted to know if she had returned to Boston. Several weeks passed and we had no idea where she was, and then Stick called again: He'd heard from her; she was in Mexico, and she wanted him to tell me that she'd "found him."

After that I heard nothing for over a month. My mother was drinking heavily then, and finally Uncle James and Aunt Kathleen convinced her to come down to their condominium in Florida. I'd talk to her on the phone several times a week; she'd always ask if I had heard from Abby, and I always said no. She knew I was lying. Once she said, "You think you're protecting your mother but you're not. I've protected you, you *and* your sister, all these years. You can't do this to me."

Uncle James got her checked into someplace down in Tampa–St. Pete and after that my mother never took another drink. She was the strongest of all of us. She was the only one who could ever quit something. Americans have a low opinion of quitters, but they have it backward: Quitting takes courage because there's always that huge fucking vacuum that has to be filled every second of every minute of every day.

LATE JUNE MY father called. He said he was "with her," and at first I thought he was in Florida with my mother. But he was calling from Mexico and he was talking about Abigail. He insisted that she needed to get back to the States for help, but he couldn't take her across the border. So I had to go down to Nogales and get her.

I flew into Tucson, stayed overnight, and the next morning drove a rented car an hour south. I parked in a McDonald's on the U.S. side and walked through customs at the border. My father had said to find a place called La Casa Negro and sit on the porch. It looked out on a busy square filled with blue exhaust, and in the distance there was a steep hillside that was covered with pastel-colored shacks. Smoke drifted up from them, filtering the sunlight. It seemed impossible that this could be a ten-minute walk from a Quarter Pounder with fries.

I was on my second beer and tequila when a pale blue 1958 Chevy Impala pulled up to the curb. A Mexican in a frayed straw hat was driving; my father and sister were sitting in back. My father got out and walked in under the shade of the porch roof. He sat down and the waiter immediately brought him a Corona and a shot of tequila.

"This is quite a place," I said. "You order a beer and they throw in the shot for free. All for an American buck."

He picked up the Corona and squeezed a lime wedge until it fit down the neck of the bottle. I watched his hands; his fingers were long and tanned. My mother always said I had my father's hands, and she always said he had beautiful hands. They looked bony to me, but strong.

"How long has she been on this stuff?" he asked.

I reached for his shot glass. "You're not going to drink this?" He shook his head. I tossed it back and followed it with some beer. "Why can't you take her across the border yourself?"

He gazed toward the smoking hillside. I hadn't seen him in over five years. He didn't look that different. His hair was whiter, shaved close to his skull. There was no fat on him; his cheeks and neck were still lean and taut. Only his eyes seemed to have aged. They were darker, more hollowed out than I remembered; and they seemed uncertain, indecisive in a way that I'd never noticed before.

"I've made arrangements," he said without looking at me. "There's a place called the Twenty-Nine Palms in Tucson that's very good. It's all paid for and there's a good hotel nearby for you—you've got to stay with her until she's cleaned up."

"Cleaned *up?*"

"Then take her back to Boston and don't let her come down here again."

"Clean," I said. "The term is 'clean.' She needs more than a *bath.*"

I thought he was going to turn toward me and perhaps snap at me but he didn't. "This guy Stick, don't let him near her again," he said quietly.

"Why don't you do her a favor and shoot Stick?" I drank some beer. "Why don't you do the *world* a favor and shoot Stick? By the way, whatever happened to that music teacher in high school? Mr. Frye—he just disappeared, and I've always wondered if you had anything to do with it. I like to think he's teaching in Wyoming and still looking over his shoulder."

He inhaled and exhaled slowly. I realized this was something he felt he had to endure. I also had the impression that he was rushed; he kept studying the square. There were a lot of street people panhandling—some were missing limbs and one man with a crutch appeared to be blind—and my father watched each one of them carefully. His driver was also paying attention. My guess is that my father's life was a perpetual state of caution, suspicion, and dread.

"How's your mother?" he said finally.

I laughed then. I laughed, and I must have pounded my fist on the table because the three empty shot glasses in front of me tipped over and clinked against one another. "You don't *know?*" His head came around and the smoke from the shacks on the hill seemed to be rising right off his skull. It was hard to see his eyes because the light behind him was so bright. "You think she's sitting patiently up there in Salem? You think she's strolling on her widow's walk, looking out to sea, awaiting the return of your ship?"

He looked alarmed, and I'd had just enough to drink to enjoy extending the moment. Our waiter came and my father shook his head. *"Un cerveza, por favor,*" I said to the waiter. When he went back inside the bar, I said, "Call Uncle Jimmy in Florida. He'll tell you all about Mom." For a moment I was really pissed off, and I almost got up and walked off the porch. But the waiter, a young man who seemed to sense the tension at our table, rushed out with my Corona and shot of tequila and I stayed put. "I mean it," I said. "Why don't you kill that fucker Stick so she can't go back to him after I get her *cleaned up* again? And why don't you take out who-ever's been supplying her all these weeks while she's been with you?"

For a moment I thought he was going to be the one to get up and walk away. Instead he changed the subject. "What's this book she says you're writing?"

"I'll send you an autographed copy when it's finished. Just give me your address."

"You have any idea what you're doing?"

"*No!* No, I don't. Why don't you *tell* me what I'm doing?"

"Sam, you can't understand—"

"What? *What* can't I understand?"

"How things were, how they really were—after the war. It's easy for you, for your generation now, to say it was all a mistake, but if you had seen it as we saw it coming out of the war, you'd understand." I kept my eyes on my fresh bottle of beer. I wanted to just hear his voice, which was calm but urgent. "There were two wars. We believed that. We won the first one, but we didn't fight the second one."

"Against the Communists."

"If we had, if we had gone right on into Russia, things might have been different."

"No Vietnam."

"I don't know, but maybe not. Not if we did it right. Vietnam was a mistake but a necessary mistake. We couldn't back out of it, and that's what was going to happen."

"Who's *we?*"

He took a drink from his bottle of beer.

"I mean are we talking about the military? FBI? CIA? SOS? The Mafia? Or is it all of them? All of them lined up against the president, who was elected by democratic vote? Who decides when this becomes necessary? What happened to the Senate, the Supreme Court? What happened to the checks-and-balances system we studied in eighth-grade civics? Let's say, just for discussion's sake, he *was* going to pull troops out of Southeast Asia after he was reelected. Makes him look like a pretty sharp guy now, doesn't it? We lost, eventually. We lost that sucker big time. April of '75 we ran for the helicopters in Saigon and we *lost* on *TV.* That's what everybody's really pissed about—we lost on fucking prime time."

"We shouldn't have."

"But we're still here. We lost, and *we're . . . still . . . here!*"

He'd been holding his beer bottle all this time, and now he put it down on the table and rubbed his temples with his long fingers.

"I tell you what," I said, and waited until he raised his head. "You tell me where you were and what you did November 22, 1963, and I'll quit the book. Just tell me. *Me.* I want to know. I want to know what you did that has sent you into hiding all these years—that's what this is, right? I want to know what you did that has meant that Mom has had to sit around waiting all these years, that has made Abby—" I stopped there and looked out toward the car. Her head was resting against the back of the seat. I realized she hadn't moved since the car had pulled up. "You tell me what you did and I *promise* I'll never tell a soul." He stared down at the bottle on the table and I waited, but he wouldn't raise his head. "All right, be the good soldier. *Still.* But if you don't tell me, then I'm going to find out. And I swear to *God* you won't like it."

"You'll kill me."

I got up from my chair so quickly that it fell over. "You have been dead to me for years. Frankly, I wouldn't know the difference." I walked off the porch into the hot sun. The smell of exhaust fumes was overwhelming and suddenly I felt light-headed. I got in the back of the Impala. Abby turned her head slowly and opened her tired, vacant eyes. She whispered my name and I took her in my arms and kissed her forehead.

My father got in the front seat now and the Impala moved through the square. The shocks were bad and it seemed we hit every pothole on the drive back to the border. My father stared straight ahead and I realized that this was something that he wanted to get over with as quickly as possible. He was economical, efficient, and this business with his children was too messy.

When the Impala stopped a block from customs, I helped Abby out of the backseat. My father walked down the crowded street with us. Sidewalk vendors tried to sell us cigars, leather goods, blankets, boom boxes, jewelry. But it was a young boy with big soft eyes who stepped up and handed me the reins of a burro. His father gestured with his arms that we should all stand close together and smile. Obediently we crowded around the head of the burro, its ears twitching because of the flies, and the man took our picture with an Instamatic camera. He gave the snapshot to the boy, who came to me, and I handed him the reins and a ten-dollar bill. The photo was still developing, and when I turned to my father, I could see that he wanted it. I tucked it in my shirt pocket.

Abby stepped into my father's arms and he held her for a moment. I wondered if it occurred to him that he might not ever see her alive again.

When he let her go, I took her arm; she wasn't steady on her feet. He stared at me and I thought he was going to say something. The storefront behind him was bright pink stucco, cracked and chipped, with a hand-painted sign over the door that read FARMACIA. We stood there in the sun, the smell of fresh burro shit rising off the hot pavement. For just one moment my father looked helpless, but perhaps he was only blinded by the glare, because he raised his hand to shield his eyes. A vague salute was the best he could manage, then he turned and walked back toward the waiting Impala.

I steered Abby into the shade of the customs building and followed the signs toward ESTADOS UNIDOS.

16

By late October in New England the days are dreadfully short, and at six o'clock I stood under a lamp on the west side of Salem Common, across the street from the Salem Witch Museum. Hume's car, a dark sedan with tinted windows, pulled up right on time. He was punctual not out of any regard for me, but because he probably had another engagement back in Boston. The rear window rolled down and Hume said, "Come on, we'll take a spin around your lovely old town."

"No," I said. "Let's walk."

"Oh, all right." There was a touch of mirth in his voice. "This isn't like a *whack,* you know." The rear door opened up and Hume climbed out. I couldn't see who else was in the car. He was wearing a wool topcoat over a suit, white shirt, and silk tie. His shoes made a crisp sound as we headed east, taking one of the cinder lanes through the Common.

I said, "Nailing my father so you can win an election is a bad idea."

"Good, Sam. Let's cut through the bullshit."

"You shouldn't even *be* running for attorney general."

"Perhaps I should hire you as a political consultant."

"The people working for you now are giving you lousy advice."

"I admit it's not a high-percentage shot," Hume said. "But you know that sometimes the situation calls for that element of surprise. Besides, this isn't a matter of professional advice. I didn't get this idea from pollsters and spin doctors."

"You just want back in the game."

"Fuckin' A, Sam. Put me in, Coach."

He was maybe five-eight and his stride was quick, vigorous. His head seemed designed to sit on top of an expensive suit; over the years it had been shaped and trimmed and appropriately aged so that it would fit nicely in your television screen or on the front page of the newspaper. He kept looking forward, never at me, which was something I had discovered about people in public life—they expect to be the ones to be looked at, not the other way around, and it was for them a source of control. So I stared down at our feet as we walked—my worn hiking boots, his shined shoes.

"If you found him," I asked, "what good would it do? My father's not going to tell you anything. He'll never admit to anything."

"I'm not so sure." Hume reached into his pocket and took out a small tin; he offered me a tiny cigar, which I refused. He stopped to light one. "Perhaps even he can be persuaded." He waved the match out and exhaled.

The cigar smelled good and I was tempted to ask for one. Instead I said, "Persuaded how?"

"Perhaps I've some new information. Something that will convince him it's in his best interest to talk?" I started walking again and he fell in beside me. "How old is your father, eighty? Thereabouts? He doesn't have much longer, most likely. So he has two options. He can die and let history establish who he was, what he did, *why* he did it, and he'll never have any control over that. Or he can speak out now and state his case for the record. No matter what history comes up with in the future, there will always be his side of the story to contend with. A man his age has to see it as an opportunity, perhaps his last."

"My father has always been a man who believes in history, which means he knows he can't really do anything about it—not, at least, in terms of controlling what it will make of him." I turned my head but didn't look at Hume. "That's true for all of us, wouldn't you say?"

"Sam, if I find him, I can treat him with respect. I can ensure that he will be comfortable. In a sense only someone like me can protect him. You know I'm right."

I suspected that this was true, but I didn't say anything.

Two witches emerged from the dark, floating toward us in long black capes, tall, pointy hats, gray wigs, and with painted moles. As we passed each other in a pool of lamplight, they tried to make their laughter ominous, but they only sounded like a couple of teenaged girls on the way to a party.

"Petra Mouzakis is your 'witness,'" Hume said.

I didn't say anything.

"I'll tell you, she was something when she worked in my office. She could really figure the angles. You knew she was going places. I wanted her to come to Washington with me after I was appointed to the Senate. But she had other ideas. You gotta be careful there, Sam. She's the reason for my second—my most expensive—alimony suit, and she was worth every penny of it. That's my highest compliment."

I didn't say anything.

Hume stopped suddenly. I turned to him and he was staring up at me in the near dark. "Listen, we're just two guys pushing fifty walking the park, Sam. To the world—to those little witches—we're just a couple old losers. But you and I got something in common. We both think we can win one more time. I know I can. And I bet you can, too. Remember, I've played tennis with you. You're toughest in the third set." He dropped his cigar on the path and ground it out with his shoe, then began walking again. On the far side of the Common I could see his car waiting for him.

"What new information?" I said. "What have you got that'll persuade him?"

Now he didn't say anything.

"I've tried to persuade him over the years and he's never budged."

"Your father's been well trained," Hume said. "And he probably felt he had something to protect when your mother and sister were alive. Now—now there's just you, and he might feel that his son can take care of himself." He laughed. "But don't quote me because I might be labeled sexist."

We were nearing the street and I stopped walking. "This is changing nothing," I said. "The fact is your guy broke into my mother's house. I can prove it and I will. All you need is a whiff of dirty tricks in the news and your election bid is toast. People are skeptical enough about you already."

Hume got out another cigar and lit it. After snapping the lid closed, he offered me the tin. "Okay, Sam. There's a number in here. You call it and see if that helps." After a moment I took the cigar tin from his hand. "If it does, you get in touch with me." He let smoke drift out of his nostrils and rise up his face, which gave the impression that his head was smoldering. "I gather others have been in touch with you about him."

I didn't say anything.

"I'm sure they've said they have your father's best interests in mind, but they're not out to do you or your father any favors." He waited. "Sam. He's no good to either of us dead. Then—as they say—he's just history."

Hume nodded and walked out to his car, which was waiting at the curb.

WHEN I RETURNED to my mother's house, there was a note on the kitchen table:

> *Felt strange alone here. Perhaps this house is haunted? Took a walk. Back soon—P.*

I was relieved. I liked being by myself (as opposed to alone) in my mother's house—I always had—and now it enabled me to call the number that was written on the gold paper inside the cigar tin. It was a 617 area code: Boston. The phone rang four times, then a recorded message came on: "You have reached the offices of R. L. Saavo Consultants. Please leave a message and we will return your call."

Saavo.

I went up to Abby's room. In her bureau I found the notebooks, tied together in two stacks with old bootlaces. They were the kind of composition notebooks we'd used in school—black-and-white-marbled cover, white pages with blue horizontal lines and a red vertical for the left margin. Abby bought a new notebook every January—one for each year, going back to 1972. When she'd fill up the notebook, she'd stop for that year—she usually dated the last entry sometime in November or December. I'd read all of them, but this one I'd read often while writing my book. She kept this notebook the year she went to Belize. I flipped through until I found an entry written while she was in treatment in Tucson.

> remember what peter o'toole/lawrence of arabia said when the journalist asked him what he liked about the desert—"it's clean." when they let me out for a walk there's all these spiky plants and you scare up animals—mourning doves (i love that name), rabbits, jackrabbits (they're much bigger, with long ears), coyotes, javalina. and the snakes. you hear them rattling in the shade, beneath rocks or under mesquite bushes. my father told me the names of some of these animals and spiky things when i was down in mexico. sometimes it was like when i was a little girl, he'd treat me like a child and explain things very carefully. especially after he realized i had a "habit." a jack-habit (they're much bigger, with long ears). the light in the desert is a long black veil. it pushes all the color down into the mountains so that what should be red is mauve, what should be green is brown. only in darkness do the true colors come out. that's true everywhere—in boston, salem, belize, mexico, here in the sonora desert with the lights of tucson rising up off the valley floor. at my father's hacienda i could get out at night, walk in the desert beneath the stars. i could do this because there was no place to go, there was just desert. no city lights. here, i'm a prisoner and there's no getting out at night because there's places to go. except sometimes when sam comes for me and we drive down into tucson and go to that mexican restaurant we both like. they have that mariachi band that walks among the tables. i'm in love with the boy who plays the big fat guitar. his black pants are so tight and the silver studs up the leg seams are like stars above the desert. has a nice ass that boy and I could use a good fuck, really. the night i tried to slip the boy a phone number sam intercepted the bar napkin and he told the kid my father was an assassin. sam was drunk on tequila and beer and he defined it as "one who shoots asses." good, sam.

you're usually on to me. try to protect me though we both know
you really can't.

I thumbed back through the notebook, looking for the passage about my father's hacienda. It was difficult because the pages were all so densely packed with my sister's heeling script, each looping *l* a full jib. She'd go on for pages without starting a new paragraph. Her most frequent complaint about my stories was that, like all journalists, I believed in too many tiny paragraphs.

i know daddy is upset with me and my jackhabit but he tries not to show it. i think he's baffled. he understands drugs, knows how they work. i think he has employed them in his work is what i think. but he doesn't know how to get me off. when i ran out of my own supply he couldn't bear to watch what was happening to me. i knew my puke, my shit, my screaming and crying would work and then saavo came. dr. saavo i called him because i think he might have been a doctor. but this is mexico amigo and who can say when it comes to titles? dr. saavo gave me the shots and i will always love him for that. i prayed for his return. he was a kind, gentle man, nothing like stick who would usually administer to me on the promise of a blowjob or something nasty down on all fours though he was using so much there toward the end that there wasn't exactly a lot to work with. i'll kill the limp dick fucker he ever comes near me again. but it's dr. saavo i could love and not just because he looks a bit like richard manuel and calls me lonesome suzie even though he knows my name is abigail. and the one time i put my hand on his thigh he only smiled and got up off the bed. put his hypo away. maybe you're gay? i said. he smiled his own lonely smile and said maybe your father's in the next room, suzie.

I heard the front door open and it was Petra's footsteps that echoed up from the vestibule. As she climbed the staircase, I put the notebooks back in Abby's bureau and went out into the hall. She looked surprised to see me—startled, caught even.

"Oh, you're here," she said.

"Maybe I'm a ghost?"

She smiled, with effort. "Are you trying to scare me?"

I walked down the hall to her. Her eyes studied my face. When we were almost close enough to kiss, I whispered, *"Boo."*

"Boo, yourself." She began to step back, but I took hold of her arm and pulled her closer.

"Tell me where you were?"

"Out for a *walk*. You see my *note?*"

"Tell me about Hume, your old employer, your former fuck."

She yanked her arm away from me but I grabbed it again. "Hey, I don't need to explain to you where I go or what I have done before I knew you—"

"No, you don't," I said. "But you came for this ride, so you got to pay the fare."

"What's going on? What happened with Hume?"

I grabbed the front of her sweater, Abby's black turtleneck, the one I'd given her for Christmas too many years ago. "Take it off," I said. "It's not *yours.*"

She struggled to get away, eventually slipping out of the coat. She ran down the hall, then bounded down the front stairs. I chased after her, following her to the vestibule, then through the kitchen, where she yanked open the back door. I caught her in the backyard, and we fell to the ground in the dark. She hit me with her fists and we were both yelling, and I kept trying to get the bottom of the sweater up over her head. Finally she rolled away from me and shouted, *"All right! All right, Sam!"* Standing, she pulled the sweater off, baring her breasts to the light coming from the house.

17

I could hear the sirens in the distance and they grew louder by the second, zeroing in on my mother's house with the precision of a mosquito drawn to earwax. Petra had rushed into the kitchen and I heard her run up the back stairs. I was still lying on the grass and, looking toward the house behind my mother's, I shouted, *"Thank you, Mrs. Fanshaw!"*

As the sirens died out on Andrew Street, I walked through the first floor and opened the front door. Two police officers were coming up the steps; they were the cops I had spoken to in Red's early that morning.

"Good evening," I said pleasantly. "You received a complaint from our neighbor, Mrs. Fanshaw, I assume."

The taller of the two men had a mustache. "May I ask your name, sir?"

"Samuel Adams."

"Agnes Adams is your mother?"

"Was. She died last Tuesday."

"Sorry, sir."

"Why don't you come inside?" I led them into the vestibule. They looked at the furniture, covered with white sheets, then the shorter one said, "Are you alone here? We received a call about noise—a man and a woman shouting. . . ."

I was undecided: tell them there was a woman somewhere in the house, bare-breasted and upset, or lie and say I was alone, and that my neighbor, who had resented our presence in the neighborhood since we moved in nearly thirty-five years earlier, was hearing things. It wouldn't be the first time.

I didn't get to answer because both policemen raised their heads at the same time and gazed toward the top of the stairs. Something happens to men's faces when they are unexpectedly presented with feminine beauty. It was comical: Their jaws went slack and their eyes lost any pretense of hard objectivity, melting into an innocent pleading and pure want.

I turned around, too, and we watched Petra descend the stairs. She was wearing Abby's maroon bathrobe now, which was taut about her hips and breasts, and as she turned the landing, there was a glimpse of thigh. "If we were disturbing the neighbors," she said, placing a languid hand on the newel post, "it's my fault, Officers. We were in the backyard and I guess things got a bit noisy."

The cops shifted their weight. Finally the taller one said, "So everything's all right?"

"Everything's fine—as fine as they can be at such times. Emotions tend to run high when someone dies, you know?" She tilted her head.

After a moment, both policemen nodded stupidly, and the taller one took the lead by putting on his hat. As we went to the front door, I thanked them for coming, as though they'd been dinner guests. When they were on the front stoop, they stole one more glance past me, then I closed the door gently.

I went back to the stairs. "That was effective."

Petra, who was standing on the first step, draped her arms over my shoulders. "You want to get men to do something, you help them activate their most basic instincts. I read an article once that claimed men have something like forty erotic thoughts per hour."

"Only forty? Listen," I said. "I don't know what got into me—"

Petra drew me to her, pressing my face to her warm shoulder. I put my hands on her hips, raised my head, and she kissed me. After a minute, she stepped away and led me into the living room. We tugged the white sheet off the couch and sat down.

"Do you suppose this is just some form of 'lust in the face of mortality'?" she asked.

"I don't know."

"This is starting to feel like more than simple lust."

"Did that article say how often women have erotic thoughts?"

"Impulses. It said we had *impulses*. And it wasn't the number, the quantity that was important, but the intensity." I untied the sash around her waist; she wasn't wearing anything beneath the bathrobe. "This is beginning to feel like love, Sam. Does that worry you?"

"Should it?"

"Occupational hazard."

"I don't have an occupation these days."

"Then can you say it?" she asked. "Can you say 'I love you'?"

"It almost sounds like a dare."

"I love you. It's frightening, isn't it?"

She leaned toward me and pressed her mouth to my ear. We held perfectly still, poised as though there were still one last chance to retreat before falling over the edge. But I realized it was too late. "Yes, it's frightening," I whispered, "and I do love you."

IN THE DESERT Abigail told me she was in love with a man named Saavo. Something about the way she said his name indicated that he wasn't just another junkie. We were sitting out on the grounds of Twenty-Nine Palms; above us loomed the Santa Catalina Mountains, north of Tucson.

"He called," she said. "I asked him to come across the border and see me."

She'd been in treatment for nearly a month, and it had been years since she'd looked so healthy. Her face was fuller, tanned, her hair and eyes regaining their old luster.

"Who is he?" I said.

"A friend of Daddy's. I gather they work together."

"I want to meet him."

"Yes, under one condition." I kept my eyes toward the mauve mountains, deepening with the coming sunset. This was a remnant from the stoned Abby, always trying to cut a deal. "We meet him at El Coronado—not here at the clinic—and then you give me some time alone with him in your room."

"Makes me feel like your pimp."

"*Sam!*" I turned to her. "I'm like a prisoner in here. I love the guy."

"Does the guy love you?"

She smiled. "He doesn't know how much he loves me. Yet."

While Abby was in treatment, I had been staying a few miles farther up in the canyon at El Coronado, a resort that was spoiling me rotten. There was a pool that was visited daily by a number of women who were looking for something to do; there was horseback riding up into the mountain passes; there were tennis courts, where I had established myself as the guy to beat. It was as if I'd shed my Boston skin and become this new species, sleek, coiled, and reflexive. I was thirty-five and my game had never been better.

The day that this Saavo came across the border, I picked up Abby, and we met him back at El Coronado for lunch on the bar's veranda, which overlooked the turquoise swimming pool. It was obvious what she saw in him: tall and lean, dark, penetrating eyes, full beard and shaggy black hair. Ramon Saavo ordered lunch in Spanish and insisted on picking up the tab, even when I told him that my father was footing the bill for this family excursion into the desert. Saavo was then in his early forties and he said he'd been an associate of our father's for years. In fact, he claimed he worshiped the man, would do anything for him without question.

"Why is that?" I asked when I finished my second margarita.

"This is a great man, your father." As Saavo gazed across the table at me, I knew Abby was holding his hand in her lap. I was soon going to have to make my exit—I'd already given her the key to my suite. "The shame of it is that the nature of his work must never be made public. He has done many great things for the United States, patriotic things, and yet this must forever remain concealed."

"And you're an *associate,* you work with him?"

"For years."

Saavo had grace and charm, and I'd had my second margarita before noontime. I didn't want to spoil things for my sister, so I pushed back my chair. "Well, any associate of our father's is an associate of the family," I said. "Now I'm going to go down and pay a visit to the pool."

Abby considered the glinting blue water. "That one in the black bikini?"

"My sister's very perceptive," I said as I got to my feet.

"Looks like a real screamer to me," Abby said, and she bit down on a taco chip.

"Perhaps we'll see you back here around cocktail hour," Saavo said. "Five o'clock?"

"Long as I return Abby to the clinic by six."

For several weeks we maintained this routine. Three or four times a week I'd break Abigail out of the joint, take her back to La-La Land in the Desert, and we'd both get our rocks off for the afternoon. Abby was right: The one in the black bikini could really let go.

I'd never seen my sister so happy. She repeatedly told me that she was in love with Saavo, which in our family is a remarkably direct admission. Terms of endearment, testaments of love, sweet nothings, these are but a foreign language to us. The best one can hope for is a good sweaty fuck during a languid desert afternoon. Screaming is optional.

I admit I was taken with Ramon Saavo, too. He really seemed to care for my sister. He was gentle and kind, and though some of his Latin considerations were a bit dramatic and perhaps calculated (flowers were delivered to my suite prior to each of his visits), he pulled it all off with an understatement that I found quaint and gentlemanly.

Maybe I was a bit jealous? He was clearly helping my sister climb out of her worst state ever, and he proved to be a stalwart friend of my father's. At times I began to think of him as a brother—or, from my father's perspective, the son he could never have. What was most intriguing—and at the same time disconcerting—was how candid he was in talking about my father. While there was a line he could not, would not, cross, still, he seemed to understand that both Abby and I craved anything that pertained to this enigma we believed to be our father.

So Ramon and I entered into a kind of collusion. He knew I'd been writing my book, and there were times when he'd listen to me and Abby piece together what I'd found and he'd gently correct some assumptions or confirm some suspicions. It was often with a nod of the head, a gesture of the hand, but I realized that he was tacitly steering me down a sinuous path toward a truth that I felt sure was at the end. I also assumed that when he returned south of the border, he was doing my father the service of inform-ing him as to my sister's recovery and my attempts at historical discovery. He was, in short, a double agent. We all willingly played along. And it only seemed possible there in the desert heat, on the veranda, by the pool, on those cool linen sheets in the air-conditioned suites. As Abigail neared the completion of her treatment at Twenty-Nine Palms, Ramon told me that they planned to marry soon after her release. He told me point-blank that he would always love Abby.

WE HAD BARELY gotten started when there was another knock on my mother's front door. Petra whispered, "They'll go away." I nodded, my face buried in her hair.

There came another knock, and then Ike called from beyond the door, "Sam!" He knocked again. "Sam! Come *on,* man!"

Petra and I disengaged, and while I shrugged into my jeans and shirt, she quickly wrapped herself in the white bedsheet that been draped over the couch. I went to the door and opened it. Ike stepped inside, filling the vestibule with the faint scent of brine.

"Sorry," he said. He regarded Petra, now standing, clutching the sheet around her. "Very sorry to disturb you, but they're out there."

"Who is?" I said.

"I don't know, but someone's watching the house." He took another look toward Petra and then watched me finish buttoning my shirt. "I had the police band on my CB and I heard the call, so I came over just as those cops were leaving. I parked around the corner and started to walk back when I saw them. Two of them in a car across from the Common."

"Men?" I asked. "Man and woman? What?"

"Couldn't tell."

I went into the dark living room and pulled the curtain back just enough to see the street. I could barely make out a silhouette of two people in the car down on the corner. "I need a closer look." Returning to the vestibule, I took my coat off the rack. "We'll go out the back way," I said to Ike. "I'm going to walk up to the car. That'll probably scare them off. You follow them and call me." I looked at Petra a moment.

"I guess I'd better get dressed," she said.

Ike began to say something, then shook his head. "Never mind what I'm thinking."

"Forty times an hour," I said, and she smiled.

"What?" Ike said.

"Never mind, it doesn't apply to you, anyway. Just follow me." I led him into the kitchen and out the back door. We crossed the yard, went through the gate behind the garage, and walked through Mrs. Fanshaw's yard to Briggs Street.

Ike said, "I'm parked on the Common a block over. Give me three minutes." He hustled off into the dark.

I walked around the block so I could approach the car from behind—there were two people in it, but it was too dark to see them clearly. The driver was smoking and there was the brief glow of an inhaled cigarette. I stood next to the trunk of a maple tree for a minute. It was a clear, cold night, and the only sound was of leaves scratching along the sidewalk bricks on a gust of wind.

I began walking toward the parked car, slow, unhurried. I could see that a man wearing a lid was behind the wheel. He turned his head but must have thought I was just a pedestrian. When I reached the car, I quickly stepped up to the passenger door and leaned down to the glass. The man there turned his head toward me, surprised. He made a sudden gesture with his hand as he spoke to the driver, who started the engine and pulled away quickly. The sedan sped down Andrew Street. After a moment, Ike's pickup truck swerved into the intersection and followed. I walked back to my mother's house, and Petra let me in the front door. She'd put the maroon bathrobe on again, and she was smoking one of my mother's cigarettes.

"It's the guys who took you," I said. "The passenger was the guy I spoke to on Newbury Street."

"You sure?" She was visibly shaken.

"When they had you on the sailboat, you remember anything about a guy's skin?"

She stared at me for a long moment, then it came to her. "Red hands."

"Like he'd been burned or had some kind of graft."

She nodded. "He did all the talking."

"Right. Now we wait."

TEN MINUTES LATER the phone rang in the kitchen. "Two guys," Ike said. "I'm sitting in the parking lot out at the Willows, watching them row out toward a moored sailboat."

"*Simple Truth,*" I said.

"I can't tell in the dark."

"A ketch."

"That's the one," he said.

"I'll be right down."

When I hung up, Petra walked into the vestibule. "I'm coming, too. Don't even think otherwise." She had changed into her jeans and a faded blue chamois shirt of mine, one of those catalog purchases that seem to last forever.

I followed her, pulling on my coat. "You really should stay here."

"Forget it. I'd like to meet this guy with the red hands again."

"Fine."

We drove out to the Willows and stopped next to Ike's truck. It was empty. Farther down the lot the sedan was parked beside a van. We got out of my car and looked out at the dark water and the lights of Beverly on the far shore. *Simple Truth* was barely visible, just two masts and a white hull with graceful lines.

"Stay put," I said.

"Where you going?"

"Just stay here."

I walked down the lot toward the sedan, keeping my right hand around the grip of the .38 in my coat pocket. The car was empty. So was the van, a panel truck that said *Olde Salem Chandlery & Sailmaker* on the side.

After a moment I started back toward Petra. When I was halfway there, the phone in Ike's truck began to beep. She tried the door, found it unlocked, and answered the cell phone. I jogged the rest of the way to the truck, and when I reached her, she was staring at me, listening to the phone. Slowly she turned toward the water and whispered, "Ike?"

Then there came an explosion out on the water. The percussion thumped my ribs and hurt my ears. Petra dropped the phone and fell to her knees beside my car. Debris splashed down on the water, pieces of wood and metal hitting the other moored boats, as flames and smoke rose from *Simple Truth*. I felt pummeled into a strange deafness, so at first I didn't comprehend that the van was now speeding down the lot toward the exit, with its headlights off. I began to run toward the vehicle. It was a stupid thing to do, but I didn't care. The .38 was out of my pocket, held in both hands before me. I think I was shouting, but sound had been rendered a distant thing by the explosion. I have no idea what I was saying. The van veered away from me and slowed as it approached the street. I was perhaps within ten yards, and it occurred to me that I had a pretty good shot, but I didn't take aim. As the van passed beneath a street lamp, I saw the man behind the wheel clearly. There was no mistaking my father's intent brow above the wire-frame glasses, his tight, determined mouth. I stopped running and watched the van disappear down the road.

I tucked the gun in my coat pocket and walked back to Petra. She was standing now, staring at a large crack in my windshield, fanning out from one point of impact. A piece of metal lay on the hood, glinting in the firelight. In the distance we could hear sirens, drawing closer.

"Sam, we need to get out of here."

I looked out at the burning boat. "That was Ike on the phone?"

"I think so." The sirens were getting louder. It was still hard for me to hear and she seemed to be nearly shouting at me. "Right *now*, Sam. You *know* those same two cops'll be down here, and they're going to be curious about the coincidence of finding us here."

I picked the piece of metal up off the hood of my car: a turnbuckle from the ketch, the metal warm in my hand. "All right," I said. I hurled the turnbuckle out into the water.

18

There have been times when I really thought I could have killed my father.

Not kill, assassinate.

Something detached and professional. Point a gun at his head and pull the trigger. The shot clean, unexpected, death instantaneous. It was not the same impulse as revenge, where you make sure the person knows who is committing the murder and has time to savor the implications. Knives are effective in such cases.

The impulse often came upon me when my father took me by surprise. He did so several times when I was a boy. Thus, I associate him with silence, with the dark, because he seemed to materialize out of them (and to disappear into them as effortlessly). One night, when I was about ten, I was in my bedroom in San Diego, putting the decals on a model submarine I had built. My room was full of model battleships (one of my favorite things to do in San Diego was to go down to the harbor and look at all the navy vessels), and I felt that somehow they were perched on my shelves and bookcases, poised to defend me. I was working at my desk, with only the small pool of light from the Tensor lamp illuminating my hands.

I didn't hear him enter the room. I didn't know how long he had been standing there beside me, watching as I tried to slide the wet decal into place on the conning tower of the sub. When I realized he was there, my heart jumped and my fingers tore the decal. For one brief moment I could have picked up my X-Acto knife and plunged it into his chest.

"What?" I said.

"Nothing, Sam. I just want to see how you're doing." When I didn't answer, he said, "That's very good work. They're all well done."

The torn, wet decal clung to my forefinger. I waited until he left, then tried to slide it on the sub again and carefully align the two halves so that the tear wasn't apparent. I came close, but I was always aware of the slight flaw on that model boat.

A little more than a decade later I was sitting in a doctor's office just off Huntington Avenue in Boston. This was before *Roe v. Wade;* the doctor was black, and he performed abortions at night, after his regular hours. I was alone in the waiting room, staring at a newsmagazine, barely able to comprehend the captions beneath the photographs. Again, the room was quite dark, lit only by the singular pool of light from the small lamp next to my chair.

When my father opened the door, he didn't say anything, and I think he must have seen the assassin in my eyes at that moment. He sat down across from me in a chair with chrome armrests and cracked brown vinyl that was intended to resemble leather.

Finally I said, "How did you find out?"

His glasses reflected the lamplight; rainwater had collected at the bottom of the lenses. "It's not important." He removed the glasses and began cleaning them.

"Does Mom know?"

"No." He put the glasses on; they had the kind of arms that curled around the ear. Reaching inside his wet raincoat, he took out a manila envelope. Laying it on the coffee table between us, he said, "You'll need this. No argument, okay?"

I had borrowed most of the money from friends at the *Boston Beacon.* There was a moment where I wanted to pick up the envelope and hand it back to him, maybe even throw it at him, but I didn't have the strength. Instead I left the envelope there on the table, on top of the old copies of *National Geographic, Jet,* and *Life.* At the very least I would not pick up the envelope in his presence. That was my final position.

Which he understood. And after a few minutes he got up and went to the door. "Tell Abby that—" I could see his eyes now, and at that moment

I think they were as close to tears as I'd ever seen them. He didn't finish what he wanted to say. I looked down at the magazine again and listened to him go out into the rain.

Abby's second abortion (that I'm aware of) was in Tucson and it almost killed her. The week before she was going to be released from the clinic, Saavo disappeared. To be more accurate, he simply failed to show up. No flowers were delivered to my suite, and when I picked her up, I told her that I didn't think he'd be waiting for us this time on the veranda overlooking the pool. She wouldn't hear it, and we sat there through the afternoon, the heat building to 108 degrees. It was mid-August and most days in Tucson the heat surpassed 105 degrees, and there were periods when it broke 110 degrees. Skin discomfort is a remarkably subtle thing, and by then I could tell the difference between 105 and 108 degrees. Even in the shade the air on the veranda was brutal.

In late afternoon I finally walked her back to my air-conditioned suite so she could sleep off the margaritas. I went for a swim. None of my playmates were at the pool. The girl in the black bikini had said she was going to a sales conference up in Phoenix. I dozed for about an hour in a lounge chair in the shade, and then I returned to my suite, where I found Abby passed out on the bathroom floor. She'd taken every pill in the medicine cabinet and drunk a good portion of my fifth of Stoly. I managed to get her back to the clinic, where they pumped her stomach. It was then that her doctor, a Dutch woman named VanLanderSchoot, informed me that Abby was pregnant.

It took over a week for her to recover from the abortion; she'd lost a lot of blood. When she was strong enough, we went for a walk up the hill behind the clinic. She stopped and leaned over to look at a barrel cactus. "It's hard to believe they're alive, isn't it? They just sit here day after day. Hardly get any water, don't move, but they're alive."

"You sound envious."

"I am." She took my arm and we continued on. It was early morning, already hot, but the sand along the path was still moist with dew. "You can smell the desert today, can't you?"

"Yes." We sat on a crumbling stone fence that was shaded by an old collapsed adobe wall. Beneath my hand the stones were still cool. We were high enough above the clinic that we could look west across the valley toward the Tucson Mountains.

"I love the desert," Abby said, "but it doesn't seem real. And I miss salt in the air."

"Me, too. Think it's time we go back to Boston?"

She nodded. "So much sunlight gets depressing. I'd kill for an overcast day with a fine Boston drizzle." She was wearing a loose white gown; her legs were crossed and she was bent over so she could study her toenails in her sandals. "I've been down here so long, the black polish has all worn off. Definitely time to go home." That word hung in the still desert heat for a moment. "Know what she told me?"

"Who?"

"VanLanderSchoot. No children. I'm barren as the desert now."

She lowered her head to my shoulder and I put my arm around her as she cried. I stared toward the distant mountains, bleached in the morning sun.

"I wish Saavo at least knew," she said finally. "Fucking men don't care about that."

"Some do," I said.

"If a woman told you she was going to abort your baby, what would you say?"

"I don't know."

"Come on, Sam."

"I was never told, until after it was done." She took her head off my shoulder and wiped her eyes. But I couldn't look at her and after a moment I stood up. "We need to go back to Boston," I said. "Soon. I'll set it up."

"And you never told me. Who was it, Jessica? Not what's her name, Laura?" I continued to stare at the mountains. Abby got to her feet slowly. "Jesus, Sam. We're just a family of killers, aren't we?"

Her voice sounded stronger and I realized that in an odd way this was the best I could do, that this small tawdry revelation would at least temporarily pull her back from her own despair. She took hold of my hand as we started down the path. When we were small, when we lived in warm, sunny places like San Diego, our mother insisted that we hold hands when we left the house. It was the same that morning in the Sonora desert, and we didn't let go as we walked back to the clinic.

AT MY MOTHER's house Petra and I turned on the TV in the den. It was just eleven o'clock and the news was coming on WHDH. Petra poured us a couple of Scotches, pulled the sheets off the couch, and sat down. I was so wired I had to remain standing.

The station already had a film crew at the Willows and it was the lead story, with a live broadcast from the parking lot. The reporter, a young blonde trying to conceal a Southern accent, said that thus far three bodies had been recovered from the water and one had been identified as a James Nolan. Behind her, firemen and policemen came and went, and in the distance several boats with floodlights searched the black water. *Simple Truth* was no longer burning, though smoke still rose into the night sky.

When the reporter concluded her story, a photograph was broadcast on the screen: former Senator Marshall Hume posing with James Nolan, the guy I had caught in my mother's house. There had been no official statement from Hume's office regarding their association, and the other two bodies had not yet been identified. The newscasters moved on to a shooting in Roxbury.

"Three bodies," I said, pouring a second Scotch for each of us. "They don't even say if the other two are male or female. There were two men in that car outside here. The guy with the red hands and a guy wearing a lid—I didn't get a look at him."

"So maybe Ike's not one of them?"

"God, I hope you're right, but then where is he?"

I sat now, and we both drank and stared at the television. For the next twenty minutes or so there was the usual litany of crimes, accidents, and fires, alternating with ditzy commercials. Even the broadcasters seemed relieved when they got to sports and weather. J. P. Proulx was doubtful for the next Bruins game against the Blackhawks, and it was supposed to drop down into the thirties overnight, with a seventy percent chance of rain in the morning, followed by partial clearing. On that faint note of optimism, I hit the off button.

Pouring rain awakened me before dawn. First thing I noticed when we moved into the Federalist house in Salem was how the rain sounded. It came down on the shallow-pitched hip roof and made this thunderous noise. New Englanders build their houses like their boats—*tight*—and listening to a hard October rain come in off the Atlantic could be a powerful spiritual experience. Abby used to be frightened by storms, and my mother always used to say, *It's just a little rain, dear.* My mother had a great many fears; I would never understand how she concealed them from us so well. After someone dies there's always a friend or relative who says something about how the dead have no worries, no fears. I used to think that just an empty platitude. But as I listened to the early-morning rain, I realized it was the gospel truth.

Petra was sound asleep next to me in my mother's bed. I got up quietly and went down to the kitchen, made coffee, and walked a few blocks to get the *Globe.*

In the front-page story, Hume's office confirmed that James Nolan was an assistant to the former senator, but Hume himself had not yet been reached for comment. One of the two other bodies had been identified: Russell Nygaard. The photograph was of the man with the red hands whom I had met on Newbury Street—he looked much younger, a good fifteen years at least. He was alleged—the journalist's favorite word—to be retired SOS, but there was not yet any confirmation from Washington. The other body was burned so badly that identification had not been possible by the time the newspaper went to press.

When Petra came downstairs, it was pouring out. She was wearing my sister's maroon bathrobe again and she stood next to me, a hand on my shoulder, and for minutes we just stared out at the rain in the backyard. Mrs. Fanshaw's house beyond the fence was barely visible.

"What's this?"

Along with the newspaper and my coffee, I had the phone book open on the kitchen table, as well as Hume's cigar tin. "This," I said, putting my finger on an ad in the Yellow Pages, "is Olde Salem Chandlery and Sailmaker—it was written on the side of that van that tore out of the lot last night."

"I didn't notice much after the explosion."

"Then you also didn't see who was driving."

Petra sat down at the table, her back to the rain in the yard. "No, I didn't."

"He was familiar."

She poured herself a cup of coffee, then ran one hand through her hair. "Familiar?"

"It was my father," I said. "And I damn near shot him."

"You know, I've felt that he was close." She sipped coffee. "Ever since I thought I saw him in the hospital outside your mother's room. There's something about him that gives off, I don't know, almost a smell, an aura."

"All my life my father's absence has felt like a presence. It killed my sister, and I think it killed my mother. Or at least put her out of her mind—her misery."

"He's close, then, isn't he?" With her free hand she held the lapels of my sister's maroon bathrobe together.

"I think he has been for some time." I watched the rain for a moment. It was beginning to let up. "The closer he is, the harder he is to find."

FIRST THING, we drove down to Ike's fishing boat in the harbor. No one was on deck. We went aboard and rapped on the cabin windows; after a moment, there was movement down below. I opened the door and led Petra down the companionway. Ike was lying in his berth, trying to get up. His face was red, as though he'd been badly sunburned, and dried blood caked his nostrils. His eyes didn't look right.

"Hey there," I said pleasantly, taking hold of his shoulders. "Not so fast, sailor. We're looking a bit dazed and confused, aren't we?"

He didn't resist as I helped him lie down again.

"We need to get him to a doctor," Petra said.

"No doctor," Ike whispered.

"Tea, then." She went in the cramped galley and turned on the stove.

"Tea," I said, "and then we get you to a doctor." There was blood on his pillow, and he'd been cut on the back of the head. His eyebrows were singed.

Ike could hardly move his mouth when he spoke. "Haven't been to one of those since they bolted my hip together. They're not going to touch this head."

"You got some burn there," I said. "What happened?"

Ike's eyes roamed the tight cabin. He had an apartment nearby but he virtually lived aboard his boat. The place needed to be aired out—it reeked of fish and motor oil. He was looking around as though trying to remember if he'd been there before. "I don't know, I was rowing a dinghy."

"You followed someone—two men—out to a sailboat, *Simple Truth?*"

After a moment, he said vaguely, "That's right, two men." Petra brought him a mug of tea. He sat up again and stared up at her face as though he were in the presence of a goddess of mercy. "Thank you."

"You see anyone else out there?" I asked.

Ike winced as the hot mug touched his puffy lips. "They were arguing."

"Who was?"

He gazed out the porthole above the berth a moment. "Three men. On the ketch."

"Arguing about what?" I asked. "You must have been close to get burned like this."

He tried the tea again and took a longer sip now. He stared at Petra. After a moment, she sat next to him on the berth, and he tried to smile at her. "You were in the parking lot," he said. "I saw you standing by my truck."

"The cell phone beeped, just before the explosion," she said.

Ike nodded, looking more alert, almost excited by the fact that he could remember. "I called. That's right, I saw you two and I called."

"You called yourself?" I asked.

"I got cell phones galore—in the truck, on my belt, up in the cabin. I'm wired, man." He took a long sip of his tea. "The tide was rising and I'd tied on to the stern of another moored boat. I must have been maybe fifty yards from the bow of *Simple Truth*. I couldn't hear them clearly because the three of them had gone down below in the cabin. What I did hear was the sound of oars. It was dark on the water, but off to my left I could hear oars and finally I could make out another dinghy. It moved up toward *Simple Truth* and I lost sight of it for several minutes—he'd gone around the stern. At that point the three men were nearly shouting down below." Ike took a last swallow of tea and handed the empty mug to Petra as though it were a gift. "Then I caught a glimpse of the dinghy once more—it was falling off quickly on the tide, headed back toward the parking lot. That's why I called you—to let you know the dinghy was coming in."

Petra looked up at me. "Your father."

I nodded.

"Then, *Jesus,* the whole thing went up," Ike said. "The noise, it was like when a charge goes off in the water—all the fish float to the surface. All I remember is lying in the bottom of the dinghy, coming in and out of it. I must have been thrown back and whacked my head good 'cause I got a Christer now. There was a lot of commotion, fire and smoke, and I was in and out through all of it. Later, when it was quiet, I felt rain on my face. It really stung. I managed to get my painter untied and just drifted on the current, going out by then. Some early-morning fisherman spotted me and he towed me in."

"You should see a doctor," Petra said as she stood up. "You may have a concussion."

Ike shook his head slowly.

I said, "Okay, then we take you back to Mom's so you can rest."

"I'll go under one condition," he said, staring up at Petra. "If you take care of me."

"That just proves there's nothing really wrong with him," I said.

We helped him off the boat and into my car; it was like walking someone with a bad hangover. Then we drove to the Willows so I could pick up his truck. I wanted to use it.

Petra got behind the wheel of my car. "You're going to that sail maker's?"

"It's better I not go in my car. Take Ike home and put him to bed. I'll be back soon."

MUCH OF SALEM's waterfront was long-gone touristy-artsy-fartsy, but there were still places like Olde Salem Chandlery & Sailmaker that managed to avoid the indulgences of upscale gentrification. The dilapidated two-story brick building had a FOR SALE sign in the window. The owners were sitting on a gold mine, but whoever finally bought it would have to invest a small fortune just to bring it up to code.

I walked around the building, looking in windows like any fool prospective buyer. Though it was dark inside I could see that there were shelves full of nautical supplies, and beyond that a repair shop with outboard motors on sawhorses. Out back a set of stairs led to the second floor; I climbed up, feeling the entire wood structure shimmy beneath me, and found a door that was locked. Through the window I could see large cutting tables, sewing machines, and long bolts of canvas. An old-time sail loft—none of those high-tech synthetic materials here.

I looked around from my vantage point at the top of the stairs: several old buildings clustered together, and between them boats sitting on their winter cradles. Seagulls stared back at me from adjacent roofs. Quickly I struck a windowpane with my elbow, reached through the broken glass, and unlocked the door. I stepped inside the sail loft. The place was absolutely silent.

I walked the length of the room to the front windows. There I ran my hand along a bolt of canvas. Much of sailing is experienced through the hands. The weave of sailcloth, Dacron halyards, three-strand laid dock-lines. At the end of a day on the water there was always evidence of the work in my raw hands. I remember my father once saying he sailed because of what it did to his hands. At eighteen, that didn't mean much to me; some thirty years later it was profound.

To my right was a door in a crooked jamb. I jerked it open and entered a small room with both shades drawn. There was a scarred rolltop desk, a wood swivel chair on casters, and an old space heater that looked like a fire hazard. The plaster walls were covered with framed photographs of boats under sail and a calendar with a redhead in a bikini sprawled on a teak deck. In the corner was a cot heaped with a sleeping bag.

Then I saw it: On the floor, next to a glass and an empty bottle of Merlot, lay a stack of books about marine navigation, weather, and sailboat maintenance. Among them was a copy of *Sailing Alone Around the World,* by Joshua Slocum.

I studied the room again.

No clothes.

No ashes.

He'd cleared out and I'd just missed him.

I lifted the corner of a window shade and peered down toward the harbor. He was so close to the ocean, yet he couldn't even risk a view of the water through an open window. This could not be the life my father chose. Years of living in hiding, constantly alert, anticipating discovery. And now an old man holed up behind drawn shades, knowing there would be no end to it, until he died. I couldn't resist a second look at the redhead in the bikini. Despite the abundance of fleshy hip, thigh, and cleavage, I tried to imagine this girl fully clothed. My mother had been a redhead long ago. I remembered the black-and-white photograph of a stunning young woman seated with her new husband in a cozy Italian restaurant, both dressed for a night on the town, their cigarettes poised, their drinks fresh, their whole lives before them.

Part III

"The Citty upon a Hill"

19

When I returned to my mother's house, Petra was in the den. "I put Ike in your bedroom," she said. "Couldn't convince him to see a doctor, so I played Florence Nightingale with what I could find in the medicine cabinet. The two shots of brandy from the liquor cabinet were the most effective." She was smoking one of my mother's cigarettes and she had the television on with the sound muted. "They confirmed that the one with the red hands used to be in SOS, but they still haven't said anything about the other body except that it's a man."

"Then it's probably the guy who was driving, the one wearing the lid." I sat down beside her on the couch and shut off the television. We were whispering because Ike was asleep upstairs. It felt conspiratorial, parental. "He was behind the wheel out in front of the house here, and I think he was the same guy driving you that day on Newbury Street."

Petra turned her head sharply toward the back windows. The sun was trying to break through low clouds. It was a New England day where "partly sunny" would be an achievement.

"What?" I said.

She shook her head. But then, after a drag on the cigarette, she said, "St. Cyr." Leaning over, she crushed the cigarette out in the ashtray on the coffee table. "The guy with the red hands, the one they claim is named Nygaard, he called the driver St. Cyr once when we were on the boat. I'm pretty sure because in my drowsy way I was trying to recall if I knew who *Saint* Cyr was—I went through Paul and Christopher and Francis and Jerome, but couldn't recall any 'Cyr.'"

I leaned forward, both elbows on my knees. There was a small notepad on the coffee table. My mother had been an avid list-maker and she kept notepads handy everywhere. When sticky notes came along, she was enthralled with the idea of being able to adhere her notes to mirrors, cabinet doors, inside books. Abby considered it a form of haunting; as retribution, she gave my mother a huge box of Post-its one Christmas. I picked up a pencil and wrote on the notepad:

SIMPLE TRUTH

Russell Nygaard/St. Cyr (SOS)   *James Nolan (Sen. Hume)*

George & Gracie

Drawing a circle around the last two names, I said, "They're government, like Nygaard and St. Cyr, but they're not Secret Operations Service. They're competing with those guys."

"First to find your father wins."

"Maybe," I said. "If Nygaard and St. Cyr met Nolan on *Simple Truth* to make a deal, it could mean that Nolan had my father, or *thought* he had him—he was real close. The way Nolan got in this house, he must have been a snoop."

"An essential tool for someone like Hume," Petra said. Her hand was on my shoulder and her fingers toyed with my hair. "Even back when he was up on Beacon Hill, Hume was always looking for the dirt on his colleagues. I remember him saying something about how the 'promise of silence' could be a persuasive thing in politics—but he had to have the shit on someone before he could promise to keep mum. That was Hume's idea of control—I got the goods on you, but I won't say anything, unless. And *that* was Nolan's job, I'll bet: find the shit."

"All right," I said. "Let's assume that when my father learned that Mom was dying, he came to Boston—from wherever he's been these past few years. And Nolan finds out he's holed up here in Salem. Hume has Nolan set up a meeting with Nygaard and St. Cyr so that then Hume can cut a deal."

"Which is what?"

I stared at the notepad for a long moment. "Hume gets first crack at my father."

Petra took her hand out of my hair and picked up the pack of cigarettes on the coffee table. "Yes, that's Hume. Trots your father out before the media and gets himself elected attorney general of the Commonwealth next fall. Then Nygaard and St. Cyr can have what's left of your father. Certainly the FBI would love to be able to clear up all the hints and suggestions that they were involved in JFK's assassination. They get your father to say what they want and give him a light deal—he's an old man and he can't do real time in prison. But who are this George and Gracie you met early yesterday morning? You think they're government, too?"

"Yeah," I said. "They said they were my father's 'friends.' They wanted to help him." I leaned back on the sofa. "Their idea of helping him might just be to help him keep quiet." Petra lit her cigarette and turned to me. "Dead men don't talk," I said.

She exhaled blue smoke out of the side of her mouth. "Who did Ike see in the dinghy? Who blew up *Simple Truth*?"

"My father," I said. "My father because he was wrong—he *thought* it was Nygaard and St. Cyr who wanted to silence him, so he struck first. He killed the wrong ones." I laughed. "Shit, he's an assassin and he's old, and I'll bet he killed the *wrong* guys." Tapping my finger on the notepad, I added, "Which could mean that my father's 'friends,' George and Gracie, are the ones out to kill him, and they're still very much alive." I got up off the sofa and went to the bookshelf and read the titles on the spines. "It's what these people do. They permanently silence people. My father calls it history. 'You're not part of history until you're dead, Son.'"

Petra stood up and came across the den to the bookshelf. "What did you find at that sail maker's?"

"A saint, of sorts," I said, taking the book down off the top shelf. "Joshua Slocum."

A LEATHER-BOUND copy of Slocum's *Sailing Alone Around the World* had been a gift from my father. He sent it to me at my mother's house after Abigail and I returned from Tucson. It was the first and only present I'd received from him since I was a boy. At the time, I thought it was funny. My father must have thought everything was all right—his daughter was "fixed." Saavo must have painted my father a rosy picture: Abigail's recovery in Tucson was a success. When the bills stopped coming in, he'd have known I had taken her back home.

Abby did seem all right for a while. She stayed clean and she got a job, two actually. She lived with a family in Brookline that had an autistic son, and the mother, who was a pediatrician, helped her find part-time work at a school for autistic children. It was, I believe, the one time in my sister's adult life that she might have had moments of real purpose. She was fully occupied, and she became genuinely attached to this boy, Nicholas. She even talked about going to school to study special education.

She told me this one cold Saturday afternoon when we were having lunch at El Phoenix on Commonwealth Avenue. Their chili was brutally hot, and I was swilling Coronas, while Abby drank Cokes.

"No mariachi band." With her fine, sharp jaw and her short hair, she resembled a slightly wasted Audrey Hepburn. She added sour cream to her bowl of chili. "No boys in tight pants with those silver studs down the sides."

"That's the first time you've mentioned men in a while," I said.

"Celibacy has its rewards." She smiled at me. "Fewer complications."

We ate for a moment. I knew my sister well enough—we were leading up to something. Finally I said, "What?"

"Saavo called me." She blew on a spoonful of chili. "I don't know how he found my number in Brookline, but he called and said he was coming up to Boston and wanted to see me this weekend."

"And?"

"I told him I was busy this weekend."

"Good."

"Good?" she said. "It's a first. First time I didn't go running back to some former dick. You suppose that really is a good sign?" I nodded. "Is that what it takes—getting your veins drained and your uterus scraped out?" It was hard to see her eyes against the sunlight streaming through the window, but her voice was both angry and resigned. "Maybe I'm just getting old."

"You're thirty-four."

"Mom had both of us before she was thirty."

I put my spoon down. I was sweating from the heat of the chili. "What do you want me to say, Abby?" She only stared at me. "You're not your mother."

"And I never will be one."

I picked up my bottle of Corona. "Neither of us is exactly prolific in that respect."

"You ever wonder about that?"

I didn't answer right away. I didn't want to say something that seemed like a dodge. "I do," I said finally. "But I guess I haven't found the 'right girl,' as they say. I don't seem to be looking that hard for that kind of responsibility. Maybe *I'm* getting old?"

"Maybe we've got what we need for now. I have Nicholas and the kids at school and you have the book."

"For right now, that's enough for me," I said.

"Is it?" She meant it.

"It is." And I meant it.

We got through that first few months back in Boston in that fashion. *How are you? I don't know but I'm real busy.* It's American to be busy. You don't have to know how you're doing as long as you're busy. So we kept busy. Abby started taking courses at BC; I was working on the book. Usually when we got together it was all right, although conversation with her was always like testing the ice on the pond—she'd start out where it was safe and sidle out toward the middle, until the sheet would begin to crackle and boom, and she'd inch her way back toward shore.

Abby and I would often drive up to Salem on Sundays; usually Mom would cook, though sometimes we'd take her out to eat. I realized later we were all avoiding what was on our minds: my father, of course. None of us, to my knowledge, had heard from him since Abby and I had returned from Tucson. But, like Abby, my mother seemed to have become resigned to the fact that he would no longer be a part of her life in any meaningful way. In a sense, we were all in mourning.

"WHO WAS HE?" Petra asked. She was making tuna-fish sandwiches and clam chowder. I had been sitting at the kitchen table, leafing through *Sailing Alone Around the World,* but more often staring out the back windows.

"Joshua Slocum? He was the first man to circumnavigate the globe single-handed."

"All alone?"

"Very." I closed the book and put it back in its slipcover. "His boat was called *Spray.* Joshua Slocum is a hero to my father, maybe the only one."

Likewise, I think my father was a hero to Ramon Saavo. I knew I was going to try his number again, the one Hume had written inside the cigar tin; but I was putting it off, waiting for all my energy to concentrate on the only other man besides my father whom I had ever really wanted to kill. More than my father, Saavo was the one who had eased Abby toward her death. There was a contradiction about Saavo that I had never understood: His willingness to let my sister descend into heroin addiction ran against the grain of his respect for my father. What the two men had in common, I gathered, was their work, the nature of which gave them a unique sense of privilege, even access to a unique morality. It went beyond allegiance to country or affiliation to political principle; it had to do with shared philosophy, which I could not fathom. Perhaps more than philosophy, the two men shared the same religion; Abby once said they were both members of the Elect.

When lunch was ready, Petra prepared a tray for Ike, which I took up the back stairs. He was lying in my bed, flipping through my old 1970 Bruins yearbook—the year they won the Stanley Cup on Bobby Orr's overtime goal. "That was one of those moments," he said, sitting up, "where it was like we all *willed* the thing to happen. Orr is on the right boards and feeds it to Sanderson in the corner, then he breaks for the net and Turk puts it right on his stick. He tips the puck past Glenn Hall, then there's that horizontal dive through the air. It was like he'd suddenly learned how to fly. *Jesus.*" Ike's bright red face was slick with ointment. He still hardly moved his lips as he spoke.

I put the tray on his lap and sat at my old desk. "You going to be okay?"

Carefully, he tasted the chowder. "Been having these incredibly erotic dreams."

"I don't want to hear them."

"The best one involves my first wife. It's the middle of the afternoon, she gives me a great blowjob, and then she says, 'Why don't you take a little nap, honey, while I go downstairs and bake a chocolate cake.'" He laughed tightly; I could see it was painful even to smile. "You wonder why neither of my marriages lasted."

"It's amazing what a good whack on the noggin will do for you," I said as I got up from my desk. "I'm going down to Boston this afternoon. You stay here with Petra."

"This is a good house to recuperate in." He attempted a small bite of his tuna-fish sandwich. "Your mother treated me like one of her own. But listen, if you're going to leave me alone here with Petra, I'm not making any promises, bro." He laughed again, briefly. "Where do you get off hooking up with something like that, you old goat. She isn't even *forty*."

"Been asking myself the same thing."

"What's in Boston all of a sudden?"

"Need to see a guy. Old business."

He waited, and when I didn't elaborate, he said, "You still carrying that .38 I got you?" I nodded. He touched his cheek carefully with a finger, as though testing to see whether it was done yet. "Plan on using it?"

"Plan? No."

"Then it could be you're not ready to go back to Boston yet."

"Got to get my mind right, huh?"

"Something like that—if you want to survive down there."

"Let me ask you something," I said. "You ever kill anybody?"

"In the line of duty, yeah." He put his sandwich down. "When I first started out on the force, I had a partner, a black guy named Jamal who had been a running back at Roxbury High. I loved the man. He didn't believe in the 'line of duty' crap they gave us at the academy. He said he just wanted a job where he could kill the people that needed to be killed. He said it was his calling. He would know who they were when he saw them, and they'd be doing something that would justify his shooting them."

"He was an assassin."

"If you want. He was good at it and for a while it worked. Then he had a nephew who was doing some stuff he shouldn't have been doing and Jamal did the wrong thing—he needed a moment to think about things, and that's all it took. The nephew went away for a long time for killing his uncle the cop."

"I remember that story. It wasn't long before you and I met."

"Most of my Boston friends are dead, Sam." He tried a spoonful of clam chowder. "Sure you want to go back there alone?"

"I live there, remember?" I said, going to the door.

"I just worry about guys like you on your own. You're so helpless."

"You're the one who nearly had his face burned off." He tried to smile. "I'll see ya," I said, going out the door. "Don't get any on the sheets."

I went down the front stairs and into the large vestibule closet. There was a small stained-glass window, which cast a somber green light. Petra came out from the kitchen and watched me put on my coat and shove the .38 in my pocket.

"Supposed to get cold," she whispered, turning the collar up around my neck, "and it might even snow." She stayed close, her face uplifted in that dim church light. Something happened to those dark Greek eyes; some acknowledgment, some decision. Her hands tightened about my neck as I enclosed her in my arms.

20

I know the drive between Boston and Salem like no other, but this trip was different. For years there had always been a clear sense of destination, of traveling between two distinct points, equal and balanced: my mother, my city; my past, my present. Who I was in my mother's presence, who I was walking the streets of Boston. One provided refuge from the other, but as I wound south on Route 1 with midday traffic, the realization that my mother was no longer there, behind me in Salem, made the city before me suddenly imposing and mysterious. The Pilgrims liked to think they had crossed the Atlantic to build their "Citty upon a Hill"—the place where they would be closer to God. But they were wrong; to climb the hills of Boston on a cold day in October was really a descent toward Evil. Ike knew this. And Abigail found the prospect alluring.

She had lots of help, from her junkie friends, and from shrewd suppliers and manipulators like Ramon Saavo, who to the very end claimed that he loved her. He came to Boston for her. Nearly a year after we had returned from Tucson, she suddenly changed her tack—she stopped attending special-ed classes at BC, and she moved out of Nicholas's parents' house in Brookline. At first she wouldn't say why, though I had a pretty good hunch. She had nowhere to go (other than home to Mother, which was out of the question), so of course she ended up on the couch in my Brighton apartment.

She was using again, though she denied it; and we were both drinking steadily. I was writing *One True Assassin,* so her constant presence was a distraction, an inconvenience, and for the first time really I lost all patience with her. After an argument—the worst we'd had since we were kids—I left the apartment, and when I returned, she was packed and gone. Fine, I thought (knowing even then that I would soon regret it), if she couldn't help herself, I couldn't help her. And I got back to work.

I didn't know where she had gone to stay and had no luck in finding her. She had become invisible. I couldn't see her, couldn't hear her, but I felt her presence. This was the way it was between us for much of the last years in Boston. When she finally called, she didn't sound good. There was noise in the background, voices and telephones. "Where are you?" I asked.

"In court."

"Where in court?"

"Brookline."

At least she wasn't in New York City. Or Belize. "I'll be right down."

When I reached the Norfolk Municipal Courthouse that afternoon, I found her sitting on a wood bench in back. The room had raised paneling and fluted columns, but the dark wood appeared to have suffered from years of human erosion. She wore a black wool coat and beret, with a long maroon scarf around her neck. Taking hold of my hand, she looked extremely pale and tired, but happy to see me. "Before I die, Sam, I just want to steal a peek at the Invisible World," she whispered. And then she offered me her sly grin. "Until now it never occurred to me that the best view would be from right here at the back of a courtroom."

I sat down next to her. She was breaking my heart and she knew it. Since we were kids my only defense in these instances was to get blunt. "Fill me in, Abby."

"This has to do with Dr. and Mr. Brookline. It started with the pediatrician's husband, Cameron. Guy says he's a real-estate agent, but I don't think he's sold more than a couple of condos in a year. Hangs around the house all day talking on the phone, unless he goes someplace like the track with his pals."

"You were fucking him."

"Listen, it wasn't like I *forced* him into anything. I knew what was on his mind the moment I walked in that house. I should get *some* credit for holding the guy off as long as I did."

"The pediatrician found out."

"Something really strange about those two—they can't keep a secret from each other. What kind of a marriage is that?" She sighed. "Yes, she found out and I didn't deny it."

"Of course. So you got thrown out."

"Which I thought was the end of it, and fine with me." Letting go of my hand, she picked at her eyelash for a moment. "I miss Nicholas, though." Something in her voice had tightened and I knew we were getting close to it. "But the shit's just beginning, I guess. They've filed this lawsuit."

"What lawsuit?"

"The one that claims I abused their son."

"Abused, how?"

"You name it. The police have photographs showing welts and bruises on his back and legs. Now, *where* did those come from? I bathed that boy regularly and I never saw any bruises other than what any other kid has— Nicholas has limitless energy, and being autistic, he tends to run into things and fall down."

"So there were bruises."

"*Nothing* like in these photos! Nothing that *I* did to him." Her voice was breaking, and as she leaned against me, I put my arm around her shoulder. "There's more, Sam. They're saying I molested him. An eight-year-old autistic *child.*"

"You have a lawyer?"

"Yes, and he's late. Saavo hired him."

"Any lawyer of Saavo's ought to have experience getting people off."

She daubed her eyes with a knotted tissue. "Sam, he's trying to help."

"I'll bet. Where are you living now?"

"He's set me up in an apartment in the South End."

"Christ."

So it began. Abby, me, and Ramon Saavo. The Boston version was nothing like Tucson. No desert heat. No languid afternoons during which everybody gets laid. No drinks on the veranda overlooking the pool. Instead we spent long hours in drafty courtrooms, often waiting for tardy lawyers (there were several before it was all over). While Abby's case devolved into a tedious stream of rescheduled hearings and continuances, *One True Assassin* was published, first to considerable acclaim, but then a kind of media erosion set in. The recently appointed Senator Hume made lots of noise about President Kennedy's assassination, which was followed by an intense flurry of new information and revelations. It became a free-for-all. Eventually, my reputation as a journalist was shot and I couldn't find any work.

AFTER CROSSING THE Mystic River Bridge, I got off in Charlestown and went to my apartment. There were two editions of the *Globe* in plastic bags on the front stoop, which meant Mrs. Hennesey had gone to stay a few days with her sister down in Braintree. In my kitchen I listened to a half-dozen phone messages. Most were from news reporters looking for something on Czlenko's murder. One was from Celeste at the *Boston Beacon*. One was a hang-up. Nothing from my father. I'd just missed him, I was sure. I had felt his presence in that sail loft, but it was too late. This was something I'd known since I was very young: identifying traces of my father. After he'd leave, my mother often went to bed, feigning illness when she just needed a good cry, but I would rummage around in the cellar, go through the pockets of his pants and shirts in the laundry. I'd keep anything he'd left behind: coins, a stick of gum, matchbooks.

I called Celeste and was told she was in a meeting. Hanging up, I sat at the kitchen table and looked down into the street for a while. The desire to open a beer was strong, but I didn't dare. There seemed no way to avoid calling Saavo.

I went downstairs to Mrs. Hennesey's phone on the assumption that Saavo was into caller ID technology. (Convinced that she was going to drop dead of a heart attack, and fearing that she wouldn't be found until days later, she had given me a key to her apartment years ago, telling me to come down if I heard her hit the floor or, more likely, if she was too quiet too long.) She had turned the thermostat down and her apartment was cold. I sat at the kitchen table and dialed the number written inside Hume's cigar tin.

I was right about the technology. After the fourth ring, Saavo said, "Okay, I'm curious. Who *is* Mildred Hennesey?"

"What are you doing in Boston?" It had been almost a decade and Saavo didn't say anything. "You don't recognize my voice?" I said.

"I don't like games." But his voice was smooth, playful.

"You'll like this one," I said. "And you're already playing."

"I know this voice but can't place it—give me a clue."

"You have too much history," I said.

"It's the problem with getting old."

"You must be, what, fifty-something? But you sound good, Saavo."

"I'm well."

"Business has been good?"

"Depends on the business."

"Heroin."

"That's not a business, amigo. For some it's a passion."

"How about RSP?" I could hear him inhale and then let it out slowly. "Sound familiar? If you need help, you might talk to Dr. Miriam Ault. She's in pathology at Dana Farber." He didn't say anything. I expected him to hang up but he didn't. "You got it now?"

"Hello, Sam."

"You must be older, Ramon. I thought that merely the mention of heroin would bring Abigail to mind. Guess she's a long way down the road now. But then I imagine your women on heroin are all pretty much the same. It's the ultimate need. They'll do anything for you, right? It's not love but a form of worship."

"Is that why you're calling me now, to reminisce about Abigail?" I decided to wait. "What is this business about RSP?"

"You provided it for my father. Or perhaps you injected it into my mother yourself?"

"This is no game, Sam."

"No, it's not. But you're in it already." He inhaled but decided not to respond. "You really *are* in it, Ramon. You worship my father—that's your weakness."

"This is a man who accomplished great things." Saavo was trying to sound earnest.

"I'll grant you this: He might have assassinated a great man, someone you despised. You have that in common with my father—assassination—but your methods are different, and you just do the little people. Besides, you're in the game simply because you did something you should never have done: You came back to Boston."

"It's a fine city." His voice sounded uncertain now.

"It is, and before you leave again, we need to see each other."

"Why should I do either?"

"Because of what the Dana Farber Pathology Department found in my mother—"

"This is not something that can be connected to me—"

"And because I got your number from Marshall Hume, the Commonwealth's former senator who will be running for attorney general next year. You do see the connection, don't you, amigo? How he would love to grab you for supplying designer drugs to Boston's well-to-do. He's a politician looking for a job. Even if he couldn't pin anything on you, he would get some great publicity—and think of the business you'd lose."

After a moment, he said pleasantly, "It would be good to see you again, Sam."

"Boston Common, by the Partisans sculpture on Charles Street."

"That would be fine, Sam."

"Four o'clock, then." I hung up Mrs. Hennesey's phone.

I went out into the front hall, and as I climbed the stairs, the phone rang up in my kitchen. I used to run up stairs to answer phone calls, but no more. When the answering machine came on, I heard Celeste say quickly, "Hi, Sam, I'm glad you called—I *really* need to talk to you, but I have another *fucking* meeting right *now*. I'll be at Dirk's wake tonight and maybe I'll see you there? *Bye.*"

DR. AND MR. BROOKLINE's suit against Abigail had ground down to a stalemate, where nobody was happy except the lawyers. I was nearly broke, living off my savings and spending a lot of nights in the grandstand seats at Fenway Park (it was 1987, the year after the Red Sox had lost the World Series to the Mets in seven, and I felt right at home amid the lingering bitterness of the crowd in that little green ballpark). Saavo was footing Abby's legal bills, though I suspected that my father was reimbursing him.

On a humid August afternoon there was a particularly contentious session, which included testimony from employees at Nicholas's school for autistic children and from Dr. and Mr. Brookline's cleaning woman, who said she had seen Abigail in bed with the child.

"We were napping!" my sister shouted as she stood up so quickly that her chair fell over. "You have *any* idea what it takes for a boy like that to settle down and *sleep?* We were just taking a *nap!"*

The judge, a large black woman in a slightly askew gray wig, ordered that Abigail remove herself from the courtroom. I walked my sister out—holding her elbow, I could feel her whole body shaking—and as soon as she stepped into the late-afternoon heat, she fainted. She spent that night at St. Elizabeth's Hospital, and the next couple of days she stayed in bed in her South End apartment. My mother and family came and went, as did Saavo and the last of the lawyers, a three-piece suit named Miles Threadgold. Uncle James had brought him in, touting him as an expert in wills and damage control. Threadgold was the first realist to handle the case, and he said that we should have settled out of court months ago. He offered to negotiate a price with Dr. and Mr. Brookline's attorneys.

Abigail was calm. Saavo had made sure of that. She neither agreed nor disagreed, but merely looked on from her bed as we argued the specifics of the case, which, we knew, could not be won. After everyone left, I sat with her for a while—she was almost asleep. Her arm lying on the sheet was remarkably thin and her eyes were closed. Tears rolled out from beneath her lids.

Wiping them away, I said, "We'll get past this, that's all. We always get past it."

The tears kept appearing and I continued to wipe them away with my fingers. "They would never understand," she whispered. "The intention was right."

"What intention?"

"Sometimes I could only get Nicholas down for a nap if I'd get in bed with him. And then he'd discovered that he could open my shirt and suck on my nipple as he dropped off to sleep. That's all. He was just looking for milk. I didn't have any—I'll never have any—but it didn't seem to do him any harm and it got him to sleep. That was my only intention, Sam. Those bruises, I never did anything like that. *Never.*"

"I know." I placed my hand on her short dark hair and left it there until she was asleep.

It took several weeks for the lawyers to negotiate a settlement, and during that time Saavo lost his cool. He became agitated and insulting, and I assumed it was because of money. The settlement was going to be for hundreds of thousands of dollars, including attorneys' fees, and suddenly Saavo was talking about how much Abigail had already cost him. He said he was going to wash his hands of the whole thing. I had assumed that he had been a conduit for my father's financing of Abby's lawyers. But something had changed—I suspected that there had been a breach between the two men. By the time the settlement was reached, Saavo had pretty much disappeared and Uncle James had to orchestrate the financing of the payment due to Dr. and Mr. Brookline. He sold his Florida condo and hit up other members of the family. As always, Uncle Jimmy was there when my father was nowhere to be found.

Abigail tried to get clean but couldn't; Saavo was long gone, and where she got her stuff I don't know. The street, obviously. How she paid for it I can only imagine. She'd avoid me for days, and then when I'd catch up to her, she'd try to brush me off. She talked about moving back to New York, and at one point she was in touch with somebody in Las Vegas.

But she only managed to move to an efficiency apartment just off Columbus Avenue. She didn't tell me where she was for a couple of weeks, and then she called and asked me to come right over—and would I bring the gun I had obtained recently for my own protection. I went there on a warm night in late September and found her out on the sidewalk in front of a dilapidated triple-decker. There were black kids playing in the street, and their parents sat out on porches. Abby and I were the anomaly; we were the only people on the block who weren't black. I was wearing jeans, my old Yaz Day T-shirt, and a sport coat with an inner pocket big enough to hold my .38. I remember feeling conspicuous more for the T-shirt than for the bulge under my coat.

"What's going on?" I said.

Abigail kept looking down the street toward the heavy traffic on Columbus Avenue. She was wearing all black, of course: a fine, sheer blouse and a very short leather skirt and heels.

"Abby, what's up?" I asked.

She wouldn't look at me. I took hold of her arm and tried to turn her to face me, but she pulled herself free and began walking quickly down the sidewalk. I followed after her, and she said over her shoulder, "Just beat it! Go *on!*"

I stopped walking. She was pretending that she didn't know me. I felt overwhelmed with confusion. I turned toward the nearest porch, where several men and women stared back at me, their gazes seeming to harbor some knowledge I would never possess—I felt shame, yet like a child I also felt understood and even forgiven. It seemed that these people knew me, had seen me before, and they were certain that my presence was only fleeting.

Walking awkwardly in her heels on the cracked sidewalk, Abigail had reached the street corner just as a black sedan pulled in off of Columbus Avenue and stopped at the curb. I ran then, ran with one hand against my breast, to keep the gun inside my coat from thumping against my ribs, and I called Abigail's name as the rear door to the sedan opened. Just as I reached the curb, she was climbing in to the backseat. It was one of those brief moments that in recollection seem excruciatingly long. There were two men in the car, a young white guy behind the wheel and a black guy in the backseat. Then, as my sister lifted her legs into the car, I could see that she wasn't wearing anything under her short black skirt and that her vagina was shaved clean. The car already began to pull away from the curb, and as she reached out to pull the door shut, she said, *"Just fuck off, brother!"*

I STOOD WITH my back against the wrought-iron gate that surrounds Boston Public Gardens. Directly across Charles Street was the Partisans sculpture, which depicts a grim, war-weary group of soldiers on horseback. It was late afternoon and the sidewalk was bustling with people who walked quickly because of the raw east wind that promised snow. Faces were flushed; chins buried in scarves and upturned collars. I didn't expect Saavo to be punctual, and it was likely that he first wanted to observe me (trying to observe him) from afar, but by ten after four I began to think he wasn't going to show. I also knew I was a sitting duck. Any car could pull out of the stream of traffic, slow down, and pop me à la Czlenko. But that was why I set the meeting on a busy street in broad daylight, with a good chance that someone could get a look at the shooter, the car, the license plate.

I was about to give up when this guy stopped in front of me. I thought he was going to ask for a handout: early thirties, soiled wool coat, half-grown beard, and that wasted stare that I'd seen too often in Abigail's eyes.

"You Adams?" he asked.

"Could be."

"The Sevens." He hawked up a head full of snot, dropped a wad on the sidewalk, and moved on, hands stuffed deep in his pockets.

I walked down Charles and, a few blocks past Beacon, crossed over to the Sevens, a long, narrow bar that served only beer and wine. As always it was dark inside and the place wasn't very crowded. The only natural light came through the front windows, and toward the back there was a skylight that cast a weak glow down through blue cigar smoke. That would be Saavo. I walked the length of the bar and found him perched on a stool, a glass of white wine on the table.

"Hello, Sam." He pushed out a stool with his foot but I didn't sit. "Want a beer?"

"A bit early for me these days," I said.

"You haven't gone and quit drinking, have you?" It was difficult to see his eyes.

"Not exactly. I have a wake to go to later."

"That's something to stay sober for."

I suddenly felt very impatient, but I didn't want to show anything like irritation or, worse, anger. When the waitress came, I caved and ordered a Pilsner Urquell.

"That's better," Saavo said. He might have passed for a banker—an international banker. Beneath his wool topcoat he wore a double-breasted suit, white shirt, and blue silk tie. In little more than a decade, he seemed to have hardly aged except around the eyes, where the skin was darker. He drew on his cigar and scratched under his chin momentarily. I had forgotten how he did this little ballet with his hands during conversation. "Sam, you should just leave your father alone."

The waitress brought my beer; I paid her and filled my glass. "When's the last time you saw him?"

"Think of the man as a dying animal. Something like a lion or an elephant. They wander off across the veldt, lie down, and die in peace. Quietly, with dignity."

"You must have been in touch before my mother died. You must have given him the RSP and the syringe. Or did you have one of your doped-up couriers make the delivery?" I drank some beer and regretted how good it tasted. "I suppose it's possible that neither he nor you actually went into Dana Farber and shot up my mother. That's awful risky. Somebody like that guy out on the street, one of your junkies, they'd do the deed for the appropriate compensation."

Saavo concentrated on rolling the tip of his cigar in the ashtray at his elbow.

"Stop looking so disappointed," I said finally. "I'm not here to have a drink for old times' sake. This isn't some Tucson reunion."

He left the cigar in the ashtray and picked up his glass. After sipping from it, he worked the wine around in his mouth before swallowing. Slowly, he shook his head, and I couldn't tell whether it was in response to what I'd said or to the wine. I had also forgotten how deliberately disinterested he could appear, and how that helped him control a situation. I'd seen it too often, while sitting on that veranda overlooking the pool in Tucson— Abigail unable to keep her eyes off him, and he'd just look bored and slightly distracted.

My beer bottle was about a third full. I picked it up and poured its contents into the ashtray, extinguishing the cigar with a hiss. "Maybe I didn't make myself clear on the phone," I said, putting the empty bottle on the table. "I got your number from Marshall Hume. He can reel you in at any time. He gave me the number first, I think, because he wants my father without any damage. He wants me to bring my father to him in one piece. That way he'll be of greatest use to Hume."

Using his elbow, Saavo nudged the ashtray aside as though it were a meal he was done with—a meal that had been unsatisfactory and therefore didn't deserve further attention. "And that's what you plan to do? Give your father to Hume?"

"What I plan to do is *my* business." I leaned toward Saavo. The smell of cigar smoke and wine was not unpleasant. "The point is, you're out of here regardless. You *don't* help me out, you're Hume's—and he'll have a field day with you. Believe me, there's nothing quite like a Boston politician who's hungry to get back into office. If you *do* help me, you can slip away so nobody'll miss you except for your doped-up clients."

Saavo was staring at me now and I suspect he used such a look for people who could not come through when they owed him money. His face, handsome, exotic, worldly, was all of a piece, set in stone. "Sam, you must realize I have always considered myself a friend of your family's—"

My arm came up off the table and knocked his glass to the floor, where it broke. Saavo looked down at the pearly droplets of wine on the sleeve of his coat. "All right," I said, "then I can't help you."

As I walked toward the front door, people sitting along the bar turned to watch. When I got outside in the cold air, I headed back toward the Common.

"Sam," I heard Saavo call from behind. I kept walking. *"Sam!"* When he caught up to me, he took hold of my right arm; I stopped and turned to him. Out here in the late-afternoon light he seemed older, less vigorous. His eyes appeared weary. "Look, what you're asking," he said. "It's very difficult. I feel a responsibility to your father. I'm sorry, but you don't know him like I do."

We were standing in front of a narrow set of brick stairs that descended below the level of the sidewalk to a dark doorway of a small restaurant. The place wasn't open for business yet, though inside I could see a pretty young woman setting up the tables. When she turned and went back through a door to the kitchen, I took hold of Saavo's sleeve and pushed him down the stairs.

I took my .38 from my coat pocket and pressed the barrel against his cheek. He leaned back until his head hit the brick wall next to the restaurant door. There was the pleasant smell of baking bread and tomato sauce. "You ever see one of your junkies die? Or do you always avoid that unfortunate circumstance? To you it's just a loss of revenue. Or, in my sister's case, a matter of cutting your losses." I jammed the gun hard against his cheekbone, tugging his upper lip into a snarl. When he exhaled I smelled his foul breath. "I should have found you after she died, Saavo. I should have tracked you the fuck down and shot you. I could have done it. And I'm telling you right now I still can, and there'd be no regret, no remorse." I cocked the hammer on the .38. Saavo's eyes were large, pleading. "I do this now and there'd be nothing done about it—just a dope deal gone wrong. This place might lose a couple nights of business, but then people would really want to come here and try the pasta. This would be the place where the dope peddler got blown away right outside the door. That's *all* that'd be left of you, Saavo, an interesting conversation piece in a little Beacon Hill restaurant."

Saavo tried to turn his head away from the pressure of the gun barrel.

"He was in Salem last night," I said. "He has my mother's ashes. Where'd he go?"

"You'll never catch up."

"I will."

"Not *this* time. It's different."

"How different?" I turned the gun so that it was pressed against the side of his nose.

"He's *going,* I tell you. If he's not already gone." Saavo almost yelled.

"How? Where?"

"I don't *know*—he only mentioned 'spray,' and I don't know what it *means."*

"Spray?"

Something in his eyes told me that that was all he knew. It made me even angrier. "You leave town," I said. "You *leave* Boston right away, *understand?"*

I released the hammer of the gun with my thumb and relief flooded

Saavo's eyes. But as I took the gun away from his cheek, he immediately began to regain his composure. It was in his eyes—not relief but a sense of verification: He knew I couldn't pull the trigger. He was never really scared; he only needed to look that way.

I drew my arm back and struck him hard on the nose with the butt of the gun. A strand of blood spurted down across his blue silk tie and he fell to his knees. I looked down at the top of his head; his hair was thinning at the crown.

"You're a lucky man," I said. "It would be easy to put a bullet through your brain, right down into the spinal column. But that would be too quick—you'd never feel a thing." He raised his head, tears in his eyes now, blood running freely from both nostrils. It was clear that he was in real pain. "I'm not an assassin, Saavo, just the son of one."

I stuffed the gun in my coat pocket, climbed the steps up to the sidewalk, and fell in with the crowd that was walking toward Beacon Street and the Common.

It had begun to snow.

21

I don't have a long history of violent behavior. Just the usual—a few fights during adolescence. Because I was taller than most kids, I was seldom challenged. The worst was during a high-school dance the fall of my sophomore year. A junior named Frankie Noyes had been egging me on all week, and we fought out behind the gymnasium. I was never sure why he wanted to take me on, though I suspected that it had to do with the fact that I was an athlete and he was not (though he was clearly strong enough to play some varsity sport). Most likely he selected me because I was a tennis player, arguably the least virile of boys' sports, and thus he avoided a contest with Salem High's true gladiators, who played football and hockey. It was more a wrestling match than a fight, and what punches were thrown either missed or were so poorly executed that they had little effect. We were locked in each other's arms for only a few minutes before the other boys, who were hoping for a real donnybrook, broke us up and drifted back inside, disappointed. I had a nosebleed and a torn shirt I would have to explain to my mother; Frankie's mouth was bloody, primarily because he wore braces. He ignored me after that, so I considered our engagement a successful deterrent.

After *One True Assassin* was published, within days I started to get phone calls from strangers who threatened me with everything from murder to having my dick cut off and shoved into an orifice of their choosing. At first I ignored the calls. In most cases they were from people (always men, with one exception) who just sounded irate but ineffectual. I was sure they were harmless, and that most would barely remember making the call once they sobered up. But there were two repeat callers—one man and one woman—who managed to get to me. They always called at night and they wouldn't leave a message on my answering machine (which others often did—and some were so funny that I'd play them again for a good laugh). Some nights I'd return to my apartment and there would be at least a half-dozen recorded hang-ups on my machine, and when they did reach me, they spoke in calm, measured voices, which I found equally alluring and threatening. I began to think of them as Melvin and Mabel, and I told no one about them except Ike Santori.

This was years before Ike took his shot in the hip on duty. He was what he liked to call "Robert De Niro lean," yet he could eat (and cook) like no one else. I'm certain there wasn't an Italian restaurant between Revere and Quincy that he didn't know about. But the place we went to most often was Santarpio's, a neighborhood bar only a few blocks from the mouth of the Sumner-Callahan Tunnel and the entrance to Logan Airport. We'd meet there nights when he got off duty, order pizza, a plate of lamb and Italian sausage from the grill, and beer, and watch whatever game was on the TV. The jukebox had everything from Aerosmith to Jerry Vale. Ike was newly divorced, and for the time being he was living with his mother in East Boston.

"This Melvin and Mabel," he said while the Red Sox were making a pitching change, "you think they're working you together?"

"Crossed my mind," I said. "Just days after I got my new unlisted number, they began calling more frequently. And lately, both have demonstrated that they know more about me than the other callers. They know where I live in Brighton, they know about Abby. The last time Melvin called, I got the impression he's been following me."

"If this is a stalker, it changes everything."

"It's probably just my imagination." I folded a new slice of pizza with one hand and took a large bite. The true test of Boston pizza is in the tomato sauce, of course; but it's also about how *little* cheese is used, and whether the crust is thin enough to fold a slice with ease. Boston pizza is a delicate thing: You should be able to eat a whole pie and not walk away stuffed.

"You gotta watch it, Sam, these people are sharp. You've already said that they keep their calls short but frequent, so they know how to avoid being traced. Plus, they're certain not to be calling from a phone that they could be connected to. These are not stupid people, just angry and—worse—methodical. Now tell me something." Ike paused to pour more beer in his glass, then turned toward me. He had the eyes of a cop now, and I realized he was watching carefully for my reaction. "In your gut, do you think this is becoming a serious situation? Not just a nuisance, but dangerous."

"I'm not sleeping well."

"I can *see* that, bro. But who is?" He smiled. "Only my dear, sweet mother sleeps through the night, rosary beads in hand. And besides, you have a lot of shit going on right now—your sister and her court case, a problem with work, and all this stuff with your book. It's got to add up."

"I would like to *have* some work," I said. "Haven't written a thing in months. Frankly, if somebody asked me to do a piece right now, I don't know if I'd be able to put together a coherent paragraph."

Ike laughed. "I felt the same way in fifth grade, so I became a cop. Tell you what we're going to do." He finished his slice, and I watched his jawbone roll beneath his skin as he chewed. Finally he swallowed, drank the rest of his beer, and said, "What we do is we go fishing this weekend."

Which was Ike's answer to most everything. It was either *Let's get something to eat* or, if his boat was in the water, *Let's catch some fish*. I have never been able to devise such clear, useful solutions to life, and it's why I've always considered Ike a genius and treasured him as a friend.

Sunday morning was overcast but calm as we ran his Boston Whaler out past Logan Airport, almost to Deer Island Light. Ike cut the motor, and rather than breaking out the fishing gear, he tossed several foot-long pieces of two-by-four in the water. Then, reaching inside his fishing vest, he took out a Smith & Wesson .38 snub-nose revolver. We spent the next hour practicing deadly force on those pieces of wood. When the tide turned, we drifted back into the harbor over a good run of spring flounder, which that night Ike's mother fried up for us.

I got a permit and carried the .38 for months. But I took to going out less, and when I did I tended not to go directly to my destination. At times I felt as if I was being followed, but I was never sure. Often I'd duck into a store or a shop and watch who was behind me on the street. Once, standing behind the plate glass of a Dunkin' Donuts, I thought I spotted Melvin. He was on the other side of the street, looking at the window display of a bookstore. Mid-forties, balding, tan windbreaker, and jeans. After a moment, he went the other way, turned the corner at the end of the block, and disappeared.

The next time Melvin called, I had just come in after seeing Abigail. There had been yet another continuance of her case that day, and I'd gotten thoroughly hammered at dinner. When I answered the phone, I simply said, *"What?"*

"Don't we sound pissy tonight? Bad day, huh?" His voice was deep, raspy, yet oddly affectionate and soothing. "Must be all that trouble your little sister's having over at Norfolk Municipal Courthouse. It's bad enough that we have so many men in America who take sexual advantage of children, but when someone like Abigail messes around with eight-year-old autistic boys, you *know* things have gotten out of hand. What do you suppose she did with him? She tell you? Suck his cock? But he's too young to get it up. No, I'll bet she made him lick her clit—what do you think, Sam?"

"I think I saw you." He didn't say anything. "Two days ago, across from the Dunkin' Donuts, right?"

"Well, we *are* getting *paranoid,* aren't we? You must be seeing me everywhere. It's an awful feeling, isn't it? You never know what someone like *me's* going to do. You suppose John Kennedy felt that way every time he went out in public? And his brother? And Martin Luther King, too? You suppose they looked at every American, thinking, That could be my assassin? And you know the worst thing is *knowing* that real assassins never *look* the part. I mean, Lee Harvey Oswald—how *nondescript* can you *get?* But of course, JFK never saw *him,* never saw it coming, did he? But I'm sorry, you don't think Oswald did it, do you? He was just the patsy, right? He was the cover for the real assassin—the *true* assassin—who just happened to be *your* father."

"Funny you should mention Oswald," I said. "I just realized that there's the slightest resemblance. The thinning hair, and that nondescript tan jacket."

Melvin hung up.

At least a week went by, and just when I was starting to think that it was over, Mabel called. I was convinced she and Melvin were connected because the first thing she said was, "How'd it go for the 'assassin's daughter' today, Sam?"

"You tell me," I said. "Weren't you there, or was today Melvin's turn?"

"Melvin?"

"Melvin and Mabel. That's what we've named you," I said.

"Who's we? You and your sister?" There was something in her voice that I'd not heard before: Her curiosity was genuine. Clearly, one of the things that motivated these two people was their own inescapable loneliness. In some way they needed to participate vicariously in my life; even my sister's legal difficulties provided them some relief from an overwhelming sense of isolation.

"If you don't like the names Melvin and Mabel, I'm open to suggestions." She didn't answer. "How about Ward and June? Ricky and Lucy?" I waited a moment, and when she still didn't respond, I said, "Well, both of you think on it and let me know if there's something you'd prefer." I hung up gently.

And I did something I probably should have done when they had first started calling: I unplugged the phone. I kept it that way the rest of the summer, only plugging it in when I wanted to make a call. Daily I would talk to my sister, my mother, and Ike, but for months the phone never rang in my apartment. As a result I got a better night's sleep, and after a while I put my .38 away in a shoe box. I acted as though Melvin and Mabel no longer existed, and indeed they simply seemed to have disappeared. I still didn't have work, and my sister was struggling—she would be dead in September—but at least I wasn't sitting around my apartment waiting for the phone to ring.

ACCORDING TO THE obit page in the *Globe,* Dirk Czlenko's wake was at a funeral home in Somerville, where he had grown up. At my apartment I showered and put on my black suit, the one I wore to weddings, funerals, and just once to a benefit dinner.

Before I left I called Marshall Hume's office and got Ms. Cluff's voice on a message machine. "This is Samuel Adams, Ms. Cluff. You tell the senator that I have found Ramon Saavo and he was of no use whatsoever. You tell him we need to talk."

Rush-hour traffic was unusually bad. Abigail called nights like this "negative Boston," because of the way the snow created reverse images. Streets were white, marred by black tire tracks and footsteps. Slate roofs bore angular patterns of lace. Color was reduced to the brick, granite, and black hues of a Brueghel painting, and pedestrians appeared hunched beneath some great weight brought on by the advent of winter.

The funeral home was packed with print journalists and not a few TV talking heads. Czlenko's casket stood on a low pedestal in front of heavy red velvet drapes. The atmosphere in the room was somewhere between art gallery chic and burlesque show tawdry. It gets strange when people who are accustomed to being seen come to *see*. Czlenko had been one of the profession's dirty little secrets: On record everyone deplored his kind of sensationalism, while privately they all read his stuff because he was so damned good at it.

Fortunately, Celeste found me immediately. "All this place needs is cocktails," she said. "You look great in black."

"So do you."

"Come with me." She took my hand and led me back out into the hall, to a door with a sign that read SMOKING LOUNGE.

We entered a long, stuffy room and sat on an antique love seat. At the far end of the room there was one other couple, huddled on a deep sofa that faced the fireplace. They were in their early thirties and the woman daubed her eyes. The man next to her had a lean, angular profile, and I was certain he was Czlenko's brother.

Celeste opened her purse and removed a silver flask. She took a sip and I could smell the thin, clean scent of vodka. "Listen," she said, handing the flask to me. "You said that whoever shot Dirk really thought it was you, right?"

I tipped the flask quickly to my mouth; the vodka was perfectly chilled. "You're going to tell me they were after Dirk?"

Celeste sat back on the love seat and crossed her legs. Her black dress was tight around her hips and thighs, and she studied me with an intimacy that I found unnerving. "You thought they shot him because he was wearing your coat," she said quietly. "But it was something else—that's why they were waiting outside our offices. They were waiting for *him*."

"So his murder is unrelated to my father—"

"*No,*" she said, and I caught a glimpse of the gold stud in her tongue. "I thought so at first, but then I went into his computer to find the last story he had been working on, which was about Marshall Hume." I handed her the flask and she took another drink. The vodka, plus the heat from the distant but roaring fireplace, had managed to put some color in her cheeks. "But I found all this other stuff, too, things I didn't know about. That's why he was killed—because of what he and Petra were working on."

"Petra?"

"They were working together on something about your father." She put her hand on my wrist. "Sam, do you know where she is?"

The couple got up from the sofa by the fireplace and began to leave. The woman was at least eight months pregnant and she walked carefully toward the door. I got to my feet and went to them; Celeste joined me. We introduced ourselves and conveyed our condolences. It was all a stilted formality, but what could we do? I was right: He was Dirk's brother and the woman was his sister-in-law. Neither really appeared to comprehend what we were saying; their eyes were glazed, distant, and unbelieving. I'd been there. It was over quickly and they left the room.

"Look Sam, I'm in an awkward position here," Celeste said. "Technically, as Metro editor, I'm now Petra's superior, but nobody buys that for a second. She and Dirk were on to something no one at the paper knew anything about. Now he's been murdered, and she—well, she's been missing for days. I think you know where she is—am I right? I don't want to seem to pry into your private life, but—"

"I think I need to know what you found in Dirk's computer," I said. "You have to understand that a lot of people seem to be after my father right now, and he may be in some danger—"

"I *know* that," she said. "That's what I'm trying to tell you." The door to the smoking lounge opened and several people entered, all in subdued states of grief, and they immediately began to get out their cigarettes. Celeste took my hand again, and for a moment I thought about how my sister used to do the same—in some ways what I missed most about Abigail was the feel of her fingers laced in mine. "Come with me, all right?" Celeste's mouth turned up at one corner. "I've downloaded Dirk's stuff into my laptop. I suppose there's no law against my showing you what I have there."

CELESTE GOT HER briefcase from her trunk and we went across Somerville Avenue to a bar called the Black Rose. We sat on the same side of a booth and she turned on her laptop, its glowing screen an anomaly in a dim neighborhood pub. The jukebox played Frank Sinatra, Nat King Cole, Bobby Darin, and Bing Crosby, while a few men drank boilermakers and watched the Bruins-Sabres game. On a high corner shelf behind the bar sat gold busts of JFK and Pope John XXIII that, no doubt, had been there since the sixties.

Celeste ordered shots of Stoly from the waitress, and then opened up a file called "True Assassin Revisited/1." She scrolled down through the first pages of Czlenko's notes:

Adams, John Samuel
1919
b. Aug 26, NYC; s. Winslow Arnold & Elaine (Beckert); sister
Evelyn (deceased, influenza epidemic, 1918).

1937
H. S. grad, P.S. 137, Brooklyn.

1939
US Navy. X-2 counter-espionage section of OSS. Trained at
Station S, Fairfax, VA (disguised as an army rehabilitation camp
for mental patients).

1940–45
Served in Mexico seeking location of German shortwave
broadcasting stations rec. & transmit intelligence to U-boats in

*Gulf of Mexico. Fluent in Spanish; cryptography. Blew up
stations; assassinated Nazi operatives.*

1946–49
*Married Agnes Margaret Byrne (Feb 20, 1948). B. S. from
NYU, 1949 (Courses: Atomic Physics, Vibration and Sound,
Optics, Vector and Tensor Analysis, Electric Wave Filters,
Potential Theory, Theoretical Physics, several languages).*

1949
Son, Samuel Xavier, b. Sept 6, 1949.

1950–53
*Shell Oil, Houston. Fluent in Arabic and Farsi. Operation Ajax
(planned by Kermit Roosevelt, Teddy's grandson): successful
coup in Iran to overthrow Mohammad Mossadegh & reinstall
the Shah.*

1951
Daughter, Abigail Byrne, b. Nov 12, 1951.

1954–59
*CIA (formerly OSS); Houston, New Orleans, San Diego; oil
exploration, Gulf of Mexico & Pacific Ocean.*

1960–61
*Operation Pluto (led to failed Bay of Pigs Invasion, Apr 17,
1961); communications advisor to Cubans at Happy Valley
(training camp in eastern Nicaragua).*

1962
Cuban Missile Crisis (Oct). Traveled to Miami week of Oct 22.

1963
Wife, two children move to Salem. Remains in SW, Houston,

New Orleans, San Diego. Miami/Mexico/Gulf Coast/Caribbean.
Contact: Felix Saavo (deceased).

1967
Salem (winter–summer). Panama (fall).

1969–72
Insufficient Evidence. Inactive? Southeast Asia?

1972–76
Chile, mil. Attaché. Contact: Ira Mandel (deceased).

1977–80
Iran, intelligence, special asst. Contact: Al-Mossa Assad
(imprisoned).

1980–81
Gdansk, special asst. to operations officer. Contact: Bruno
Wjoldkereski, Solidarity party boss.

1981–92
Caribbean/Mexico (still active SOS?). Contact: Ramon Saavo.

1992–Present
Known Residences: Progreso Island, Yucatán; St. Barts (lives
aboard a sailboat—Tartan 36).

"Felix and Ramon Saavo," I said, and when Celeste gazed at me, I couldn't help smiling. "It never occurred to me that they were a father-and-son routine. Just didn't see the likeness. At Disney World Felix called himself Trini Lopez." Celeste was trying to stay with me, but I could tell that the name Trini Lopez didn't register. "Earlier tonight I think I broke Ramon's nose."

"How?"

"Brass knuckles."

"You're serious?"

I turned back to the computer and scrolled down through the entire file—it was eighty-seven pages long. There were letters to and from SOS officers. There were names and addresses. There were dates of airplane flights (some with various aliases: James K. Hill, Compay Fuentes, Tomas Montoya, Carl Jendrow).

"That's right: Jendrow," I said. "I remember—it must have been when I was in high school—someone called for Mr. Jendrow. It was someone from Pan Am and I told her that no one named Jendrow lived here, then my father took the phone."

"Dirk was piecing together your father's entire professional history. A lot of this he got from your book, it seems."

"It's the only history he has," I said, nodding. "All this isn't just for an article."

"He must have been doing research for a book."

"Dirk was working on a book on my father?"

Celeste's face was extremely pale in the light from the computer screen. Her eyes seemed to glow from within, each striation a vibrant blue-white filament. "*They* were," she said. "Dirk and Petra were working on this together. And I'll bet Petra still is."

"Yes, I suppose so."

Celeste put her hand on mine, and it occurred to me then that she was sort of a negative Abigail. Where my sister had been so dark—the hair, the eyes—Celeste was pale and light. She was petite, too, though not wasted away. I suspected that she was so worried about becoming chunky by the age of forty that she built into her busy schedule regular workouts at a gym. "Are you very disappointed?" she asked.

"Only in myself," I said.

"I'm sorry, Sam—I really am." Leaning forward, she kissed my cheek with the affection of a kid sister. Then holding my hand tightly, she did the only other sensible thing to do: She got the waitress's attention.

22

In those last weeks before Abigail died, it got to the point where I couldn't believe anything she said. On the phone she'd talk about how she had to get out of Boston, how she was afraid, how she needed money. We'd agree to meet someplace and she often wouldn't show up. Since the day she'd told me to fuck off, as if I were some john who was pestering her, I felt this growing anger toward her, but I realized that I couldn't sever our tenuous connection. Something was troubling her and I was sure she was in danger. And the more certain I became of it, the more she avoided me.

One day, right after I finished talking to Abby, the phone rang. I answered, thinking it might be my sister—she often did that, call back immediately with an amendment to our conversation. But the call was from a woman who barely whispered into the phone. "Sam Adams?" At first I thought it was Mabel and I was tempted to hang up. But she said, "Is this Abigail's brother?"

Not "the assassin's daughter," just Abigail. This wasn't Mabel, but someone quite young. "Who's calling?" I asked.

"My name's not important."

"Why's that? Why shouldn't I just hang up?"

"Because I know your sister can't help it."

Truth was I liked this woman's voice. It was frail and husky, as though she were getting over a cold, and it sounded honest. "Help what?" She took in her breath and exhaled slowly. I was afraid suddenly that she might hang up. "*What* can't my sister help?" I asked.

"Please, just come and see for yourself. She stands outside the fence and watches him. Wickham House."

"What's that?" I said.

"I can't tell you any more because I work there." Her voice was so faint that I cupped my hand over my other ear. "You'll see," she whispered. "You have to come and stop her." And she hung up.

I looked up the Wickham House in the phone book and found that it was in Cambridge. The next afternoon I went there—a dilapidated Colonial on a side street not far from Harvard Square. Behind the house was a brick courtyard surrounded by a high wrought-iron fence. Inside children were running, screaming, playing tag. Their recess, if that's what it was, was supervised by two women, one with graying hair tucked up under a straw hat, the other in her mid-twenties, very thin in a plain green dress. The younger woman kept close to two boys who weren't participating with the other children. Both boys wandered, seemingly aimlessly, about the yard, and the young woman walked close behind, as though she were shepherding them. She was good at not interfering except when necessary. When one boy picked up a small rock, she immediately said his name and took it from him. She called the boy Nicholas.

After a few minutes the two women ushered the children inside, but I knew that the younger one had seen me, and I waited. After several minutes she came out again and spoke to me through the fence.

"Mr. Adams?"

"Sam."

"Your sister, she's been coming here and she watches Nicholas. She usually walks by a few times, and she often sits on that stone wall down there at the end of the lane." She was so young her face didn't have any real definition yet, but her eyes were remarkably green and direct. "I know about Abigail's case. Mrs. Johnson is extremely protective of the children. She'll call the police if she finds out it's your sister who's been lurking out here these past few weeks."

"What is this," I said, nodding toward the house, "state foster care or a special ed program?"

"We're Quakers." She smiled almost apologetically. "But, yes, the program is partially state subsidized." She appeared very nervous; beneath the green dress her shoulders were remarkably narrow.

"I'll talk to my sister," I said. She began to turn away. "Thank you for calling me."

Pausing, she said, "When they brought Nicholas here, they told us about your sister's case, the accusations. I remembered seeing it in the news." She took hold of the wrought-iron bars between us. Something about those hands—they were so bony and delicate—made me realize that she was not well. For a moment there was a look that crossed her face that seemed to confirm what I suspected, that she was sickly, and that she worked with these children because it was the only meaningful thing she could think to do in a short lifetime. Then she said something that struck me as odd, almost prophetic. "I'd seen film clips of her on the evening news. I'd never seen anyone famous, you know, in *person* before. But when she walks by this fence and looks in at the children, I can see that she's only looking for Nicholas, and she's nothing like she was on the news. She's . . . she's different."

She spoke with such intimacy and urgency. Finally I said, "How is she different?"

Her eyes were so pale and, though it was a warm afternoon, she had begun to shiver. She only turned, hurried across the courtyard, and entered the house.

I CALLED MY sister repeatedly; I went to her apartment, but I couldn't find her. I had a key to her door and I let myself in, thinking that she might have passed out. The apartment was empty. There were messages on her answering machine and I sat on the bed to listen to them. Several were from a TJ, and I immediately thought of the black guy in the backseat of the car. He was setting up appointments—with men, I assumed, though he didn't say so outright—stating times she was supposed to be certain places, some addresses, mostly hotels. In one message, TJ was enraged because Abby had failed to make an appointment. Other messages were from men who clearly were trying to set up a date; some of these sounded straightforward and businesslike, while a few guys sounded hopelessly timid and nervous.

The last message sent a chill through me: Melvin. It was definitely his playful, sauntering banter, but there was, toward the end of the message, a change in his tone. He was pissed off about something—he said that Abby had failed to fulfill her obligations, and that there would be a severe penalty. I was convinced Melvin was talking about money. But what worried me also was his familiarity—this seemed a call from someone who had been in ongoing negotiations of some sort and I was only privy to one of the latter installments. It had been months since I'd heard from Melvin (or Mabel, for that matter), and it never occurred to me that he (they?) would begin to call Abby. What worried me most was that she'd never said a word to me about these calls, as though I were the one who needed to be protected.

The apartment was like most of the other places she'd lived since moving out of Salem. There was clothing lying about and the bed was unmade. On the bedroom walls were posters that she took from one place to another: sand dunes on Cape Cod, Plimoth Plantation, the old brown and white poster of The Band from their *Stage Fright* album. On her nightstand was an ashtray full of cigarette butts and roaches, an empty bottle of Chardonnay, and four candles, the melted wax hardened to water-stained oak veneer. I opened the drawer and took out her journal—she always kept it in her nightstand. Though I'd known about her journals for years, up to that point I'd never read them, even when I'd had the opportunity. I looked at the marbled cover a moment, feeling guilty for what I was about to do. What I committed to paper was always "public"; Abigail's journals were purely private, and I feared that greatly.

I started at the back of the notebook and flipped through the pages. She was dating her entries, something that surprised me. I read what she'd written over the past few weeks.

SEPT 6

you say it's your birthday.
well happy birthday to you sam.

SEPT 7

labor day fucking.
lots of labor but doesn't lead to labor.
ha-ha.

SEPT 8

tj says supplies are tight. i can't work enough for him he says.
jeannie has been picked up again and they put her in the hospi-
tal. heard from linda she slashed her wrists again. girl can't do
anything right, even that.

SEPT 9

second call from this guy. not a job. don't know what he wants.
talks about our "common knowledge" & somehow he thinks
i'm going to come up with $. yeah right. says he's been in touch
with sam & that conspiracy theorists don't know the damage
they can cause. what can he do to sam that hasn't already been
done? poor sam. everybody has a drug of choice & for sam it's
the kennedy assassination thing. i'll take heroin anyday thank
you. i ask this guy about this "common knowledge" & he just
gets cute & hangs up.

SEPT 10

two calls. one from the guy who says i can call him melvin if i
want. says sam gave him that name. not clear what he wants,
sex or $. talks dirty which some guys like to do over the phone
but i don't think he was jerking off. their breathing gets short
& eventually they get distracted when they come. later i'm
awakened by another call, this from a bitch sam named mabel.
she calls me all sorts of names & starts talking about sam, how

they have something on him. at first i thought she was a girl-friend but then it was clear she was just really screwed up. when she mentioned melvin i started to get it & got pissed off. asked what she wanted. $? tell her i don't have any, i never have any. but the court settlement, that was for a lot of $, most of which was never paid after nicholas' parents disappeared. if my family can get that kind of money together once, they can do it again. i tell her to fuck off & hang up. should have said to go fuck melvin & leave me alone.

SEPT 11

tj's all pissed off. he owes big $$$ (timmy says he gambles on football mostly) so he's cutting down on supply. all the girls are afraid. he hit me & threw me out of the car on tremont street. i can't work without it. give him everything i make & finally he sends timmy over with a package.

SEPT 12

richard manuel hung himself with his belt from the shower curtain rod in a florida motel room. experiment: i tried to hang from my curtain rod with both hands & right away the screws started coming out of the walls. the scales say i weigh 102. what kind of curtain rods do they have in florida that can take the weight of a man richard's size?
p.m.
melvin has this sick slick delivery over the phone & he scares the shit out of me now. this time he talks about nicholas. knows he's at the wickham house. not clear: is he saying they could steal him so it'll look like i did it? i go by wickham, watch the kids behind the fence. didn't dare go too near but at one point i'm sure nicholas saw me sitting on the stonewall. he pointed. nicholas nicholas nicholas. how can i save you baby?

SEPT 13

tj's losing it. he cut jeannie after she got out. stitches in her cheek. even timmy says he can't do anything about tj. says somebody's going to get dead if the $ don't get straightened out. i don't know who owes who what but i just give it all to tj so timmy'll set me up. i'd be out of this city on a hill already but i keep thinking about sam poor fucking sam. and how all this wasn't necessary when saavo took care of me. & nicholas nicholas nicholas. want to tell sam but can't. he can't always play savior. not now when it's getting dangerous. i want to call ronnie in las vegas & see if i can go out there and work but i went by wickham again to see that nicholas is alright.

SEPT 14

the guy from rhode island was one sick fuck. told timmy i'm bleeding & i'm not going out for a while. he's trying to cover for me but says tj is just off the map. sam keeps calling but i can't deal with him right now. he'll only want to try & help me but this is getting too deep. didn't go to wickham house today. too sore to get out of bed.

SEPT 16

melvin called & says they'll either get nicholas or hurt him if i don't come up with $20,000. dear god. hurt him how? melvin says acid in the face & eyes. nicholas nicholas nicholas.
p.m.
timmy came by with a package. says tj needs me to work tomorrow. if i don't i'll bleed even more. timmy says tj will make him do it too because he knows he's sweet on me. that's what he said "sweet on me." like we're kids in school. i got to work because timmy'll do what tj says. he'll apologize but he'll do it. he has to. we have that in common.

That was the last entry, dated two days earlier. I put the journal back in the nightstand drawer and was startled when the phone rang. I thought about picking up right away, but waited until the message machine clicked on.

"Hello," a man said, "Abigail?"

I picked up the receiver and said, "Who is this?"

"I—I'm not required to say that, am I? Who is *this*?"

"Her brother."

After a moment he sounded bolder when he said, "Come on."

"You don't think so?"

"No, you don't call someone like Abigail and get her *brother*."

"All right," I said. "What exactly do you want?"

"I was given this number—and I want to talk to Abigail."

"You want to talk? About what?"

"Listen—I just—I just want to talk. Really *talk*. I'm not into anything, you know, kinky or dirty. But I'm in town for a couple of days, and this guy I know who was here a while ago, he said that Abigail came up to his hotel room and, well, they had the best conversation. That's *all* I want, a conversation. A real conversation with a woman. *Honest.*"

I held the phone away from me for a moment. I could hear him say, "Hello? Hello? You still there? *Hello?*" And then I used the receiver as a hammer as I broke that message machine and Princess phone to pieces, cutting my hand in the process.

THE FOLLOWING AFTERNOON I found Abby sitting on the wall at the end of the lane behind Wickham House. Bright green moss sprouted from the crevices between the granite slabs. She kept watching the empty courtyard and hardly noticed when I sat next to her. It was a warm afternoon for September, though there was already the smell of fall leaves in the air; her long coat was opened, and her black leather skirt barely came halfway down her thighs. The purple eye shadow looked like bruises. One hand fingered the half-dollar coin that hung on a thin silver chain around her neck.

"Nice jewelry," I said.

She studied it a moment; one of her long nails was broken off. "Look at that man's head, will you? What was he, forty-six?"

I glanced at the profile of Kennedy on the coin. "Yes."

"When it happened forty-six seemed so old." She let go of the coin and took a pack of Marlboros from her coat pocket. Just opening the box and getting a cigarette out took considerable effort.

"Abby, listen, we can deal with this stuff. Melvin and Mabel, they're probably bluffing, but you never know."

"I've got to get Nicholas out of there." It took two matches to get the cigarette lit.

"And TJ—you owe him money?"

She exhaled smoke and turned her head toward the courtyard. "I should be able to hold him off as long as I contribute to his cash flow."

"What about Jeannie? He cut her."

"Only *after* she cut herself. See, there's a pattern here. TJ won't do anything to damage us because then we don't generate income. That's bad business. But as soon as you do damage to yourself—it's a different story. Then your only purpose is to be an example to the other girls."

"What's that stand for, TJ?"

She smiled briefly. "He says it's for Thomas Jefferson." After taking a drag on her cigarette, she added, "He sent Timmy over to my place yesterday, just to give me a warning."

"How do you know?"

"Busted my phone."

I got up and walked across the lane. "And you think he did that?"

"That's Timmy for you. TJ tells him to rough me up, he just takes my phone apart."

"Well, he is sweet on you." I turned around quickly, but Abby continued to stare down the lane toward the courtyard behind Wickham House. She was so out of it, she didn't even make the connection: I could only know about Melvin and Mabel's calls, about TJ's threat, because I had been in her apartment and read her journal. For a moment I wanted to plead with her, to beg her to snap out of it, but I knew that was impossible. I walked back across the lane. "Abby, *I* busted your phone."

She dropped her cigarette butt on the bricks and carefully crushed it out with her shoe. Her movements were slow, deliberate, choreographed to appear calm and normal, but she never took her painted eyes off the courtyard. "The message machine, too?"

"What do *you* think?"

"Guess you owe me a trip to Radio Shack, Sam. Though I don't miss those calls."

"I took one of those calls. He said he just wanted 'conversation.' Said you were recommended to him because you give good *conversation!*" I sat next to her again, this time on the side toward the courtyard so it would be harder for her to avoid my eyes. "Abby, don't you see what's happened? Since Saavo cut out on you, it's just been going to shit. Fucking Saavo, our *father's* compatriot. *Jesus!* The only thing to do now is to get you out of here," I said. "Out of Boston."

"What, back to that la-la land clinic in the desert?"

"No." I took her hand. It was frail and there was no response in her fingers. "No, but someplace where they won't find you, where all of *this*—TJ and Timmy and Melvin and Mabel and men who want conver*sation*—won't fucking matter."

"You're right. You're always right." Her eyes slid toward me, though she didn't quite look me in the eye. "What about Nicholas? I can't just leave him in there. Look, he could be playing in the yard and Melvin could just walk up to the fence, talk to him a moment, then throw acid in his face. You should hear Nicholas scream. It's horrible, Sam. When something hurts, when he doesn't understand something, he just *screams,* and it's very hard to get him to stop. I used to try everything. I'd hold him. I'd tell him it was all right, but he wouldn't stop. He doesn't understand pain. There's no reason for it in his world. Think about that, Sam, in his world there's *no* reason for pain. So he just screams and screams." She stared at me long and hard then, as though she had just realized I was there. "You want to make a plan, fine. But it has to include Nicholas. I can't go anywhere without knowing he's okay. Maybe we could take him with us?"

"Then we'd also have the law after us."

She took her hand from mine and folded her arms as though she were cold. "You know, I figured out how to stop his screaming. It was *so* easy. One day he fell and got a splinter in his finger and had been screaming for I don't know how long. So finally I started to scream *with* him. I gave it all I had, and after a minute he stopped and watched me like he does. Where can we get twenty thousand to pay Melvin?"

"That won't guarantee anything. It's not good business."

Dropping her head, she said, "I suppose. They're never satisfied, are they?"

"No. The only thing to do is get Nicholas moved." She raised her head and watched me. "I'll talk to these people at Wickham House, and I'll ask Ike to look into it. He could talk to them, too. They're Quakers, they're good people. I'll tell them what's going on and they'll move him somewhere else. Somewhere Melvin'll never find him."

She nodded her head slowly, but her lower lip began to quiver and she stood up. I turned and watched children running out the back door of Wickham House and into the courtyard. Abby walked down the lane, her feet unsteady on the bricks. She stopped and put both hands on the wrought-iron fence. I followed and stood behind her. Nicholas sprinted along the other side of the fence, and as he passed by, he didn't notice her.

"Nicholas," she said.

The young woman who had called me watched from across the courtyard. She was holding hands with the other autistic boy, who had a green balloon tied to his wrist. I stared at her and she made no move to intervene.

Nicholas ran to the corner of the courtyard and then back along the fence, his hand briefly grabbing each wrought-iron bar. He stopped when he was in front of my sister, and he squatted so he could reach through the fence toward a maple leaf lying by her shoes. She crouched down opposite him, picked up the leaf, and held it out to him. He took hold of the stem but didn't look at her as he ran his fingers over the serrated edges of the leaf. Finally he got up and walked across the courtyard holding the leaf at his side.

Abby stood up slowly and started back toward the end of the lane. I fell in beside her. "How 'bout a ride back to your place?"

"No, I'll take a cab."

When we reached the street, I said, "You mean you have an appointment, don't you? Come on, just skip it. Abby, I mean it about leaving town. Just come and stay with me and I'll set it up. We could be out of here tomorrow."

She looked down the street toward Harvard Square and waved to hail a cab. As she lowered her arm, her hand touched my cheek briefly. "*You* leave Boston? *Never* happen, Sam. This is home—be thankful for that." She went to the curb as the taxi approached. "Listen, you talk to these Quakers. It's a good idea. You and Ike, get them to move Nicholas, all right? I can take care of the rest of it. I can handle TJ and Melvin and all this other shit."

"How?"

She now seemed remarkably lucid. "Witchcraft," she said. Despite the makeup, her eyes were clear, even humorous, as they had been when we were kids. Leaning toward me, smelling of cigarettes and perfume, she whispered, "I know how to make them all disappear. *Poof!* I'm a Salem witch, remember?"

The taxi stopped at the curb and she got in back. Just as the car pulled away, she turned and looked up at me through the window glass. Raising both hands, she curled her fingers as though they were cats' claws and opened her mouth. Silent scream.

23

After a couple more rounds in the Black Rose, Celeste and I were getting blasted in the journalistic sense of the word. Long ago I realized that this is when the toughest questions are asked, and there's a chance that someone might give an honest answer. Often they're the ones you can't quote, but you never forget.

"Tell me about Saavo," Celeste said. "You really broke his nose earlier tonight?"

"Think so. It was the least I could do. He's responsible for my sister's death—all right, not *solely* responsible, but he had as much to do with it as anyone. He's the one who claimed to care about her. So, just like my father, he abandons her."

"She died of an overdose?"

"According to the papers, yes. A junkie's death is pretty predictable. It's more a descent to a foregone conclusion. It was like she'd left this earth long before, and dying was just an afterthought. It was her idea of witchcraft. It was how she made everything disappear, *poof*. See, she wasn't the only one who went away. There were all these people she was associated with—Melvin and Mabel, and a pimp called TJ. They just disappeared. Never heard from any of them again. Because my sister was tidy—very clean about it. That was her sense of humor. I know she did it for me. I know she was saying, *At last I'm clean*. If you looked up her obit, it would say she died of an overdose, but who's to say which really killed her, what she died of first."

"Which?" Celeste asked.

"I could have killed Saavo tonight," I said. "There was a moment when I had my gun in my hand and I could have, but I realized that I was at least a decade too late. I guess I don't have that *thing*—whatever it is that my father has—that allows you to pull the fucking trigger."

"*Which?* You said 'who's to say which really killed her.'"

"Last time I saw her was a warm fall afternoon near Harvard Square. That night she got in the bathtub and OD'd. I have a friend Ike, who used to be a cop, who called me as soon as the report came in from her landlady, who had complained about water flooding down into her apartment."

I looked out the window at the snow. Something strange was happening. I knew I was a couple of drinks too deep, and I hadn't had anything to eat, which didn't help. But that wasn't it. There was something else going on that I couldn't see. I am not one to believe in spirits and premonitions and omens, but at that moment I felt something actually *move through me.* It was both physical and emotional. And it frightened me like nothing I'd ever experienced before.

"Hey," Celeste said, her hand on my sleeve. "You all right? Sam? What *is* it?"

"I don't know," I said. "I'm just— I feel strange. . . ."

"Like you're going to be sick?"

"No. Like something's going to happen. Do you believe in premonitions?"

"I'm a journalist, Sam. I believe in sources, after-the-fact sources I can quote."

"Good answer. It's about what I usually say. But—"

"But what?"

I took a sip of my drink. "I don't know."

"You're talking about your sister. Maybe that's it?"

"Perhaps. You know, I still think about her all the time, but I've never *once* talked about her death. How she died. It's like I don't want to give it away."

"Would you rather not talk about it?"

"No. That's just it—I want to." And I smiled at her. "You want to listen?"

"Absolutely." Her fingers slid down my forearm and took my hand. Again, I was reminded of the safety and comfort of holding my sister's hand. "All right," I said. "But realize that it was nothing remarkable. For the cops it seemed pretty routine. The police found Abby naked in a tub that had brimmed over because the faucet wasn't completely off. There was only this chain around her neck, with a Kennedy half-dollar coin on it. And she had a tape player on so she could die listening to The Band—I still have the tape. She went slowly, listening to 'Lonesome Suzie,' 'Tears of Rage,' 'Whispering Pines,' and 'I Shall Be Released.' Nobody sings songs like that anymore—nobody else *sings* like those guys. What bothered me—what *still* bothers me—is that the newspaper obit got it wrong. Technically, Abby didn't die of a heroin overdose. The coroner said her lungs were full of water. She drowned first."

Our waitress, a small woman with a reedy voice and an assessing eye, came to our booth and said, "You two darlings just about there?"

"We've been behaving, haven't we?" Celeste said.

"Sometimes it's you quiet ones who go out, smash up the car, and get the bar sued."

"We're fine," I said, handing her our glasses. "One more and then we'll go."

She tilted her head skeptically but took the glasses back to the bar.

"Abby's memorial went just as she had requested," I said. "She kept a journal and it was all in there: how she wanted to be found in the tub, listening to The Band, and what she wanted done afterward. It was simple: cremation and the ashes scattered at sea. My friend on the force, Ike, arranged to rent a fishing trawler, and about thirty of us went out in Salem Harbor at dawn. Mostly family, along with some of her junkie friends. But not the pimp. And not Ramon Saavo. And not my father—he didn't even show for his own daughter's memorial. Which is why he was so determined to get my mother's ashes now. It's guilt—for the first time he's acting upon guilt. It's about fucking time, but it's too late."

The waitress brought our last shots and the bill. "Have a good night," she said. "And take a cab." She went back to her perch at the end of the bar and gazed out the window at the snow. It occurred to me that she and I were about the same age, and I could feel the weight of her disapproval. A man of my vintage sitting in a booth and holding hands with a woman about twenty years younger. I should be ashamed of myself.

"Hey," Celeste said, leaning toward me. "Hel*lo?* You look pissed off."

"No, I'm only telling you about Abby just because I *want* to, which is strange. Something's happening—I don't know what it is."

"Maybe we should get you something to eat," Celeste said.

"No, I'm not hungry." I turned to her. For a moment she almost looked frightened. "Know what pissed me off even *more* than the obit?" I said. "This couple in Brookline who had taken Abby to court, claiming she'd sexually and physically abused their son—their autistic son? About a half year after Abby died, it came out in the papers that this couple—a *pediatrician* and her phony realtor husband—had been abusing their own boy. Well, no *shit.*" My free hand came down in a fist on the tabletop, causing our glasses to bounce. "There was testimony from teachers at his school *and* from other parents whose kids had told them what was going on with this boy. The state got involved and took the kid away from Dr. and Mr. Brookline, and eventually, before they could get nailed in court, the couple just *disappears* and they're *never* heard from again. How the fuck does a parent *do* that? Disappear on his *own* kid?"

"I don't know, Sam." Celeste was near tears. "And the newspapers—they never said anything about the case against Abby."

"Not a *word,*" I said. "They owed it to her. They owed her that much."

CELESTE WAS IN the rest room when "Mack the Knife" began playing on the jukebox for the umpteenth time. Out the window I watched the dark sedan pull up to the curb, and I knew immediately that it had come for me. I don't know how—it was part of what I had felt pass through me earlier—but something in the way the car moved slowly and purposefully reminded me of the night Czlenko was shot. I knew I had to go, that there was no choice.

I slid out of the booth and walked over to the end of the bar and said to the waitress, "Would you call her a cab, please?" I put several twenties on the bar. "This should cover everything, the drinks, the cab, your tip."

For a moment I thought she was so disgusted that she was going to refuse the money. But her eyes, which had been dulled by the years of bar-room night shifts, were suddenly curious. "You're leaving her?" she asked.

"Please just make sure she gets that cab," I said, and went out the front door. As soon as I stepped into the cold air, I felt sober.

The rear door of the sedan opened, and the guy I called George said, "Get in, Sam."

I climbed in the backseat; as I shut the door, the car moved out on to Somerville Avenue. Gracie was driving, and next to her sat Marshall Hume.

George turned to me and quickly felt my coat pockets. Removing my .38, he said, "Told you he'd still be carrying this thing." He tucked the revolver inside his topcoat. He wore fine leather gloves and reeked of some god-awful cologne. "I'm disappointed you never called us."

"Must have forgot the number," I said. "You should have written it down in a cigar tin, like Hume did. Have you been working together on this all along, or is this a marriage of convenience?" Gracie shook her head but didn't say anything. "All right, I'll ask an easy one. How'd you know I'd be here?"

Hume turned his back against the passenger door so he could face me. "The wake was a no-brainer, as they say. And when you weren't in the funeral home—but your car was parked outside—it made sense that you'd be in the nearest watering hole." Hume paused to light one of his small cigars. "I had hoped that bringing you and Saavo together would have a better result than a broken nose."

"You know that for a fact—it is broken?"

"Very," George said. "You did a nice job."

"Then you've seen him?" I said to Hume. "Tonight?"

Exhaling a long plume of smoke, the senator nodded. "You know, it's often like a chemistry experiment—you put different elements together in a test tube and sometimes you get the desired result—something useful and productive. But sometimes you just end up with that rotten-egg smell that stinks up the place. So, what do you do? Give up? There's never any progress that way. No, you try again. You try a different combination, a different experiment. Over and over, until you get the desired results."

"What are the desired results?" I asked.

"Sam," Hume said. "You know what I want. I had hoped getting you and Saavo together might help. I had hoped he might help you find your father."

"You're so considerate." I wiped the condensation off my window and gazed out at the street. "And you know for sure he didn't?"

"No, I'm not sure, Sam. He could have told you something."

"What makes you think I'd tell you where my father is, even if I knew?"

"Because he's going to be brought in, one way or the other," Hume said. "And because the man's of no use to you—never has been. In a strange way I always thought you were someone who had a highly developed sense of justice."

I leaned back and looked at Hume through his cigar smoke. "What do you know about *justice?* You got booted out of the game down in Washington when your hand was caught in the till, and now you're home with nothing much to do, so you want back in the game in the worst way. And you know you could never take the attorney general's office away from Pauline Wainwright fair and square."

Hume seemed unimpressed as he continued to work on his little cigar. I stared out my window again. We were heading toward Charlestown. No one said anything, which worried me.

Finally I asked, "So anybody know how the Bruins are doing?"

"They were ahead four-two," George said. Gracie looked up in the rearview mirror at him.

"Good," I said. "How 'bout Proulx?"

"Big brawl," George said. "Proulx got tossed."

"I like him better all the time," I said.

"Me, too," he said.

Hume was gazing at us as though we were both out of our minds. I said, "I didn't know you had such an interest in science, Senator, other than political science."

His face and silver hair were faintly illuminated by the green lights from the dashboard, which gave him an alien pallor. "Political science *is* a form of chemistry," he said. "Essentially, it's the study of opposites. The way they attract. The way they repel. The way they sometimes combine to make something new." He leaned over the back of his seat. Cigar smoke filled the car; it was an improvement over the cologne. "You appreciate history, don't you, Sam? You remember the famous Sow Case."

"Vaguely," I said. "Some dispute over a cow."

"This one took place in the 1640s. There was an argument over the ownership of a cow—poor Mrs. Sherman versus the well-to-do shopkeep named Keayne. It became a great source of litigation and was debated throughout the colony, and eventually it brought about the division of the Massachusetts General Court into two chambers, the house and the senate."

The car pulled over to the curb. Through the snow I could see that we were a few blocks from Monsignor Morrissey Boulevard. "That was more interesting than your usual sound bites," I said. "This civics lesson has a point?"

Hume got out of the car and dropped his cigar in the snow. "Plurality makes democracy possible. One side can win only if there's another side that loses. It's a beautiful experiment we started right here in the Commonwealth. All because of a sow." He shut the door and the car pulled away.

We took Monsignor Morrissey Boulevard back into Charlestown, but rather than climbing the maze of narrow streets on Bunker Hill, we descended into the dark region below the tangle of elevated highways that separates Charlestown from the river and downtown Boston. If the city had an asshole, this was it.

Gracie stopped the car suddenly. All I could see out my window was a chain-link fence and, in the distance, Boston Sand and Gravel. Overhead was the constant rumble of traffic, punctuated by the bucking and banging of eighteen-wheelers.

"Just tell us where your father is," George said. "That's all you've got to do."

"I don't know."

"That's really too bad." He reached inside his topcoat and took out the .38 "Okay, this is as far as you go," he said pleasantly as he jabbed the barrel into my ribs.

I looked at the back of Gracie's head, her fine hair, but she wouldn't turn around. George poked me again, harder, and I climbed out of the car. The snow blew in off the Charles River. George remained in the backseat of the car, the gun—my gun—pointed at me. For some reason, I whispered, "Thank you."

He leaned toward me and, to my surprise, pulled the door shut. The sedan pulled away quickly and its taillights disappeared in the snow.

I began walking alongside the chain-link fence. The wind was at my back and I turned my coat collar up. The first shot was so muffled by the snow that at first I thought it was the traffic above me on the elevated highway, but when I heard the second report, I was sure. I couldn't see anything except diagonal snow. The shots came from ahead of me and I continued on. After about a hundred yards I saw something dark lying in the snow ahead of me. I approached slowly, and when I was close enough, I could see that it was a man. His topcoat was familiar. The snow around his head was saturated with blood. I knelt down, took him by the shoulders, and rolled him onto his back. Saavo's nose was crooked, and blood covered the duct tape over his mouth and chin. His arms were also bound by duct tape. The gunshots had been to the right temple, causing a massive eruption of flesh, bone, and brain matter tangled in wet hair. The wound reminded me of Dirk Czlenko, lying on the sidewalk in the Fens, only the damage to Saavo's head was even greater. They must have had him in the trunk. I assumed that the gun—my gun, no doubt—had been fired from only a few feet away. It was no more complicated than putting down an animal. But unlike Dirk, Saavo saw it coming. His coat was already edged with snow, and it wouldn't be long before he was covered. I got to my feet and began running.

Part IV

The Elect

24

Somehow it all seemed predestined, as the Puritans would call it. They believed that before we even come into this life, an all-powerful God has determined our fates. Worse, there is no aspect of salvation achieved through the exercise of personal will and action. There is no such thing as atonement and saving yourself. The Elect are simply chosen. This goes against everything in contemporary life, where most of us are given to the assumption that we can shape our own destinies. Call it the American assumption, which leads not to personal freedom but to a life overburdened with conflict. It all becomes a test of wills, of desires, of wants. A matter of rights. A question of privilege. And if we don't get our due, we are the victims. Who is the victim now? The dead guy lying in the snow down by the river or the man climbing Bunker Hill to his apartment? Or should a case be made for the shooter? Let us now consider the assassin's dilemma, for even a cold-blooded killer must deal with gross injustice and what we now call issues. The murtherer too may be the victim.

WHILE WORKING ON *One True Assassin,* I had looked forward to its completion, when I would feel, if only temporarily, deep satisfaction, perhaps even a quiet sense of elation at a job well done. It's how I had felt after finishing many of the magazine pieces I'd done over the years. Instead, when I finished the book, I became depressed. Somewhere I read that after completing his first novel, *The Wapshot Chronicle,* John Cheever mowed his lawn for three straight days because he didn't know what to do with himself. (No surprise, of course, that a writer whose work examined the vagaries of suburban life finds that his only diversion is to cut the damned grass.) I think I knew exactly what he had gone through, but I had no such solution because I lived in a Brighton apartment. Having no yard, I spent days on the new couch I'd bought with part of my advance (my one impulse purchase, which I still have), feeling anxious and distraught.

Abigail called one night when I was struggling with the last chapter of the book. She sounded tired, spaced out, angry. She wouldn't tell me where she was calling from, and I tried to maintain the posture that I didn't care.

"You're drunk," she said.

"So, what's your point?"

"So why?" When I didn't answer, she asked, "How's the book?"

"I'm just about done, but I'm quitting the book." I was drinking Scotch, neat.

"*Fine*. Stick it in a drawer. Kiss off how many years of your life? *I* have, so why should you be so fucking special?"

"Where are you?" I asked.

"Someplace you'll never be, Sam. Trust me. You have doubts about the research?"

"No." My neighbor's dog began barking again.

"Your sources good?"

"I think so." I got up off the couch and went to the window.

"The obvious question, then."

"Of course."

"If you weren't writing about your father, would you feel this way?"

My Brighton apartment overlooked a tiny yard behind the house next door. While working on the book, I hadn't been bothered by their dog's barking, but since I'd stopped writing, he was driving me nuts. It was a black and brown mutt, chained to a maple tree. He puled as though injured. The neighbors called him Max. "I'm going to go buy a pair of those big chain-cutters," I said to my sister, "and go down there and spring Max loose."

Abigail began to sing "I Shall Be Released" in her high falsetto. I was trying to imagine where she was, what she was doing. Something in her voice was changing—she seemed to be drifting away from me. It was hard to hear her over the dog's barking. "Look," she said finally, raising her voice, which now sounded desperate, "you've *known* this was coming all along. We're not supposed to snitch on family—and we're really not supposed to tell on our fathers. But that's exactly why you did it, Sam, why you *had* to do it. Daddy isn't like other fathers. Never has been. And we're not like other kids—we knew that before we were ten. *He* did that to us. It was his choice to take on that life, and to leave us with Mom."

Down in the yard, the mutt trotted away from the tree until the chain snapped taut, jerking him back by the neck. It was a young dog and it still hadn't learned the length of its chain. "Somebody on the block called the ASPCA or something like that," I said. "They came to the house, and for a couple of days they took the dog off the chain, but now he's back on it. Why do people like that even have pets?"

"You're worried about how the book will affect Mom."

I drank some Scotch. "She doesn't know about it at all. That's been my biggest mistake. A couple of years ago I should have gone up to Salem and told her what I was doing, so she could absorb it. I tried to, a couple of times, but I just chickened out. I kept thinking, What if I'm wrong, what if I don't actually place him on the grassy knoll? Then I've done this to her for nothing. Where the fuck are you?"

"That's not important," Abby said. She now spoke urgently, as though she didn't have much time. "I'll tell you what I think: She *knows* it was him. I don't know if he told her or if she pieced it together, but she knows. And I think in some odd way she'll be relieved when it's out. Sure, shocked and maybe alarmed at first, but I think it's been something she's felt she's had to carry by herself for years. Once it's out there, out there in the world, it won't be just her responsibility anymore. Tell you what you do, Sam. You *ask* her. You tell her what you've got in that book and you ask her if she wants you to finish it. You want, I'll go with you when you do."

I could hear someone else—a man—speak to her. He sounded pissed off. "Sam," she said, "I've got to go now. And don't go doing anything stupid about that dog. You talk to Mom."

"About Max?"

And then she laughed, though there was no joy to it. "Right. She'd just tell you if you cut Max free, he'll just get caught, and tied up again. He's not your responsibility, Sam."

"Know what our father would say?" She didn't answer, and I realized that she was afraid to—I could tell by the sound of her breathing through the phone. "He'd say you just open this window, take aim, and put the beast out of its misery. One head shot should do it."

Everybody has a theory.

There's the lone-gunman theory. There's the two-gunmen theory, the three-gunmen theory. The Castro-Cuban revenge theory. The Russian conspiracy theory. There's the CIA, the FBI, and, of course, there's the Mafia. There's a firearms and ballistics expert, Harold Donahue, who believes that the fatal shot came from an AR-15, which was mistakenly discharged by a security guard riding in the limousine behind Kennedy's, leading to a government cover-up. There's New Orleans lawyer Jim Garrison trying to press charges against CIA operatives Clay Shaw and David Ferrie. Much was made of Ferrie's homosexuality and his ties to Oswald, and he committed a questionable suicide just days before Garrison could get him into a courtroom. At one point Garrison also put forth the theory that Kennedy's assassin fired from a manhole. There are the witnesses who claim to have seen Jack Ruby *everywhere* that day—in a van in Dealey Plaza, standing on the front steps of the Texas School Book Depository Building, at Parkland Memorial Hospital, at the police station, at the newspaper office, inside the theater where Oswald was finally apprehended. (Yet no one has come up with a multiple Ruby theory.) And there are Jack Ruby's claims during his last years in prison that the government was injecting him with a cancer-causing serum. He died of cancer. There's Dr. Charles A. Crenshaw, a resident physician at Parkland Memorial Hospital, who tried to keep the president alive in Trauma Room 1, and who after decades broke what he described as a "conspiracy of silence" among the medical personnel who had worked on Kennedy. Crenshaw is convinced that the president's wounds had been altered after his body left Parkland

Memorial Hospital and was flown to Washington. There's a man named Charles Rogers, who allegedly was responsible for killing his parents in what is called the Houston Icebox Murder Case (in 1965 their bodies were found dismembered and stored in the refrigerator of the home they shared with their son). A CIA operative, Rogers had several aliases, including Carlos Rojas, and perhaps he was one of several shooters in the railroad yard next to Dealey Plaza. There's the Oswald impostor theory, in which Carlos Rojas–Charles Rogers, posing as Oswald, went to Mexico City weeks before the president's assassination and visited the Russian and Cuban embassies there. There's the multiple Oswald impostor theory, which purports that a virtual fleet of Lee Harveys and Harvey Lees went about Dallas creating minor yet memorable scenes in places such as car dealerships. There's a convict with the alias of James E. Files, who in the early nineties explained on videotape how he had shot the president from behind the stockade fence on the grassy knoll. There's the Zapruder film, which more than any other piece of evidence altered the country's perception of the events in Dealey Plaza. There's the Beverly Oliver film, which was allegedly confiscated by an alleged government agent only moments after the president was shot, and the film has never been located amid all the evidence that the government gathered that day. There are witnesses who saw puffs of smoke, who detected gunpowder (which they claimed smelled just like a fart). There are numerous photographs depicting grainy faces in crowds, some of which seem to have a connection to the president's assassination, and some of which seem to have been doctored. There are bullets galore. The Magic Bullet, so named because it caused seven wounds to two men while having sustained little damage to itself. There are bullet casings and bullet fragments. They've been found on the rear seat of the president's limousine, dug out of the ground in Dealey Plaza (and in at least one case pocketed by an alleged government agent, never to be seen again), discovered on hospital gurneys, and removed from the wounds of President Kennedy and Texas Governor John Connally. Bullet ricochets cracked the limo's windshield and wounded observer James Tague in the head. Witnesses saw sparks on concrete and pavement when they heard the shots. There were two shots. There were three shots. There were four shots.

There was an absolute barrage of gunfire, so much that it's remarkable that only the president and the governor were seriously wounded. Bullets entered the president's back, his neck, his throat, his head; bullets struck him from the back, the front, the side. Bullets passed through his skull at an angle of eleven degrees, or fifteen degrees, or, possibly, twenty degrees, and at the moment of impact his head was turned to the left perhaps six degrees or more. At a firing range outside Baltimore, bullets were fired into ten skulls filled with gelatin and covered with sheepskin in an attempt to re-create the effects of the shots that killed the president; the results were inconclusive. Just before the shooting began in Dealey Plaza, the police radio system in Dallas shut down. Minutes after the shooting took place, the telephone system in Washington, D.C., shut down. It was as though several of the ten plagues had returned, or the sun, moon, and stars had lined up in a configuration that could only lead to this dire result. Richard Nixon, then a member of the board of directors of the Coca-Cola Company, was in Dallas that day, though of course years later he denied it. About 1:33 P. M., the White House press secretary announced that President Kennedy was dead at Parkland Memorial Hospital, while in the Oak Cliff section of Dallas, a voice over the police dispatch radio said, "We are all at the library," only to conclude minutes later that *"We have the wrong man!"* And it was never determined who was speaking or who was apprehended and so quickly dismissed. There was the babushka lady. There were the two Hispanic men sitting on the curb, one appearing to speak into a walkie-talkie, while the other seemed to be signaling by pumping an umbrella in the air as the limousines passed. There was Oswald sitting in the second-floor cafeteria of the Texas School Book Depository Building ninety seconds after the shooting, calm as could be. There was Officer Tippit, who was shot and killed by Oswald. Or by a man who looked like Oswald. Or by a man who didn't look like Oswald. And still more bullets—two different kinds of bullets removed from Tippit's body, neither of which matched Oswald's revolver. There were the "three tramps" (not to be confused with the hoboes), who were found in the railroad yard and escorted across the plaza by the Dallas police, only to be released from custody before any record of who they were could be made. There was Jacqueline Kennedy, in her pink suit and pillbox hat, climbing out onto the trunk of the limousine to get help. There is John Fitzgerald Kennedy's brain, which had been kept at the National Archives, until it disappeared, and hasn't been located for more than twenty years.

MY MOTHER AND I were sitting on a bench in the lobby of the Boston Museum of Fine Arts. Her feet were tired and she was content to look at the Monet water lily series surrounding us. She seldom came into the city anymore, and when she did, we tried to make it an occasion—a museum or some performance in the theater district.

"I need to tell you something." I turned to her then because the longer I put it off, the more difficult it would be.

"What?" she said. Sometimes looking into my mother's hazel eyes was like a trap; you felt caught and you knew you couldn't escape.

"I should have said something a long time ago," I said.

"Oh, God."

"It's not about Abby."

My mother raised a hand and touched her hair. She was still coloring it ten years ago and she was always concerned about looking "presentable," as though her appearance should be a gift—to whom or what for, I was never sure. Her puffy face always seemed to be making an effort, attempting to be buoyant. Abby and I used to think it was a generational thing, this need of my mother's to maintain a "facade," no matter what, but now I realized how necessary and difficult it was for my mother.

"Your father?" she whispered.

I nodded.

"You've heard from him?"

"No."

And then I began telling her about my book. After a few minutes my mother looked at Monet's water lilies. She might have been alone, sitting there, studying a great work of art. Her expression never changed as I explained my theory. I watched her closely for some twinge, some shift in the pupils that would indicate that I was wrong. But, instead, a strange thing happened. Abby was right: My mother, though she would never say so outright, was relieved that we understood what she'd been harboring all these years. What I didn't anticipate was my own reaction. I was like a small boy, confessing to my mother, owning up to a fib, and what crushed me was not her outrage but the quiet authority of her disappointment. I wept as I told my mother what she already knew about my father, and when I was done, she simply opened her purse and took out her Kleenex.

"The men's room is over there," she said, handing me the whole wad. I hadn't cried in front of my mother since I was eight, but it didn't seem a big deal to her.

When I came back and joined her on the bench, I said, "Now am I presentable?"

She looked me over for a moment, and I knew then that I would publish the book and that she would endure whatever came of it. Turning her head toward the paintings, she said, "Amazing, isn't it? So much color. So still, yet it has movement. It's as though you can see the heaviness of the summer air."

MY THEORY BEGAN with who my father was as a young man—his faith in democracy and sense of duty to country. Too often now these are considered paltry clichés. But to begin anywhere else would be to avoid an essential and fundamental aspect of my father. When I wrote that section of the book, I kept on my desk the few photographs I had of him during World War II. In all of them he's wearing a tropical uniform or a T-shirt with his dog tags around his neck. His eyes are bright, his face is lean, and his jawbone is striking. He has a mustache and behind him are palm trees. My favorite photo is of him standing under a tent, a tropical downpour behind him; he's wearing a safari hat and is holding a machete across his chest. He's young, vigorous, and the look in his eye says there's nothing that can stop him.

I'm convinced that from that point on he believed he was a part of something much larger than himself. Call it loyalty to a cause. He felt he had something to fight for, to die for, and I suspect that the fact that he had survived the war meant that he had no choice but to carry on for those who didn't. No wonder my mother fell in love with him. Only later did she realize how it would transform her life and those of her children. But there was no question about her remaining loyal to him, and that, I was certain, had everything to do with why he came back for her ashes.

He felt he owed her something.

Perhaps he was fulfilling a promise.

25

The next morning I was awakened early by the slap of the newspaper landing on the front stoop. For years I always liked hearing that sound; it seemed an appropriate way for someone in my profession to start the day. But now I sat up startled and it took me a moment to get my bearings. I couldn't remember much about the walk up Bunker Hill to my apartment, only that I'd passed an old man with his dog on a leash. The mutt jumped up on me, sniffing my coat. As the owner pulled the dog away, he apologized, but then he saw the blood on my sleeve. We were standing beneath a street lamp and he got a good look at me before I walked on into the dark.

I had fallen asleep in the coat, and when I switched on a light, I could see that the dried blood had turned black. Quickly I went down to the stoop for the *Globe*. There was only a small boxed piece on the front page about a cabdriver finding the body of a man in his mid-fifties near Boston Sand and Gravel. That's all they had when they went to press, his gender and approximate age.

The phone rang as I climbed the stairs to my apartment. When I reached the kitchen, my message came on the answering machine. I envy people who play music or even sing their recorded messages; I merely say, "What is it?"

After the beep, Petra said, "Sam, you there?"

I hesitated a moment, then picked up. "Yeah." There was silence for a moment and I thought it meant she regretted that I had answered. Every second that passed, things seemed more difficult, more complicated.

Then she said, "It's Ike."

"Ike?"

"He left," she said quickly. "I just got up and there's this note on the kitchen table that says 'Tell Sam I've gone to P-town.' You know what that means?"

"Did anyone call or come to the door?"

"Someone might have called. I'm not sure because I stayed up late and couldn't sleep—and then suddenly I really conked. But I think I remember the phone ringing. Ike must have answered it. Why would he go to Provincetown?"

"Because Ike knows something about my family's history."

"Who would call?" she asked.

"Good question." But I suspected it had been my father.

"When are you coming back?" Petra asked.

"I'm not." For a moment I thought about leaving it at that, but she was up there, alone in my mother's house. "You come down here."

"How? I don't have a car."

"Neither do I."

"What happened to yours?" she asked.

"It's over in Somerville and they'll be looking for it."

"Who will?"

"The cops. Listen, my mother keeps a spare set of keys in the drawer nearest the back door. Take her car out of the garage and pick me up."

"What's going on?" She sounded alarmed but pleased that she was going to be getting out of that house. "Why is your car in Somerville and why are the cops—"

"Just pick me up, but not at my apartment—I'll be at the monument up the hill."

There was that silence again. "All right," she said, sounding genuinely frightened. "You're in trouble, aren't you?" Which meant she didn't know what had happened last night.

I PUT ON JEANS, a sweatshirt, and an old waterproof jacket with a decent hood because outside last night's snow was disappearing in a steady drizzle. After getting coffee and a roll at Billy's Spa, I walked up to Monument Square, where the day's first busload of elderly tourists had just arrived. They complained in Southern accents about the rain and didn't seem impressed by the wet concrete obelisk in the center of the square. One of them asked their guide if this was Lexington or Concord.

I stood by the wrought-iron fence on the east side of the square, reading the paper, and inside of ten minutes my mother's 1988 Oldsmobile arrived. Petra slid over and I got in behind the wheel. She watched me for some signal, I guess, some sign that we should kiss or hug. It was only last night that she had come into my mother's vestibule closet and kissed me good-bye, but I pushed the wet hood back off my head, put the car into gear, and drove down the hill.

"What's going on?" she asked. "Why will the cops be looking for your car?"

"Hume and his pals set me up. I can't go near it."

"What's *happened?*"

"You don't know? You really don't, do you?"

"What's *that* supposed to mean?"

"Come *on,* Petra. You've been in touch with Hume. You're working for him again, right?" She stared at me wildly and for a moment I expected her to lunge at me. There had been moments in bed when she looked this way, as though she were about to take a chunk of flesh out of me. "What, did he make some deal with you?" I asked. "You help him find my father and he'll make sure you get the exclusive story?"

"Fuck you."

"You already have."

"I didn't *want* this, Sam."

"I just hope it wasn't too awful for you."

"That's not what I *mean.*" She leaned toward me slightly and her lower lip was trembling. "I didn't want this to happen—between *us.* I thought it would be neater, tidier—I don't know, *Jesus.* More professional or something, I guess."

"You and Dirk were working on a book about my father."

"*Yes.* Yes, we were. For the past year or so we'd keep talking about your book and we kept saying it made sense, that the stuff that came out after your book just seemed too perfectly designed to undermine it. Then

Czlenko came to *me* and showed me all this stuff he'd already gathered. And that's—I *admit*—what got me hooked."

I turned my head and looked at the traffic. "You know who killed Dirk?"

"No."

"My guess is it's this guy I've been calling George."

"Of George and Gracie? You thought they were government, too."

"Right," I said. "They've been following me around, thinking I'd eventually lead them to my father. But they must have known Dirk was really on to something because when they saw him with me, they popped him— I don't know why. Maybe to scare me? To see if I would run to my father? Who knows how those people think?" I looked over at her. "But you've been in touch with your old friend Senator Hume?"

She ran her hand over her mouth and chin. "He contacted me, Sam. He'd heard I'd been visiting your mother at Dana Farber. There is no *deal*. He just wanted me to know he was looking, too. It's the way he does things."

"I know, his idea of chemistry. So you haven't talked to him since last night?"

"No."

"Since Hume and George and Gracie all decided to work together."

"How do you know this?"

"I told you. Because they set me up. They shot Saavo."

"Who's Saavo?"

I pulled the wet, rolled-up *Globe* out of my coat pocket and handed it to her. "Probably figures I don't have any choice but run to Daddy now."

She opened the newspaper. "You've found him, your father?"

"I'm close. I think I'm very close."

As Petra looked at the paper, we drove beneath the city skyline; the taller buildings disappeared into fog. Morning traffic was slow as always, but it was worse because of the Big Dig, the massive construction project that was eventually going to bury the Southeast Expressway underground and impoverish Boston.

Folding up the paper, she asked, "The dead man's not identified in here. How do you know it's Saavo?"

"They used to call a head shot like that a 'gangland slaying,'" I said.

"Why are the police going to come after you?"

"They used my gun. Hume will make sure the cops get it."

When we got through the worst of the traffic and picked up speed down near Quincy, she said, "We're going to Provincetown?" I nodded. "How'd Ike know?"

"He's got a good memory. He spent all that time years ago recuperating at my mother's, and my guess is she told him a lot."

"And it includes Provincetown?"

"My parents were married in New York," I said. "But they went to P-town on their honeymoon. When we were small and living out west, they would refer to going back to Provincetown like it was this dream, this ideal place. Abby and I didn't even know where it was until we moved back to Massachusetts with my mother. We went there as a family, once. Maybe that's where he's taken her ashes, maybe that's 'home.'"

THE SUMMER BEFORE our senior year in high school, our father did something that, at first, took us all by surprise: He planned a family vacation. He announced it at breakfast, when we were all seated around the kitchen table, eating blueberry pancakes. My mother, who in 1967 still hoped that somehow we could escape our own past and become a "normal" family, said, "Someplace out west? The Grand Canyon?"

"East," my father said, pushing away his empty plate. He was a fast eater, which he said he had learned in the navy. Hurry up and wait. "Thought we'd go see this cottage your brother Jimmy and Kathleen have bought in Wellfleet."

Abby, who was fifteen at the time, made a face as she lowered her head and cut into her pancakes. "That's not exactly a vacation."

My mother toyed with the lapel of her bathrobe a moment. Her seat was always nearest the stove and she turned her head to look out into the yard. The backyard was in full bloom—it was late June and the roses were out. "When did you talk to Jim or Kathleen?" she asked.

"I didn't," my father said.

"Jack, don't you think we should be invited before we pull into their driveway?"

"I didn't say we were staying at their cottage."

Abby whispered, "A *motel!*" She grinned at me with blue teeth.

"No motel," my father said.

Abby was still grinning, but she wasn't smiling. She squeezed blue chewed-up pancakes between her teeth, just for my benefit. "*No* camping. I'm *not* spending all night in a tent with *bugs* around my head."

"No, you'll sleep on the boat."

It was my turn to flash a blue grin at Abby.

"*Jack,*" my mother said.

My father got up from the table and went into the den.

"It's one thing to go sailing outside the harbor," my mother said loudly, "but the Cape—it's a long way—across open water . . ."

Abby leaned over her pancakes and pretended to barf.

My mother began clearing the table in that abrupt, efficient fashion that said it all. "I mean it only takes a couple hours to drive out to Wellfleet."

He came back into the kitchen with one of his nautical charts, which he unrolled at his end of the table. "I've figured it all out," he said, drawing a line on the chart with his forefinger. "First day, we sail southeast across Massachusetts Bay to Provincetown, where we anchor for the night." My mother put a stack of plates on the kitchen counter and, to my surprise, she revealed a hint of a smile. It was as though he'd said the magic word. Abby saw it, too, and we exchanged glances. "Then the next day," he said, "we'll sail down the inside of the Cape and tie up in Wellfleet Harbor. Consider it a reenactment of a historic nautical event." I watched my mother's profile carefully; she was trying to keep her expression neutral as she gazed out the window at her roses.

"A historic nautical event," Abby said with mock dignity.

Pointing at the upper arm of Cape Cod, my father said, "Exactly. We'll trace the course of the Pilgrims' first landings in the New World."

From opposite sides of the table, Abby and I leaned over the chart. My father had drawn lines from Salem to Provincetown, and then down to Wellfleet, and in the lower right-hand corner he had written various figures—compass degrees, nautical miles, tides.

For the next week we devoted our full attention to making *Shallop* ready, and we watched the weather: The first days of July, leading up to the

Fourth, promised to be clear. My father's concern was that there wouldn't be enough wind. The closer to the departure date, the more excited I got; never before or since had my family worked together like this on something. Even my mother, who still maintained that my father was out of his ever-loving mind (a phrase she used often, and one that I never understood), got into the spirit of the provisioning. She packed the galley shelves and cabinets and icebox, and it was assured that we weren't going to starve to death in the middle of Massachusetts Bay.

We departed Salem Harbor before sunrise. The air was still and we motored out toward the brightening eastern horizon. As the sun came up, I kept looking astern; I'd never seen the sunrise on Salem and Marblehead Neck from several miles out, and it was a grand sight: Windows appeared to be ablaze with reflected orange light and the city's church steeples rose prominently above the green treetops. Something about that one view explained why men go to sea.

The first few hours the northeast wind was light, the water pale blue and glassine, though by midmorning the wind freshened and we were heeling nicely. Around midday my mother was in the cabin making tuna-fish sandwiches when I sensed something was different. Abby did, too. We looked all around: Blue sky met blue water for 360 degrees.

"You can't see land," Abby whispered. It was the closest thing to a prayer I'd ever heard from her.

Our father told me to take over at the tiller. "Hold this course and keep an eye *there*," he said, pointing to the southeast, "and you'll raise the Provincetown tower." He went below to help my mother prepare lunch.

Abby hung the binoculars around her neck and scrambled forward to the pulpit. She wore denim cutoffs, dirty sneakers, and an old white dress shirt of mine with the frayed collar turned up. Her tanned arms and legs were shapely but still girlishly thin. As she leaned against the chrome railing, her hips, elbows, and knees appeared to gyrate in a slow, rhythmic dance that compensated for the hull's rise and fall through the swells. She watched the eastern horizon with an intensity that bordered on religious devotion. Once she turned her head and smiled at me; the deck was twenty-six feet long, and even at that distance I could see the joy in her eyes.

IT TOOK YEARS for me to piece together my father's activities from World War II to the early nineties. Most of his time was spent in Mexico and the Caribbean, with forays overseas. I combed through documents that were available through the Freedom of Information Act. Occasionally, I found a "friend" in some bureaucratic position who would slip me material that would help me fill in the gaps. The work was relentless, tedious, often frustrating, but once I started I was afraid to stop. Much of it was a matter of identifying a string of aliases my father used, and their connection to certain operations. This led me to embassy logs, hotel registers, airline passenger lists, hospital admissions records. In August of 1961, Carl Jendrow was treated for food poisoning in Mexico City. In Vera Cruz, Jorge Pessaro had an abscessed tooth removed in September of 1962. Robert Hill flew between Belize and Texas eight times during the fall of 1974. And so on. My father spent much of his time on the Mexican Gulf Coast and, by the late seventies, several small islands off the coast of Belize. His addresses tended to be post office boxes, though occasionally there'd be evidence that his mail was being delivered to a marina.

When I had everything I could find pieced together in chronological order, it was possible to see the trajectory of his career. It built from the late forties to the early sixties, and then there was a long, slow decline in activity. When he was young he moved swiftly and often. During Operation Pluto he came and went from Happy Valley, the training camp in Nicaragua. After the Bay of Pigs invasion failed, he traveled between Houston and New Orleans, with occasional flights to Miami and Havana. He was then involved in Operation Mongoose, which was the CIA's effort to assassinate Castro. This was about the time we moved from San Diego to Salem, and we saw or heard little from him. In 1963 he was in New Orleans, in contact with people like David Ferrie, Guy Bannister, and Clay Shaw. On November 20 my father (Jorge Pessaro) and Felix Saavo (Enrique Quantaal) drove from New Orleans to Dallas. They traveled in an Oldsmobile with a Goldwater bumper sticker, and in Dallas they stayed at the Adolphus Hotel, room number 24. On Friday, November 22, shortly before the Kennedy motorcade reached Dealey Plaza, Lee Bowers Jr., who worked for the Union Terminal Company, was in the tower that over-looked the railroad yard directly behind the grassy knoll. Police had cut off traffic to the area, but Bowers observed three cars enter the parking lot between the grassy knoll and the switching yard. One was an Oldsmobile with a Goldwater bumper sticker. Several witnesses who were waiting to see the president claim they saw men behind the fence at the top of the grassy knoll, and their descriptions fit my father, who was tall and lean, and Felix Saavo, who was quite heavyset. The thin man wore a short-sleeve shirt and he carried what looked like a rifle case.

After nearly five years of research, I was certain that I had placed my father at the fence above the grassy knoll, with an AR-15 in his hands. But I had nothing that proved he actually fired the rifle. It was possible that he was simply a part of the president's security team. I've long believed that the film that Beverly Oliver took of the motorcade would reveal a great deal about the president's assassination, but she claimed that minutes after the shooting an unidentified government agent confiscated her camera and film, never to be seen again. For almost a year I was suspended at that moment in time (my father would call it *history*) when he walked into the shade of the grassy knoll. I couldn't seem to take it any further, and at times I was relieved, even thankful. I wondered what those moments had been like for him, as the motorcade turned left off of Houston Street and began its slow descent down through Dealey Plaza. In America we slaughter our presidents on Elm Street.

Then I heard from a new "friend" in Washington. There had been sev-eral during my years of research. I seldom learned who they were; occa-sionally they called to suggest that I look into some piece of JFK assassination minutiae, or they sent stuff in the mail—Xeroxed copies of articles, documents, letters, official records. Sometimes it was helpful; more often it was not. But one day when we were having a blizzard in Boston I got a brief phone call from a woman who was in some noisy public place, a bus terminal or an airport.

"Give me an address," she said. She didn't sound young; her voice was hoarse and it took an effort for her to pronounce every syllable. I thought:

This woman drinks and she smokes heavily. She sounded tired, bitter, perhaps even frightened.

"What for?" I asked.

"Not your own, but someplace where I can send you what I found."

"What is it?"

"You'll see." She coughed harshly and then inhaled deeply. Asthmatic, too.

"You know where I live. I'm listed in the phone book."

"Yes, I *know* where you live, dammit, but I can't send it to you there. Want them or not?" A snowplow rumbled through the street and my apartment shook as though we were having an earthquake. "All right, then, I'm hanging up," she said.

"Okay," I said quickly, and gave her Ike's address.

That weekend, the Bruins were playing one of their Saturday-afternoon games and Ike got two tickets from one of the officers in his precinct. It was the last time we went to a game at the old Garden. They were good seats—first balcony, center ice, a few rows above the press box. The stands were so steep in that building that it felt as though you were suspended right above the face-off circle at center ice. The Bruins were playing the Nordiques, and the score was 1–1 after the first period. Ike offered to go for this round of beers, and as he got up he took a small padded envelope out of his leather jacket and dropped it on my thigh.

"This came in the mail. I'll bet it's dirty pictures. You been gettin' any lately? Somebody with a jealous husband?" He put his big hand on my shoulder a moment.

I watched him climb the steps. He knew it had to do with my father. I looked at the envelope: a typed label—my name, in care of Ike's East Boston address. No return address. I opened the seal, then stopped and glanced around. Because it was a Saturday matinee, the stands were full of kids. The sound of the crowd was different from a night game, the pitch of the voices higher. There was more laughter. All around me there were kids, many of them wearing black, gold, and white Bruins jerseys and hats, eating, talking, gazing down at the ice surface as though it were a rare gem.

Inside the padded manila envelope there was a white envelope, which contained a short strip of film. I held it up against the bank of lights on the opposite side of the Garden and could see three frames. It was too tiny to see detail, but I immediately recognized the setting. Anyone would—anyone who had a recollection of that day in Dealey Plaza. There was the grassy knoll, the fence, the trees, the pergola in the background, while in the foreground the president's Lincoln passed farther to the left in each of the three frames. I put the film back in the envelopes, which I tucked inside my coat pocket.

Ike returned with two beers and a bag of peanuts. "She as beautiful in Technicolor?"

"I'll never tell. Besides, I think they're black and white."

"Just remember, blackmail's a crime. Don't cave in."

Ike had a cousin Gino, who was into photography and who could keep his mouth shut. Over the next week we spent a lot of time in his darkroom developing and enlarging the film. In the second frame the white smoke was visible drifting away from the barrel of the rifle above the fence, but the third frame had it all: In the foreground the spray of blood arching like a penumbra around the president's exploding head, and, there, above the fence, the gun smoke has drifted away enough to reveal my father's face. Eventually my publisher spent a lot of money paying experts to examine the film for evidence that it had been doctored or tampered with in any way. They were unanimous in their determination that it was the real McCoy. Though the resolution of the enlargements wasn't absolutely clear, I had no doubt that the shooter was my father.

None.

It wasn't just the complexion and shape and proportion, but the expression.

His face was absolutely neutral.

Ever since I was small it was the face that I feared the most.

26

My father was a different man on a boat. It had to do with the water, the wind, the currents, and the tides. There was a faith in these natural elements that he never seemed to display on land. I also think that from a boat deck he liked the fact that he commanded a view of every direction—360 degrees to the horizon. He liked to see what was coming.

Aboard *Shallop* he gave orders that were direct and specific; when he told you to raise the main or trim the jib sheet, he did so with such assurance that I was eager to comply. His voice was often stern, and if a task weren't done properly and with alacrity, he'd say so. His orders were clear and, at seventeen, clarity was something I needed badly. Even when he got angry—and his anger would come and go easily—it had worth because it was understood that we were working for the same cause. Nothing is clearer or more fundamental than a ship on the ocean. All efforts are devoted to keeping her on course, afloat. That's the beauty of it.

Abigail spied the Provincetown tower through the binoculars and screamed, *"Land ho!"* She and I shouted and cheered as though we'd discovered a new continent. That evening we moored in the harbor, near a pier full of people, licking ice-cream cones and sucking Coca-Cola through straws. As the sun set in Massachusetts Bay, we ate hamburgers and corn on the cob, and were sound asleep in the cabin before it was dark. At sunrise the deck glistened with dew. We rowed ashore and walked the streets of Provincetown, spending over an hour in the vast army-navy store on Commercial Street. My father took a photograph of the three of us standing in front of the large bronze plaque that commemorates the Pilgrims' signing of the Mayflower Compact. The framed photograph has since been on my mother's bureau; she stands between us, her arms around our shoulders, and we are all suntanned, we are all smiling for our father. We might have passed for any American family on vacation. We appear to be almost normal. From her smile, her eyes, you can see that it was one of the moments in her life when my mother was truly happy.

Early afternoon we coasted down to Wellfleet Harbor. This was where the Puritans first discovered planted corn, baskets of acorns, and crude huts. The beaches were littered with large dead fish they called grampus. They found human footprints in the sand and they saw Indians in the distance. A search party continued south in a shallop as far as present-day Eastham. Early the next morning, while the party was preparing breakfast, natives emerged from the woods, screaming. Arrows and musket fire were exchanged. Both sides kept their distance, no one was injured, and the Indians soon disappeared into the trees. Puritan records of this first encounter proclaim that God had vanquished the enemy and given the explorers deliverance.

In our two days of anchorage at Wellfleet we swam, rowed the dinghy up salt-marsh tidal creeks, and hiked beaches; we caught flounder, and dug clams at low tide. We didn't see one Indian. We went ashore only to visit Uncle James, Aunt Kathleen, and our cousins. And then, on a clear morning that promised another perfect, hot summer's day, we started the voyage back across Massachusetts Bay for Salem. Winds were calm, and we could barely make three knots as the Provincetown tower dropped below the horizon astern of us.

To reach Provincetown by land you drive in a huge arc, from Boston down the South Shore to the Sagamore Bridge, and once across Cape Cod Canal, local geography defies compass logic, which means "lower" is north of "upper": You drive east across the Upper Cape and then, from the rotary in Orleans, north along the forearm of the Lower Cape. One hundred twenty-six miles from Boston. Henry David Thoreau once walked it.

A little before noon we entered Provincetown's narrow streets, crammed with old shingle and clapboard houses. From Memorial Day to Labor Day there's a huge tourist trade in trinkets, fried seafood, and side-walk art. Gay couples parade alongside families from Connecticut. Shops and restaurants do their best business on overcast days. But it was late October, and Petra and I walked several blocks through the rain without finding anything open. We finally ducked into a bar with a low, beamed ceiling. An old man in an apron came out from the kitchen and said they weren't open yet, but then he offered us coffee. We sat at the bar, and he brought us two mugs and returned to the stove, where he had several giant pots simmering. The place smelled of clams.

Staring out the window at the fish pier, Petra said, "It's a big harbor."

"Not many sailboats still in the water this late. Shouldn't be hard to find."

"I'm not thrilled about a long walk in this rain." She got up and went down to the phone booth at the end of the bar, where she opened up the Yellow Pages. "I say we call the marinas and boatyards," she said. "Until one tells us where your father is."

"Sounds too simple."

She was already dialing. "Czlenko and I used to make bets on who could get an interview first—a state congressman, a celeb pumping a new flick, a woman gang-raped on the T. Czlenko was really fast, but I could beat him."

I brought our coffee mugs down to the end of the bar. "The secret is that you lie."

"Not quite." She smiled, but then someone answered the phone and she said in a slow, dull voice, "Hi, this is Boston Nautical Supply. We got a driver on his way out there with an order for a boat called *Spray*. He needs directions." She paused. "There isn't? Okay. Thanks." After hanging up, she looked in the phone book again and began dialing. "Use to work with a girl named Nancy, who believed the perfect feature story was one you could write without ever leaving your desk. Girl was a magician with the phone. She ended up in D.C., covering the White House. Go figure. *Hi, there!*" she said brightly. "This is Jeannie at Nor'east Marine Supply, and our driver's headed out there for a boat called, let me see—*Spray?* He's new and he left without directions, so he just called in—sounds like the jerk's lost somewhere between Hyannis and Chatham." She began to raise the mug to her lips, but stopped and stared at me. "*What* is he delivering? Jeez, hon, I don't know, hang on." Holding the phone away from her mouth, she said, "*Billy,* what's that new guy taking out to P-town there?"

I said the first thing that came to mind: "A boom vang."

She almost laughed. "You hear that?" She said into the phone. "Christ, and I think he's got the *winches* in the truck."

I shrugged and gestured toward the phone she was holding against her shoulder.

"Hi," she said into the receiver. "I don't know, he might even have the wrong friggin' order. I swear his IQ's lower than Pedro's ERA. Those winches are supposed to go up to Gloucester someplace." She listened for a moment and then said, "Now I gotta call the moron and tell him to get his truck back in here. Thanks, hon!" Hanging up, she whispered, "The secret is *how* you lie."

"I see."

"What the hell is a *boom vang?*"

BY LATE AFTERNOON the wind had died and *Shallop* was becalmed in the middle of Massachusetts Bay. Reluctantly, my father started the engine and it was a relief to move through that hot, humid air, across flat water that seemed to have the density of oil. We kept our gaze to the west, watching for thunderheads over the mainland. When they appeared my father calmly told us to double-reef the mainsail and to replace the genoa with the storm jib. My mother went below and got out the life jackets and raingear.

We'd been in squalls before, but it had always been a matter of running for the protection of Salem Harbor. Out here Boston's faint skyline was some twenty miles off the port bow and there was nowhere to hide. For the next half hour, as the clouds rose up off the horizon, we busied ourselves, checking hatches and lines. My sister ate half a bag of saltines.

The first whitecaps seemed to almost glow beneath the blackening sky, and the water quickly turned to leaden chop. At first heavy raindrops spattered the deck, then suddenly a driving rain came up with the wind out of the southeast. I glanced at my mother, who sat on the high side of the cockpit, with one arm around Abigail. Their faces were wet, and for the first time, I think, I saw the woman my sister would become—her cheeks, the set of her mouth, surrounded by the arc of the slick yellow hood, mimicked my mother's features. Abby was watching the horizon, I'm sure in an attempt to keep her stomach under control. My mother, to my amazement, appeared serene and blissful. They might have been members of a convent, devoted to austerity and contemplation.

The wind rose quickly, and we were rolling sidelong through the building swells. My father cut the motor and we came about, heading due east so that we could keep our bow at an angle to the swells. Everyone shifted over to the starboard side of the cockpit; we were heeled over so far that the lower rail was buried in whitewater. We braced ourselves with all four limbs, and there were moments when it seemed that if you let go, you'd fall right out of the boat. *Shallop* was doing better than eight knots, and with the twenty-five-knot gusts, it felt as if we were going fifty. Waves crashed over the bow regularly, and the spray sounded like sand against my hood. Each time the boat ran in the lee of a rising swell, there'd be a few moments of relative calm; then, as we'd angle up the face of a wave and break over the top, the mast and rigging would tip as though suddenly pushed by an invisible hand. The water hissed as it ran along the hull. Something had come loose down in the cabin and banged against cabinet doors.

My father kept his eyes forward, often studying the mast, the sheets, the rigging. Occasionally we heeled over so that water rushed in over the coaming, and he would pull up on the tiller with both arms, easing us off the wind. We all moved with the rhythm of the boat as it drove into the squall. Everything was in motion, yet the sails were rigid and the lines were taut. Cresting waves would loom above us to the windward, the whitewater poised to tumble down on us, but the hull would slide up and up until it broke through the peak, only to fall again as we'd surf down into the trough beneath the next wave. Abby made her way down to the lower rail so she could puke over the side. I got down behind her and held her about the waist. At first I didn't understand, but when I looked up, I saw that my mother had one hand around my ankle.

"I'm not going anywhere!" I shouted.

"Just hold on to your sister!" she shouted back.

When Abby was through we both moved like crabs, clawing our way back up to the starboard side of the cockpit. We continued east for perhaps half an hour. Twice more my sister had to vomit and I clambered down to the lower bench and held her. We hardly spoke and all our effort was devoted to hanging on.

Then my mother turned her shoulders so she was facing southeast and she said, *"Jack."*

We all turned and squinted into the wind. The waves were running eight feet and better, and as we ran up the face of the nearest swell, the ship came into view, a freighter, perhaps a half-mile off, its bow pointed straight toward us. There came a long, deep blast of its horn.

"He sees us," my father said.

"What do we do?" my mother asked.

"Hold our course."

THE LONG SHINGLED building had a faded sign above the door that read:

SNOWE'S MARINE
FIBERGLASS — WOODWORK — ENGINE REPAIR
WINTER STORAGE — SALVAGE — SLIP RENTAL — ANCHORAGE
EST. 1916

As I opened the door, Petra nodded toward the parking lot. Ike's truck was at the far end, between two sailboats perched on cradles. We went inside, where pine floorboards creaked and there was the pungent scent of varnish, lacquer, and shellac. For a moment I felt a light, heady high that reminded me of the sensation I got as a boy from using the glue on my fleet of model boats.

"Stay in here too long," Petra whispered, "and you won't have any brain cells left."

We walked up to a counter and looked into the workshop. It was empty, but through a back window we could see a man sanding the hull of a catboat. He was perhaps in his late sixties and wore a mask and safety glasses. We went out the side door into the boatyard, and as we approached, he shut off his sander.

"Hi," I said. "You got a boat moored here called *Spray*?"

He pulled the mask down off his nose and mouth and lit a cigarette. His cheeks were streaked with sawdust that had caked against his sweaty skin. "Why's everyone all of a sudden asking 'bout *Spray*?"

"Don't know," I said. "Are they?"

"That Italian went out there first thing this morning, if that's what you mean."

"He's a friend," I said. "Santori."

"You're all friends, huh?" There have been generations of Portuguese families fishing out of Provincetown, and my guess was he was a member of one of them.

"*Spray* belongs to my father," I said.

This took him by surprise. His eyes drifted out over the harbor a moment, and then he studied my face carefully. "Could be," he whispered. "What's your name?"

I didn't know what to say.

Raising my arm, I ran my fingers along the sanded wood hull. The air was cold and damp on the back of my neck. If I told him my name, he wouldn't recognize it because my father was certain to be using an alias. He'd think I was the liar, that the man on *Spray* wasn't my father.

"The other man, Santori," Petra said. "How did he get out there?"

"Rented a dinghy." He looked her over carefully. "By the hour."

"How much?" she asked.

"A hundred."

"I don't have a hundred," I said.

He dropped his cigarette in the crushed seashells under our feet and positioned the mask over his nose and mouth. "He'll be gone soon," he said through the mask. "He's paid up on everything and he'll be gone when this fog lifts." He switched on the belt sander and began running it back and forth across the boat hull.

Petra stepped back from the dust quickly. I walked over to the extension cord and separated the plugs, stopping the motor. He turned to me and now seemed to hold the sander at his side as though he might use it as a weapon.

Petra slid her bag off her shoulder and got out her checkbook. He said nothing as she wrote out the check. When she handed it to him, all he said was, "Greek." Nodding out toward the harbor, he added, "Italian." As he folded the check and stuffed it in his breast pocket, he stared at me, his eyes shrewd and mocking. "And what are *you* supposed to be?"

WE LOST SIGHT of the freighter each time *Shallop* descended into the troughs between waves. As we'd climb toward the next crest, though, the ship would reappear, a little bigger. The name on her rust-streaked bow was *Aurora Borealis*. Every minute or so there came another long blast of her horn.

"*Jack,*" my mother shouted, "there must be something we can do!"

"Hold our course. He'll slow down and give us time to pass. He's under power, we're under sail—it's rules of the road that he give way to us."

"Rules of the *road!*"

"There's plenty of time. He's still well off."

I turned my head away from the wind and faced the stern. My father was staring toward the ship through his soaked glasses. "Get on the radio," he said. "Channel sixteen."

I started to move forward in the cockpit, but my father grabbed my arm.

"No," he said. "Your mother. I need you up here."

My mother went below and Abigail followed her—she was very ill now, incapacitated with seasickness, and I saw her collapse into one of the berths.

"We're going to harden up," he said.

"We can't!" I shouted. "Look at the sails now!"

"We can get a little more speed out of her."

The reefed mainsail and jib were well out, and the mainsheet running to the portside winch was taut as a wire. "The rigging!" I shouted. "Look at the bend in the mast now—it won't take any more."

"We need more speed. You steer, I'll grind the winch." I shook my head. I loved to handle the tiller but had never done so in anything like this sea. He gripped my upper arm again and pulled me toward the stern of the cockpit. "Don't argue with me, Sam! *Take the helm!*"

I worked my way past him and put both hands on the tiller. It was a thick, curved piece of maple, deep red, with bold grain and a high-gloss spar varnish. The pressure on the rudder was incredible; I was leaning back with my legs braced and my arms fully extended, and I still could barely hold her on course. The tension between the wind and the water seemed to be concentrated in that tiller.

My father went down to the lower side of the cockpit, yanked the winch handle from its pocket, and began cranking in the mainsheet. He had to put his back into it as he rotated the drum slowly and hauled the boom in closer, causing the boat to heel even more. I've always loved the sound of the winch gears, but at that moment each precise click of metal seemed like the last, and I expected something—the line, the sail, the winch, perhaps even the rigging that supported the mast—to give way. But it didn't, and I could feel the boat gaining speed through the swells.

Below, I could see my mother braced in the cabin, speaking into the radio microphone, but the responses when she released the button were nothing but static. "I don't think I'm getting through!" she shouted up to my father.

"Keep calling," he said as he slammed the winch handle in its pocket. "Keep calling out our course." He looked at the compass. "Sixty degrees."

The freighter was closing in, a huge curl of white water surging ahead of its broad bow. It was getting close enough that we could now hear its engines.

"Nine and a half," my father said as he tapped the knot meter with his finger. "We're doing better."

"In *Ben Hur* they call this 'ramming speed,'" I said.

"Never mind the movies!" he shouted.

"And they unchain the slaves rowing the ship so they might have a chance to save themselves after the collision."

Squinting through the rain, he said, *"Just hold your course."*

We descended in a huge trough and the freighter disappeared except the very top of the bridge, which was well back on the stern of the ship. There came five angry blasts of its whistle, and as we climbed the next wave, the bow of the ship came into view. They could no longer see us from the bridge. We were about a hundred yards from the ship, close enough now to hear the water breaking off the bow. My father put the handle in the winch again and cranked the boom in even tighter. As we shot down the back of a wave, I could see we were going to get by the bow, though the ship was so wide I wasn't sure if we would completely avoid the hull.

I looked at the knot meter—we were doing ten knots down the back of waves and dropping back to eight-plus on the climb. The wind increased, blasting around the side of the ship like a gust turning the corner of a city building. My father came up to the topside of the cockpit and shouted down into the cabin, "Everybody to windward." My mother helped Abby into the upside berth, which I could feel through the tiller helped our trim.

And then the ship was alongside of us, cutting off our wind. We slowed down to about five knots as the freighter slid by, perhaps thirty yards to the starboard. Her deck was at least fifty feet above the waterline, and she was longer than a football field. It was amazing to me that so much steel could float, that the ship didn't just sink to the bottom. As her stern passed us, we could hear the vibration of her engines.

Suddenly we were out of ship's lee and the wind came up again, knocking the mast over sharply. My father tried to let the mainsheet out but was thrown to the floor of the cockpit as the ship's white water broke over our bow. Then, high up the mast, there came a loud tearing sound, and within a second the mainsail was trailing into the water in two giant rippling streamers. We lost our headway and were in danger of broaching—turning sideways to the next wave.

27

I rowed a heavy wooden dory out into the fog on Provincetown Harbor. After we had gone a few hundred yards, the town, dominated by the Italianate watchtower, had the hazy splendor of a Constable. Even Petra, who was sitting in the stern, was seen through wispy air. She kept her hands in her coat pockets, and the moisture in the air was so great that beads of water glistened in her dark hair. Head tilted, she gazed down at the water. The word for her expression was pensive, and if I could paint, this was the moment I would want to capture.

Each stroke of the oars produced small pretty whorls that trailed behind the boat. She reached over the gunwale, extended an arm, and tried to poke her fingertip into one of the spinning holes in the water.

"My sister used to do that," I said quietly. "Little maelstroms. It was a word I encountered when I was about thirteen. Poe had a story called 'The Maelstrom,' and I can remember looking the word up in the dictionary. It's this scary tornado thing that can suck you in and destroy you." Petra took her hand away from the water and stuffed it back in her coat. "My sister already knew the definition of a maelstrom," I said. "She was so much smarter. I don't know how I outlived her."

The water was flat and gray.

The air was only a shade lighter gray.

I could no longer see the town and in every direction the fog was the same.

"How do you know where you're going?" she whispered.

"I don't. Except to watch my wake and try to keep it straight behind me."

After a few more strokes I stopped rowing and the dory glided to a halt. We sat, motionless, as though suspended in a gray orb that smelled deeply of sea salt. Eventually, off to our left there was a sudden flapping and splashing, and a seagull appeared, wheeled above us, screaming, and then it disappeared. Petra couldn't quite conceal the fact that she'd been startled.

IT WAS A KIND of haunting, all the times my father's presence seemed palpable, yet he was nowhere near. As long as I can remember there were moments when I'd be sitting in my bedroom, or eating at the kitchen table, and I'd suddenly have this overwhelming sense that something was missing. I've never been able to express how that felt. At such moments I wasn't particularly upset. Or sad. Nor did I feel rejected, taken for granted, or deceived. It was odd how often kids I grew up with were mad at their parents, really angry, and I took particular note of how frequently boys were pissed off at their fathers. I found it ironic, even funny, how the fathers were there, at home, near at hand, and yet their sons seemed determined to get as far away from them as possible. On more than one occasion, while walking to school or, when we were a little older, when we were out drinking, boys I knew in Salem would talk about their fathers to me with an intensity and earnestness that was remarkable. They hated their fathers. More than once they told me how lucky I was, how much they envied me because my father was hardly ever around.

And more than once boys told me how they had actually considered— seriously considered—killing their fathers. It would usually come up as an extended exercise in logic. They would enumerate all the benefits of their fathers being removed from the world. Their mothers usually would be much better off. Their siblings could be dealt with, finally, without interference. The death of their fathers usually suggested absolute freedom. They could come and go as they pleased, stay out late, take the car, not think about college, or a particular career. Dead fathers meant sex would come easier. Boys drunk in cars, in the woods, at the beach, often throwing an empty bottle or kicking or punching something nearby. One kid who was a descendant of one of the early Salem families took a long beer piss after a party one night and said that this was what he was going to do after his father died, get drunk and piss on his grave.

For most men, absolute freedom is money. Or so they think. They talk about how once their fathers are no longer an obstruction, they will inherit the wealth they deserve. I knew an editor at the *Herald* who once figured out on a bar napkin what his father, a prominent Beacon Hill lawyer, was worth. He did the calculations in about eight minutes, the length of time it took him to down a gimlet at the Bull & Finch (which was not such a bad place before the television show *Cheers* transformed it into a tourist attraction). He pushed the napkin toward me on the bar and it was covered with figures. "Houses, cars, insurance policies, stocks, bonds, debentures," he said pleasantly. "When all is said and done"—his finger tapped the figure that was underlined twice on the napkin—"that's my cut, and I've earned it."

PETRA AND I sat in the fog and didn't speak. Didn't move except to look around. It was as though we were inside a pearl, outside of time. Only the tide moved—imperceptibly, the still water beneath our dory flowing away from land.

Land that we could no longer see.

Pulled toward a moon we could not see.

Forces of nature at work in a world we could not see.

Except for the fog.

ALL THOSE TIMES when something seemed to be missing I felt curious. I wanted to know how things would be different. How my life would be altered. If my father were sitting at the kitchen table, how our conversation would be different. I was curious about how little everyday things would have been affected. If I'd forgotten to do a chore or had come home late, I wondered if he would have been angry with me. Some boys I grew up with were spanked by their fathers; a few were beaten. I didn't envy them, but in some vague way I knew that at least their fathers cared enough to lay a hand on them.

I STARTED ROWING AGAIN. Slowly, dipping the oars carefully. Nothing changed except for the wake rippling the smooth water behind us. When I stopped rowing again, it was as though we hadn't moved at all.

ONE BOY I played tennis with, Rick Larabee, said something once that was interesting and, I think, true. Larabee was a senior; I was a sophomore. After our matches were concluded, we were lying in the grass next to the court waiting for the doubles teams to finish.

"You realize that sex will be different for you?" He had a long face and a badly sunburned nose. His backhand was stronger than his forehand, something most kids didn't figure out until it was too late, so he was difficult to beat; but I could take him, though it was never easy. Larabee could chase down and return almost any shot.

"You know this for a fact?"

"Adams," he said, gazing at the sky, "you have no father—no father who's hanging around the house every weekend, anyway. And you live with two women. In many ways I suspect you'll have an easier time of it."

"Why?"

After a moment, he laughed. "I don't know. After I get out of Harvard with a degree in psychology, I'll tell you. Trust me: I just know I'm right."

Larabee did go to Harvard, and he went on to get several degrees, but he was wrong. Once, years later, after I had split up with yet another woman, I told this to Abigail. We were walking through the North End, though I don't remember where we were going. Sometimes we just liked to walk the streets of Boston together.

"Sex will be easier," she said, laughing. This was about a year before she died and she seldom found things funny anymore. "Doesn't Larabee have a Ph.D. in something now? Sex will be easier—yeah, *right!* Sex with *strangers.* You've had plenty of girlfriends, and it's safe to say I've been with more than a few men. *That's* the easy part, but the *results* are harder."

"What results?"

"You're a son, but not a father."

I stopped walking, but she continued down the sidewalk to a bakery on the corner, where she paused to look in the window. An old couple passed by me, speaking Italian. The woman wore a black shawl; the man a fedora and he used a bamboo cane. They kept their heads down, watching each step they took on the pavement. There was the marvelous smell of fresh bread in the air. People talk about moments in their lives, gut-hollowing moments when the bottom falls out. It was true. I was only a son, nothing more. It seemed meager and cruel. I was not only *only* a son, I was a son who hardly knew his father. There on that brick sidewalk in the North End I felt suspended in the universe—there was nothing behind me, and I realized then that there was really nothing ahead of me. I had no father; I had no son, no daughter, nothing. It was at once difficult and liberating. It didn't matter what I did with the rest of my life. I'd arranged things so that I had no real responsibilities, to the past, to the future. There was only the present, which seemed paltry and thin. For the first time in my life, I think, I was truly afraid, and the only thing that saved me from that moment was the smell of those bread loaves and the fact that my sister was standing there at the bakery window, waiting for me.

Finally I started walking again. When I reached Abby she took my hand, and we crossed the street like when we were children.

PETRA RAISED HER head to the left and leaned forward slightly. I turned and saw the suggestion of a boat, perhaps just a trick of the eye, and rowed in that direction. We had been heading west, but now I believed we were going southwest. Between strokes I glanced over my shoulder and soon realized we were approaching the hull of an aluminum skiff, which from a distance appeared empty. It wasn't moored—just drifting. As we drew near, I could see that there was one oar still in the locks.

Then, just as Petra whispered, "Sam," I saw it: a hand gripping the oar.

As we drew alongside, our wood hull bumped aluminum. Ike was sprawled on his back in the bottom of the skiff, his legs draped over the middle thwart. He'd been shot through the forehead, about an inch above the left eyebrow. His eyes were open and he stared up into the fog as though he'd just seen a religious vision. He appeared in awe. But his arms and legs looked uncomfortable and I kept waiting for him to move, to get up. His coat was open and he was wearing a shoulder holster. The gun was in his right hand, which lay in bloodred water beneath him.

There was a sharp sound off to our right, which sounded like a hatch being shut.

Petra sat perfectly still in the stern of the dory.

"You could wait here while I go look."

She shook her head vehemently.

I reached down into Ike's skiff and removed the gun from his hand. It was an automatic and I tucked it in my coat pocket.

I began rowing toward the sound, taking long pauses between each stroke so that I could simply listen. Watching Petra's face, I knew she could see something ahead of us now. I looked around and saw it: a sloop, about forty feet long. It became clearer as we glided through the still water.

"All right." It was my father's voice cutting through the fog. "That's close enough."

I couldn't see him on the deck at first, but then, as we drifted nearer the white hull, his head and shoulders were visible in the cockpit. His arms were extended across the coaming and he was pointing a pistol at us.

"It's me, Dad."

There was no response. We stopped drifting and neither of us moved.

Finally he stood up. "Sam, what are you doing here?"

"We're coming aboard," I said.

"Just turn around. Go back."

"No, I'm coming in."

"Go back. I'm about to get under way here and—"

"You shot him?"

"He was a cop."

"How do you *know?*"

"Sam, I know cops. He was a cop."

"He *used* to be a cop. He was a friend of mine, and of Mom's."

My father looked away for a moment, a gesture that indicated he was recalculating in some way.

"We're coming on board," I said, and immediately began rowing toward the sailboat. The name, written in blue script across the stern, was *Spray*.

"Who's that with you?" he asked.

"My name is Petra Mouzakis." As I shipped the oars, she studied my face carefully. Then, raising her head as my father came to the stern rail, she added, "And I assure you I am *not* a friend of your son's."

"I see." There was now a hint of amusement in his voice. "You are, shall we say, something more than a friend?" After using his foot to fend off our bow, he tossed a line down to me.

ONCE WE HAD lost our mainsail, *Shallop* had great difficulty making any headway into the wind. The white water would crash over the starboard side, pushing the bow farther away from the direction of the wind.

"We'll broach!" I shouted.

"Keep steering," my father said.

"I can't!"

"Keep steering."

He went below and disappeared into the forepeak. I heard the knock of a cabinet door swinging against a bulkhead. Quickly he came back up into the cockpit, with a blue canvas bag over his shoulder. It contained the drogue, which we'd never had to use before. He went up on deck and worked his way to the bow, where he knelt and tied the line to both cleats. Then he dumped the drogue, a large folded mass of canvas, overboard and held on to the chrome rail with both hands as the line paid out—at least two hundred feet of anchor rode, attached to a large parachute-shaped drogue. The waves kept smacking the hull, and with only the jib up, I had very little control of the boat. Though I held the tiller all the way over to port, the bow would not come around into the wind and waves.

Then my father turned and shouted, *"Hang on!"*

The white line suddenly rose up out of the water, snapped taut, the bow veered sharply to the starboard, and it was as though the keel had slammed into a rock. I heard my sister scream below in the cabin, and there was the sound of canned goods banging around. The initial jolt sent me to the floor of the cockpit, and I lost my grip of the tiller. I clawed my way to my feet and looked forward—the bow had swung around so that it pointed into the weather. My father came back down the windward side and jumped into the cockpit.

"Let's just hope it holds," he said. "Come on down below now."

"The tiller," I said.

"Doesn't matter now as long as that drogue holds."

We went below and my father dogged hatches. "We'll be all right, unless that rode snaps or yanks the cleats out of the deck."

The hull rose steeply up the face of oncoming waves, then crashed down into each trough. The motion seemed far more extreme there in the closed cabin. I kept looking out a porthole, trying to keep an eye on the horizon. But within a minute my stomach began to turn and for the first time ever I felt seasick. I wanted to throw up but couldn't. Abigail lay on the bunk, her arm across her face. My mother had been wiping her face with a damp cloth.

"We'll be all right," my father said. "It'll be rocky for a while, but these squalls pass quickly." He sat down at the table, seeming not to be affected by the pitching and yawing of the hull. "We'll be fine," he said.

My mother leaned over Abigail and laid the cloth over her forehead. It was as though she hadn't heard him. There was something in her expression that from then on became permanent.

The squall did pass quickly. When the seas began to calm, we put on the 150 percent genoa, came about, and headed northwest for Salem, arriving inside Marblehead Neck at last light. Little was said during the remainder of the cruise; we were all exhausted. When our father left for Panama several weeks later, Abigail and I knew things had changed, that he wouldn't be back with any regularity. We never spoke of it directly with our mother; it wasn't necessary. Over the winter *Shallop* was sold to a doctor up in Newburyport. I remember going down to the boatyard on a raw afternoon in March to watch the truck haul the vessel away on a trailer. Out of the water sailboats reveal their secrets, their true selves. She had a deep keel and lines that could break your heart.

28

"Been a long time since we've been on a boat together," my father said, tucking his gun into his shoulder holster. He reached down to give me a hand, but I grabbed a hold of the stern rail and climbed over. Smiling, he kept his arm extended and graciously helped Petra as she came up the ladder.

When finally I was standing in the cockpit, I shoved my father so hard that he lost his balance and fell against the large chrome steering wheel. Something about touching him made me freeze, though, and I simply remained there, in the stern of the boat.

"You took her *ashes,*" I said. "*Now* you kill *Ike?*" I moved toward him, but Petra threw her arms around me. Trying to shrug her off, I shouted, "And you ruined her *mind!* You went into her room at the hospital to make sure she wouldn't *talk!*"

Petra was gripping my shoulders tightly and speaking my name.

My father backed up toward the cabin and braced himself in the open companionway. There was something different about him. This close he seemed frail and brittle, as though he were still recovering from a long period of idleness. Or illness. Only his eyes, behind those wireless glasses, seemed to possess the vigor and quickness I recalled.

"Sam," he said. His voice wasn't as strong as I remembered. His suede jacket was zipped up to his throat; though his neck chords strained when he spoke, his voice was hoarse and weak. "Listen, you need to get away from here. I'm pulling out now."

"You should *never* have come back," I nearly shouted. I got free of

Petra's arms—she was still speaking to me, though I ignored her—and moved forward in the cockpit. "You should have stayed in Ensenada that Christmas! Fourteen years old—*that's* the last time I should ever have *seen* you!" I took Ike's gun from my coat pocket and aimed it at my father. My arm was shaking. Petra was clutching at me from behind, and speaking loudly, rapidly. "You *give* me my mother's *ashes!*" I shouted. "Right *now! That's all I want from you! Give them to me and then you can sail away to fucking hell!*"

Petra reached out and grabbed my elbow, pulling my extended arm down, and in a moment my father had drawn his gun again, and he aimed it at my face. The barrel wasn't two feet away from my eyes. His arm, his hand were steady and sure.

I struggled with Petra, who was wrapped around me from behind. She and I were both shouting then, and as I tried to raise my arm again, she yanked on my elbow so that the gun went off. The sound of the shot, though muffled in the dense fog, startled both of us. As I slowly lowered the gun to my side, Petra released her hold on me. The bullet had splintered the teak handrail that ran along the top of the cabin.

For a moment no one said a thing, no one moved. There was silence except for a seagull cawing in the distance. My father's face settled into a look that I recognized; it reminded me of times when Abby and I were young and we were fighting, squabbling, being noisy kids, and he'd suddenly had enough. He stepped toward me, raising his arm, and struck me on the side of the head with the butt of his gun.

As I HAVE SAID, when we were young our father never struck us. It wasn't until I was much older that I realized that this was unusual, that so many of my friends' parents—particularly the fathers—tended to physically reprimand their children. But our father rarely touched us, either in anger or in affection.

I vaguely recall the image—I couldn't have been more than four or five—of my baby sister climbing into my father's lap, where she'd put her arms around his neck and hug him. We still lived in warm, sunny places then, so her chubby arms and legs were often bare. I remember feeling resentful; it seemed only *she* had the privilege to embrace my father. It had to do with the fact that she was smaller, that she was a girl.

But I also remember that my father only briefly tolerated those embraces—all sticky fingers and drooling lips—before he managed to disentangle her and put her down. For me, it was always a moment of vindication when Daddy would finally place his hands under Abby's arms and remove her from his lap.

I WAS KNOCKED out cold when my father struck me. The next thing I remembered—aside from the pain in my skull—was my father's hands reaching under my shoulders, while Petra took hold of my legs. And there was the sensation of being lifted and carried, though it faded quickly as I passed out again. But as I descended back into that darkness, I was keenly aware of one thing: my father's labored breathing, his breath virtually odorless. It was neither pleasant nor unpleasant. Perhaps a bit stale. Neutral.

THE NEXT TIME I opened my eyes, I was staring up at the ceiling of the boat's cabin. Petra was leaning over me, daubing at my scalp with a damp and bloodied towel. My father stood at the top of the companionway steps, gazing astern. He appeared exhausted, I suspect from lifting and carrying me. Yet his profile and the expression on his face reminded me of when I was a boy, of the holiday season in Ensenada, in particular. The man was forever alert. Like an animal—a predator, a hawk, say—he was always looking in six directions. Furthermore, he remained still so that he could hear. Lying on my back, watching my father peer into the fog, I suddenly understood what he had been trying to tell me earlier: Some threat was near, and we had arrived at the worst possible moment. Just as in the past, my presence made him weak and therefore vulnerable to attack.

"The perfect assassin," I said slowly, and waited until he turned his eyes on me, "the one *true* assassin has no family."

"Hypothetically?" he asked.

"Sure, why not?" I said.

"Hypothetically, yes," he said, barely in a whisper. "The perfect killer is completely alone. There is no past. There is no wife. No son. No daughter. No home."

"Then we're getting close," I said. "I'm all that's left between you and perfection."

There was the faintest smile before he said, "And there's no future."

"Except to survive."

With reluctance, he nodded.

"And to kill again," I said.

"Not by choice." He turned his head, scanning the fog. "Not by choice, Sam."

"Self-defense?" I tried to sit up, but the pain in my skull was overwhelming and I could only prop myself up on one elbow. "Is that what it is? Is that why my friend is out there lying in that skiff with a bullet in his head—self-defense? An act of preservation?" He wouldn't answer. *"Preservation?"* I shouted. "For *what?"*

Petra's hand gripped my shoulder and I lay back on the cushion. She went to the galley sink and wrung out the blood-soaked towel. "What're you looking for out there?" she asked my father. When he didn't answer, she said, "Well, whoever it is, they've been after you since you've been back in Boston. Perhaps it's more accurate to say that they've never stopped chasing you."

He came down into the cabin, but he still seemed to be listening for something out on the water. "You have no idea," he said.

"No, I don't." Petra draped the towel over the sink faucet to dry, which seemed a charming but absolutely pointless domestic gesture. "But I'm trying to understand. I'm coming out of the women's room in the Dana Farber Cancer Institute and I see a man—I'm sure it was you—down the hall. Your wife suddenly loses her memory and traces of a suspicious drug are found in her after she dies. She had been talking to me. She had been talking to me because I'd been working on a book about you. She was an amazing woman, your wife. She was dying, she was in considerable pain, yet she was determined to remember all that she could— it was remarkable how she fed off of her recollections of her family. Though there was clearly much sorrow, they still gave her joy. It was all she had left." Petra leaned a hip against the galley sink and faced my father. "Then *suddenly* it's all *gone*—her mind, just *poof*. Was it because of what she was telling me? Or was it because of what she might say to those who were after you?"

Somehow my father seemed pleased, although his expression didn't really change. "Perhaps that depends on what she was telling you?"

"I think she knew more than you realized," Petra said. "Or perhaps it wasn't a matter of *knowing,* but of understanding. Yes, that's it. She understood you."

My father put his hands in the front pockets of his tan chinos. "Is it unusual for a wife to understand her husband? This is not news that will change the course of history."

I sat up, slowly this time. My head was throbbing. Gently I touched the lump on the side of my head.

My father opened a cabinet and took out a bottle of brandy. He poured some into a blue plastic coffee mug and handed it to me. "Perhaps a dram of grog will help?"

I took a sip and winced. "Might."

"Good," he said, "because I need to make way before this fog lifts."

I stood up slowly, using one hand on the bulkhead to brace myself. "At this point I don't care what you did or didn't do—I wrote my book already. And I don't care where you're going. It really is too late for some kind of father-son reconciliation, you know. All I want is my mother's ashes."

"Why?" he asked.

"No." I took another sip of the brandy. "The question is why do *you* want them?"

He sat down at the varnished table; the seat cushions were blue with little white anchors stitched into the fabric. Taking two more mugs from the shelf, he poured a little brandy into each; had I known better, I would have thought he was some retired professional, a banker, a lawyer, someone who had made a killing in real estate, enjoying his golden years aboard the sailboat of his dreams. Sliding one of the mugs toward Petra, he said, "Think what you want of me, but I keep my promises."

"No one ever doubted your loyalty," I said. "It's a matter of what you've been loyal to." He sipped his brandy and ran a finger along the grain of the table. I leaned down toward him. "You did make a promise to her?"

He nodded but kept his eyes on the table. "Long time ago, Sam. I wasn't much of a husband in life, so I owe her this." He pushed his glasses up his thin nose. "Wasn't much of a father either, I realize that. And I realize it's too late for some 'reconciliation.' Frankly, I like you better for not wanting that."

"Frankly, I don't give a damn if you *like* me."

He didn't exactly smile, but his eyes appeared bemused. "I never made any promises to you, Sam, because I knew I couldn't keep them."

"Don't forget your daughter. You didn't make or break any promises to her, either."

"I haven't forgotten," he said.

"I'm not so sure."

Now he raised his head and his eyes seemed to be pleading. "I simply couldn't get back for Abigail's funeral, Sam. I'm sorry about that. Believe me, I'm sorry about what happened to your sister—more than anything, if you want to know. My one comfort was that she had you. I know you took care of her the best you could."

"Whatever I did, it wasn't enough. She deserved better."

"I know," he said quietly.

"Bullshit."

He was about to speak but then seemed to reconsider. For a moment he looked helpless. Suddenly he turned his head sharply, got up from the table, and went quickly up the companionway. We followed him up to the cockpit. "Where *is* that?" he asked.

After a moment, I could hear a faint sound of an outboard motor. "Somewhere off to the right," I said, glancing at the compass. "East."

My father remained still, listening, until we couldn't hear the motor any longer. "I'm sorry, Sam, but I have to get out of this harbor. Now."

"Just give me the ashes," I said, "and we'll be on our way."

As he turned toward me, there was a moment when his face tightened with indecision. Then he shook his head. "Told you, I made a promise."

"So did I."

"To your mother?"

"To my mother, to myself." He wanted to get by me, but I didn't move. "We're not leaving this boat without her ashes."

His face pinched in again, and there was something I hadn't seen in a long time—anger. "All right, then, suit yourself." He lowered his head and walked toward me. At the last moment, I stepped aside. After he passed me, he stopped and turned around. There was now something new in his eyes, something I didn't understand at all. "Fine, Sam. You and your friend here come along if you want. You make your own decisions—you always have. But I guarantee you're *not* going to like where *this* boat is going." He smiled briefly as he tilted his head toward the east. "They'll be back, and this fog won't last forever. Now let's get under way."

29

The tide was falling, and once the orange mooring ball dropped out of sight, *Spray* glided slowly through pure fog on still water. The only sound was the low rumble of her diesel engine. My father was at the wheel, watching the map of Provincetown on the navigation screen. The harbor lay inside the curved fingers at the end of Cape Cod's arm, graceful on a map, yet full of treacherous sandbars and shoals. I went out on the bow pulpit and gazed into the soup, a pointless, romantic exercise, really. With all the electronics in the cockpit, my father was able to push buttons and the boat would steer itself down the middle of the channel. Aboard *Shallop* we navigated with a compass, wind vane, telltales, and dead reckoning. I wanted to get some distance from him, which on this vessel was about forty feet.

I was angrier with myself than with him. It was just as it always had been on a boat: He was in command. I had no power, no leverage; my desires were subordinate to his expectations and requirements. He gave orders; I followed them. This was the way it had always been, the way it would always be. Had I not been so obsessed with my father's "alleged" role in a political assassination, I myself might have lived a very different life. As a journalist I might have found different stories to write.

Turning around, I leaned comfortably into the curved chrome rail of the pulpit. I could barely see the cockpit in the fog. Petra sat with her arms spread along the coaming, as though she were on a pleasure cruise. They were talking, but I couldn't hear them over the throb of the engine. That they seemed to take to each other only spiked my anger with a pang of adolescent jealousy. I considered telling him to stop so that I could board the dory that was tethered to the stern cleat and row ashore alone. But to do so, to leave without my mother's ashes, would cement my sense of failure.

I made my way back to the cockpit.

Tapping a finger on the navigation screen on the steering console, my father said, "They're out here."

"Who is?" The screen indicated stationary boats moored in the inner harbor. Then I saw that one boat was moving slowly to the south of us. "Who's that?"

"Must be that outboard we heard earlier," he said. "My guess is they don't have electronics and are wandering blind in this stuff."

"It's got to be Hume," Petra said.

"If it is," I said, "he's probably not alone."

"Hume never does anything alone," Petra said.

I said to my father, "They must have followed us from Boston."

He studied the navigation screen. "Don't seem to be moving now. Probably cut their engine to see if they can hear us." He turned the ignition switch and shut off the diesel. We drifted through the fog in silence. There were the slightest ripples on the water, suggesting a hint of a breeze out of the southwest.

"All right," my father said, "raise the main."

Petra followed me up on the deck. I hauled down on the halyard and the mainsail ran up the mast. Then, from the cockpit, my father unfurled the genoa, and both sails billowed listlessly in light air. There was only the faintest sound of water washing along the hull.

"We aren't doing two knots," I said.

"But it's beautiful," Petra said, gazing up at the sails. "I keep thinking I should be nervous, even scared, out here in this fog, with no idea where your father's going, what he has in mind."

"Welcome to my family."

"But it's really just beautiful."

"It's wind and water, the essentials."

"Do you have any idea where he's going?"

"At the moment, west. And after he clears the harbor, he'll head north and try to get around the tip of the Cape—see if he can catch a breeze out there."

"Out in the open ocean?" There was a hint of alarm in her voice.

"The wind should pick up a bit once we're off Race Point."

Her face took on a complexity I couldn't read. It wasn't just a fear of deep water.

The air was so moist that tiny beads of water clung to her hair. She spoke quietly, "Your father was saying how my being a journalist placed limitations on my ability to perceive things in a historical context."

"He was talking about history?"

"Yes." Her eyes were troubled now. "That's not good?"

"Never has been in the past. I think at some point, when he was young, he had deep beliefs, about freedom and democracy, but now I don't know that there's much left. It's like he's been scoured out. The only thing he still believes in is history. The present has little consequence."

Now she tried to smile. "Sam, this is not instilling great confidence in our captain."

Somewhere behind us an outboard engine started up. Its sound was very faint. We returned to the cockpit, where I stood next to my father so I could look at the navigation screen.

"He's moving in this direction," I said. "And he's gaining."

"How do you know it's Hume?" my father asked.

"I saw him last night," I said. "He'd hooked up with these two who claimed they were on your side."

"A man and woman," my father said.

"Right. I called them George and Gracie."

"You would."

"They killed Saavo."

My father began to turn toward me but thought better of it.

"They used my gun," I said.

Now he looked at me. "The one you brought on board—"

"That belonged to Ike."

"*You* have your own gun?"

"Surprised?"

"So the pen wasn't sufficient," he said. "I could have told you that years ago and saved all of us a lot of grief."

"Too late now," I said.

"They used your gun on Saavo—I won't ask *how* they acquired it. And they hope that you'd come running to your father, and lead them to where they wanted to go." My father removed his glasses and with his fingertips massaged the bridge of his nose. His face seemed vulnerable; his eyes tired and pallid. The arms of the wire frames had left a deep horizontal crease embedded in the side of his skull. Strange, but this was the most familiar physical aspect of my father. Putting the glasses back on, he said, "People underestimate Hume. He has resilience and old-fashioned pluck. He thinks he's made a deal with them."

"You know who George and Gracie are?"

"Unfortunately," my father said.

"You know their real names."

He nodded. "But George and Gracie will do."

"And what branch of the government are they?" I asked. "FBI? CIA? SOS?"

My father didn't answer.

"Maybe they're not government," Petra said. "Mafia?"

He smiled at her. "Does it really matter?"

Suddenly there was an opening in the fog overhead. Pale sunlight played over the boat, and wind filled the sails, causing the hull to heel to starboard.

"The fog," Petra said, "is it breaking up?"

"We're outside the protection of the harbor," my father said.

Sound carries well over water, but through such fog it tends to come and go. The sound of the outboard was so faint one moment that it seemed to almost have disappeared, then it would suddenly come clear through the fog. For a moment I thought I caught a glimpse of a boat to the south—a launch, running parallel to us about a hundred yards off our port bow— then the outboard suddenly revved higher.

"He's turning," my father said. "He's working in big circles." Pointing farther forward, he said loudly, *"There!"*

The launch emerged from the fog, headed straight for us. It was an old boat, the kind that had been common in New England waters when I was a boy—heavy lapstrake hulls designed for open water. I could see two men, and after a moment I realized Hume was driving while George was standing with his arms braced on the top of the wood-framed windshield. He was holding a pistol in both hands, trying to take aim at us.

My father drew his gun from his shoulder holster. "Get *down!*" he shouted.

The first shot came from the launch. I grabbed Petra and we fell to the cockpit deck. My father fired several times and there was the sound of breaking glass. I got to my knees and looked toward the launch—George was knocked back into the bench seat, blood covering the front of his windbreaker. Hume was leaning over the steering wheel, clutching his upper arm. His silver hair was blown flat by the wind. He looked frightened, and he seemed to be shouting something that we couldn't hear over the whine of the outboard. The launch kept coming toward us and he was unable to control it. Still on my knees, I turned the wheel hard to port, causing the sailboat to turn toward the oncoming launch. When the two vessels collided, it was a glancing blow, which still caused the sailboat to shudder and heel. I was thrown forward, hitting my head on fiberglass—in the same place my father had struck me with the butt of his pistol.

The pain was such that what transpired next seemed almost surrealistic. I sat on my haunches holding my head, and I think I was swearing. The launch was taking on water fast in the bow. The stern rose out of the water, the outboard still revving loudly, and smoke billowing as the engine overheated. As the bow sank, Hume climbed toward the stern. George's body slumped forward against the broken windshield, then the entire boat went under quickly, as though it were pulled. Only Hume remained, flailing about in bubbling, foamy water.

Then I blacked out.

WHEN I OPENED my eyes, I stared up at a painfully bright blue sky. I was lying on the cockpit deck and I got to my feet. The boat was heeling nicely and we were doing about five knots in a steady breeze. Petra sat next to Hume, whose upper arm had been wrapped in a bandage. His hair was still wet and matted, but he was wearing dry clothes, a gray sweatsuit, which made him look anything but senatorial. Petra's gaze was difficult to read; she seemed to be trying to warn me about something. There was a sound down below that I couldn't identify. Only my father, who stood at the wheel, seemed pleased that we now had a fresh wind.

I looked around to get my bearings. Provincetown was about two miles behind us to the west. A massive fog bank, burnished silver in the sun, hovered well to the south. North and east there was only the horizon, where dark blue water met pale blue sky.

"You need to reason with your father, Sam," Hume said instructively. "I've told him that when that launch fails to return, the Coast Guard will come looking for us."

"Gracie?" I said. "She's waiting for you back in P-town."

Hume was confused by the name. "Look, this is bad enough." He was trying to assume a demanding tone, but it was undermined by the fact that the front of his sweatshirt had big red letters that read: *Billabong*. "Tell him he can't just sail away from this. I'm his only remaining chance."

My father was preoccupied with steering. He seemed to be thoroughly enjoying himself. I turned to Hume. "Only chance for what?"

"To tell his story," Hume said. "Like I told you, I can guarantee that he'll be comfortable for the rest of his life."

"Until someone puts a bullet in his head, like Saavo?" I said.

"*That* wasn't *my* idea," Hume nearly shouted.

"No?" I said. "But it worked. And you always find value in what works. After all, you're a politician." I leaned forward so I could see down the open companionway into the cabin. "What's that noise?"

Hume repeatedly slapped his hand on the teak bench. He was a man who knew how to bring a body of lawmakers to order, but he was accustomed to using a gavel. "Just *look* at him," he said, nodding toward my father. "Doesn't say a *word*. Thinks he's going to escape *forever*. Doesn't care if he takes you *down* with him. His son, his *only* surviving—"

"The dory's still tethered." My father's voice was calm, reassuring, maybe even playful. He spoke to me, but he was staring at Petra. "It's turned out to be a nice day for a row in an open boat."

She drew a swatch of hair off her cheek. "What *is* your destination?"

"Destination?" My father studied the eastern horizon a moment. "I thought it was all in the journey. Isn't that what you kids believe? Your whole generation—didn't you sing songs about peace and love and the value of the journey? It's not the destination. It's all about getting there. Who cares what the end result is, right? That was for Nazis, right? Please don't tell me Bob Dylan did it for the money."

"A destination?" Hume sounded confused and frightened. "You don't have one?"

"We're under full sail and there's a fresh breeze," my father said. "Isn't this *destination* enough?"

"*Sam,* tell me," Hume demanded. "You know what he's got in mind?"

I ignored him and got to my feet. My head was very sore and tender, and I could feel my pulse pounding in my temple. I made my way down into the cabin, where I could clearly hear a motor running, accompanied by the unmistakable sound of water being sucked into a bilge pump. I knelt on the teak floor and lifted the panel by its recessed brass ring. Below was the top of the keel, a slab of iron that on a boat such as this must have weighed several tons. There was a series of bolts protruding from the slab, and the whole thing was covered with water.

I climbed up the companionway and said, "The launch must have damaged the hull."

My father raised his head toward the top of the mast.

"You mean we're taking on water?" Petra asked. Again, I saw it in her eyes, which seemed to have opened up into a pleading helplessness. Pure fear.

"We have some time," I said, "but the bilge pump can't keep up."

"We're *sinking?*" Hume said.

"Eventually," I said, sitting across from them.

Turning to my father, he said, "You've *got* to turn *back!*" Slapping his palm against the bench, he shouted, "For God's sake, what are you *doing?*"

I studied the blue horizon a moment, then said, "He's keeping his promise."

"*What* promise?" Hume shouted.

"He has a promise to keep to my mother." Suddenly I felt something let go. Something that had been locked down tight for a very long time. Before my mother's death; before even my sister's death. Something that had been with me all the way back to when I was a boy. To the moment when I was sitting in the car that was going to take us away from Ensenada, away from my father. I remembered his rubbing my head just before the car pulled away; and, as we descended the dusty switchback road, I looked back up the hill at him as he stood at the edge of the terrace before the hacienda. Since that moment I had known that my father operated according to principles that I could not fathom, that his sense of duty and loyalty would always be a barrier between us. He had never made me any promises, and for the first time I understood that he was giving me something that went beyond duty and loyalty. He was being honest.

Turning to my father, I said, "You have been ill."

He didn't answer but only squinted up at the sails.

"You have been ill," I repeated. "And you don't have much time, so now there's only this one promise left to keep." I turned to Hume and Petra, who were both sitting across from me, leaning back against the heel of the boat. "He promised to bury my mother's ashes at sea," I explained. "You see, *this* is home. A long time ago he asked that if he died first she would bury him at sea. And likewise, she asked him to do the same. And that's exactly what he's going to do."

Hume leaned forward and shouted. "You mean he's going to go *down* with her? Is *that* it?"

I nodded. "In a manner of speaking, yes."

"This is some suicide run? I don't *need* some Captain Ahab obsessive shit!" Hume tried to get to his feet but couldn't, due to the heel of the boat. "You tell him to turn this thing *around* and return to *Provincetown!*"

Petra folded her arms and gazed out at the water.

I said to my father, "Okay, take her ashes with you. It's all right."

His hands on the chrome wheel were long and tanned. Aged, yet still vigorous. He steered slightly to port, compensating for the roll of the sea; then, just as easily, he brought the rudder back the other way. We were on a straight, true course. "Thank you, Sam," he said. "But this is not for you.

You're all that we have left, son. You take your friends and row them ashore." He placed a forefinger against his wire-frame glasses and pushed them up his nose. "Before you do, I want one favor."

"What's that?" I asked.

He gazed up at the wind vane at the top of the mast. "We're starting to get a good southwest breeze and I want to run northeast with it. Would you mind raising the spinnaker? And take him up on deck with you." Looking at Hume, he said, "You ever raise a spinnaker, Senator?"

Hume shook his head.

"Well, you should, at least once. Take him up on deck, Sam."

"Aye-aye."

ON THE FOREDECK I was explaining halyards and whisker poles, tacks and clews, but Hume wasn't paying much attention. He was having difficulty with the roll of the sea.

"Even for a professional assassin, he's certifiable," he said. "You're going to let him go through with this?"

In the cockpit my father was talking to Petra, but we couldn't hear him over the wind.

"Doesn't seem I have any choice," I said. The spinnaker, light, silky Dacron, was neatly folded into a blue canvas bag. I removed the sail and laid it on the deck, making sure the three corners were free. "With my father, there has never been much of a 'choice.'"

I motioned for Hume to step back until he was next to the mainmast; then I raised the spinnaker, the halyard racing through the block pulley, bearings clicking with a smart precision. Suddenly this abundance of sheer fabric, pale blue, swirled and twisted upward above us, until, like a parachute, there was a quick, almost chemical reaction to the wind, and the giant triangular sheet ballooned out and filled with air with a loud thud. In the middle of the spinnaker was a large white ensign. Immediately the boat picked up speed, and as the bow plunged through the swells, we were bathed in a cold salt spray.

Hume began crawling back toward the cockpit, his hands and feet desperately seeking purchase on deck, handrails, and lifeline. I wanted to say something to him, to someone as I gazed up at that spinnaker, which now billowed against the clear sky. Blue on blue. But I was alone and speechless on the deck, gazing at the sail as it gave shape and purpose to the wind.

WHEN I RETURNED to the cockpit, something had changed. I sensed it in both my father and Petra: Their posture was different, relaxed, as though they had formed a difficult alliance. Neither would look directly at me. My father appeared nearly serene as he handled the wheel and gazed up at the sails. Petra no longer seemed afraid; she was still, and her eyes sought the horizon pensively. She had something, a secret, a promise, a sense of mission—I couldn't tell exactly.

But Hume noticed this as well. "What?" he said, almost in a panic. *"What?"*

"We've been talking," Petra said to me. "And here's the deal: We're going to bury your mother's ashes, and then the three of us are going to row ashore."

"The boat's *sinking!*" Hume shouted. "We don't have *time* for a *ceremony!*"

"*Spray* will remain afloat for a good while, Senator," my father said. "You have plenty of time."

Hume turned to me, furious. "They've *lost* their fucking *minds,*" he said.

"You can always go below and bail while we do this," I said. Then to my father: "All right, then. Where are they?"

He nodded toward the cabin. "The locker in the forward berth."

I went down below, opened the locker, and on the second shelf found a white box wedged between stacks of neatly folded yellow raingear. It was just like the one that had contained my sister's ashes. I took the box off the shelf and was surprised at its weight. A body, a life, reduced to a few pounds. All of us, the same. It seemed just. Pure and absolute.

I sat down on the V-berth bed, holding the box on my lap. The white cardboard had a smooth, waxy feel beneath my fingers. Water dashed against the bow behind me. Looking back into the main cabin, I could see that water had begun to seep across the teak floor. It was comforting, being surrounded by all this seawater. I sat there, running my hands over the white box. The last time I had talked with my mother, she was sitting up in her bed in Dana Farber. The room smelled faintly of grapefruit, and there was an unfinished half on her bed tray. She held on her lap one of the art books I'd brought her—she had told me that she could no longer concentrate enough to read, but she would love to look at paintings. I had brought her several, but it was the large volume of Monet's work that she opened most often. She paused at certain pages, particularly those depicting boats, the ocean, the shore, the sky.

"Just look at this," she said, turning the book so that I could see. I sat beside her on the edge of the bed. She was so small and frail by then. "That sky. The water. How does he do that? And the air—you can *see* the atmosphere."

This more than anything else about Monet always impressed my mother, the fact that he would make the invisible visible. For several minutes we looked at *Antibes, Vue de la Salis* and *Sur la Falaise près de Dieppe*.

"There was a dog," she said.

I was accustomed to her abrupt segues. "Where was this?"

"Out on Route 128. I was driving down to see my brother in Wellesley, I don't know, maybe two years ago? It doesn't matter." Her hands on the page full of Monet's colors were frail and delicate. They shook slightly as she caressed the paintings. "The traffic was heavy, and I was over in the right-hand lane because I didn't want to miss my turn for Route 9. And there in the breakdown lane was this dog. It must have been hit by a car. It wasn't dead, but it must have been paralyzed. It lay there, with its head raised up off the pavement, watching the traffic come at it." She didn't speak for a moment, and I helped her turn the page, but she didn't look down at the book again. Staring toward the window, she said, "And the look of horror in that dog's face. I tried to pull over, but the traffic was so heavy—you know how Massachusetts drivers get. I was afraid. But the terror in that dog's eyes, I've never seen anything like it." She closed the book, which I took from beneath her hands and placed on the nightstand. When I turned back to her, she was staring at me. She lifted her hand and placed it against my cheek. Her fingers were warm, their touch light. Neither of us spoke for a long time, until finally she smiled weakly. "I think I'll try some more of that grapefruit now."

I TOOK MY MOTHER's ashes back to the cockpit. My father had turned on the autopilot and he was sitting in one of the corner benches in the stern rail. When I held the box out to him, he shook his head. "You go ahead, Sam."

I opened the box. The ashes were in a plastic bag, closed with a white twist-tie. I realized that Petra was standing beside me, and my hands seemed remarkably clumsy as I untied the twist and opened the bag. When I took it out, I handed the box to Petra. Then I leaned over the stern rail and poured the ashes into the boat's wake. They were gray, mostly like sand, though there were some small chunks. They hissed as they entered the water, and a cloud of fine dust drifted toward the dory, which was tethered some twenty feet back. I remained at the rail, holding the empty plastic bag in my fist, staring down into the water.

When I turned to my father, he had removed his glasses. His eyes were large, moist as he looked astern. He didn't say anything. I don't think he could; nor could I.

MY FATHER LET out the mainsail and fell off to a broad reach so that we were only going a few knots while I pulled the dory alongside. I could feel Hume's anxiety, his desire to climb down into that boat as soon as possible.

"How far do you think it is to shore?" he asked, squinting toward the low coastline behind us.

I ignored him.

"You have the tide with you," my father said.

I looked at him. "You could return with us," I said. "Does it matter now?"

The slightest smile crossed his thin lips. Raising his head, he gazed up at the mainsail for a moment. "This is too good a wind."

I nodded.

His right arm moved. I thought he was going to shake my hand, and something made me want to resist. But his hand went into the front pocket of his tan slacks. He took out an old compass, in a leather case on a long cord, and held it out to me. "You might need this."

After a moment I took the compass and hung it around my neck.

Petra came up from the cabin, a small nylon bag slung over one shoulder. "I've got water."

I unclipped the lifeline, and she climbed down into the stern of the dory.

"Sure you don't care to accompany me, Senator?" my father said cheerfully. "I could use a good crewman."

Hume stepped tentatively up onto the coaming. "Thanks, no," he said, his voice unusually high and polite.

My father grabbed his wrist firmly. "Are you sure?" Hume, alarmed, shook his head. "Maybe if I took you with me, I might make amends? Perhaps history will see it as an attempt to balance the books?"

He grinned up at Hume, whose eyes drifted over me, pleading. Then, still holding his wrist, my father helped him into the boat.

I climbed down quickly and sat next to Hume on the middle thwart. I looked up at my father as he untied the painter from the cleat. Tilting his head toward the south, he said, "Mind that fog bank."

As soon as he dropped the line into the bow of the dory, we began to fall behind *Spray*. My father did not watch us go. He made no parting gesture; instead he hauled in the mainsheet and brought the boat around until she was running northeast again. I put my oar in the water and began to pull. Hume fell in time with my strokes and we pointed southwest. Occasionally I glanced at Petra, who kept her eye on *Spray*. I tried not to look and concentrated on rowing. But finally I paused and turned: She was already well away, heeling nicely, sails full.

Part V

Compact

30

We moved to San Diego when I was seven. My early recollections are sharp, but they lack connection. I remember running my hands over the stubble of the stucco wall on the back of our house. Workmen who came to replace the Spanish tile roofs called me Xavier, and *poco amigo*. We went to the beach often and I fell in love with the ocean. I could watch the waves crest and break forever. One of the few times I recall my father touching me was when he would pick me up by the arms so that I would rise up over the next rush of white water. He gave me a sailor's cap, which I wore everywhere. The only place I remember both my mother and my father laughing together was when we were at the beach.

We all loved the water.

We are water.

Water is home.

HUME DIDN'T LOVE WATER. And he was a lousy rower. The physical effort seemed a personal insult.

"I've got blisters on my hands already," he said after about twenty minutes.

"That's what you get for all those years of chauffeurs, and doormen waiting at the curb," I said.

"My arm is killing me. Can't we take a break?"

"Just for a drink," I said.

Petra removed a plastic bottle of water from the nylon bag.

Hume grabbed it from her and drank nearly half. "How far have we gone?" he gasped. "The beach, it doesn't look any closer."

I took the water from him, took a sip, and gave the bottle back to Petra. "We're doing all right," I said. "The tide is taking us in, but there's a current and we have to keep rowing southwest if we're to make Race Point." I began to pull on my oar, and reluctantly Hume did, too.

Petra looked to the southeast toward the fog bank. "I think it's closer," she said.

"It'll reach us within an hour," I said, "unless the wind shifts." I knew Petra was watching me, looking for signs of concern or fear. I kept my head down and pulled hard and steady. "Ever read Stephen Crane's story 'The Open Boat'?" I asked.

"God, yes," she said. "I was a freshman at BC."

"Remember the opening line?"

"What is this?" Hume demanded. "A quiz?"

After a moment, Petra said, "Something about the sky—the rowers' perspective."

"Don't know why, but I've always remembered it," I said. "'None of them knew the color of the sky.' That's what it's going to take, Senator. Keep your head down and pull."

"Or what, a recitation from *The Odyssey*?"

"Hume, you don't understand our predicament. If we don't make Race Point by nightfall, the tide's going to turn and go out." I glanced up at Petra. I could tell I had confirmed her worst fears, but she seemed relieved to know that she'd been on the money. "With this current it's going to take us hours to make it to the beach, so we have to keep moving. We don't reach the tip of the Cape before dark, they may never find us."

"I can take a turn with an oar," she said.

"You'll get your turn," I said.

Hume said nothing and he seemed to be putting more back into it.

ONCE, WHEN WE were living in San Diego, my father had to go away to "work." I had no idea what he did then; the word *work* was sufficient, suggesting that adult realm that I couldn't fathom. Mother said we were going to go away, too, and the three of us flew to Boston to visit her family.

We stayed with Uncle James's family in a rented cottage on Cape Cod. Relatives came and went; there were many cousins our age, and they talked with funny accents. Uncle James gave me a Red Sox hat, and he told me that Ted Williams, number 9, was from my new home, San Diego—a small detail that seemed to confirm that I was destined to be a lifelong Sox fan. We'd watch games on a small black-and-white TV; the picture was often snowy and Uncle James would have to toy with the antennae. Curt Gowdy did the play-by-play, and between innings my cousins always sang along with the jingle for Atlantic gasoline: *"Atlantic keeps your car on the go-go-go! So keep on the go-o-o with Atlantic!"* Abigail and I sang along, too. Somehow I came to understand that my father's "work" was connected to gasoline, which sharpened my affinity for the Red Sox. Uncle James drank Narragansett Lager beer from Dixie cups; sometimes he'd let me sip the foam, which would cling to my upper lip like a mustache smelling pleasantly of beer. Our days seemed ruled by the tides, which determined when we would go dig clams (at low tide) and when we would go flounder fishing (high tide). The beaches on the Cape weren't as expansive as in San Diego, but the smell of salt and low tide was rich and powerful. We played Wiffle ball with our cousins for hours, and after dinner everyone went into the backyard to eat watermelon and chase fireflies.

Down through the woods behind the cottage was a salt marsh. Abigail and I were warned not to go near the water by ourselves, but the two of us liked to sneak down there and find snails and caterpillars. The marsh grass stretched out toward a river, and I'd never seen anything so lush and exotic. We became bolder with each visit, venturing closer to the water. There were a number of wood dinghies tied up at a small dock, and when no one was around, we'd climb into one. I pretended to row, while Abigail would sit in the stern, gazing down into the water. There were schools of minnows, and periwinkles and starfish clung to the dock pilings. Once she asked, "How old is this water?" It seemed like the most profound question. It still does.

Finally, one day I did it. It was foggy and a fine warm mist fell on the marsh. I sat in the bow of the dinghy and fiddled with the knot that was tied to the dock cleat. Then, suddenly, I gathered in the line and pushed off from the piling. The dinghy turned slowly on the still water. Abby laughed with delight.

This was all the encouragement I needed. I moved to the middle thwart and took hold of the large wooden oars. I loved the way the brass oarlocks creaked every time I pulled. I got the bow pointed down a narrow tidal creek, and because the tide was quite high, our heads were just above the tall green marsh grass. Abigail trailed a hand in the water, trying to poke a finger in the small whorls that spun off the oar paddles—it would be years before she would connect these to the word *maelstrom*. I pulled slowly on the oars and was quite proud of how I could work the dinghy around tight bends in the creek, often pushing off the soggy peat walls on either side. The sweatband of my Red Sox cap became soaked, and my bare forearms were slick with mist. I never felt better. Everything was wet, our clothes, our hair. Wet and warm. The air was water. Everything was water.

And then we reached the river.

WHEN PETRA TOOK a turn at the oar, we made better speed.

"My my," Hume said, sprawled in the stern. "You two are in such sync—you must be something in bed."

"Fuck you," Petra said.

"Please," he said. "For old times' sake."

I took the water bottle from him and placed it behind me on the bottom of the dory.

Suddenly the fog enveloped the sun. It hadn't reached us yet, but it wouldn't be long. I concentrated on Petra's feet. She understood how to brace her heels against the boat's ribs so she could get good purchase for each stroke.

Hume watched her for several minutes, the slightest smile on his thin lips.

"Enjoying yourself?" she whispered finally.

"Reminiscing," he said.

"Well, do so in silence," she said.

"Remember Vermont?" Hume asked. "We stayed at some Shaker village that had been turned into an inn. Large, severe buildings overlooking a lake. What was that, some New England preservation group bullshit? They invited me up as keynote speaker. Great perk. God, all those blue-hairs with checkbooks. But we hardly left our suite, remember? And one night we went down to the lake and went skinny-dipping."

"You didn't go in," Petra said.

"Didn't I?"

"No. And it was New Hampshire."

"Was it now?" Hume sighed dramatically. Then he said, "Adams told you."

Petra and I kept pulling, but I could feel a tension in her body next to me.

"Why don't you shut up," I said. "Or I might make you walk the gangplank."

"Who made you captain?"

I smiled. "Well, I do have the compass."

He ignored me and concentrated on Petra again. "Now, what the *fuck* did Adams tell you?"

Petra said nothing. If anything she was pulling even harder.

"While the captain here and I were up there *hoisting* ye old *spinnaker,* Adams told you what you wanted to know, didn't he?"

Petra leaned forward and our shoulders touched as we stretched out our arms and together rolled back in a long, smooth pull. Then we leaned forward again. I saw a drop of sweat run off her chin and land on the thigh of her jeans. She seemed not to notice.

THE RIVER CURRENT was swift, and at first I thought this was fun: We were going fast and rowing seemed effortless. Small boats were moored ahead of us, and I took pride in how well I steered past them.

Our journey down the river probably took less than thirty minutes, but it seemed much longer. As we began to round the first bend, Abigail stared back toward the salt marsh until it disappeared from sight. I could tell from her shoulders that she was trying to decide whether she should be worried or not.

"We'll go a little farther," I said, trying to sound in control and reassuring. "Then we'll turn around."

"Can you?"

"The tide," I said, because it was the big discovery of that summer. Uncle James explained how the moon caused the tides and that they rose and fell approximately every six hours. "We can always row to shore," I said, "and when the tide turns, it'll take us back."

Abby looked skeptical and her eyes were large with fear. Yet she was also excited. Every moored boat that we passed seemed monumental. Seagulls, perched on the roofs of clam shacks along the shore, observed our passing with cautious reserve.

After we rounded the next bend, the river narrowed, making the current faster. On our left the land loomed high above us, while to the right lay another salt marsh. Well in the distance we could see a lighthouse and open water. The fine mist had turned to a warm, steady drizzle. Abby was wearing pale green shorts, Keds sneakers, and a white short-sleeve shirt with little sailboats on it. Her hair was matted to her skull and water ran down her face. We were both soaked through and it felt wonderful. When I took off my Red Sox hat and put it on her head, she gave me a smile.

THE FOG SURROUNDED US. As the wind died the swells were reduced to a light chop. Hume took over at the other oar again. He seemed inspired by the fact that we could no longer see the coast.

"Adams gave it to you," he said to Petra, without looking up from his labor.

I had given Petra the compass, which she held in her palm before her. I watched our wake, making adjustments in my strokes to keep us straight. She concentrated on our direction: southwest.

"He told you the story back there," Hume continued. "It's the crime of the century—no, of America's history. And he left it with you. It's yours, darling, and it's your call."

She lowered the compass. Something passed across her face that I didn't understand. A recognition—of what, I wasn't sure. "Supposing he did?" she asked. "What's it to you?"

"I can help you make the right connections," he said, still keeping his head lowered to his task. He spoke with measured force, which rose and fell with the effort of each stroke. "It's going to be a very difficult sell, unless you get the right help. You don't and you'll just end up another conspiracy nut, like our captain here. Do it right and you know it'll transform you. It's a Pulitzer. It's a book deal. It's an incredible movie deal." He raised his head as he pulled back on his oar. "And think long term. You'll get access to stories that will put your career in the top echelon. You'll be Woodward and Bernstein rolled up into one, and you'll be a hell of a lot prettier to look at on the tube. Larry King will eat you up." Leaning forward and extending his arms, he whispered, "I know you, Petra. Remember? You had the fire, and you still do. Here it is, babe."

"Petra," I said.

"Forget him," Hume said. "He had it and he blew it. He's history."

"*Petra,*" I said. Her eyes found mine. They were dark, shrouded, confused. Or *conflicted* might be the more popular and appropriate word. Her beautiful Greek eyes were conflicted in a way that I'd never seen before; they held both hard calculation and a soft longing. "The compass," I said. "Check our course."

She was startled momentarily; then she raised her hand and leveled the compass.

WE WERE NEARING the mouth of the river when I saw the boat coming around the bend. Abigail turned and watched it speed toward us, white water peeling away from the bow. It was a scallop boat, about twenty feet long, with long-handled rakes standing up on the transom. There were two men aboard, and even at a distance of several hundred yards I could tell that the large one in a white T-shirt was Uncle James.

Abby asked, "Are we going to get in trouble?"

I wasn't sure. I didn't even want to think about what our mother was going to say. She rarely cried in our presence, but I suspected that this might do it.

As the boat closed in, I kept watching the other man, who was driving. He was thin, and he wore glasses beneath a long-billed cap that was common among local fishermen, and suddenly I stood up in the dinghy to wave.

Abby turned around, causing the dinghy to tip. I lost my balance, and I had no other choice but to dive overboard, rather than fall against the gunwale. For the moment that I was airborne I believed I had not just succeeded in clearing the dinghy, but in doing the impossible—our father had returned to save us. I was certain that he would throw me a lifeline, or perhaps even jump into the river and carry me back to the boat. It seemed a long, suspended moment there in midair—there's some mental and physical preparation just prior to breaking the surface that we all must feel—and I remember seeing the distorted reflection of my face in the river. But when I entered the water, my left shoulder hit the oar. As I descended among slippery reeds, I was stunned with pain.

The river was not deep, and my hands and knees touched bottom, which was littered with the sharp edges of seashells. The muck was slick and cold; I was petrified that something lurking there, some eel or crab, would bite me. I could see the bottom of the dinghy drifting downstream quickly. I pushed off from the muck and kicked wildly, realizing that I couldn't use my left arm. When I broke surface, the dinghy was turning slowly because Abby was trying to row. She placed both hands on one oar and extended it toward me. I grabbed the flat wood paddle with my right hand. She was crying, and her mouth turned ugly as she began to scream above the noise of the approaching boat. Looking up, I saw Uncle James, throwing a line toward me. His voice was calm, reassuring, and he did not seem at all angry.

WE COULDN'T SEE anything but fog and the chop around the dory. My lower back was starting to cramp, but I didn't want to give up a turn at the oars. We were all weary.

"The current's too strong," Petra said.

"Not necessarily," I said. "Just keep pulling."

Hume was slumped on the stern thwart. His Billabong sweatshirt was soaked around the neck, and his hair, plastered to his scalp, had lost the silver highlights that were so evident on television. It was just sparse and gray now. And his face, drawn with exhaustion, was that of a mean old man. He was glowering at Petra, and she was staring back, and I tried to keep out of it by concentrating on each agonizing stroke.

"We ever get out of this boat," he said to her, "tell you what I'm going to do."

"What's that, Marshall?" she asked, her voice hoarse and weak.

"*I'm* going to tell the story. *You* don't want it, *I'm* telling it!"

"What story?" she said.

"The story of the shooter behind the stockade fence. The story just about every damned American believes. All I got to do is fill in the blanks."

"But you don't know the story," she said.

"Yes, I do. And I can tell it so there will be no doubt." He glanced toward me. "His *father* won't be around to deny anything. And *you* two? Who's going to listen to his *son* the conspiracy *has-been* at this point? And who's going to listen to *you* after you've been running around with him?" For a moment, his face seemed to brighten with insight. "In *fact,* denials from both of you could even strengthen my story. I can prove I was out here. I can tell John Adams's story—I'm the *only* one of us who can tell it because I'm not *per*sonally in*volved.* From me, the story will be a contribution to history."

Petra and I leaned forward together and pulled back. It was as though we were joined, physically, even spiritually. Our timing was perfect. And I swear I knew what she was going to say next.

At the beginning of the next stroke, she said, "But it would be a lie."

"It would be history," Hume said. "And history is more powerful than lies—or truth, for that matter. It's not *what* happened. It's what people *believe* happened."

"You can't *do* that!" Petra nearly shouted.

Now Hume laughed, revealing gold crowns back in the molars. "I can and I will."

"You can't!" she screamed.

"Baby, it happens all the time. It's not a matter of whether it's true or false."

"But *you* don't know." She stopped rowing. "It's all a *lie!*"

"*No, cunt.* It's all an *official* lie."

Petra let go of her oar, leaned forward, and slapped Hume's face hard. Then she rose up off the thwart to hit him again. The dory tipped toward the stern and I grabbed a hold of her oar before it slipped into the water. The two of them were a flurry of arms, and they swore at each other as only ex-lovers can. As I shipped the oars, Hume got his hands around Petra's throat. He began to stand up, causing the dory to tip wildly from side to side. I hollered for everyone to sit down. Everyone was yelling at that point. Petra, in a half-crouch, was gasping for air while her arms flailed out at Hume. He only managed to tighten his grip. His face was red with anger; hers was turning blue. Finally I leaned forward and punched him in the stomach. His belly was soft and the blow doubled him over, knocking Petra back across the middle thwart. She hit her head good on one of the ribs. Straightening up, Hume lost his balance and went overboard with a tremendous splash that doused my face with cold salt water.

When he surfaced he was already several feet away from the side of the dory. I took my oar and extended it toward him. His arm came out of the water and he took a hold of the blade of the oar. As I began to draw him in, he kicked his feet frantically—clearly, he wasn't a very good swimmer, and he just looked heavy in the water. When he was close enough, his other arm came up and his hand clutched the scarred wood of the gunwale.

"Wait," I said. "You'll have to come around to the stern to get in or we'll capsize."

He let go of my oar and worked his way, hand over hand, to the stern. "You get me *into* this fucking *boat,*" he said. It was a command, pure and simple. But then he looked above me and his face was transformed. There was both outrage and terror in his bulging eyes, his open mouth, as he shouted, *"No!"*

The flat of the oar blade caught him in the center of the forehead with a loud smack.

I looked up at Petra, who now stood beside me. She appeared stunned and she let go of the oar, which clattered in the bottom of the dory. "He'll kill us, Sam," she whispered. "He'll just kill us." She touched the back of her head, and there was blood on her fingers. She sat down, her hands hanging limp between her knees, her mouth slack with disbelief. "Oh God, what have I done?"

I leaned over the stern. Hume was inert, his eyes were closed, and blood issued from his scalp and seeped into the water. One hand still clutched the transom.

Then I stood up and looked about at the fog. It was as though we were in a place separate from the world, a place where there was only gray water and gray fog. The gray had sapped the color out of everything else—the dory, the oar in my hands, even my skin. I asked quietly, "How old is this water?"

And then I raised the oar in my hands, raised it above my head, and swung down with everything I had, striking the head clean on the crown. The hand slipped from the stern as the body rolled in the chop. The gray sweatshirt, with *Billabong* in red across the chest, descended so quickly, it was as though it had never been there.

THE FACT THAT Uncle James expressed no anger brought home to me the seriousness of the situation. As the scallop boat cruised back upriver, dinghy in tow, he held Abigail on his lap, telling her everything was all right, that no harm was done. Though she eventually stopped crying, I wondered if I wouldn't have been better off drowned in the river, thus earning some sympathy.

The scalloper, a man Uncle James called Gil, was a year-round Cape Codder who owned the cottage we were staying in, and he looked like the whole thing was a bother but slightly interesting—something that only happened during the summer season. His lean, weathered face was stern, and I could smell beer and cigarettes on him.

"Had yourself an adventure?" he asked me. "Where'd you think you were goin'?"

I muttered something about the tide, which he ignored.

"Cross the Atlantic Ocean there?" He laughed then, and I hated him.

I moved to the back of the boat and sat beneath the scalloper's rakes, their long curled tines rusted and snarled with clumps of dried seaweed. Staring into our wake, I tried to get up the nerve to jump in the water, this time for good. Instead I moped as only an eight-year-old can, and stood with my back to the others all the way in to the dock where Gil let us off.

When we returned to the cottage, my mother was calm. I could tell she'd already had her cry. She picked Abby up in her arms and smoothed back her hair. She told me to go to my room until dinner.

I didn't have my own room. I had been sleeping in the unfinished attic with Uncle James's and Aunt Kathleen's three boys. There, I lay on my cot and stared up at the roof beams that angled overhead until I fell asleep.

I was awakened by the creak of wood as my mother came up the stairs. She sat on the cot next to me, but I didn't look at her. I concentrated on a large knot in the board directly overhead. There's something about certain wood knots that can be watchful as an eye.

"I don't know what ever possessed you." There was no anger in her voice, which disappointed me—this was worse, much worse than I'd suspected. I glanced at her and what I saw in her face was fear and not a little pleading. She was trying to get through to me, and suddenly I was frightened, too. "This isn't just about going down to the water when you were expressly told not to, Sam. You know that, I know you do. This is about you and your sister—"

And that's all I remember of what she said, though she said much more. But I was crying so hard then that she took me in her arms and I never wanted her to let go.

WE PULLED AT our oars without speaking. The dory moved more swiftly through the water now. I checked the compass regularly, keeping us on a southwesterly course. The fog never let up, and after another hour we could sense that day was moving toward evening. We were both sweaty and chilled, and I could hear a quiver in Petra's breathing. There was no discussion of how we would deal with what we had done, no attempt to get our stories straight if we made land.

There was no story.

Out there on the Atlantic Ocean there was only the gray fog, the water, and the incessant repetition of pulling the oars.

Petra spoke first. "Hear that?" She stopped rowing.

So did I, and behind us we could hear the faint sound of surf. We looked at each other for the first time. I saw some relief in her eyes, but also there was indecision, uncertainty. I wondered if she saw the same in mine. We didn't begin rowing again but only stared at each other, as though waiting for the other to say something. I half expected her to speak in a language I didn't understand. Greek perhaps.

We began rowing again, and the sound of the surf became more distinct with each stroke. When we were getting very near the shore, our backs were warmed by sunlight, breaking through the fog, and suddenly we were out of it. Turning, I could see the sun setting behind the dunes above the beach.

We rowed carefully, watching the swells emerge from the fog behind us. As we neared the shore, the waves became steeper, and finally one caught the dory and carried it along, until it crested about us with a roar. The oars were of little use; the dory sped along on the white water, tipping and tilting. Petra let go of her oar, which disappeared behind us, and grabbed on to the gunwale. She let out a yell then, and I did, too. Our voices were neither joyous nor frightened. At best they were surprised, and thankful for deliverance. As the white water subsided around us, the dory scraped sandy bottom several times before it came to a halt.

I jumped out into knee-deep water so cold that my ankles ached immediately. I took hold of the painter, and as the next wave lifted the dory, I pulled it farther up onto the beach. Petra climbed out and led me out of the water. There was nothing in sight, just the beach, backed by high, magnificent sand dunes in the last light of the day. It was a landscape that seemed undiscovered. We walked west, our heads lowered, without once looking up toward our destination.

31

There were numerous conspiracy theories.

They all had one—journalists, government spokespersons, TV talking heads, radio blowhards. One theory painted Hume as a hero, a flawed yet ultimately honorable public servant who had over the years relentlessly sought the truth. The contention was that he and federal agent Martin Inge were killed by John Adams in Provincetown Harbor. Inge's body was recovered with the sunken runabout. Hume's body presumably was taken out to sea by the tide. There were several reports of trawlers bringing up articles of clothing, but none were proven to belong to Hume. None was a Billabong sweatshirt. This theory also credited John Adams with the murder of Ike Santori and Ramon Saavo. The man was an assassin, pure and simple.

PETRA AND I were questioned repeatedly, alone and together. By local police on Cape Cod. By Massachusetts State Police. By FBI. By CIA. By ATF. (Uncle James retained Miles Threadgold to act as my legal counsel during these interrogations.) I never denied that Petra and I had been in Provincetown on that October day. However, no one could prove anything more than the simple fact that we had rented a dory and rowed out into the fog-bound harbor, where a sailboat named *Spray* had been moored. The following day I paid Snowe's Marine to have the dory towed back into harbor, and I was billed dearly for a new set of oars.

I KEPT WAITING for some word about Gracie. But there was none. No mention of her in any of the news stories about federal agent Martin Inge. She simply disappeared.

THE FIRST TIME was in Revere. I had gone to visit Ike's grave. A silver car entered the cemetery and parked farther uphill near a small mausoleum, complete with columns. No one got out of the sedan. A rear window was cracked and smoke drifted up into the winter air.

I tried to concentrate on Ike's grave, the marble headstone a pale mauve. He lay beside his mother, Maria, who lay beside his father, Ignatio, who lay beside his older brother, Renzo. Ike had been an only surviving child. Once, when we had been drinking after work, he told me about his mother's miscarriages, and about Renzo, who had died of polio in the early fifties. It was a family that no longer existed, except for these stones. They were good stones, handsomely carved. In the New England climate little survives better than a gravestone. It was all that was left of the Santoris, but it seemed enough. My family wouldn't even have stones. Our remains would forever be borne upon the water.

I didn't pray at Ike's grave. Unless thoughts are prayers. I thought about the Bruins, the Red Sox, what was going on in Boston. If he could hear me, that's what he'd want to know about. I once asked him why he loved fishing so much and he said because of the smells and because of the way his mind worked when he was out on the water. He was focused on the moment, handling the boat, hauling in lines, baiting hooks, whatever, but he said time was different and he could think things through better than on land.

I stood in the cold raw air for nearly an hour, but the silver car didn't move. There was something about its tinted windows that seemed an affront, an insult. When I finally began walking down the path toward my car, the sedan rolled by me, trailing smoke from its window as it passed through the open wrought-iron gate.

The next time was when I was driving south on Route 1. The car behind me was dark blue, and when I abruptly took the Malden exit, it got off, too. I went into a grocery store and when I came out, the car was parked down the street. When I got back on Route 1, the car followed me into Boston, where I lost it in traffic.

It became habitual: looking behind me; checking the street before going out my front door. Boston, I concluded, is a good place to follow someone. Most everyone looked suspicious.

ANOTHER THEORY had it that John Adams was pursued by Ike Santori, who had killed Ramon Saavo in the line of duty (this despite the fact that he had been retired for years). Hume was in cahoots with John Adams, and they had disappeared with a considerable amount of drug money. It was suggested that I knew where both men and the money were, and that in time I, too, would disappear and collect my share.

THE GUN—my gun—used in the shooting had not been found. Like Gracie, it was something I kept waiting to read about in the newspaper one morning.

THROUGH THE WINTER, Petra and I rarely saw each other, but we called often. She took a leave of absence from the *Boston Beacon*. Over the phone her voice was strained and distant, though occasionally she sounded wildly overconfident. At such times she joked about taking Hume's advice and cashing in with the best story she could tell.

The fluctuations in Petra's moods reminded me of Abigail. It seemed as though I was waiting for her, waiting in some way that I could not easily define.

EVERY DAY for months I'd check the Boston newspapers for some indication that my father and *Spray* had been found, that Marshall Hume's body had been found.

The ocean is vast.

It's a lot of water.

But I couldn't help thinking that such complete silence was odd.

I didn't know what I feared more: what I might find in the paper, or what didn't get in the paper.

IN LATE JANUARY there was the story about federal narcotics agent Sylvia Tomasi, who had been found shot in the head in a motel room in Westfield, a small town up in the Berkshires. First reports were that it was self-inflicted, but eventually there was evidence of foul play. I had no doubt that the woman in the photograph in the *Boston Herald* was Gracie.

Her sister in New Jersey was quoted in some stories, claiming that Sylvia had been in hiding since Senator Hume's disappearance, and that she was petrified of being murdered. It was reminiscent of all the people who claimed to have known of plans to assassinate President Kennedy and who, after November 22, 1963, were frightened out of their wits. And who eventually died violent, suspicious deaths.

THE FIRST TIME I saw him was on Tremont Street. He was in his early thirties and he wore a leather coat and a Kangol lid, very common in Boston. I led him over to Washington Street, the end that used to be the center of the Combat Zone, which was now under construction; soon those blocks would be lined with expensive condominiums. But on the street there was a crossroads of sorts: groups of black kids in baggy pants and turned-around ball caps; lots of Asians walking to and from Chinatown.

I stopped in a CD store, and when I came out, Kangol Lid was waiting a half block away on the other side of the street. I walked to Filene's Basement, where shoppers rifled through bins of discounted clothes as though searching for buried treasure. I hid in a dressing room for a long time. When I went out again, I didn't see him.

The next time was in Quincy Market. It was a sunny day with a bitter northwest wind. He wore the same jacket, the same Kangol lid. I turned around and began walking toward him. There was a moment when our eyes met; we were perhaps twenty yards apart, but it reminded me of when I saw Hume's man in the hall of my mother's house. There was a moment of recognition, an acknowledgment that is hard to define. I wanted to take a swing at him, but I also wanted to simply talk to him, to find out what he knew. His face was city pale, his small eyes alert. Something about him suggested that he wasn't from Boston originally, but that he'd observed Bostonians well and thus dressed and moved as though he fit right in. As I approached, he appeared indecisive, and I wonder if he, too, wanted to talk to me, to find out what I knew, to compare notes. But then he went quickly to the cabstand and rode away in a black-and-white Town Taxi. I couldn't see his face as the car passed me because he held a cell phone to his right ear.

MRS. HENNESEY put her house on the market and stayed with her sister in Braintree.

I moved up to my mother's house in Salem, but I seldom removed the covers from any of her living-room furniture. I changed real-estate agents and the house was shown frequently.

ONE AFTERNOON in January, I met Petra in front of Trinity Church in Copley Square. She'd lost weight. Her face was almost severe, and her eyes never stopped taking in everything and everyone around us.

"We can't talk here," she whispered.

"In the middle of Copley Square?"

"Are they following you?" she asked.

"Who?"

"Come on, Sam. Don't play with me."

"Yes, I think so."

"I see them everywhere. I'm afraid to use the phone. They're probably here now."

I wanted to say something to refute this, but there was no denying that it was possible. I turned to look up at the Hancock Tower, rising above Trinity Church, its glass walls reflecting the late-afternoon sky. Pretending to admire the architecture, I scanned people walking behind us. We crossed the square toward the Dartmouth Street entrance to the Boston Public Library. I was following her lead.

"You have any idea who they might be?" she asked.

"None."

We went into the library, a perfectly ordinary thing to do, but with Petra beside me it seemed loaded with implication. After climbing the marble stairs to the second floor, we entered the long reading room under a high vaulted ceiling. The uniformity of the tables, each with green-shaded brass reading lamps, gave a sense of civilized enterprise. People read, and even the sound of a page being turned had its own singular echo. Students wrote in notebooks or clicked away at laptop keyboards. We sat at an empty table and Petra watched the doors; they were leather with brass tacks.

"I had a job interview, in New York," she whispered.

"Great. What paper?"

"I'm through with the fourth estate. It's a PR job."

After a moment, I said, "That's okay."

"It feels dirty, sleazy."

I unbuttoned my coat. "Perhaps you're just coming to your senses?"

"I don't know if moving away would change anything. Somebody really wants to shadow you, they'll find you, no matter what."

"If they're real pros, yes," I said.

"Have you considered the legal difficulties?"

"Which ones?" I ran my thumb along the grain of the table.

"If they found out what happened out there on the water?" She continued to watch the doors, but her face became so intense her skin almost seemed to percolate. "Sam, they'd try to determine which oar killed him."

"True," I said. "But they'll never know, and neither will we."

"That's the hardest thing to bear." She touched her forehead briefly.

"I know."

"It's like original sin." Her trembling hand came to rest on the table next to mine.

"Exactly." I wanted to touch her hand but couldn't. "There can be only one murtherer."

After a moment she got up and left.

ANOTHER THEORY, one with considerable imagination: Ike and Saavo had the goods on John Adams. They tried to sell it to Hume because he could go public and benefit from it. Ike got greedy, killed Saavo, then took Hume out to *Spray*. But when Adams offered Hume money, Ike ended up dead in a skiff. Hume and Adams sailed away.

I MET CELESTE in a bar in Kenmore Square. "When you were a baby," I said, "this place used to be called K-K-Katie's, a sort of rathskeller where you could hear some good blues or R and B."

"Do you know that every time we get together you always make a point of reminding me of how much older you are?" She lit a cigarette and crossed her legs. She was drinking vodka with a twist.

"I thought I was complimenting your youth."

"You don't suppose you're self-conscious about it?"

"I'm not sure. When you get to be my age, you tell me, okay?"

She got the bartender's attention. For the first round we talked around it. We stuck to the Red Sox, winter trade rumors, the endless speculation about whether they'd build a new ballpark or somehow do the right thing and erect a modern stadium around the existing Fenway.

"If they can put a man on the moon," Celeste said, putting down her empty glass, "they can bring Fenway Park into the next millennium."

With that I had to get the next round.

Then it seemed time for her to say what was on her mind. "You interested in doing something on the ballpark?" she asked, which surprised me.

"The history, the politics?"

"Sure. It's Boston in microcosm," she said. "You could have a field day, ha-ha."

I paid for our drinks.

"Sam, it would give you something to do, something to write about. Think about it as a warm-up, say. Just a few innings in spring training."

"Which suggests there's an Opening Day."

"Which suggests I'd like you to do something regular for us. It wouldn't hurt for your name to be in print again—as a byline, instead of in a story written by some crime-beat hack." She put her hand on my elbow for a moment. "God, does this town miss Czlenko!"

"I'll think about it." Her grip tightened on my elbow. "I said I'll think about it." I raised my glass and said, "To Dirk."

She let go of me and picked up her drink. "To Dirk."

As she scanned the bar, her eyes turned cautious, even worried. "Listen," she whispered. "I got this freelancer pitching an idea at me about you and Hume and your father's mystery sailboat. No, I can't say *who*, you know that. But what's interesting is that this freelancer says there're things the feds have discovered that haven't hit the press."

"Discovered?" I asked. "You mean like found?"

She crushed out her latest cigarette. "I can't say because I wasn't given enough specifics. Just enough of a teaser."

"What kind of a teaser?"

Celeste worked on her drink a moment, and I could tell she was seriously considering crossing the line. Then she shook her head. "I can't, sorry."

Good for you, I thought.

Then she took a deep breath and said, "Is it possible that one of you is talking?"

"What?"

She put her hand on mine. "If so, I don't think it's you."

I CALLED PETRA several times that night. There was no answer, no message machine. The sound of a phone that just keeps ringing is becoming that rare thing; it suggests infinite possibilities, none of them very good.

The next morning there was a message from the phone company, saying that the number had been disconnected.

I went by her apartment in the South End. She didn't answer her bell, and there weren't any lights on up in her third-floor windows.

After several days of this I was convinced that she was gone.

YET ANOTHER THEORY was that Ike and Saavo worked together to import drugs supplied by John Adams. The conspiracy theory combinations seemed endless. They mutated, like strains of a virus.

MY MOTHER'S HOUSE sold in February. I gave most of the furniture to relatives. My share of the money should have allowed me what Americans often think of as "freedom." It wasn't a fortune, but it was enough to allow me some time. And movement. I could leave Boston, settle somewhere else. I thought about the Southwest. I thought about Mexico. But it would feel like running, like hiding, which is exactly what my father had done for decades. Now I understood the necessity, the desire to flee, to hunker down and cover up. I was certain it was my oar that had killed Hume. Rather than killing my father, I had followed in his footsteps.

I DECIDED NOT to leave Boston. To do so would disappoint my sister.

Instead I rented a new apartment in Charlestown, this one higher up Bunker Hill, with a view of the harbor. I began to read and take notes about Fenway Park. I continued to scan the newspapers every morning, looking for a story. About a body found at sea. About a sailboat. I found nothing. This was how my father felt, always watching, waiting for someone to appear suddenly.

This was the assassin's dilemma: There were only theories; there were no stories.

Nothing.

Nothing but the fear of what was possible.

EXCEPT THERE WAS a photograph of J. P. Proulx, who had scored his first hat trick. He stood above the goalie, who was sprawled in the crease, arms and stick raised above his head in the warrior's gesture of pure victory.

SATURDAYS I OFTEN walked across the Charlestown Bridge to shop at Haymarket Square. One weekend in early March, the streets were wet and the bins of produce and fish were pungent in the morning air. Bostonians milled about the booths as though participating in a sacred ritual, their faces solemn yet joyful.

After buying a fresh haddock fillet, I saw him again. Same leather jacket, same Kangol lid. He was picking over some heads of lettuce. He had no bags in his hand; he wasn't really buying.

I tucked the fish wrapped in paper under my arm and started back toward Charlestown. Halfway down Canal Street I stopped in a restaurant and ordered coffee. Sitting at a window, I couldn't see him anywhere on the street.

I continued my walk. It was starting to look like rain. By the time I got across the bridge to Charlestown, there was a fine drizzle. Crossing the small park where City Square used to be, I looked behind me—he was just coming off the bridge. I walked faster, breaking a sweat as I climbed Bunker Hill.

When I reached my block, I saw a cab pulling away from the front of my building. Petra was sitting on the granite steps. I hadn't seen her in weeks. She looked gaunt. It had begun to rain harder and her hair was wet. She stood as I approached, put one arm around my waist, and kissed my damp neck.

"Where have you been?" I asked.

She shrugged.

"You shouldn't be here."

"Thanks."

"I mean it."

"I don't care."

I glanced down to the end of the block but saw no one. "All right."

We went upstairs. I hadn't unpacked or arranged furniture yet. There were boxes stacked everywhere. I put the fillet in the refrigerator, then cleared books off the kitchen table so she could sit down while she toweled off her hair.

"Thought you were in New York by now," I said.

"I was." She stood up, removed her raincoat, and paced the kitchen as she rubbed her scalp. Her hands were like small animals parting and separating swatches of wet, tangled hair. Looking out from beneath the towel, she said, "I didn't take the job."

Folding my arms, I leaned against the windowsill. Across the street seagulls lined the ridge of the slate roof, all facing the harbor, their feathers smoothed back by the east wind. "You should have," I said.

"I couldn't stay away." She drew several wet strands of hair down off her forehead and inspected the ends closely; it made her slightly cross-eyed. "Sam, I just couldn't leave Boston."

This sucked the air out of me. I couldn't help it. "I know," I whispered.

She stopped pacing and draped the damp towel over the back of the chair. It reminded me of the moment on my father's boat when she hung the towel over the faucet. She came over to me. "We need to be close to each other."

"Is that what you want?"

She nodded. "I'm frightened all the time."

"Me, too."

I looked down into the street. I couldn't see him, but I knew he was there, keeping out of sight, out of the rain.

She laid her arms over my shoulders. "Your father told me things. And I promised I wouldn't tell. Ever."

I put my hands around her hips. "Why'd he tell you, then?"

"I asked him that and he said just so someone would know."

"And he knew you'd keep your promise," I said. "He saw that in you right away."

"That's not all, Sam. I think he also believed it would keep us together." She buried her face against my neck. Her body trembled, and I suspected that it had been a while since she'd had anything substantial to eat. Lifting her head, she looked right at me. "He told me something else."

Whatever she was going to say I wanted to believe with all my heart. But I knew I couldn't. And I knew that that was the way it was going to be from then on, the desire to believe precluded by an inability to trust. It was how he had lived; it was all he had left me. I still held her, though, and realized that the trembling might have originated in my hands. "What else?"

Her face was so close to mine I could feel its warmth, could see the moisture in its pores. She waited until I stared into her dark eyes again. "He said you would always take care of me, no matter what, no matter how difficult or horrible it got."

"He was right," I said. "And you realize that this will never end."

"I know." Petra's arms tightened around my neck. She pressed her cheek against mine as she whispered, "What else can we do?"

I took my weight off the windowsill and turned so that I could look over her shoulder and into the street. A heavy rain now swept the sidewalk brick. Farther down the block I spotted him, hiding in a doorway. Water ran off the brim of his lid and spattered his black shoes. Suddenly there was the loud cawing of a seagull, which caused him to raise his head. I drew Petra back from the window. The flock of gulls took off from the slate roof, rushed straight for my window, then together wheeled east. They fanned out over the harbor, flickering white against the city skyline, until they seemed to disappear.

About the Author

JOHN SMOLENS is the author of four other works of fiction, *Winter by Degrees, Angel's Head, My One and Only Bomb Shelter,* and *Cold.* Educated at Boston College, the University of New Hampshire, and the University of Iowa, he is a professor of English at Northern Michigan University.